FATAL FEAST

A BIOLOGICAL THRILLER

I0616044

Table of Contents

AUTHOR

BETTY KUFFEL

FATAL FEAST

F atal Feast is a work of fiction. References to real people, real places or historical events are used fictitiously. Events, settings and characters are a work of imagination. Any resemblance to actual events, places, or persons living or dead is coincidental.

OTHER TITLES BY THIS AUTHOR

Fiction

Deadly Pyre – A Kelly McKay Medical Thriller
Book 1 - Seattle
Deadly Spin – A Kelly McKay Medical Thriller
Book 2 – Alaska
Coming soon
Deadly Crosswinds – A Kelly McKay Medical Thrill
Book 3 – Montana

Alaska Flight – A Romantic Medical Thriller
Papa Dearest – A Novel

Non-fiction

Eyes of a Pedophile – Detecting Child Predators
Your Heart – Prevent & Reverse Heart Disease
in Women, Men & Children
Modern Birth Control

DEDICATION

To researchers who have dedicated their lives to science and helping mankind.

Chapter 1 – Deathwatch

D riving through a designated kill zone on the twisting mountain road to Dad's cabin fueled my concern. I hadn't talked to him in weeks and there was no cell coverage in the remote area. A Montana State Fish, Wildlife and Parks command post officer stopped my vehicle on Highway 93 south of Medicine Falls to warn me of the hazard. He glanced at my Ohio plates and explained a whitetail doe infected with Chronic Wasting Disease had died within a mile of our location. To eradicate infected animals and stop the spread, a group of local hunters had orders to shoot all deer, elk and moose within a ten-mile radius. He suggested I turn back.

I explained the circumstances. He reluctantly acquiesced and let me pass.

Decades of CWD research at the Rocky Mountain high-risk lab made my father a local and international expert. He would know if this orchestrated kill was adequate to stop the epidemic spread in wildlife. It sounded doubtful.

He'd voiced concerns about the rapid spread of this variant of mad cow disease into vast herds of wildlife after prion-infected deer were killed in the fall hunt in eastern Montana. That was months ago, hundreds of miles away, and across the Rockies. Then, there had been no outcry, no headline story, no significant public education about the mis-folded proteins that behaved like untreatable super-bugs. It appeared Montana authorities had suppressed information just like British leaders during the mad cow epidemic in the 1990s.

An outbreak of this fatal disease in big game would be catastrophic in vast ranching country, where pickups driven by hunters cruised with rifles hanging in their back windows year-round.

Growing up with a prion researcher father had stimulated my interest in his work. He had dressed me in oversized protective gowns to make rounds on sick animals with him at a large animal veterinary research center in Colorado.

I'd felt very grown up, especially one memorable day after second grade when I skipped down a long hall beside him in my scuffed cowgirl boots with a large gown covering my pretty sundress. We went out a side door along a cement corridor to an animal pen. As we approached, a skinny black cow spun around and collapsed against the fence near Dad's feet.

Frightened, I jumped back.

He knelt and calmly spoke to the struggling animal. "I failed you. So sorry."

I had squatted beside him looking from her frightened brown eyes to his sad face. "She looks really weak, Dad. Can we help her get up?"

He stood and took my hand, pulling me away from the cow. "She's too sick to eat and her jerky muscles made her fall. My medicine didn't work. She's dying of mad cow disease."

I moved away from him and the cow. "Don't be afraid, Callie. She's not mad at you. It's a contagious disease that damaged her brain."

Tears welled in my eyes. "Quick, give her something else. Fix her."

"Nothing will help, honey." He hesitated as if trying to find words to tell a seven-year-old about the disease epidemic. "This bad disease is even killing pet cats in England."

The day he left for a Great Britain sabbatical to help solve the mad cow crisis, I put my arm around him. "Promise you won't eat any hamburgers."

"Cross my heart." Dad smiled. "And, I'll write to you and keep journals on my work so you can read them someday if you're interested."

That was the day I knew he would save the world, and the cats.

Now, decades later, after my medical school, infectious disease training and finally finding some success in prion research, we were both still trying to save the world. Our dream had been to work together, following an animal rights break-in at my lab, the CDC made the dream come true by transferring me to the more secure Rocky Mountain Ridge Lab where he had worked for years. This was my first day in town, road-weary after a three-day drive from the Human Prion Center in Cleveland.

Eight miles after the turnoff, I parked in front of the one-room cabin and tromped up three plank steps into view of a German shepherd barking ferociously at the window. My knock brought louder barking when I cracked open the door to peek inside. "Dad, are you here?"

The growling dog backed away, positioning itself across the room near a silhouette on the bed.

A hand patted her head. "It's okay, girl. Callie won't hurt us. Come on in, honey. This is Blaze, my rescue dog."

Their images clarified in the dim interior as my eyes adjusted. I approached but stopped cold, not because of the dog. In the four months since my last visit, Dad had metamorphosed from a fast-talking white-haired professor with a goatee, to a haggard mountain man with long hair and a bushy beard. He pointed a walking stick. "Lock the damn door before those guys come in again. They've been sneaking around for days."

I moved closer. "I didn't see anyone. Who's been up here?"

An uncoordinated arm shot forward. "Stay back." His voice broke in a sob. "It's my brain. Hallucinations, I guess." A cascade of spasms jerked his shoulder, a hand, a leg. "I couldn't bear to tell you. I infected myself in a lab accident."

Years of suppressing my emotions as an infectious disease physician caring for challenging prion-infected patients in the Cleveland hospice wing failed when I saw him debilitated and dying. I wailed in grief. "Oh, no, Dad. If you'd told me, we could have tried my animal drugs."

He struggled to his feet. "I have little time left. I'm so sorry we won't be able to work together." Dad hung his head. "I injected monoclonals from my deer study, but the damn wasting disease progressed too fast" He lurched toward the door. "Please walk up to the lookout with me one last time."

Dad stopped frequently to catch his breath and gain footing on the rocky path to the ridge. We sat on a boulder at the top to rest looking at an endless view of distant mountain peaks jutting against the eastern sky. It was here we had shared stories, achievements, and the profound sadness after Mom's death of pancreatic cancer. This was one of those times. He wanted to say good-bye to our favorite place.

When there were no more tears, we discussed the tragedy of losing our dream of working together. There was so much to talk about but his brain deterioration from prion clumps ravaged his memory and ability to communicate. I listened to a stranger with skeletal features, his shirt hung on a scarecrow frame. Sunken eyes looked my way. "I plan to take my life before I get worse and kill somebody."

My experiences working at the Human Prion Center had forever embedded images of despair in my mind. I stifled a gasp and scanned the area, fearing he might try to lunge from the steep cliff to his death.

He shook his head. "I won't jump. I have other plans." Then, with tears streaking his cheeks, he laughed and laughed, a familiar croaking laughter that had haunted my dreams for years.

No one laughed in the hospice wing of the human prion hospital *except the patients*. During their downward spirals through combative behavior and confusion, strange spasms of laughter echoed in the halls before silence and coma ensued. The same neurological symptoms of *laughing death* were first seen in primitive New Guinea tribal members with *kuru* who developed the infectious disease from ritual cannibalism. My unfortunate patients had suffered with inherited forms of the disease or rare infection sources but like kuru victims, in the end they drifted into peaceful unconsciousness, leaving behind infected corpses requiring cremation to destroy the prions.

I understood why my father wanted to leave me before his condition worsened, but it did nothing to soothe my grief. On the descent to the cabin, he steadied himself with the walking stick and was emphatic about me not touching him to help. Exhaustion stopped him from climbing the cabin steps where he sat to rest.

Dad took a ragged breath. "We made the summit. Let's have a glass of brandy for a toast."

In the past, we'd sipped the calming liquid, sitting by a roaring fire while relaxing in the cabin after a day of hiking, but today I brought two paper cups and the bottle out to the porch. Anguish choked each breath as I poured and handed him one. Dad's words faltered and jerky movements sloshed his drink. "Cheers. Cure this damn disease ... before it wipes out the world." His eyes drifted to the dog's beautiful face. "Blaze, take care of Callie."

The dog wagged her tail.

I stroked her head. "We'll take care of each other." My voice broke. "I'll find that cure, promise."

Sipping brandy, he coughed repeatedly while trying to talk. "I stripped the apartment. Burn everything you can after I'm gone ... paint the inside of the cabin and house." He crumpled the cup. "I can make it up the steps now."

Dad lay on the bed, his jerky speech making it difficult to understand. Sometimes, I just nodded when I didn't comprehend, -anything to give him peace. After drifting into a restless sleep, he awakened just after sunset. In kerosene lamplight, I followed him to the small kitchen area where he had organized the death meds, the same drugs he'd used to euthanize animals.

My ambivalence watching him prepare to take his life, wanting to help him, and wanting to stop him, ping-ponged in my heart. His uncoordinated movements made it difficult for him. I turned away. Dark images reflected in the nearby window. Dad's jerky hands stirring suicide meds into a small bowl of applesauce. My face of stone, holding back tears. I understood the rational decision formulated in a once-brilliant mind. He had the right to make this final choice.

Before swallowing the drugs, he donned gloves to feed Blaze from a large bag of vegetarian dog food. She waited patiently until he added a little water and then placed the bowl on the floor in front of her. Dad went back and sat on his bed. Thin legs hung limp between involuntary movements as he struggled to swallow each spoonful of death slurry.

I controlled my emotions to help ease his sorrow. Wanting to pull him back to the time before prions had entered his body. Back when we'd consulted, working on parallel projects, separated by so many miles but close in spirit.

A smile crossed his lips when I turned on his battery-powered stereo playing the orchestral CD of Wagner's "Ride of the Valkyries." One of *our* songs he had played for me many times on the piano. Tonight, mythical winged valkyries from Norse folklore accompanied him on his journey, like they carried soldiers to the hall of Valhalla who died in battle. An appropriate tribute to a man who'd fought a valiant battle against ravaging disease.

The music played on. Dad looked out to the mountains with Blaze beside him.

His eyes closed.

Drugs slowed his breathing, stopped the leg spasms, and let him rest for the first time in months. Thundering music filled the cabin as his breathing slowed. Rhythmic movement of washboard ribs tenting the fabric of his red wool shirt faded. My tears fell on him as I waited for another breath. My gloved hand on his chest stopped moving. I'd never considered this end.

A profound darkness enclosed me, stopping my breath.

I dropped my gloves into the burn barrel near the door and lay on the couch thinking of the time as a seven-year-old when I was excited to see my first mad cow prion slide. When I begged him to quit his job so he wouldn't die. Sobs racked my body as I contemplated a future without him.

Blaze pawed my knee. I hugged her and cried harder, resigned to stay in the cold cabin until daylight when I could safely navigate the mountain road back to town into cell phone range. The contagious disease death had to be reported and I hoped the medical examiner would comply with his wishes not to report his cause of death to the Rocky Mountain Ridge Lab.

Blaze walked around Dad's bed whimpering, then returned and curled up by me. My hand on her back brought me comfort. Later, I awakened shivering in dim lantern light, when seeing his body, a fresh horror swept over me, realizing my world would never be the same.

I stepped outside for more firewood. A faraway wolf howled. Forest noises compressed to an eerie chorus of rustling branches and whistling treetops. Near the wood pile, I startled at the whoosh of an owl's wings sweeping past. Filtered moonlight illuminated the large gray bird as it perched on a nearby bare pine limb wrapped with fingers of fog. I recalled the Indian saying: *If the owl cries, an Indian dies.*

Owls symbolized death. I stood still, barely breathing. The owl gave a cry and disappeared on silent wings.

Chapter 2 - Death Knell

Daylight painted shadows across Dad's stiffening body in the chilly one-room mountain cabin. Blaze lay on the floor nearby. Seeing them together deepened my anguish. The dog that had brought him comfort during his futile effort to save himself from the killer-disease led me to the door. Her breath condensed in the cold fall air as she scanned the area before disappearing into pine trees shrouded in ice fog. Blaze plodded back a few minutes later. Inside, she circled the bed then lay on the floor staring at his body.

I locked the door, leaving them together for the last time, and walked to the car. Three distant rifle shots reminded me of the kill zone proximity, stopping the spread, and the urgency of finding a prion cure.

Along the narrow gravel road to Medicine Falls, brilliant trees sparkling with hoarfrost penetrated my dark thoughts. Tall evergreens lined the steep terrain. No sign of life. No other humans. A stark contrast to city life.

Dad and I had collaborated on prion research long-distance for years. But after penetration of my lab containing an aggressive prion variant, the CDC mandated a move to a safer location. The high-risk NIH lab, remote and more secure, was a disruptive change, and now more difficult without Dad.

I showered at the Wagon Wheel Motel and changed into a black outfit that fit my mood. Just after 8 a.m., I dialed the state lab and asked to speak with the medical examiner.

A pleasant male voice answered, "Dr. Dalen, here."

"This is Callie Archer. I'm calling to report a prion death. My father died last night."

"Callie, I'm so sorry. Your Dad and I were friends. He was excited about finally working with you."

Emotion slowed my response. "It was a dream of ours." His next comment saved me from explaining my concerns.

"I won't need to do an autopsy. Nolan told me his diagnosis."

Why would Dad have confided in this man and not tell his own daughter the truth?

I waited at the Wildlife Refuge, one of the few restaurants in town, to rendezvous with two men dispatched to pick up Dad's body. I thought it was a better location than meeting in my motel room. I had no appetite but drinking coffee and eating toast helped pass the time while I sat at a window table waiting for their arrival.

My list of things I had to do grew as I waited. Bring Blaze's food from the cabin was at the top. Dad had smiled through tears assuring me he'd protected her from prions. He said he'd turned her into a vegetarian. His words had reassured me after envisioning the dog with progressive disease.

Go to the lab and check on my animals. Get a copy of Dad's will from the safe deposit box at his bank, a death certificate from Dr. Dalen, talk to Director Reilly. My compilation of things to do ended when a dark van bearing a state government license plate parked at the restaurant an hour after my conversation with Dr. Dalen.

Locals eating breakfast eyed the two strangers who entered looking for me. Over my third cup of coffee, we discussed the route to the cabin and my concerns about infection containment.

They assured me Dr. Dalen had ramped up staff education on prion safety because of recent medical examiner reports of suspicious deaths nearby in Idaho. I explained my second concern. "Blaze is a big protective dog. I'm not sure what she'll do when we try to separate them."

The men followed me up the mountain where they waited in the van while I entered the cabin alone. Wearing protective gloves from a box near the door, I moved the bag of dog food to my car and returned to clip a leash on Blaze. I wanted to give Dad a good-bye kiss but because of prion risk, I patted his bony arm in sad farewell feeling his past strength-infusing hugs I would miss terribly.

Blaze reluctantly followed me up a trail where we sat on cold ground scattered with golden aspen leaves. I held the big dog's quivering body to me and whispered that things would be okay someday.

She growled when the men in protective clothing walked up the steps and entered. Minutes later, they carried the remains of my beloved father in a black body bag down the steps and into the van.

Blaze nearly pulled me off my feet as she bolted down the trail trying to follow the departing vehicle. I tugged her to my car where she jumped into the back seat. We snaked north on Highway 93 along the Bitterroot River toward Missoula following the vehicle carrying his body.

The face of a worried dog in my rearview mirror stared straight ahead at the distant van along the fifty mile route. My thoughts returned to good days at the cabin and a rocky lookout above it, where birds sang, and one could see *forever*. Dad had seen forever for the last time on the preceding day after struggling up the rocky trail to reach the place he loved. Memories haunted me as I gripped the steering wheel and held back tears, stunned by his rapid demise.

My anxiety unwound as I navigated the curves nearing the state lab in Missoula. The vehicle carrying my father's body disappeared, presumably proceeding to the corpse entrance at the back of a large brick building. Sad thoughts of a future alone faded when a cold nose nuzzled my neck as I parked in front. I left Blaze in the car with the windows lowered partway and entered through a heavy glass door with ominous gold lettering, *Montana State Crime Laboratory*.

An attractive younger man greeted me with a professional handshake that evolved to a comforting hug. "Callie, I'm sorry we didn't meet before this happened." Hugh Dalen led me to a soft leather chair in his office near a large desk. I pictured my father sitting in the same chair talking to him about prions. Dalen sat down. "Nolan was excited about your transfer here and finally being able to work with you."

A tear escaped down my cheek, betraying anguish. "Why didn't he tell me he was dying of prion disease?"

"He was ashamed he'd made such an error. Nolan hoped he could cure himself and proudly tell you news of his success." Hugh slid a death certificate across the desk to me. "I completed this after your call. A forensic exam is unnecessary since I know the cause of death."

Hugh's words brought relief. I didn't tell the pathologist my father killed himself with potassium and sedatives. Dad would *not* want suicide on his record. "Did he tell you he wanted to donate his body to the Prion Center in Cleveland?"

"We talked to Paul Wilder, your director there. If you are up to talking, we could call him now to coordinate."

I nodded. Talking to Dr. Wilder, my friendly mentor during the years of rodent research and the beginning of the monkey trial before my forced move to the Ridge Lab would help. Hugh dialed the number. Paul's familiar voice answered on speaker phone. "Wilder here."

"Hugh Dalen in Missoula, Paul. Callie Archer is here on speakerphone with me. Her father just died."

"I'm so sorry, Callie. I wanted to tell you, but he swore me to secrecy."

My tears started. "He told me yesterday his internist Dr. Maxwell sent a sample of his spinal fluid to you for diagnosis."

Hugh handed me a box of tissues and placed a hand on my shoulder.

I dabbed my eyes. "Sorry, thought I'd get through this without more tears."

"It's a difficult situation. He did his best to hide the disease as long as he could and retired three months ago, telling the lab he had Parkinson's." Paul hesitated. "Nolan gave his approval for whatever studies we want to do here."

Hugh added, "My copy of his will says body donation if the Prion Center wants it, otherwise, cremation."

I looked down, resigned. "I agree with his wishes."

Paul asked, "Callie, did you know he was working with stem cell preparations and near the end injected the monoclonal antibodies into himself he was testing on diseased deer?"

"Dad mentioned using monoclonals, but not stem cells. He had trouble speaking and was secretive." I looked at Hugh for his reaction. "Prion paranoia, or maybe he couldn't bring himself to talk to me about it."

Hugh agreed. "Likely both."

Paul continued. "I need his body refrigerated and air-transported to us today. I'm anxious to examine his nervous system and other organs under electron microscopy to see if his treatment had any effect."

Hugh's eyes found mine, his eyebrows raised in question. "Paul, are you okay with me taking tissue samples for Callie's research before we ship his body?"

The opportunity would have been lost to me without Hugh's suggestion. "I hadn't considered it. Yes, I'd like to compare drug effects on the prion strain in his tissues with the aggressive one in my study."

"Collect the specimens she wants, then ship the body as soon as possible."

I envisioned Paul in his lab coat, a shock of white hair, and twinkling eyes with smile crinkles. "Paul, I will miss working with you."

"I'm sorry you have to put up with Clint Reilly, the asshole director there. Unfortunately, I have bad news from this end."

His terse remark about Dr. Reilly brought a smile to my lips. The smile faded when I heard Paul's next statement.

"Larry Westphal returned from his rehab stint. Headquarters approved his request to transfer to the Ridge Lab, so you'll have to deal with him again."

My muscles tensed just thinking about Larry. "Shit! I thought I'd never see that bastard again."

"Report him if he harasses you."

"I will." We said good-bye to Paul. I slumped in my chair thinking I'd always felt uncomfortable around men my age outside professional settings. In the past, a few nerdy researchers were likeable, but now, when feeling and looking my worst, my self-consciousness resurfaced in Hugh's presence.

Dad knew I seldom dated and at twenty-eight, had no close friends. My workaholic nature interfered with relationships, so it was easy for me to leave Ohio. Even under these horrible circumstances I felt more comfortable with Hugh than with most men. Maybe his friendship with Dad made the difference.

Hugh ran fingers through his wavy auburn hair. "It's difficult to know what to say, Callie. I was surprised they'd move you away from the Human Prion Center to the isolated Montana facility with your background in human research."

"I quit my infectious disease practice and patient care after I started the primate project so moving here sounded good to me because I'd be with Dad."

"It's awful things didn't work out that way."

"I can't believe he didn't tell me."

"He felt terrible about his fatal mistake."

Hugh's kind words helped. "I know, but it'll take a while for everything to make sense. I resigned myself to leaving the older facility after repeated threats by animal activists. It would be a disaster if they contaminated themselves or released test animals infected with the aggressive cross-species prion in my studies."

Hugh leaned forward. "Cross-species? Isn't there a strong species barrier?"

"I probably shouldn't be talking about it, but Dad trusted you. This prion is more virulent. It killed exotic ungulates, carnivores, birds, and the zookeeper. My source is from his brain."

"Sounds horrible." Hugh leaned toward me. "I'd hoped the three of us could work together."

I shrugged. "Well, I guess now's the time to start sharing our expertise."

Hugh tilted his head, questioning. "What do you mean?"

"Dad will be with us in a scientific way." I waited for his response, hoping he wouldn't consider my statement crude.

Hugh asked with a surprised look. "Always the scientist? I wasn't thinking about working together in quite those terms, but you're right. He'll be helping."

"I'm hard-wired like Dad."

"I see that. From what he'd said about you and your achievements at such a young age, I thought you must be like him."

"Thank you for suggesting samples of his prion subtype for my use. I'll need brain tissue, lymph nodes, skeletal muscle, and bone marrow."

Hugh made notes on a yellow pad. "I can complete the collection by early afternoon. You want the specimens in liquid nitrogen and brain tissue in formalin, right?"

"I could return to pick them up later today after I check on my animals at the lab."

"That works for me. Do you want to see him one more time?"

"No. We said our good-byes."

Hugh walked with me toward the front door. "So, who's this Westphal guy?"

I stiffened, not wanting to rehash the ugly scene. "A drunk prion researcher who forced his way into my lab one night and tried to rape me."

Hugh opened the building door. "Why isn't the bastard in prison?"

I exited to the parking lot walking beside him. "A security guard dragged him away. He went to rehab instead of prison."

Hugh walked in silence.

I opened a back door to let Blaze out. She woofed a greeting and ran to him.

"Blaze and I know each other." Hugh petted her. "She's a great dog. Nolan loved her."

I took her tail wagging as a positive sign. Dogs know who to trust.

Blaze returned and jumped in. Hugh closed the door and leaned against the car. "This isn't a good time to talk business, but I'm concerned about a call I got from the CDC in Atlanta this morning. I think you'd want to know."

"Why did they call?"

"To alert me to three worrisome human prion deaths that occurred over the past few weeks in Idaho. They just determined the diagnosis on a guy who died last week south of Medicine Falls, just across the state line."

My eyes widened. "What are the prion subtypes?"

"A bovine spongiform encephalopathy variant, mad cow disease in cow country. Variant Creutzfeldt-Jakob just like the Brits."

I gasped. "I thought you'd say it was the sporadic form. That's horrible."

Hugh looked around the parking lot. He whispered, "It looks bad. They're considering Idaho a hotspot and are sending out an investigative team."

"That's ominous. We have to find the source immediately because any hint of mad cow disease in this area would stop transport of all beef and mean economic disaster." I opened my door to get in but turned back to him. "Call me if you have any more news. I hope we're not ground zero."

"We have to get ready. Let's hope it's a single source."

I mentioned the kill zone near Dad's cabin.

Hugh frowned "I know. Montana beef and hunting industries would collapse."

I drove away distracted from my grief by the potential disastrous outbreak of the fatal disease.

Chapter 3 - A Voice from the Dead

The dead-end road two miles south of Medicine Falls carried me ten miles upward on hairpin turns to the renowned high-security Rocky Mountain Ridge Lab. Late afternoon sun streamed through loops of concertina razor-wire atop the two perimeter fences. The spiraling wires cast shadows on the asphalt. I parked and scanned the twelve-foot-tall chain-link outer fence. I doubted anyone could penetrate the barrier and the moat of dead ground extending to the electrified eight-foot interior fence.

Westward, a man mingled with deer in two corrals within the double fence. How wonderful it would have been to catch a glimpse of Dad out checking the deer instead of a stranger. Blaze waited in the car with the windows lowered watching activities while I entered the Administration Building to tell Dr. Reilly of my arrival in Montana and Dad's death.

On my preparatory visit prior to moving, Dr. Reilly said my lab in the new high-tech four-story brick integrated restrictive facility, the IRF, would not be ready when I arrived. His email sent just before I left for Montana said my temporary lab would be in an Admin wing just down the hall from his office. Way too close for comfort from what Paul Wilder said about him.

When I had toured the large veterinary facility at the back of the thirty-acre compound where my animals were housed, I found it impressive and believed my study animals would receive proper care. At that time, Dad seemed a little unsteady when walking out to the complex with me but nothing in his behavior alerted me to what I would find when I arrived.

A guard directed me through a metal detector, then the two fences. The buzzer at the Admin entrance roused the security chief Sgt. Les Collucci who opened the door and introduced himself.

"Hi, Sarge. Good to meet you. Is Reilly still here?"

"He hasn't left yet." Sarge's eyes widened. "Is something wrong?"

I took a deep breath, holding back tears. "Dad died last night."

"Dr. Archer, I'm so sorry." He put a hand on my shoulder. "We've sure missed seeing him around the lab since he retired."

"Thanks. I didn't want to come here today, but I need to talk with Dr. Goff about my animals. I wiped my eyes. "While I'm here, I'll tell Reilly of Dad's death, though I doubt if he cares."

Sarge, a middle-aged man in a white NIH uniform shirt and dark pants, rolled his eyes. "You may be right. I'll walk out to the animal compound with you. I need to talk to Bernie about a faulty alarm."

I looked forward to knowing him, friendly conversation might brighten dark workdays without Dad.

We cut through the ancient coffee room where researchers congregated in caffeine withdrawal. Butt-indented cushioned chairs lined Formica tables near the side door exit to the fifty-yard path to the Vet Building. I told him about Blaze.

Sarge suggested I move into Dad's small duplex apartment in town where the dog had lived before moving to the cabin.

"I like the idea. He hasn't painted in years, but I'm sure it would be better than living in a motel room." And, I thought, I would have to sanitize everything before moving in.

Dad was meticulous in his work, but prion disease is always fatal. I could take no chances with the infectious proteins resistant to all common methods of sterilization. I didn't want to face the death my father had endured.

Sarge and I entered the vet compound through double doors with thumb print and keycard locks and asked for Bernie. The young male receptionist scanned an electronic board. "Dr. Goff's badge shows her in the monkey pod."

I followed Sarge down a long hallway. "I'm glad you know where you're going."

The large, air-conditioned building housed hundreds of project animals. Sarge introduced me to many workers in scrub outfits scurrying around like rats in a maze.

He held a door. "Have you met Bernie?"

"About a year ago when I visited Dad and we touched bases four months ago. She's efficient and funny. I think I'll like working with her."

Sarge opened a heavy metal door into a clean area where overhead classical music mixed with monkey chatter. Occasional screeches echoed off the walls. "We caught you playing with baby monkeys again."

The fortyish exuberant woman held a tiny monkey with a fuzzy golf ball-sized head. Her compact body spun toward him, a grin on her face. "You know I never play with the babies, Sarge. I'm examining her." Bernie held the baby out for us to see.

"She's adorable." I stroked her soft fur with one finger. "How old is she?"

"Two days. Weighs about a pound. Put on a gown if you want to hold her." Bernie pointed to a cage. "Her mother is one of the disease-free controls in another project. Your control pair are in the cage against the far wall. They've done well since arriving a few days ago."

The uninfected rhesus pair I used to compare with the test animals chattered and played. They swung around inside their large cage as if moving from branch to branch in their natural habitat.

Bernie watched my interactions with the tiny baby while checking her movements. The monkey's large inquisitive eyes studied my face and slender fingers gripped my thumb. "Don't be getting too attached to her. You'll be asking me for a pet monkey for your office."

"Hmm. I hadn't thought about that." I uncurled the delicate fingers holding my thumb and handed the baby back to Bernie.

"She's docile now, but the older ones are pests. You'd get no work done with a monkey scrambling around your office." Bernie placed the baby back with the mother. "Sarge, your board alarm turned out to be a faulty freezer sensor. They checked it out this morning and installed a replacement."

"Glad it's solved. I enjoyed the walk out with Dr. Archer. Have a good meeting, ladies." He disappeared toward the exit.

Bernie removed her gown and washed her hands. "You can trust him, unlike a few others at this facility."

I took a deep breath, preparing myself to again say the words I dreaded. "Bernie, Dad died last night."

"Oh, no, Callie." She threw her arms around me. "I'm so sorry. I've really missed him. My staff loved him." She wiped her eyes. "We worked side by side for years. He was a meticulous researcher. Why are you back at work so soon?"

"I'd rather be working than home crying."

"I understand. I suppose you want to check your animals?"

I nodded.

"The rodents are fine. They're eating, looking good."

"And the study monkeys?"

"Not so good. I was hoping I'd see you as soon as you arrived."

Bernie led me to an isolation wing. "In morning review, the vet techs in charge of the infected pair said they're eating less than usual." She keyed open the door. "They're agitated and falling from the bars."

I followed Bernie along a corridor. "These athletic monkeys rarely fall. Don't you think it's too early for them to be showing such advanced signs of disease?"

"You're the expert on that. We haven't done prion studies on primates here before. You're the first."

My two-foot-tall monkeys huddled in a far corner of their cage. As we approached, the female reached with a trembling arm for a climbing bar and missed. She sprawled on her back. Her behavior gave me a sudden jolt of emotion, reminding me of Dad's poor coordination. "I hate seeing the monkeys sick and have great hopes my successful rat treatment will stop the disease in primates."

Bernie joined me at the cage. "In human disease vision distortion evolves to paranoia, both are difficult to test in monkeys. Since this pair has obvious abnormal neurological symptoms we can follow, it's possible to evaluate the effect of treatment." She scanned a chart. "When do you want to start the drugs?"

"All I need is an accurate weight for each one to calculate their doses."

Bernie handed me two clipboards. "Here are their weights from this morning." The female struggled to get up. Bernie's eyes widened. "Oh my god, Callie. Look at her belly. She's pregnant!"

I stared at the struggling animal. "Damn it! How could they have been so careless at the Cleveland lab to give me a pregnant monkey?"

"That kind of mistake could have happened here." Bernie watched the uncoordinated female right herself and huddle against the male. "Don't be too hard on the Cleveland vet team. These monkeys don't show evidence of estrus. It's difficult to tell when they're fertile."

"How far along is she?"

Bernie squinted, thinking. "Their gestation is about five and a half months. I'd guess she's halfway." She counted on a wall calendar. This is September fifteenth,so delivery would be around the first week of December."

"Pregnancy was not part of my research protocol."

Bernie smiled. "It is now. It may be fortuitous. You'll have a test baby."

"It's bad enough dealing with the adult monkeys. My dad talked about loving his deer, yet for decades he infected, drug-tested them and watched them die. Hell, I even love my rats." I thought about the baby monkey I had just met and dreaded what lay ahead.

Bernie peered over the top of the frames perched on her nose. "So I've heard." She smiled. "Don't be getting soft on me, girl. Animal studies have to be done. Your success could save many human lives."

Crossing the compound surrounded by the tall fences en route back to the old administration building I felt like an inmate in a new prison confined for some terrible deed. Surrounded by strangers in an alien environment, alone, but for Blaze. Ridge lab was nothing like the high-rise security building I had worked in for years. Listening to twittering birds and breathing in fresh mountain air reminded me I'd escaped the noise and exhaust fumes of Cleveland.

I entered through the side door, crossed through the coffee room again, heading to Reilly's office. My footsteps echoed in the long mustard-colored hallway where dim bulbs hung from ceiling cords. Crumbling plaster displayed spider-webbed damage extending from the ceiling to the ancient hexagonal-tiled floor.

How could his building be more secure than my lab in Cleveland?

Strange childhood thoughts about sidewalk cracks that led to an underworld where demons could be released and bring bad luck flitted through my thoughts as I walked on the uneven surface. I'd had enough bad luck so stepped over the next crack near the end of the long hall.

The staccato sounds of someone walking on the hard surface gave me just enough warning to step aside. Dr. Reilly rounded the corner. "Good to see you made it to Montana, Archer. Collucci told me you'd arrived. Come to my office. I want to talk to you about a number of things."

Reilly snapped at me like a nasty elementary school principal I'd once known. I resented his behavior but followed him into his office.

He spun toward a file cabinet causing his gray comb-over to flip up. Reilly slicked his hair back down, pulled open a drawer, and removed a packet in one smooth move. He slammed the drawer shut and continued a pirouette terminating at his high-backed leather chair at a gleaming desk.

Scanning the director's office provided insight into the irksome man. No mess. No stacks of papers. A bookcase held volumes arranged in a perfect line, from tallest to smallest. Over his desk hung a large photo of the smiling director dressed in orange camo kneeling beside a dead elk. One hand rested on a tine of an enormous rack, the other held a rifle pointed skyward.

Before he had time to open the file, I blurted, "My father died last night."

"My condolences," he said without feeling. "Nolan was a highly respected researcher. When's the funeral?"

"He requested no funeral and no memorial service. I came to tell you I may need some time off to handle affairs and move to a bigger place that accepts dogs."

"You manage your hours. Take the time you need." He opened the packet of papers. "It's a good thing you're on salary because from what I hear, if you were an hourly employee, you'd destroy my budget with overtime." Reilly snapped. "You're just like your father, a damn workaholic. What the hell are you doing keeping his dog? Dogs are more trouble than they're worth."

"Blaze was like a child to him."

"Same statement goes for kids. Good luck finding a place to live in this town. You're lucky to have a motel room." Reilly removed a stapled sheaf of papers from the file and slid them across the desk to me. "This is background information on the Ridge Lab for your talk next Thursday night. I scheduled you top billing as speaker for the quarterly Community Laboratory Relations Program."

I opened my mouth to refuse but Reilly's hand shot up. "Elk and deer hunting seasons will open soon. You need to reassure the hunters and ranchers the lab is safe." He stood up and leaned his small frame across the desk as if to intimidate me. "They worry about our biologics escaping the lab. It's your job to calm their fears."

Other researchers had complained to me on a visit in the past about the brutal community meetings. "It's a valid concern, but I'm not prepared to deal with angry locals. Will you be there for crowd control?"

"Miss Callie, you came here with a five-star rating. In Montana, we make you earn your spurs." He smirked. "You can't get out of this. Crowd control is part of your job."

My eyes stabbed the bastard. "Exactly what topic do you want me to present?"

Reilly spewed, "I paired you with Stan Heath, the regional director of Fish, Wildlife and Parks. Slides are optional. He'll talk about Chronic Wasting Disease. Be prepared to talk about human prion disease. It'll be a packed house."

My stomach clenched. The topic was too close for comfort after Dad's death.

"I'd like to meet Stan and coordinate before the meeting."

Reilly scribbled on a notepad. "Here's his number. Call my new secretary Joy if you need anything else." He slid his chair back and stood, dismissing me. "Stop at Human Resources to report your father's demise. They'll notify insurances." Reilly walked to the door with me. "There'll be paperwork for you to sign."

"Dad willed his body to science."

"Thoughtful of him." Reilly closed his door.

On my way out I stopped in security and asked Sarge to pass the news of my father's death to the staff.

The monkey pregnancy meant unexpected challenges. I couldn't wallow in grief, there was no time. I had important research to do related to primate development and how placental barriers might prevent disease transmission. Based on my knowledge of humans, the same protective process could prevent the passage of medications given to the mother from reaching her developing fetus.

Also, should the drugs not work, I had the opportunity to use a targeted antibody against the abnormal protein in the newborn, a monoclonal—if I could get an antibody in time. I had two months.

Reviewing Dad's journals and pathology slides from the pregnant doe that infected him might contribute to my search for a cure. His horrible accident had proven CWD from infected deer crossed the species barrier and could infect humans. This was a significant finding and unknown prior to his infection. It made sense. A primate study in Canada proved monkeys were susceptible. They ate CWD infected venison and all died. I infected my study monkeys the same way, but I hoped they would all survive with my treatment.

Monoclonal antibodies designed to target and interlock with an abnormal protein structure could be the answer all prion researchers had been looking for. In theory, this interaction could flip the abnormal protein configuration back into the normal molecular shape and reverse the incurable disease.

Dad and I had little time to talk about monoclonals he had been developing. By the time I arrived in Montana, he had moved to the cabin in hiding, with memory fading, co-ordination faltering and wasting away like the deer. These thoughts swirled on the drive from the lab to Medicine Falls where I parked at a small duplex with yellow peeling paint.

The house appeared deserted. Long grass. Drapes, closed. A curtain hanging across a front window moved, revealing an elderly bearded figure who lived in the other half of the side-by-side.

Blaze whined to go in with me, but I had come only to retrieve the safe deposit box keys and go to the bank to find his will.

I pulled the key from my pocket, reminding myself that Level 3 biologics didn't jump or fly around contaminating surroundings like airborne pathogens. I'd cleansed the key at the cabin with bleach but put on gloves before entering the spartan unit.

On a desk against one wall, I found a notebook with Dad's scrawl. *Callie, we have two safe deposit boxes at First National on Main. One for financial and ownership documents, the other with research information also has Hugh Dalen as signatory.* Trusting Dr. Dalen with his research solidified my feeling of trust for the pathologist.

I dumped the keys from a tiny envelope into my gloved hand and scrubbed them with lye solution I found on the kitchen counter. Reassured they were not contaminated, I placed them in my pocket and left for the bank.

I drove a few blocks to the old brick building where a clerk led me down a cement stairway to a dark vault where she retrieved two metal drawers. She placed them on a desk in a corner alcove. I plopped into a cushioned chair and opened the first box. An envelope inside addressed to me contained a copy of Dad's will and a large life insurance policy with me named as beneficiary. I tended to be frugal like him and had no idea he carried the policy. Deeds to his duplex and cabin designated me as co-owner.

The second box contained numerous thumb drives and a small digital camera. A note taped to the camera said: *Dear Callie. I'm gone now, but with you in spirit. The videos will help you decipher my research notes. Love and strength to you, Dad. Hug Blaze for me.*

Tears flooded. Promise, I'll hug Blaze for you, every day.

I tucked all the USB flash drives and camera in my purse, then rushed back to the studio apartment. Blaze and I entered together. She explored then curled near my feet where I sat at Dad's desk. I took the earliest dated video stick and placed it in the camera to view.

December 3: Someone had filmed Dad nine months earlier ministering to a whitetail doe. She lay on the snow in a fenced area with him squatting near her head. His gloved hands stroked her silky face. Her ribs protruded like Dad's had at the time of his death. The deer struggled to rise on skeletal legs. Saliva dripped from her mouth. The camera zoomed in on her brown eyes staring up at him. My father's trimmed gray beard shimmered in the winter sun as he attended to the disabled doe.

His sad voice echoed off the walls. "I'm sorry the medicine didn't work, my friend. I thought we'd have a fawn. I can't let you suffer any longer." The deer's head rested on the snow. His fingers found a vein in her neck. Dad injected fluid from two syringes, then petted her golden coat and waited in silence.

Her breathing stopped.

The video ended.

Tears ran down my cheeks as I thought of his death scene at his cabin.

December 4: Twenty-four hours later, the camera recorded a nighttime scene of Dad sitting at the desk the following day in his apartment where I'd found the note and keys. Lamplight shadowed his sad face. Behind him, my smiling mother looked at me from their wedding photo. She had short curly dark hair. I look just like her. Glimpses of two additional photos in the background showed happy times for them. One pictured her holding me as a toddler, and the other, a photo of her with my handsome, dark-haired father taken many years earlier at the Oregon Coast.

Dad's trembling voice interrupted my thoughts of Mom. "Callie, something terrible happened last night. I cut myself doing the necropsy on a prion-infected pregnant doe I'd euthanized. The contaminated scalpel slipped and sliced into my hand through two glove layers. I can't believe I did this."

I cried as I watched and listened to his next three months of reports. On the last one, dust motes stirred in the late afternoon sun streaming around him through the dirty apartment windows. I recognized marked deterioration in his health as he spoke from the desk where I sat with Blaze beside me.

After finishing the first set of videos, I stretched my legs and explored the L-shaped apartment. Cabinet doors stood open. Bed stripped. Cleaning supplies cluttered the kitchen and bathroom. When I sat back down, I scanned the video index and scrolled to one labeled nine months after the fatal cut, the last video. I wanted to hear his final words.

Dad's cheeks appeared sunken. A thin arm jerked toward the camera, his voice strained, "I have someone I want you to meet."

A smeared image focused on a German shepherd. Friendly eyes looked into the camera.

"Callie, this is Blaze." Beside me the dog sat up and cocked her head, listening to the video voice. She wagged her tail.

"I found her the week I retired. We've been together for a month now. I named her Blaze for two reasons. A blazing fire brought us together, and only fire kills prions for certain. Crazy, but I wanted her to have a strong name and survive.

"When I was tending my fire at the campground, I heard whining and found Blaze chained to a tree. I assumed campers left her behind. I sat down beside her. She just lay there covered with wood ticks, too weak to get up. I poured water into her mouth and fed her some cheese and a few crackers I had in the car.

"I spent days feeding her and ridding her of ticks. She let me bathe and brush her. We sat together in the backyard and when she regained strength, began playing ball. Since she improved, Blaze and I have been closing the house and moving to the cabin. I've been less depressed with her by my side. I hoped the monoclonals were working on my brain cells, but I think it's Blaze. She's an amazing companion. I've been very careful to avoid infecting her.

"I cleaned junk silverware, dishes, and pots before taking them to the dump. I burned towels, washcloths, sheets, clothes, most everything else in a campground fire pit near the Medicine River. If anybody from town had seen me, they'd have thought I'd gone stark raving mad. I guess I have. Voices in my head mumble, and I've started seeing things I know aren't real."

The shaky image steadied after Dad placed his camera on the tripod. He fell back in his chair, silent but for heavy breathing. His tortured face refocused.

I barely recognized the man speaking with strange, halting speech, not rapid-fire like my scientist father.

I saw a furry blur near his chair. A shaky hand patted her head.

"I told my colleagues I have Parkinson's. I won't be able to drive soon. After stocking up on supplies, Blaze and I will move to the cabin, where we'll be when you arrive in September ."

In his last video, Dad appeared gaunt and bearded.

"My emotions are shot. I cry every day. I can't eat. My brain is slow. Irritability and anger float near the surface. I'm ready to explode.

"Callie, if the outbreak of the disease spreads further, crazy people like me will fill the streets and jails. If I had a gun up at the cabin recently, I probably would have killed myself or someone else. I saw things in the woods, but Blaze didn't bark. I guess I was hallucinating.

"I know I'll soon be in diapers. I won't allow that to happen. I hoped I'd have a few more weeks to spend with you, but I'm so weak, it'll be my time to go soon. I hope you understand. I'm ready.

"All my notes, computer files and journals are yours. Don't let Reilly interfere with our work. There's an Angus rancher south of town you should meet. Mack and I have worked together a little. He has an interesting business. I wanted to introduce you but there's no time. I love you, honey. Thanks for all your help. You're the best daughter anyone could have. Find that cure. I know you can do it."

Sitting alone in his home, I cried. I felt his arms around me. I couldn't talk to him, but he spoke to me from Valhalla.

Chapter 4 – Changes

Hugh walked out of the state lab with me, carrying a box holding four liquid nitrogen canisters containing tissue specimens.

I opened the back so he could place them inside. "Thanks so much for waiting for me to get back here. After finding Dad's video documentary of his progressive disease process in his safe deposit box, it had me so captivated I couldn't turn it off."

"No problem. I had things to do. It must have been a shock to see him alive and hear his voice." Concerned eyes scanned my face. "How are you feeling?"

"Strange. Sad. Exhilarated. My emotions are doing somersaults."

He leaned in and ruffled Blaze's fur. "Be sure to call if I can help. I'd love to take you to lunch when you get back to Missoula again."

I thanked him. "I'm really concerned about the CWD infected deer they found south of Medicine Falls last week."

Hugh winced. "It's frightening. They were only on the other side of the Rockies till now."

I took a deep breath. "We'll see more. Prions are highly infective, so it doesn't take much to cause disease, and the protein is so resistant to degradation, they can last for decades in the soil."

"It's a huge worry. I'll call if I hear anything. Try to get some rest."

Seeing Hugh again generated a desire to know him better. Dad trusted him. Blaze liked him. How could I go wrong? But then, I'd never been good at choosing men.

Blaze and I followed the same highway route for the second time in one day, through Missoula and south, with my brain in overdrive. Hearing my father speak from the grave and watching his disease progress left me feeling otherworldly. Morbid thoughts about his body pieces floating in nitrogen bottles in the back of my car added to my scattered thoughts.

I wanted the specimens in safekeeping at the Ridge lab, but another trip to the mountaintop had to wait till morning. More than anything, I needed sleep.

Fall colors flashed along the highway penetrating my ruminations. A spectacular white peak jutted above the evergreen foothills behind large cattle herds that dotted grassy rangeland. A loud honk and revved engine from a passing logging truck forced my thoughts back to driving.

The truck careened around us carrying a heavy load and one large log with a message painted on the end: *Spotted owl motor home*. The satirical statement reminded me of local confrontations between environmentalists and loggers in

Medicine Falls Dad had talked about. He also warned me of agitated animal rights activists who harassed lab personnel by lining up near the gate yelling threats.

A sign announced my arrival: *Medicine Falls, Montana-Population 3,321.* I turned into town and stopped a few blocks later at the dumpy motel on Main I'd be calling home for a while.

Before I'd moved to Montana, Dad warned me his studio apartment had no privacy and was too small for the two of us, so he'd arranged for Sal to reserve a kitchenette for me, basically a studio apartment. I think he'd planned to avoid being too close to me, allowing him to conceal some of the health changes he was experiencing. He hadn't expected the crippling disease to progress so rapidly and force him into hiding at the cabin.

When I first entered Medicine Falls, I'd driven past the motel in disbelief that Dad would want me to stay in such a dump. After making a loop through town, I understood it was my only option when I'd checked in on my way to the cabin the preceding day.

Blaze and I parked at our door near the partially burned out neon sign: *The Wag— Wheel.* I wondered if Sal, left it that way on purpose.

Childhood nightmares crawled back when I placed my key into the shiny new lock on the damaged door of #6. I'd hated motels since age five, when my grandmother and I had bolted into the night after finding bedbugs. The stark contrast between living in a comfortable, secure high-rise in a large city and being stuck in a single-story motel with shag carpeting made me fear what else was in store.

When I had checked in, a teenager was working so I hadn't met Sal. She and Dad had become friends, so I had to tell her of his death. The cowbell on the door jangled when Blaze and I entered. I heard Sal's coarse voice from behind a curtain of dangling strings of wooden beads separating her living quarters from the outside world. "Be there in a sec."

A skinny woman resembling a retired rodeo queen wearing cowboy boots, tight denims, and a fitted red shirt with pearl snap buttons, parted the beads and emerged. Her dyed black hair was drawn back in a waist-length ponytail that swished as she walked. "Callie! I saw you had hit town yesterday. Did you go up to see your dad?"

Tears flooded. "Dad died last night."

She came around the counter and hugged me. "Oh, no. He was so sick and isolated at the cabin." Sal wiped a tear, smudging her black mascara. "I knew it wouldn't be long. I wanted him to stay with me, but he was too independent." She hugged Blaze. "We are all going to miss him. I told him I would take her."

"I want to keep her."

"I'm glad. Blaze and I are good friends. I'd love her company when you're working."

I patted her head. "She's traumatized without him, and I have to go to the lab tomorrow."

Blaze parted the beads and walked into Sal's apartment. Sal watched her disappear. "I'll put her to work guarding the motel so she can earn her dog treats."

I felt relief seeing their connection.

"I just made coffee. How about a sandwich?"

"Sure. I haven't eaten much in two days."

Sal led me behind the desk and into her living quarters. "You look beat. Sit in your Dad's chair." She placed a mug of steaming coffee on a round oak table along with a can of condensed milk for creamer.

Instead of the sixties-vintage décor with lava lamps and the shag carpeting I expected based on my own unit, her spotless one-bedroom apartment had shiny hardwood floors, leather furniture, and a glowing electric fireplace. Classical music played in the background. Blaze lay down at my feet with her head resting on a stuffed cat.

"Nolan told me a lot about you. I learned to cook vegetarian after spending time with him." Sal dabbed her eyes. "I'll miss his wit. His bright outlook added enjoyment to my dull life."

Seeing Dad's handwriting on a cribbage score sheet lying on a shelf near the table brought comfort. Feeling a profound emptiness without him made me realize how my mother's death must have affected him. Knowing he'd found companionship with Sal eased my sorrow.

Sal talked about Dad's apartment and the fenced yard where Blaze knew the surroundings. "It's a perfect plan for you two, but she's welcome to stay here whenever you're working."

"I have a lot of work to catch up on. Maybe work will help me get over Dad's death."

"Nolan spent most of his time at the lab. The apartment's going to need a coat of paint before you move in. I'd like to help."

"That's great. Sgt. Collucci said he and his wife will help us paint, too."

"The last unit here just filled. Do you feel up to looking at his apartment to talk about what we need to do?"

My exhaustion said, no, but I wanted to move out of the motel as soon as possible.

Blaze sniffed every corner in Dad's apartment and then whined at the side door into the garage. I opened it and she disappeared for a few moments. She returned and looked at us as if to ask, "Where is he?"

I looked into her intelligent eyes. "You have two mothers. We'll take good care of you."

Blaze followed Sal into a small pantry and returned carrying a treat.

"Your dad stripped the cupboards except for her box of dog treats. I think the man lived on cheese and crackers when I didn't cook for him."

"Dad never cooked when I was around. We ate out or he just ate oatmeal at home."

Sal walked through the house with me. "This place hasn't been painted since he bought it after your mom died. I'd start with everything new in the kitchen. Take the mismatched dishes and silverware to the dump." She looked in the kitchen cabinets. "I guess he already took care of that." Sal opened his closet. "Empty. He got the apartment ready for you."

"I'm happy you and Dad were friends. In a small town like this, it could be lonely."

"Depends. I know everyone. I've lived here my whole life." She swished her ponytail. "You wouldn't want to know some of them."

"You'll have to tell me who to avoid if I ever leave the lab before dark."

"I'd worry about *after* dark. When do you want to start cleaning up the apartment?"

"By Saturday I'll have a lot of work behind me. Reilly scheduled me to present at the town meeting on Thursday evening."

"He's throwing you to the wolves. Your Dad didn't trust him."

"I think Reilly hates me."

"You'd better keep the motel door locked. The people who just checked in are from out of state. I'd bet they're here to cause trouble at the meeting."

"Some of the researchers said the meetings can be nasty."

Sal agreed. "I go to the meetings occasionally just to watch the antics. Do you have dinner plans tonight?"

"Oatmeal with raisins, fruit, and a glass of wine."

"Healthy, but I have spinach lasagna ready to put in the oven. Why don't you eat here?"

"That sounds better."

My concerns about being isolated in the small town eased. I had Sal and my wonderful dog in Medicine Falls, and I'd found Sarge and Bernie at work.

After dinner, Blaze followed me to our home in the end unit of the single-story motel where she curled up on a thick throw rug, a gift from Sal. I fell asleep on the edge of the bed with my hand resting on the dog's furry back.

I awakened in early morning darkness with the pink neon *No Vacancy* sign glowing in the office window. I left Blaze with Sal before heading up the hill to work after stopping for a scone and latte at the Coffee Outpost. The front page of the *Medicine Falls News*, a weekly, lay on my table with a story about the lab's community meeting. "This week, experts will be speaking on prion disease in humans and animals. Prions are weird protein particles that cause fatal disease in cattle and big game." Interviews with hunters, a rancher, and someone from the Beef Growers' Association rounded out the mostly negative comments.

The article did nothing to allay my concerns about the meeting.

Before I was out of cell range, I called Paul Wilder in Cleveland to tell him about the pregnant monkey.

"That certainly changes things, doesn't it?" His voice carried surprise but no concern.

"We can't say it was part of the original study, but I want to take advantage of the opportunity to try monoclonals on the baby if it survives."

"I like the idea of testing a monoclonal, unless the monkeys are cured by your rat drugs. I have a meeting now. You'll be seeing Larry Westphal soon. I'll call later."

Hearing the name was a bad start to an ominous day.

Chapter 5 - Treating Monkeys

Bernie and I wore disposable impervious gowns, HEPA filter masks, goggles, and double gloves to protect ourselves while we performed injections. Level 3 diseases are not airborne like influenza viruses. However, infectious prion particles swirl in body fluids. Droplets can become aerosolized during procedures and spread the disease, so we took all protective precautions.

I videoed the sick monkeys prior to beginning the drug infusions to document baseline neurological impairment. Frequent videos would provide a comparison for monitoring treatment response.

The male monkey huddled in a corner of his cage, then slumped within a minute of Bernie's injection of a sedative and anesthetic drug. She reached in to pick him up. "I won't handle any diseased study animals until they're sedated and no longer a biting risk." She placed the limp animal beneath bright lights on a stainless-steel table.

I tightened a tourniquet around his upper arm. "Prion researchers have been working on treatments for decades." I swabbed the injection site at the elbow with a smelly iodine solution and placed an intravenous catheter. Saline dripped to keep the line open as I injected solution from the first syringe.

Bernie followed the monkey's vital signs. "He's stable so far. I'm curious. What meds are you giving them? I won't divulge your secrets."

"Three drugs with complementary activity. First, dexamethasone, the steroid we use to suppress inflammation and allergic responses in veterinary and human medicine. In this case, it stimulates the action of P-glycoprotein, a natural substance that makes the blood-brain barrier permeable to drugs."

Bernie checked the monitors. "His oxygen saturation is holding at 100%. It's hard to get drugs into the central nervous system, so first, you are opening the door to the blood brain barrier." She listened to his heart and lungs. "Prions don't stimulate inflammation in the body, so I wondered why you were using an anti-inflammatory. Now, I understand."

"The steroid also upregulates a receptor in the normal cell nucleus called pregnane X. Its main function is to remove toxins and foreign substances, in our case, the abnormal prions."

Bernie stroked the sedated monkey's hairy arm. "The combination acts like a cellular vacuum using natural processes."

"It worked in rats. Why not monkeys?"

Bernie raised her eyebrows. "Prions in the brain and beta-amyloid brain accumulation in Alzheimer's disease are remarkably similar. Maybe you've come up with a treatment that could cure prion disease, and reverse dementia?"

I injected fluid from the second and third syringes. "That would be amazing. I follow the Alzheimer's literature." I laughed. "Instead of reading romance novels at bedtime, I read about brain disease."

Bernie faked disgust. "Callie, you are very, very sick. There's more to life than work."

"Seriously, I read molecular biology looking for methods to stimulate normal body responses to combat disease like some cancer treatments."

Her eyes softened. "I may give you a bad time, but I'm happy there are people like you."

"I never paid much attention to disease evolution in pregnancy or fetal development during medical school. With the pregnancy, I better read up on those topics, too." I placed the syringes and needles in an incineration bin. "Let me know if you see any articles in the vet journals."

"The drive to cure this awful disease has gone to your head. I go home at night, walk my dogs and play the piano."

"That sounds better than my nightlife. When I was in elementary school, I made rounds with dad on large animals, cattle and deer. I started college at sixteen, so never really learned how to play."

Bernie laughed. "We all have our faults. My mother was a concert pianist and made me practice every day." In a serious tone she added, "After all these years since the outbreak of mad cow disease in the U.K., you're the first to have any treatment success. It's exciting to be on your team."

"My new vision of a cure is finding a way to get a monoclonal antibody to cross the blood-brain barrier, bind prions, and snap them into the normal shape, reversing the disease."

Bernie listened while removing the IV and placing the monkey back in his cage to recover under the care of techs.

"Just before he retired, Dad had started a monoclonal study on wasting disease. He had the pregnant doe and I have a pregnant monkey. I wonder if he has notes on the blood-brain and the placental barriers in deer."

Bernie injected the female with ketamine. We waited for it to take effect, and then moved the monkey to an exam table near the ultrasound machine where Bernie moved the probe over her belly. "It's a female fetus that appears normal. At full term, if she goes that long, the birth weight should be about 500 grams, similar in size to the baby I was holding when you and Sarge visited me."

I started the fluid line and injected the drugs. "If treatment opens the placental barrier, it would make the vertical transfer of prions from the infected mother to her fetus easier. That's not good."

"Right, but on a positive note, the fetus will likely develop prion disease anyway and your drugs will cross the placental barrier and produce a cure. Exactly what we'd want!"

I loved Bernie's analysis and cheery attitude. "But, in this case, because we're treating the mother, if the fetus is born with prion disease, we won't know if it was natural transfer or infected because the drugs opened the placental barrier and allowed the infection to cross over."

"Nothing's easy." Bernie placed the sedated female in the care of techs.

I tossed my gloves and gown in the incineration bin with hers. "What we really need are immunizations for man and beast. Things are looking worse with mad cow disease popping up around the U.S. and the world."

"When did you inoculate the monkeys with prions?"

"Early July. I gave them infected food instead of injecting prions directly into their brains. I wanted to evaluate infection from *eating* prions to provide a test model closer to human disease caused by consuming infected meat."

"These monkeys are in bad shape after just two months. That seems fast."

I thought for a moment before divulging more details to Bernie but decided she needed to know for the safety of her staff. "It took months to identify symptoms in the rats after direct spinal fluid injections, but this cross-species prion appears more aggressive in primates than in rodents."

Bernie suggested, "Maybe the species barrier in rats is stronger."

"At this point, I really don't know, but this particular prion jumped species barriers, infecting exotic ungulates and big cats in a Wisconsin zoo. It even killed birds. And then the zookeeper."

The vet frowned. "Horrible."

"He handled beef donated by a local dairy farmer who euthanized a stumbling cow. The farmer didn't know it had prion disease."

"Scary." Bernie checked a calendar. "Based on the ultrasound fetal size, your female was impregnated within a few days of her prion ingestion. If monkeys are like most prion-infected deer, she'll abort early or produce a stillbirth."

The morning phone discussion with my old director had strengthened my desire to take advantage of the unplanned pregnancy. I told Bernie what he'd said, adding, "The original monkey project designated using only a pair on first try, so a newborn could be a valuable addition to the study. If I find the rodent treatment ineffective in the adult monkeys, I hope we can be ready with a monoclonal for the baby."

Bernie frowned. "Do you know of any human reports on prion transmission from mother to fetus?"

"I looked in some of Dad's literature and found one study where vertical transmission produced a viable offspring in tiny Asian deer, but nothing in humans."

"It's probably a Reeves's muntjac. Now there's an unusual pet for you."

"I like the idea. I'd be out walking my deer and the locals would really think I'd gone crazy."

Bernie opened her office door. "I was *kidding*. Your dad's research on whitetails might be helpful."

"I'll call Colorado U. They may have some unpublished fetal studies."

"The baby may be your real chance for fame. You'll be able to test treatment during both pregnancy and infancy, more transferable to humans than rat studies."

"I hate seeing adult monkeys with this disease. I love my mice and rats, so I'll have problems with an infected baby. They are so human."

Bernie peered over her glasses. "Don't get soft, girl."

"A couple of weeks before I left Cleveland, my office rat died of old age. Do you have a baby rat I could have in my office? I love snuggling a rat when I'm reading. They're like tiny kitties with sandpapery tails."

Bernie laughed. "Girl, I think you are twisted."

"Just a little." I read titles in her bookcases and waited while Bernie dictated the ultrasound report. When she finished, I told her of my conversation with Hugh Dalen about the three recent prion deaths in Idaho. "A team from the CDC is coming out here to investigate."

"What prion types killed them?"

"The first two were hunters, but they tested positive for mad cow, not CWD. The preliminary third report is the same. The third guy was also a young hunter, so they thought it might be CWD. None had traveled outside the state."

Bernie choked. "I'm sticking to chicken and fish."

Chapter 6 - Prion Prison

Stellar jays squawked from the dark pine forest splashed with golden tamaracks rocking in the wind scattering leaves along the path back to my lab. The crisp fall weather reminded me of the walk with Dad up to the lookout. I sadly pictured us walking together from the vet building back to work on our projects but found myself alone, reading a journal eating yogurt from a vending machine like other reclusive researchers with heads down, reading and eating.

Stan Heath, the Fish, Wildlife and Parks regional director's calm voice and vast experience doing community presentations reduced my concern about the meeting. After I'd organized a few PowerPoint slides for my talk, I delved into researching fetal growth in Rhesus monkeys. Bernie called to report she'd found no information on neonate prion infection for any species except the Reeve's deer. I asked her about Dad's vet records on the infected pregnant doe.

Bernie tapped on my office door less than an hour later carrying a large file. "Here's what I found. His records are numbered and color-coded. You won't have any trouble finding what you're looking for." She plopped down on a chair. "These are from the past year just before he retired. If he discovered anything, the data is here. He talked about computer files and digital slides."

"I have some journals and thumb drives at home. You'd probably have more luck getting Dad's computer files than I would. Dr. Reilly is surly. I doubt he'll be cooperative if I request them."

She glared. "Don't take any shit from that sexist bastard."

"Headquarters made him accept me and my prion study. Reilly just assigned me to do the next community presentation. Is that his way of making my life miserable?"

"I'm sure you intimidate him with all your accomplishments. He's not kind."

I paged through the file. "I truly dislike the man, but after I saw the dead elk photo hanging over his desk, I liked him even less."

Bernie snarled. "He shot it inside a damn fence before the practice was outlawed. Those "canned" hunts were despicable. I don't see how anyone could kill an animal just to hang a trophy on the wall."

"I'm not surprised."

Bernie got up to leave. "I'm happy to have another female researcher here. It gets tiresome with all these men."

I followed her out and went to Reilly's office. He met my request for Dad's computer with a nasty tone, but IT staff delivered the computer within the hour. After the tech reset passwords and a vet tech brought my baby rat, I felt comforted and energized. I held the adorable soft white creature with black shoulders and head. Her dark, beady eyes darted around the office. Like my other pet rats, I chose a cheese name.

I lost track of time in my broom-closet office with Brie snuggled against my neck. Dad's computer files and digital slides documented prions in the whitetail fetal deer, confirming the vertical transfer of prions.

Chapter 7 - Return to Normal

Four years of testing numerous drug combinations on genetically modified mice and rats had evolved to improvement in symptoms, followed by disease resolution. Rodent brain images changed from the appearance of sea sponges, the spongiform encephalopathy of prion disease, to normal.

At a national conference the year before my transfer to Montana, I had the honor of reporting the first evidence of effective prion treatment after decades of research around the globe. Accolades after the success generated more competition in the field and accelerated the bad behavior of my Cleveland cohort Larry Westphal. With Larry in rehab and me in Montana, my worries about sabotage had eased until I met Clint Reilly.

The night before my presentation at the community meeting, the guard delayed my departure with an offer of good coffee he'd brought from home. I couldn't turn Rudy down after drinking brown tasteless water from the coffee room all day. I met him in the hallway on my way out and had to jog to keep up with his long stride, following him along the corridor toward the control room near the front door.

Rudy Jonsrude reminded me of the big friendly guard in Cleveland who we'd called Hulk, the one who'd saved me from Larry Westphal. I hoped Rudy wouldn't have to become my bodyguard.

He slowed a bit. "I walk fast on rounds because I can't stay away from my light board for long. You and I are the only ones left in the Admin Building. My board showed you leaving the lab. I knew right where to find you."

I raised my eyebrows. "You were stalking me electronically?"

"You could say that." The radio on his belt buzzed. "Jonsrude here."

"Bill, checking in. No issues."

"Thanks."

Rudy's radio buzzed two more times, before we reached the control room. "What's happening? Are those the guys outside the fence?"

"Yeah. I watch the facility on the electronic board, and three perimeter guards call in hourly." We turned into the corridor near the control room. "Electronic alarms on the perimeter fence connect to my light board, but I speak with the guards each hour."

The compound map covered one wall of the control room. Little green lights dotted schematics of the buildings scattered over the thirty acres inside perimeter fences. Rudy pointed to unlighted areas on the board. "These are storage sheds with no biologics, so they are not surveilled."

Rudy pulled up a chair for me to sit next to him at a horseshoe-shaped desk with a wraparound panel of switches within his reach. I scanned the controls. "It looks like an airliner cockpit. Is this technology all part of the new facility?"

He shook his head. "We've had some of it functioning for years in the Admin Building, and older labs like the one you're in are online. Right now, only Level 4 in the IRF is fully functional. Video surveillance and some security aspects are still off-line." Rudy pointed out areas on the large lighted board. "This is the Admin Building. Over here is the animal compound where two NIH guards are on duty 24/7, locked inside the alarmed building. I don't worry about the animals. Our security is higher than all the other NIH facilities."

"That's what I was told before Homeland Security made NIH move me here for a higher level of biosafety. If anyone breached the area and my infected animals escaped, it could end the world as we know it."

Rudy leaned back in his cushy chair. "We're still not ready, but don't worry. We're safe."

The board's green glow cast a surreal tone to Rudy's face.

"It's so quiet, won't you get sleepy?"

"Strong coffee, checking out false alarms and making rounds keeps us awake on the night shift." He explained, "In the daytime, one person is always at the console while the others make rounds."

"So, you're not bored?"

A flashing yellow light drew Rudy's attention. "Heck, no. I love this job." He joggled a switch. "I've been back from Afghanistan for almost three years, but I'm still jumpy." He fidgeted in his chair. "I still get adrenaline surges that make me shake when the old building creaks and rattles on stormy nights."

Rudy's finger traced a circuit on the diagram. "This is the entry door to your new lab. The light, here, is the temperature control on the freezer." He glanced at me. "Lights flash even if you open a freezer door. There are similar alarms on the refrigerators and on the interior door between your office and the lab area."

"It could get confusing, considering all the labs you have to monitor."

"True, but it's simple with the diagrammed layout. A system alarm flashes red and an audio alert occurs if the doors aren't secured within two minutes." He reached forward and pointed to another area. "If I don't acknowledge the audio alert within thirty seconds, my radio buzzes." He flipped a test switch so I could hear the alarm.

I startled at the sharp tone. "I can see why you're jumpy."

"They're usually false alarms, but they still trigger an adrenaline surge." He held out a steady hand. "Sometimes I get the jitters, but not tonight."

After my Cleveland experience, I was worried about a breach. "What if something really happens?"

"If an alarm sounds when I'm making rounds within the Admin Building, I return to the control room and assess the location." He tapped his radio. "The perimeter guards keep me informed. They patrol the electrified fence line all night long."

"You're the only security officer inside the compound at night?"

He nodded, "I'm the only one here in Admin. The other two guys are in the Vet Building." He pointed to a section designated as Level 4, the highest-risk area. "This level on the top floor of IRF is fully secured. We'll have two officers on duty in Admin 24/7 when all levels in IRF go live."

"A lot could go wrong, but I feel reassured after understanding your electronic surveillance."

Rudy smiled. "Locked doors, system alarms, metal detectors, and perimeter guards. They've kept us secure for years. It's like a ship, with the perimeter guards patrolling the dock and with me onboard." He pointed to his landline. "For problems outside the compound, the guards call the sheriff's department for backup. Inside the compound, NIH personnel are responsible to the FBI. We'd call the Missoula FBI office for backup."

"They wouldn't be much help in a real emergency since they are more than an hour away. That's worrisome."

Rudy flipped a couple of switches, testing lights. "I wondered what was up. A few days ago the Counterterrorism Division of the FBI gave us a mandatory training update."

"Didn't Reilly warn you they were coming?"

Rudy leaned back, his hands resting in his lap, looking more relaxed than usual. "I thought there must have been a threat, but they denied it. The FBI task force from Helena was here, too. I'd never seen them before."

"I wonder why Dr. Reilly didn't call me to come in if it was a mandatory meeting."

"You were with your dad."

I took a deep breath, exhausted, thinking I should go home. "I was feeling pretty overwhelmed. I probably shouldn't have come."

"You're here late tonight."

I held up a file. "I have a few notes to review for my talk at the town meeting tomorrow night. From the newspaper article, it looks like there might be trouble."

Rudy answered a radio call. "Maybe that's why the feds were here. When my wife went a couple years ago, wing nuts from Earth First! and the Animal Liberation Front raised a ruckus."

"I can see why PETA or ALF would be interested in the lab, but why an ecoterrorist group like Earth First!?"

Rudy shrugged. "Not sure. Aren't they all true believers on a mission?"

"I used to think Earth First! members were pacifists, but they've killed people. It was ALF that forced entry at the Cleveland lab, prompting my transfer."

Rudy patted his holster. "They won't get to your animals here."

"Reilly suggested I carry pepper spray."

Rudy looked skeptical. "It is unlikely they'd attack you, but they'd release your animals if they could get at them."

"That's what worries me."

"Ranchers and avid hunters will be at the meeting. You don't have to worry about them. Locals aren't crazy like the animal rights people."

I finished my coffee and got up to leave. "I'd feel better if you were coming."

"You'll have protection. The law always attends. I'm a hunter, so I'd go this time if I didn't have to work."

Guards waved me through the gate. The perimeter lights dispelled some of my dark thoughts, but one persisted.

I'm locked in *prion prison* for life.

Chapter 8 - Death Threat

Attendees streamed into the Medicine Falls high school gymnasium for my first exposure to the quarterly meeting of the lab scientists with locals. A new experience for me because researchers were isolated from the public in Cleveland. Here, I sat between Drs. Clint Reilly and Stan Heath feeling my anxiety rise as squeaky folding chairs below a makeshift stage filled with a menagerie of people.

From a long presenter table, we had a clear view. Six-foot-four Stan in his attractive FWP uniform leaned my way. "Callie, I've run across that bunch by the door that look like they haven't bathed in months. I think they just crawled out of the woods. There's going to be trouble tonight."

I followed his gaze. "Aren't they just interested people who live here?"

His eyes scanned the room and then settled back on me. "They don't come to these meetings to pat you on the back. I'd say there are a lot of pissed-off people here tonight. It's a bad sign when the chairs are full."

Dr. Reilly tapped the microphone for silence. The crowd paid no attention at first, but finally quieted for his welcome and overview of the new Level 4 facility, without providing specifics about security or electronic surveillance. "I've received nasty phone calls comparing the Ridge Lab to the meth halfway house here." Reilly scoffed, "As if our lab brings danger to Medicine Falls. It brings no danger. It brings jobs and life-saving research."

A male voice shouted from the back of the room, "It's worse than meth! We can see the dolts who use drugs. We worry about bugs that could destroy all of us, including ranching and hunting."

Reilly snapped, "You have nothing to fear from the lab. This is the most secure research facility in the U.S., possibly in the world." He pointed to a row of noisy men in the second row. "You should be proud to have the lab here employing so many people."

An ancient man struggled to his feet. He rapped a cane on a metal chair quieting the crowd and exposing a pistol strapped to his hip. Tobacco juice stained the untrimmed white beard the color of his Carhartt jacket.

Seeing his handgun sent a jolt through my chest. "Is it legal to carry a gun in here?"

Stan scanned the room. "As long as it's not concealed. A lot of them are carrying, just to make a point."

My chest tightened. "I'd rather deal with animal activists in Cleveland. I never saw weapons."

The old man bellowed. "Forget the bull crap. Get on with the hunting part."

A uniformed police officer moved toward him.

The old man sat down and glared at Dr. Reilly who continued with his presentation. "I've invited four speakers tonight. They'll talk about diseases in animals that can be transmitted to humans. We'll start with anthrax and tularemia." He gave a short overview of the human health implications of both diseases. "Then, Dr. Callie Archer will talk about mad cow disease in humans contracted from eating infected beef. Dr. Stan Heath is regional director of Fish, Wildlife, and Parks. He'll end our presentations tonight with a disease similar to mad cow spreading through wildlife called Chronic Wasting Disease."

The first researcher's overview of anthrax and the potential terrorist threat to humans generated no questions from the audience. The tularemia specialist explained the disease could spread from rabbits and kill humans.

A husky man dressed in a red and black plaid shirt called out, "Elmer, we don't shoot *wabbits* in these parts." Laughter broke out.

Reilly quieted the hecklers. "You've been waiting to hear about prion disease. I'm pleased to introduce our newest researcher. Dr. Callie Archer is an international expert on prion disease and is looking for a cure."

I walked to the microphone hearing a jumble of comments from around the room. Groans followed my historical perspective on prion disease including the spread of kuru by cannibalism in New Guinea. "A similar abnormal protein causes scrapie disease in sheep, Creutzfeldt-Jakob in humans, mad cow disease in cattle, and Chronic Wasting Disease in wildlife." The crowd silenced when I ended with a short video of a man infected with prion disease.

Hands shot up, but I continued speaking. "Prions have been around for decades, but not until people in Great Britain developed the fatal neurological disease from eating infected beef did anyone become concerned. If people could catch it from eating a hamburger, they wanted to know more about it."

Voices filled the room, making it impossible for me to be heard.

The tall imposing FWP regional director took the microphone. "Listen up. I want to tell you about the disease in wildlife, but we're not continuing until you quiet down. You need to know most infected deer and elk are in a corridor along the northern portions of Colorado and the southern Wyoming border. The bad news is, we identified six infected deer in eastern Montana last year and of more concern, we killed a whitetail doe with CWD just south of Medicine Falls."

A hand went up. "So, it's spreading here?"

Stan had their attention. "Numbers were steady for years, but in the past two, Colorado showed an increase. Chronic Wasting Disease has now spread into a total of twenty-five states and Canada. Hundreds of infected animals were taken in hunts across the U. S. last year, including the West, Midwest and east coast states."

The room hummed with conversation.

"Recently, Colorado Fish and Game found a bull moose with Chronic Wasting Disease. That was a first."

A question came from the audience: "Why does that matter?"

"Prions are likely to spread among herd animals from licking and ground contamination. Moose are lone creatures. The method of infectivity to the moose isn't clear, most likely from grazing on contaminated ground. It also shows cross-species spread."

Stan had their attention.

A young man in front asked, "How many people have gotten sick from eating wild game?"

"No human disease from eating wild game has been reported. But because the disease in wildlife is spreading and the prions are like those in mad cow. It's possible humans could be infected from eating wild game."

More hands went up.

"I can reassure you, we are testing all deer taken in the area around Billings and other animals taken by Montana hunters who believe an animal may be ill with CWD. We ordered a controlled kill in the area south of town like we contained an outbreak in a domestic elk farm a few years ago. Dr. Archer will continue now."

Stan sat down.

I flashed slides comparing normal and diseased brains. "Before my success in treating rats infected with prions, the disease was fatal to all animals and humans. My study rats improved. The disease in their brains receded. Our hope is that rodent research will transfer to prevention and treatment in humans through a primate trial."

My final statement generated an outburst from the front row. "Killer! You kill monkeys."

I tapped the mic and held up my hands to shush a cacophony. "The lab is held to high standards for the humane treatment of animals." I doubted anyone heard me.

Stan took the microphone. "Let Dr. Archer speak, or the meeting will be adjourned." Motioning to me and the other researchers, he said, "Using animals in their studies is appropriate. A few lab animals are sacrificed to save many human lives."

A man in the back raised his hand. "Sir, please tell us about the risks of wasting disease spreading from wildlife and domestic elk farms to cattle."

Stan tried to calm them. "Domestic elk farms are safe. The animals are closely monitored by vets." Angry people shouted questions while one stood and proclaimed elk farms were no threat to wildlife or cattle.

Another shouted, "Shut up, Adcock. Let the scientists talk. We know you run an elk farm and used to shoot corralled animals."

Three men lunged at Adcock. Police interceded and pushed them out the door.

Dr. Reilly grabbed the mic. "We will not tolerate unruly behavior. Quiet down."

More shouting. "Close the damn elk farms before they contaminate our cattle."

Reilly tapped the mic, trying to regain order. The rotund Medicine Falls chief of police strode to the stage. "I'm closing this down. If you can't treat these scientists with civility and respect, you're out of here. Leave peaceably, now! All of you, move to the exits."

More disorderly behavior erupted as officers attempted to disperse the crowd.

People surrounded Adcock, the elk farm man. He punched a guy in self-defense. A photographer snapped the altercation.

I imagined the photo on the front page of the newspaper, giving Ridge Lab bad publicity, something Dr. Reilly wanted to avoid at all cost.

Stan motioned to me and the other scientists to follow him. "Let's get the hell out of here." I shoved my computer into its case and slung the strap over my shoulder.

To keep us from having any further contact with the unruly people, the police chief motioned to a side door.

A tall Native American man dressed in black western attire moved forward and spoke to the chief, then herded us away from the disorderly crowd to the exit.

Two officers dragged Adcock out of a brawl and placed him in the back of a patrol car.

In the parking lot away from loud groups of people exiting the building, Dr. Reilly introduced me to the cowboy. "Meet Dr. Callie Archer, Mack." He smirked. "Callie, meet Mack Janns, the cowboy who dresses in black and rides a white horse. He's come to our rescue."

I offered him my hand. "Nice to meet you, Mack. I guess Medicine Falls is still the Wild West."

Mack's long single braid fell forward over his shoulder when he bent to shake my hand. "Don't worry about the locals, Dr. Archer. They're always at each other about the elk farms." His firm grip and dark eyes sent a sensual jolt to my heart. "I'm more concerned about all the foreigners in the front row, Doc. They're here to make trouble."

Reilly cut in, "Callie, did you buy that pepper spray like I suggested?"

I shook my head. "I'll be okay."

Reilly stomped to his Mercedes convertible.

The other researchers drove off, leaving me with Mack. A bit awkward, but my heart still pounded from the uproar. I pointed. "My car is over by that big white pickup."

"That's my truck. Why don't we go somewhere for coffee to let the police have time to clear out the parking lot? It wouldn't be good to have one of these crazies follow you home."

Mack's polished black cowboy boots added a couple of inches to his height, making me feel smaller than usual. A rowdy group milled around our vehicles with one young man leaning on my car. A tall, thin woman blocked my way. I tried to pass, but she side-stepped in front of me. The brazen woman didn't look at Mack, her eyes locked on mine.

A gaggle of her friends watched.

I moved forward. "Excuse me. I need to get to my car."

The woman spat her words. "Baby killer. You use monkeys. It's like killing babies."

I glared. "How would you know?"

"My friends in Cleveland told me about you."

One of the men taunted. "Hey, Hannah, show us a good bitch brawl."

Hannah slammed my shoulder.

I backstepped to regain balance and in a flash of anger swung my laptop, striking Hannah's chest. The thrust sent the shocked woman sideways. My kick caught her knee sending her to the pavement. I flung my laptop to Mack and landed a kick on Hannah's thigh as she tried to get up.

Mack mocked, "Get your bitch out of here. We don't cater to your type around here, women know how to fight, and men know how to shoot." He flipped back his jacket revealing a weapon I hadn't noticed.

The cursing group scrambled away. Hannah scooted back and got to her feet. "We'll meet again. Next time I'll wring your neck like you kill those helpless lab rats. You'll see how it feels to die."

Mack spoke into his cell. "Chief, we need you on the east side of the school. Somebody just attacked Dr. Archer."

Two officers strode toward us.

The activists scattered.

Mack offered me a hand for the high step into his double-cab pickup. He started the rumbling diesel engine and burst out laughing. "That was the coolest knockdown I've ever seen! You floored that broad so fast, I barely saw what happened."

I grimaced. "It was automatic. I surprised myself."

He eased the truck into gear. "I came along as the great protector, but you took care of things by yourself." He laughed.

I looked back and saw the police walking toward the school. "Dad wanted me to be able to defend myself. We took martial arts together when I was in high school. That ruckus set me on edge and brought it back."

Mack drove out of the lot. "That group came to make waves. Wanted to see themselves in the headlines or in jail to gain publicity for their cause. I'm afraid we'll see more of them."

"What's open for coffee this time of night?"

"The Outpost. It's open till midnight."

"I stopped there on my way to the lab this morning for coffee and a scone. Haven't eaten since. I'm hungry enough to eat a horse, except I'm a vegetarian."

Mack looked askance. "Skipping meals and not eating meat? Sounds unhealthy." He frowned. "As for meat, I'm a rancher and couldn't live without eating beef."

I said nothing but thought it was not the most conducive conversation to begin a friendship.

We entered the Outpost to jazz playing overhead and the aroma of fresh brewed coffee. Mack led me to a corner table where I sipped an Americano and devoured a bowl of tomato bisque with bread.

Mack's sipped coffee. "Was your soup okay?"

"Delicious. Thanks for escorting me and the guys out of the meeting."

He leaned back. "Embarrassing crowd. Don't get the wrong idea about this peaceful little town."

"After tonight, I'm wary. Are you concerned about your cattle being close to a biologics lab?"

"No. The lab's been here for decades with no problems. Researchers died in the 1920s trying to solve the 'black measles' epidemic that turned out to be Rocky Mountain spotted fever."

I was surprised he knew the history. "I treated spotted fever once when I was still practicing infectious disease. It's nasty."

"Too bad the crowd ended your presentation. I wanted to hear more about prion disease."

"We can talk about it sometime."

"I knew your dad. We had long conversations about prions."

His words caught me off guard, but when we were introduced, I'd thought his name sounded familiar. Now, I recalled Dad had mentioned Mack in one of his videos.

"He helped me with some lab issues at my ranch. I was very sorry to hear he had died and had no idea you'd moved here."

"The feds moved me to the Ridge Lab recently." I told him a little about the Cleveland circumstances prompting the move.

"So, you have a new secure lab. Did you find a place to live?"

"It's a long story. Reilly put me in an old lab, and I live in a motel."

Mack's eyes jerked wide. "That's crazy."

"I'll be moving into Dad's house soon, but the bio-level 3 labs in the new building aren't ready."

Mack's calloused fingers touched my hand. "I hope things improve. It must be awful for you without your dad. People in this town loved him."

"Thanks. I'm just starting to get back to my project after weeks of turmoil." I sipped more coffee. "Tell me about your ranch."

"Seven miles south of town. I own Angus Insemination International and a certified organic Angus herd."

"Insemination and organic? Do they mesh?"

Mack's sensuous lips spread into a wide grin. His dark eyes pierced mine and distracted my thoughts.

"They don't. The organic herd is totally separated from the others and not injected with hormones. Artificial insemination with registered Angus is not considered natural, so I have to guarantee the state my two businesses are isolated."

I flushed, embarrassed by my naïveté.

"Getting certified organic is a tedious process and guaranteeing their quarantine from the registered cattle. We use different feed, and for the insemination and embryo business, we use hormones in the impregnation process."

"How can you tell the organics from the certified ones?"

"We give them unique names, and they come when called."

I burst out laughing. "I'm a city girl, but you just went too far."

Mack smiled. "We actually tag ears and chip them like expensive dog breeds. Waving a wand over their ear tags tells me who they are, who their parents were, when they were born, and how much they weighed at birth."

We talked about Dad, my move to Montana, and former job in Ohio. "It's been an adjustment. I've never owned a pair of blue jeans."

His loud laugh drew attention to us. "You're a real city girl, Doc! What are you doing in a place like this?"

"I was exiled."

"Since you're stuck here, I'd like to give you a hand at learning cowgirl ways. How about going horseback riding with me sometime?"

I took a deep breath. "That's a scary thought. My only experience is riding a pony tied to a merry-go-round when I was six."

"First, we have to get you some riding clothes. My horses would laugh if you showed up in sandals and a dress."

"I'm glad I wore sturdy shoes and slacks tonight. It's hard to kickass wearing a skirt."

"If I didn't already have a commitment in Missoula this weekend, we could go riding Saturday. How about a week from now, Saturday morning?"

"What am I getting myself into?"

Mack smiled. "You're not in Ohio anymore, Callie. Welcome to Montana.

"I'd love to join you."

"I'll fix breakfast at the ranch, then we'll tour the property on horseback. First, we'll go to Ranch & Home to shop and get you outfitted for a ride."

Mack paid the tab and we walked into the night.

The disastrous town meeting had warped into a pleasant encounter for me, someone who rarely dated. I'd met two interesting men in a matter of days. I might like Montana after all.

Chapter 9 – Aftermath

Mack waited while I started my car, then followed me out of the school parking lot and turned south. His taillights faded in my rearview mirror, but his charm and good looks made me wish we were still together.

I drove past the motel after seeing the office dark. People gathered in the parking lot beneath a streetlight. Not wanting to run into Hannah again, I rounded the block and parked at the end of the building and slipped into my room without being seen. Pumped on adrenaline and too wide awake to sleep, I prepared myself for a long night. With the door locked and a chair propped under the knob, I took a hot shower.

Dressed in a flannel gown and wool socks, I carried a glass of cold Chardonnay and one of Dad's journals to bed. Unlike his typical precise handwriting, I scrutinized a barely decipherable scrawl. This one began:

Callie, I can't focus on my work. I'm losing track of important data points and can't ask for help. Then they'll know. —I want to finish this project, I have to. It could save my life. Monoclonal antibodies against this wasting prion are on order. I think it will cure the disease, this form, anyway. It slowed the disease in transgenic mice. This prion isn't like the HIV/Aids virus that keeps mutating, prions don't contain genetic mater-

ial, but as you know, there are so many forms. In mice, there are twenty, many in wildlife, and a few in humans. I'm getting closer to a cure. My ramblings in these journals may help you proceed when I'm gone, but I hoped the monoclonals would save my life.

On my way to work the next day, I needed coffee to fuel my brain. I wanted to stop at the Outpost, but cars lined the street. I nearly drove on by to avoid starting my day facing irate residents and activists but decided I'd better force myself to stop and learn how to deal with local politics.

When I smelled the delicious baked goods and several people smiled, I knew I'd made the right decision. The same friendly female I met my first day in town, this time with her impressive dreadlocks tied in a knot high on her head, took my order.

"A huckleberry scone and an Americano to go."

"You're from the lab, right?"

I wondered how she knew. "Yes. I'm Callie Archer."

"Be careful on the road. Some animal rights people just left here talking about heading up to the laboratory gate."

"Thanks for the warning."

On the road, my coffee slopped when I took a turn too fast. I slowed for the last hairpin turn and saw a car near the summit partially blocking my lane. Four people milled around. Someone slapped the side of my car as I inched past. "Animal killer!" I think it was Hannah.

The electronic gate rattled shut behind me. Being enclosed gave me a sense of relief. The possibility of spending years confined because of high-risk projects had never concerned me in the past. Even in crowded cities, I'd felt secure. Hidden in crowds.

Memories of the confrontation with Hannah and my sense of proximity to danger in the small town lingered, giving me a foreboding about the future. Grief over losing Dad intensified my gloom. I sometimes wished I was back in Cleveland.

Anger and comfort shoved back and forth in my mind like opposing poles of two small magnets, repelling, spinning, and realigning. My resentment at being locked up evolved to comfort. The compound pulled me in, surrounding me with metal arms inside the safety of tall fences and electronic surveillance.

The perimeter guards waved me through the metal detector, like brothers welcoming me.

I belonged here.

My new home.

Sgt. Collucci sat in the surveillance headquarters. I said good morning as I passed him and headed to the coffee room carrying my scone in a little sack, sipping from the cup I'd brought from town. A male researcher called out, "Hey, Callie, come join us. We heard about the great impression you made in town." A young guy with curly red hair and a matching beard pulled out a chair beside him. "You realize, now they'll recognize you."

"It's hard to hide in a town this size. I didn't see you at the meeting?"

The young man shook his wild mane. "None of us go unless Reilly has coerced us into presenting. Putting you on stage was cruel. What did you do to him to deserve that?"

"Get transferred to Ridge Lab."

He raised his bushy eyebrows.

"Reilly hasn't liked me since my arrival."

"At least you have a presentation out of the way for months, maybe a year."

The older, more serious fellow inquired, "So, how bad was it?"

"Rowdy. Cops closed it down."

The young guy slapped the edge of the table. "Good job! That's better than the last one."

"The crowd was intimidating. Some were packing guns."

The older researcher said, "No big deal. You'll get used to that. We see guns every day, but with that kind of interest, they'll start following us to work again."

I saw a flicker of concern. "When I drove in, there were people at the gate. I recognized one of the women from the meeting. Said she'd wring my neck like I kill my helpless lab rats, so I'd feel what it's like to die."

The older man got up to leave. "That's wrong, damn wrong. It's bad when we only feel safe locked inside a compound."

I agreed. "I never believed I'd prefer being inside razor-wire fences, but as of this morning, I do."

The two left trailing animated comments. "Those damn people are despicable. What really gets me is most of them have probably never held a job, yet they attack us, involved in research that could save their stinking lives."

They turned toward the Security Office. "Sarge should get the car license and report the threat."

Like me, the older researcher felt safer locked inside a compound with lethal organisms than outside the perimeter with threatening humans.

A few minutes later, Sarge walked in and sat by me. "I'm sorry activists threatened you. They keep us on our toes, so it's not all bad. I reported them to the sheriff."

"I was surprised at the aggression of the activists last night."

"They like to intimidate people. It's good to stay below the radar in town if you can because you can't tell who might be the enemy. Now they have you in their sights." Sarge looked serious. "Speaking of sights, if you don't have a weapon, I'd be happy to help you choose one and give you some shooting lessons."

I stared at him. "You're scaring me."

Sarge shrugged. "Think about it. When you're ready for everything, it's calming.

"I took you up on the idea to move into Dad's house. His friend Sal, who owns the Wagon Wheel, is going to help me spruce it up and choose some new furniture."

"We've known Sal for years. Let me know when you are ready to paint." Sarge got up to leave. "My wife is great with a brush. Ann's an artist but likes to paint walls, too."

I appreciated his friendly gesture. We exchanged phone numbers, and I promised to call the next day.

Walking down the old hall to my lab, I thought about how nice it was having more friends after years of self-imposed isolation in medical school and then in research.

Among hundreds of digitized electron microscope images on dad's computer, I found prions in the fetal necropsy tissue. This confirmed vertical transfer of Chronic Wasting Disease to the embryo in the doe whose blood had killed him. His monoclonal antibody orders and a file of mysterious electron microscope images stained with green fluorescence caught my attention.

The labeled on the folder: *CSF-A01: Sample frozen*. Three slides showed sparse prion forms. This might be Dad's cerebral spinal fluid Dr. Maxwell sent to Paul Wilder. The *01* could mean January; was A for Archer? I had to find the frozen samples, determine the source and make sure they were hidden so no one who saw them could surmise his cause of death.

Bernie's call three hours later interrupted my review. "Thought you might want to see the monkeys. They are looking better."

She asked about the town meeting. I told her I'd walk over to visit the monkeys in a few minutes and tell her about it.

As I walked through the lunchroom en route to the back exit, Reilly's whiny voice called out, "Archer, I want to talk to you. I just spoke with Paul Wilder in Cleveland."

His tone sent a surge of adrenaline from my gut to my fingertips. Could he have found out about Dad's prion disease?

Reilly walked closer. "I knew you'd be delighted to hear the news. Paul called to tell me Larry Westphal is doing final packaging of his scrapie research project. He'll arrive next week."

I stared at him, dumbfounded.

Reilly had never appeared happier. "We were undergrads together. It will be good to see him. Don't you think so?"

My gut clenched at the thought of Larry being in the same lab with me again. "Didn't Wilder tell you I charged him with assault and sexual harassment? That's what finally sent Westphal to detox." I turned to go out the door. "I don't want to deal with him again. Keep him away from me."

Reilly called after me. "Callie, you're such a cute little woman. I suspect you just overreacted to his advances."

I stomped back. "Westphal attacked me!"

"I have his file. The details are there."

"Then I suggest you read them." I stormed away. So, he confirmed they were old buddies, just like Paul had said. More trouble.

Reilly followed me. "Wait a minute, wait. The meeting last night—what did you think?"

I snapped. "I wasn't prepared for guns and violence. Why didn't you warn me?"

"You'll get used to it. Women around here carry pepper spray instead of perfume. If you're concerned, wear a big canister of bear spray on your belt." He hesitated. "Just stay in your car if you have to stop on the lab access road. If you're really concerned, drive right over them. It's self-defense."

Did he really mean what he said?

He shrugged. "You don't have many options. The lab road is a cell phone dead zone. You can't call for help."

Blaze greeted me with happy woofs and wags at the motel office when I stopped to pick her up. On our way out, we passed a cheerful duo who entered exuding the strange smell of patchouli. The skinny woman with a protruding pregnant belly held the hand of a young man in ragged denims and a PETA T-shirt.

Sal waved goodbye as I opened the door for Blaze to leave. She turned her attention to the young couple. The male said, "We're looking for a room with weekly rates."

A white van with Colorado plates sat in front of the office door.

Chapter 10 - A Montana Date

Sal, Blaze and I made a quick trip to Missoula Saturday morning to shop and buy paint. Sarge and Ann joined us at the apartment just after lunch. We worked for hours and I bought dinner for everyone at the Wildlife Refuge. Back at the motel, a hot shower sent me into a deep sleep with Blaze on the floor beside me.

Sunday morning, Blaze and I went for a long walk around town and stopped to buy three small cans of pepper spray at the Mercantile. One each for the car, the house, and my pocket. After our walk, we drove back to Missoula and returned with a down comforter, pots, dishes, silverware, and a new dog bed.

I hauled my purchases to the doorstep and found a colorful dried flower arrangement in a painted cowboy boot from a local florist. A card read: *Dear Callie, A little something to cheer your new Montana home. Mack*

I called to tell Sal about the flowers.

She answered on the first ring. "Nice gesture. I saw him at the grocery store on Friday. He mentioned the town meeting and that he'd met a beautiful young researcher."

I smiled at his description. "He's a charmer. I forgot to tell you what happened yesterday when we were busy painting the apartment."

Sal was silent for a moment then said, "And, what did happen?"

"He invited me to go horseback riding next weekend. I don't know how to ride, and I haven't had a date in a couple years. The poor guy doesn't know what he's getting himself into."

"He's an expert. You don't have to worry about not knowing how to ride. You made quite an impression on that cowboy."

I flushed just thinking about him. "The feeling is mutual."

"Like you said, he's a charmer. Just don't get yourself in too deep. He has *a history*." Sal paused. "I hadn't seen him in a long time. It was nice he sent flowers. I don't want to mess up your date. You spend some time with him, and then we can talk."

I hung up wondering what *a history* meant.

Chapter 11 - Mack Janns

I'd soon be settled in a home of my own after weeks of chaos. After a window-fogging shower in the motel and ready for work, Blaze headed out our door and stopped at the motel office door. She wagged her tail, waiting for me to sneak her inside before my early morning drive to the lab.

Driving to the most exciting job in the world on a frosty fall morning before sunrise made me happy and pleased Blaze liked her doggy daycare routine.

I was rejuvenated after being away from the lab for a whole weekend but couldn't delude myself into thinking I hadn't felt a tug from my pathology slides and the monkeys. I had so much to do after the delays of moving and Dad's death weighed heavy. But the weekend hiatus from detailing slides, as well as meeting Mack, helped reset my internal drive to include time off.

Paul Wilder called me midmorning just before I left for a walk to the vet compound. He wanted to complete our recent conversation and asked how things were going in general.

"Fine, other than my father dying, the IRF not being ready for Level 3 researchers, Reilly sticking me in a broom closet office, and Larry Westphal arriving this week."

Paul laughed. "None of that's funny. It couldn't get much worse, but I'm glad you're resilient."

We talked about Reilly's assertion that I had misinterpreted Westphal's advances. Paul didn't laugh at that. "Advances? My God, if the guard hadn't come when he did, you'd have more than ripped clothing and he'd be in prison. I'm sorry you have to face him again and deal with Reilly."

I said, "Too bad Larry's an alcoholic."

"That's no reason. I think he has a loose screw." Paul warned, "Remember, Reilly and Westphal are old buddies. You can't trust either one."

A trip to the primate pod left me feeling sad about adorable monkeys that deserved better than to be killed in the name of science. I returned to my office thinking about an infected baby monkey and snuggled Brie while reading Dad's journal entry about antibodies, hoping to determine treatment and a source for them with so little time before the birth.

March 20 – *Damn that lab. They've been promising to ship the antibodies for weeks. We've been working on the development for over a year not knowing I'd need them for myself. After the first round, I was ecstatic. The 13D7 antibody was perfect in detecting the CWD PrP prion form, but the real test isn't only to detect it, but bind and snap that damn twisted particle back to normal. 13D8 bound perfectly but it blocked the second binding site and interfered with reverting the shape. The lab is working to alter 13D8 or configure a new one to work in concert. I know they can do it. I know it will work. They have to hurry.*

April 10 – *The two antibodies arrived. The company came up with something better by substituting the 14D8 with a different antibody that blocks the membrane receptor for proteoglycan interaction on the cell surface. It blocks the tau protein in Alzheimer's so why wouldn't it work on a similar abnormal prion protein? I told them I was willing to test it in my study. But, planned to use it on myself.*

April 17 – *I survived the first antibody injection last week. 10 mg of Dexamethasone suppressed some of the allergic response from the foreign proteins, but I still got a total body rash and the shortness of breath was frightening. Breathing improved within hours. I still have the rash and my shakes are worse. I'm injecting another dose today and weekly if I can hit a vein and it doesn't kill me.*

April 19 – *It's probably placebo effect, but maybe the antibodies are working. I still need the walking stick, but I'm less depressed and less paranoid. People are still staring at me. There is no sense in going to the Human Prion Clinic in Cleveland for treatment. I'd just be a guinea pig. I might as well practice on myself. I wish I would have spent more time with Callie the past few years. Together we'd be quite a team. I always told her to be so careful, now I'm the idiot who infected himself. I wish her rat studies were more advanced. I'd try anything, but I think the monoclonals are the ticket.*

I skimmed his rambling scribbles through May. The next readable entry made me weep.

June 16 – *I've been on the antibody serum for months. The disease progressed. I stopped after last week. I can't get an intravenous in anymore. I quit work, retired. Told them I have Parkinson's. I have to drink coffee from a sippy cup like a ba-*

by or it sloshes all over my shirt. Hell, my arm jerks are so bad that sometimes I throw liquids in big splashes. Soon I won't be able to feed myself. I keep choking. I'm losing weight. I've never been one to yell or be abusive, but that part of the disease has surfaced. I even yelled at my wonderful dog, my best friend. The 70-pound dog cowered and crawled up on my lap. I cried. I can't let Callie see me like this.

I'd thought we'd have years together. Our time was so short, and his speech and mind so impaired we couldn't talk about his research, so I telephoned the pathology director for help in locating Dad's stored specimens. I had to push on and see what parts of his work I might use in my research.

The director sounded cheerful. "You're in luck. Dr. Archer's work hasn't been moved since he retired, but Dr. Reilly was in here asking about it a week ago."

"I'll be right over." I hung up. Damn Reilly. I hoped he hadn't taken anything.

I changed into scrubs and protective gear to enter the lab with the pathology director. The mask hid my expression of joy when I saw a treasure trove of carefully labeled freezer specimens stored in rows dating back years. Bottles carried labels with the familiar numbers of monoclonal antibodies, and I found the tubes of Dad's spinal fluid.

The director helped me place cylinders of liquid nitrogen containing adult and fetal deer tissue into a tub to carry to my lab. "Callie, I'm happy to transfer your father's work to you. Call me if you need us to make more slides."

I stored everything in my lab, hidden from Reilly's eyes in case he nosed around. I hurried to the vet compound to examine the monkeys and tell Bernie about the frozen specimens and antibody order. She liked my news but had news of her own. "The monkeys are better this afternoon than they were on Friday!"

We went to the monkey pod. I peered in at the infected pair. "They're looking more coordinated. That's exciting. What's your guess on when she'll deliver?"

"Early November if she was impregnated in late May. But, we know all bets are off with the unpredictability of this disease in pregnancy."

"How often have you seen stillbirths with prion disease?"

"Most of the time. It happens in sheep, deer, and elk, but I have no information for monkeys."

I reviewed the tech documentation on my study rats related to their eating, weights and coordination. Most neurological symptoms had resolved in the infected group, but I continued their weekly treatment injections.

Sharing monkey improvement news with my cohorts at the Ridge Lab wouldn't happen. I had vowed not to make that mistake twice. In Cleveland, when I exclaimed that my prion-infected rats had improved, cohort responses ranged from anger to elation and jealousy. Then, Westphal's derogatory words and interest in my project accelerated. I feared sabotage and tightened the security on my data journals and drugs, often locking them in a safe.

I took a quick break for lunch and hoped I didn't look too happy or someone might ask why. I'd have to lie. Back in the lab, I hunched over the microscope and resumed the tedious chore of scanning slides until I felt cross-eyed and seasick.

The following day, Chris Turner, another prion researcher, waved me over to join him in the lunchroom where he sat talking to someone I didn't know. Chris continued the conversation, "Dapsone helped people with leprosy. Some of its activity appeared favorable in delaying human prion disease, too, but I'm seeing no benefit in my transgenic mice trial." He motioned toward the man. "Callie, this is Kenji Kato, a prion researcher out of UCSF. He just joined our team."

I talked with Kenji about my California college days and then transitioned to discussing numerous trial drug failures. I told them about my rodent research that had triggered the small monkey trial.

Kenji looked skeptical. "There's so much variability in prion virulence between species, I think our chances for finding an actual cure are slim."

"It seems that way." Chris agreed. "They tried everything on the Brits who contracted the mad cow variant. Nothing worked."

"Maybe we're going at this backwards," They stared at me. "I wish we could just prevent it with an immunization. We've stopped polio, measles, mumps, and smallpox."

Chris said, "Prion disease isn't much of a human risk right now, but an immunization for cows would give us a great start on safer meat."

The CDC hadn't released information on the three recent Idaho bovine prion deaths, so I couldn't tell Chris and Kenji that mad cow was a huge human risk and close by. "True, but BSE is spreading. There's a new outbreak of mad cow disease in Argentina."

I enjoyed talking with them, exchanging ideas. Maybe I'd found camaraderie.

My hopes about a friendship at the lab changed later in the week when I joined Chris at lunch. As soon as I sat down with them, jovial conversations between the male researchers changed so abruptly I thought someone had pressed the mute button.

I would have let it drop and just avoided confrontation with Chris and others like I had in the past, but after Hannah's take-down, a new confidence and strength persisted. I followed Chris out of the lunchroom refusing to cower in the face of adversity. I spoke when we reached privacy in the hallway. "What's with your bad attitude toward me?"

Chris walked on. Our footsteps dueled on broken tiles, echoing.

I continued. "When I sat down, your laughter and conversation stopped. Is it something I've done?"

He stopped so short I nearly bumped into him. "You might say so." He glared, speech clipped, demeaning. "It all depends on how you look at things. I've been here toiling over goddamn mice for years and making no headway." His voice rose. Saliva droplets sprayed. "You arrived with an entourage of rats and primates."

"I didn't ask to come here. The feds transferred me after a Level 3 break-in."

"You're successful at half my age and working on primates. All I'm doing year after year is kill mice. It pisses me off."

"I felt the same until my breakthrough with rats and a NIH grant for a small primate study."

Chris slapped his thumb on the door scanner into the lab wing. The lock clicked and the door opened.

I touched the scanner and entered the lab wing after him. We walked down the hall toward our respective labs. "My mice studies didn't go well at first, either. Real success came with two hooded rat studies. Do you have plans to work with other species?"

He walked ahead. "Hell, no. I'm almost out of grant money."

I entered my lab, ending conversation. The door had barely closed when I heard a knock.

Chris stood outside. "I'm sorry. I had to put my wife in assisted living last week and it's killing me. She has Alzheimer's."

I looked into his sad eyes. "So sorry. She must be very young to have such advanced disease."

He shook his head. When I visited her last night, she said, 'Who did you say you are?'" Chris looked at his feet. "I've been behaving like an ass. I haven't told anyone else about her. I'm sorry."

Given how Dad died, I wondered if his wife had developed prion disease because Chris carelessly brought it home. There is overlap in the symptoms. "If you want company for coffee or lunch, pick me up on your way."

"I'll do that. Thanks." He walked slowly down the hall toward his lab.

I left my lab at dark, exhausted after hours of slide documentation. The miles of driving gave me time to think about my date with Mack the next morning.

Everything was so different. The big Montana sky, wide open spaces, few people, and a date for the first time in two years.

I parked at the Wagon Wheel next to a panel truck with Arizona plates. I recognized it as one of the vehicles I'd seen near the lab gate. Damn. Maybe Hannah was staying right next door.

Blaze greeted me with joy. I reminded Sal about my date to go horseback riding the next morning.

She patted Blaze. "I'll pick her up later in the morning if you want to lock her in the house when you leave."

"What do you think about me having a dog door installed so she can go in and out at will?"

"Perfect, as long as a skunk doesn't decide to come in and look around."

"That's something I'd never consider. I didn't see skunks in Cleveland."

Sal laughed. "It's doubtful you'd have a skunk visit you here unless you leave it open at night. Don't leave any dog food outside either, it can attract skunks and raccoons."

"I don't want either." Blaze and I drove home. I fed myself and Blaze before we went for a walk.

Mack called to confirm our date. "I didn't forget. What time do you want to pick me up?"

"Are you an early bird?"

"Sleep is highly overrated. I'm always up early."

"I'll be there at nine. Don't eat breakfast. I'm cooking." Mack explained, "Ranch & Home Supply opens early. We'll head there first to get you some serious horseback riding clothes."

"Gee, I thought I'd wear a skirt and heels."

"If you do, we'll have you wearing new Western clothes before the horses see you. I don't want you to spook them. I'm heading out to check on a sick steer right now. See you in the morning."

Blaze's sharp bark alerted me to Mack's arrival. She came to my side and growled when he walked up to the door.

Mack stepped back when Blaze stiffened, on guard. "Who's this?"

"Dad's dog, Blaze. She's my new roommate."

When Mack reached down to pet her, Blaze ducked and pressed against my legs. Her ears down, no wagging. I squatted to hug her. With Sal's warning and now Blaze's reaction, I wondered what she sensed. "Sal from the motel keeps her for me when I'm at work. She'll pick her up later this morning."

"Dogs usually like me. I see she's very protective." Mack remained in the doorway. "I've known Sal for years."

I offered Blaze a treat. "Sal is coming to get you. I'll see you later." She wouldn't take the bone. Head down, sullen, Blaze walked away and curled up on her bed.

She loved seeing Hugh Dalen but clearly didn't like Mack and I hated leaving her behind when we drove off to a warehouse that sold ropes, smelled of feed and sold ranching clothes. After a few try-ons, I went to the checkout counter wearing Wrangler jeans and a dark red western shirt similar to Sal's. My new cowboy boots clomped as I walked along thinking they cost a fortune and hoped I'd like wearing them. I told Mack, "I love the boots. They're more comfortable than they look. They remind me of a favorite pair I wore in elementary school."

"Mack stuck out a foot to show me. "They're just like mine. You look terrific."

I handed the clerk my credit card.

"Nope." Mack pushed my hand aside. "This outfit's on me. Put it on the tab, George."

Mack's extravagance caught me off guard. "I'll buy them. I don't want you spending money on me."

"It's a welcoming present from a Montana cowboy."

George grinned.

I wondered how many other women had received Mack's gifts from Ranch & Home.

The pickup blew diesel fumes as we drove south out of town on Highway 93. Mack turned left on a dirt road. Billowing dust obliterated the road behind us. White rail fences around a large quarter horse ranch reminded me of Kentucky, but the imposing Bitterroot Range to the west and brown grassland that abounded instead of lush green fields told me I was definitely in Montana. Mack pointed to the beginning of his property about a mile before we passed beneath a log arch entrance announcing Angus Insemination International.

I was surprised to see no vehicles parked near his barns. "The ranch looks huge. How many people work here?"

"Depends on what we're doing. The hands may be out checking fences." He pointed toward two large buildings. "They park out of view, along the side of the larger white barn. Two full-time lab assistants work in the AI building." Mack pointed to the smaller white barn with *AI* in giant letters on the side. "They're busy when we're doing embryo transfers and insemination. During low-activity times, the girls do data input and make follow-up phone calls for customer satisfaction."

"I don't see how you can perform the insemination process with uncooperative cattle."

"We have our ways." Mack smiled. "When we're inseminating and doing embryo transfers, a vet friend of mine takes a leave from his practice in Colorado and comes here to help. We've done it together for years."

Mack parked near the house. "Some hands stay over there in the bunkhouse during calving. Four are full-time employees; we've been together for years. They're all Indians. Blood I trust."

My new black boots were dusted gray when I stepped out of the truck onto the powdery road. I followed Mack up heavy plank steps onto an expansive covered deck surrounding a white-chinked dark log home. A padded bench swing rocked in the light breeze, with sun casting faint shadows through a pair of high-backed rocking chairs flanking the swing.

"Come on inside." When Mack opened the screen door, the spring screeched a greeting.

A towering rock fireplace in an expansive room rose two stories to a wood-railed balcony. "This isn't a home. It's a lodge!"

"That's the look I wanted. Big and comfortable." Mack walked toward another room. "I'll give you a quick tour of the house before I start breakfast."

I followed him into an adjacent formal dining room, where the windows offered an expansive view of the Bitterroot Valley blocked only by a couple of gnarled apple trees.

He motioned to a large window. "I watch the sun drop behind the Bitterroots from here. It's a good way to wind down at the end of a day. "Don't take this wrong, but next I want you to see my bedroom."

The south-facing large room with a king-sized bed had sliding glass doors that opened to a deck and hot tub. Shrubbery secluded the area. "Soaking in the hot tub on a cool evening under bright stars is great for relaxation and sore muscles."

"Wow! Not the typical country home."

"We'll tour upstairs later. Let's have breakfast before you starve."

Walking back through the bedroom, I examined intricate beaded Indian artifacts hanging on log walls. A painting of a Plains Indian war party covered most of one wall, with a gun safe the size of a walk-in closet filling one corner. "That safe is almost the size of my office at the lab."

Mack laughed. "I like guns, but I'm not a hunter. Got my fill of killing in the military years ago. I was a sniper. Mostly, I'm a collector. I have an Uzi. You could shoot it if you'd like."

I stared at the safe. "Having never shot a weapon, being in the same room with guns makes me nauseous. Why would you want a machine gun?"

"For fun and to get looks like the one you just gave me. It's a simple weapon with great engineering." We walked back toward the kitchen. "The fire-resistant safe is also for documents and computer files of business data. It would be a disaster if I lost data on my registered Angus and the AI-embryo business."

"I feel the same way about my research logs and computer files. Rather than ship them, I carried them cross-country with me."

We walked into the kitchen. "I start the day with my laptop and coffee here at the breakfast bar. I think of myself as an urban cowboy, but I'm really *country*."

"Do you play a guitar and sing?"

He shook his head. "Sadly, I've tried, but it set the neighborhood coyotes yowling, so I had to give it up."

He made me laugh as I sat at the bar overlooking a large gas range in the spotless stainless-steel kitchen and watched him in action. "I think Martha Stewart would like to cook here."

Mack talked about ranch activities while he prepared thick French toast dipped in eggs flavored with a sprinkle of cinnamon. "I own a thousand acres adjoining Forest Service land and lease additional acreage for the organic beef."

On a table in a windowed alcove, Mack placed two plates of French toast topped with melted butter and drizzled with warmed maple syrup. He cut a bit of basil from a row of herbs growing in a window planter and sprinkled it on the toast. We sat side by side, looking out at his ranch, eating and sipping coffee.

I savored my first bite. "I'm not much of a cook, but I love food. I've never tasted better French toast."

"I knew you were a brain from what your dad said and your introduction at the town meeting. More into science than cooking."

I snickered. "In college, I lived on Fruit Loops. Mother was horrified when I told her."

"Bad eating stunted your growth." He raised his eyebrows questioningly. "I'm not so sure you're eating right now if you're a plant eater."

"I eat healthy. Occasional eggs, lots of oatmeal and fruit."

"Good food but boring. What do you do for fun?"

"Play with lab rats, monkeys, and read. Just coming out to your ranch is a holiday for me."

Mack grinned. "Good. Maybe I can broaden your interests."

"Did your mom teach you to cook?"

Mack took our plates and put them in the sink. He poured more coffee and sat down.

I waited, uncomfortable with his silence.

"I learned to fend for myself when I was very young." His expression was somber. "My alcoholic mother taught me how to open a can when I was four. So, you could say she taught me how to cook. She was a loving mom, but most of the time I fed her and myself out of cans. As a teenager, I lived with my grandmother after I got out of prison."

I wondered if this was the *history* Sal mentioned but hadn't given me details.

Now it was my turn to say nothing. I didn't know what to say.

"I tell people. If I don't, they'll hear it from someone. In a community this size, everyone knows your business." His sad brown eyes studied my face.

I tried to keep my expression neutral, but it was difficult. I'd never met anyone who'd spent time behind bars.

"It was a long time ago. When I lived on the reservation, I killed my mother's boyfriend to keep him from killing her—and me."

A killer. What do I say to a killer?

"You're quiet, Callie. I'm sorry to tell you this, but in order to be friends, you need to know my past and who I am. I was a juvenile when it happened, thirteen. My record is sealed. They called it self-defense." His eyes darkened and his voice rose in anger. "I never should have been locked up.

He'd hurt both of us and had choked her to unconsciousness. I thought she was dead and that I was next. I got my hunting rifle from the closet and shot him."

"That's a frightening story. I'm so sorry."

"Don't be."

"That's a tough way to grow up."

He shook his head. "No. It was peaceful. They released me to my grandmother after a year in juvenile detention and counseling. She rescued me. We walked the Reservation land. She talked to the spirits. Taught me Indian ways."

I squirmed, wanting to change the topic, but he talked on.

His gaze shifted, far away in thought, looking out over his ranch. "She taught me how to cook the venison I killed, potatoes, and fry bread. Nothing fancy. Made sure I got enough to eat and good grades. Lived till age eighty-two. She died here at the ranch."

Mack poured coffee.

I wondered how much more of his life story I'd hear.

"There's another thing you should know, I don't drink much alcohol because of what it did to my mother. During my last year of college, she died of liver failure at St. Pat's hospital in Missoula. She was forty-six." He rinsed the plates. "Let's head out to the corral and go for a ride."

We walked slowly across the grass toward the corral.

I took his hand. "Thank you for telling me about your life and family."

"I wanted you to know about me. I know a little about you because of the time I spent with your father. You were his star."

We neared two horses with saddles tied to a fence near a red barn. "You'll have to tell me what to do."

"Don't worry. Candy is your horse. She's old and talented." He handed me a couple of sugar cubes from his shirt pocket. "Candy loves these. Talk to her a little. Give her these one at a time and she'll follow you anywhere."

An attractive, slender Native American with thick braided salt-and-pepper hair was waiting with the horses. Mack said, "Callie, this is my foreman, Andy."

Andy tipped his sweat-stained cowboy hat. "Pleased to meet you, Dr. Callie. Heard a lot about you since you hit town."

I greeted him, not sure how to take his comment.

"Have a good ride." Andy walked back toward the barn.

Mack stroked Candy's face. "Candy's a twenty-eight-year-old retired quarter horse. She remembers her training and can cut as well as the young ones."

I gave her the sugar as he suggested. She nuzzled my pocket for more. Mack helped me place my feet in the stirrups and mount. He adjusted the straps to a comfortable fit. I leaned forward and talked to Candy.

Mack mounted a sleek black horse with white stockings. "I talk to my horses, maybe like you talk to the lab rats. Candy and I have been together for more than ten years. She's too old for cutting. It's her time for joy rides."

I patted Candy's neck. "I don't think you're old. We're the same age."

"You're a young one, Callie. I've got you beat by eight years."

Mack's black horse had a white forehead blaze. His stockinged feet pranced, anxious to go. Mack galloped ahead and then turned back, stopping short beside me. I admired the beautiful horse and smooth ride. Mack adjusted his hat and made another dash before returning to my side. "Candy enjoys the exercise. Touch the side of her neck to get her to turn. She senses what to do."

"How do I get her to move?"

"She'll follow me, but just flick the reins like this." He demonstrated, and his horse moved ahead.

I did the same, and Candy followed.

Mack scanned me from my head to my dusty boots. "Damn, you look good on that horse." His horse walked ahead. Mack turned back to talk. "We'll be moving cattle to winter pasture soon. Maybe you could help."

"That would be something to write about to my friends in Cleveland. I can't imagine the logistics of moving cattle. I doubt I'd be any good unless you give me a lot of training by then."

"It's easy. I'm sure you could help. I move my nonorganics to a nice feedlot in South Valley during winter months."

I pulled the rein to the right. Candy followed Mack's horse.

"You'll see some of my cattle. We'll ride the fence line along Adcock's elk farm property." Mack pointed out a small herd of black cattle. "Those are some of mine."

We stopped near a tall double fence similar to the fencing around the lab compound but without razor-wire loops on the top. This secure fence enclosed a herd of elk. Numerous bulls with expansive fuzzy racks in velvet watched us from a distance. "They're beautiful creatures."

Mack scanned the elk. "Garrett Adcock's a strange fellow but takes good care of his animals."

I wanted to hear what Mack had to say about the outlawed practice without expressing my abhorrence. I moved Candy closer to him. "No one shoots fenced elk anymore, right?"

"True. I helped Garrett get into the elk AI business after shooting elk on farms was outlawed. Now he provides semen to other elk ranchers who want to broaden the genetic mix in their confined herds."

I felt more comfortable riding as time passed. I thought Candy could read my mind because she reacted to my slightest move. "And I thought cattle insemination would be difficult—but elk? Are you joking?"

"AI in elk is more difficult than in cattle." We ambled back toward the barn. "I'll tell you about my process another time. With elk, it's similar, but we control them in a more confined space."

Mack dropped his reins. I followed his cue. The horses stopped near the corral and waited. He helped me dismount and held me close for a second. His strong hands around my waist and the scent of cologne made me smile. "Since when do real cowboys wear perfume?"

"Just for pretty ladies." Mack laughed. "You're such a lightweight, Callie, I bet Candy appreciated you, after carrying me." He talked softly to both horses and petted Candy's satin nose. She nuzzled his neck and then his shirt pocket.

I admired Mack's gentle way with the horses.

"Candy knows I usually carry sugar cubes for her." He handed one to each horse.

"How long do horses live?"

"Seldom past twenty-five."

"My pet rats die after about three years and it breaks my heart. With creatures like these, I can't imagine the pain of losing them."

"I love my horses. Actually, I get to know the bulls, too, and get attached to them."

"Aren't bulls mean and unpredictable?"

"They're less predictable than horses, but my three-year-old bull named Igor is more like a horse than any other bull I've known. The ranch hands think I'm crazy to trust him."

"Why?"

Mack shook his head. "He's more predictable, gentler, and prime stock from a registered Black Angus outfit in Eastern Montana in the Judith Basin. I paid $90,000 for him."

"I had no idea a cow could cost that much."

"Callie, Igor is *not* a cow." Mack faked a frown. "Igor could be very mean if he heard you say that."

"I was using *cow* generically."

"You're a city girl. I'll teach you Western ways; don't worry." We waited for a ranch hand. "Igor's my best semen producer and makes me more money than my Pekisko casino shares. Casino payments to tribal members paid for my college and this ranch."

"That's wonderful."

An attractive young Native American woman in Western attire walked toward us. Mack handed her the reins. "Thanks, Laney. Meet Callie Archer."

Laney said a curt hello with no eye contact and walked away swaying her hips, trailing the two horses. Her long black braid swung like the tails of the horses.

Mack and I walked to the white barn. He held the door. "Let me introduce you to the artificial insemination business."

I entered with reluctance. What had I gotten myself into?

Brilliant lights in the office reflected on glistening white floors. In the laboratory, which was like many I had worked in during my years of university training, specially marked refrigerators and freezers lined the walls. Three microscopes on a clean granite counter sat ready for use. Two young, attractive Native American women dressed in black scrubs sat at computers. One wore a braid bound in a red ribbon ending at her waist. The other had shiny black hair cut straight across at the middle of her back.

Mack greeted them and introduced me. "Meet Dr. Callie Archer. She's a physician researcher at the Ridge Lab. I wanted her to see our operation."

The women glanced up with quick smiles that revealed white, straight teeth. He placed an arm around the one with the braid. She leaned into him.

I said hello to the women. "This looks clean enough to be a surgical suite."

"It's where we do embryo sorting. We're careful to keep our insemination products free of contamination. No cowboys traipse through here."

"I've read about human in vitro fertilization but know little about the specifics."

He motioned to the workers. "These vet techs are trained to sort embryos. They also prepare semen and embryos for shipping, frozen in liquid nitrogen."

Mack used tongs to pull a few foggy strings dangling straws of semen from a nitrogen cylinder. "The straws are about the size you'd sip a milkshake through, but these contain frozen semen." He examined the labels. "All from Igor. With a blue-ribbon bull like him, we sell his semen around the world at good prices. I keep a significant supply in storage. Actually, I'll get more money for them after he dies."

"That sounds morbid."

"Not really. It's like money in a secure Wall Street stock account. Only this is a real stock market, a cattle sperm bank. Igor, two other bulls, and a number of my registered cows are what we call *genetically elite*." Over his desk against the wall near the entrance he pointed out some photos. "Those are my children. The photo on top is Igor. You'll meet him later."

To me, all the cows looked alike.

"We use them for the embryo business. Their offspring sell for top dollars because of their size, ease of delivery, and carcass configuration." I followed him into an adjacent room with more freezers and shelves. "This bank of freezers and refrigerators are used to store various specimens and drugs. I keep a big inventory of liquid nitrogen cylinders containing the frozen embryos and semen on the labeled shelves."

"So, you ship orders in liquid nitrogen internationally?"

"UPS does pickup and delivery way out here. Bar-coding specimens makes tracking easy."

Mack asked the workers a few questions. "Let's walk back to the house, Callie. I don't want to bore you."

We went out the door. "You aren't boring me. I had no idea the meat industry had this kind of technology."

"It's big business. In Montana, we have about three million head of cattle, almost three times the human population. I sell a lot of semen here and ship it everywhere. It probably costs $100 per head for the average rancher to purchase AI service. Big money, with big results."

We had almost reached the house when one of his employees caught up with us and said another big order from Brazil had come in. After their short conversation, we went on.

"One step I didn't tell you about is how we use surrogate nonregistered cows to carry the genetically desired calves. When a cow is hormonally ready, we place an elite embryo in the uterus."

"I think I get it. Like human models who don't want to mess up their bodies with a pregnancy."

"Right. That way, we deliver the model's calf here on the ranch or we ship elite frozen embryos to buyers to impregnate their own surrogate cows."

Mack sat on the porch swing and motioned for me to join him. "I make a lot more money from semen and embryo sales than I do from organic or Angus beef sales. But what you do is far more important and much more difficult than modern ranching."

"This is not like my last date, playing chess with a nerd! I love what I do, but I find your work intriguing. Could I come back and watch?"

"I'll teach you how to sort embryos if you're interested. Sometimes we need extra help."

"I don't think I'd be much help. I'd be afraid of getting stepped on."

"Oh, I won't put you in the corral. We could have you sorting embryos under a microscope in the lab in no time."

"At least I know how to use a microscope after staring at prion slides for years."

"Sorting embryos is the easy part. The AI process is time-sensitive but crude. Working with large animals is a lot different than working with rats and primates."

"Doing procedures on cattle must be difficult."

Mack set the swing in motion with his foot. "That's why I have a partner. We force ovulation by injecting a hormone at the right time and extract the eggs. That's the tricky part. But you're trying to save lives and keep the world safer for all of us."

His arm around my shoulders blunted the cool fall temperatures. Feeling his body warmth and experiencing his cowboy charm placed me in a peaceful state. An occasional creak from the swing interrupted my thoughts drifting far away. I rested my head against his shoulder and thought about Montana and his strange business.

Mack stopped the swing and checked his watch. "It's almost four o'clock. Are you hungry?"

"A little."

"I'll have a roast beef sandwich, but for a vegetarian I have to be more creative. How about a salad and a peanut butter sandwich on homemade bread?"

"Homemade bread? That sounds great. I don't remember ever having homemade bread."

"Well, today is a day to remember."

When he dropped me off at the duplex, I invited Mack in to see my newly painted apartment and furnishings. Mack towered a foot taller than my five-three height. He sat down on a kitchen chair and pulled me to him. Our interaction began with a warm hug and my thanks for the horseback ride, meeting Candy, and learning about the ranch. I rambled on.

He brushed a curl off my forehead and gently touched my lips with a finger to silence me. "Callie, I don't know you very well, but everything I know, I like. You raise feelings in me that have been buried for years."

His lips touched mine gently, and then he pulled me to him in a crushing kiss, igniting feelings I had seldom experienced. A surge of passion left me breathless.

He looked into my eyes, a soft look.

A sensual, salty taste lingered on my lips. I smiled.

Mack stood. He hugged me again, lifting me off the floor and lingering against me long enough for me to feel his physical interest. He whispered. "I'll call you soon, pretty girl." He walked out the door. His shiny black braid swayed with his stride.

After the passion ebbed, I slowly walked to the door and locked it. I went to the bathroom and looked in the mirror at my windblown hair and flushed cheeks.

I didn't even know him, but I was in love.

I fell asleep with a smile on my lips, wishing Blaze was with me.

In the morning, I walked to the motel to pick up the dog. Thoughts of Mack distracted me as I told Sal about Mack and Blaze's reaction to him.

Concern painted her face.

"Mack is amazing. Charming. His ranch is beautiful."

Sal's frown persisted.

"I was shocked when he told me he killed someone when he was a teenager. It was self-defense."

"I've heard the story." Sal expression was unchanged. "Did he tell you the man was his biological father?"

A jolt of adrenaline disrupted my happy thoughts. "No."

My legs shook so much, I sat down at her kitchen table.

Sal put her arm around me. "I don't want to lose the only daughter I've ever had. Maybe I'm an alarmist, but I have bad feelings about Mack. Please be careful."

Chapter 12 - Return of a Nemesis

One morning on a break from scanning slides, I stayed for a second cup of coffee in the cafeteria with a couple of my cohorts conversing about genetic components of prion disease. One of them emphasized, "At one location on the human genome, the inherited form of the prion gene is at codon 129. It's the same genetic variation present in those who develop Alzheimer's disease."

That fact had bothered me for years. "Could we come up with a cure for both Alzheimer's and human prion disease? Over 80% of people diagnosed with human prion disease have a mutation at that codon."

Bernie pulled out a chair and sat beside me. "This conversation sounds too serious. Do you talk about prions all the time?" She placed a bowl of oatmeal on the table. "At least I can eat my gruel without worrying about it killing me."

I scooted over to make more room for her. "Thanks for joining us."

She frowned when I continued.

"Studies in the United Kingdom show that one in two thousand people carry mad cow prions. Will they eventually develop the human variant like the others who died from eating contaminated beef?"

Bernie swallowed a bite and commented. "Maybe it's a carrier state. Brits are still excluded as blood donors in the U.S."

Another prion researcher agreed. "I think you're right. The Ridge Lab should design a study to look at the overlap in Alzheimer's and CJD." He turned to Bernie, "I have to get back to my prions, so I'll leave you in peace with that oatmeal." The two men walked out, talking about prions in plants.

I begged, "Can you take a little more prion conversation?"

Bernie shrugged. "Sure."

"I'm excited about a report I read last night on an enzyme link in some neurodegenerative diseases. It appears to flip the abnormal prion conformation back to normal."

"That sounds too good to be true. I guess sugarplums weren't dancing in your head last night."

"An Ohio friend alerted me to the U.K. article." I pushed a copy I'd printed in front of her and pointed to the conclusion. "Blocking the activity of the JNK3 enzyme resulted in a 90% reduction in brain prion deposits."

"They're onto something, but since they're working with mice, it'll be years before human tests."

"I don't think so. My friend talked with a molecular biophysics professor with a U.K. university group that constructed a 3-D picture of the binding surface using X-ray crystallography. I need it for my baby!"

"They have nothing to lose. I bet they'll jump at the opportunity of a single treatment trial in a primate."

"I'll call today after talking with Paul Wilder."

I walked toward the exit with Bernie feeling excited about the prospect and planning to follow her to the Vet Building. "If the U.K. group agrees, we might have two antibody options, Dad's and this one."

We were walking out the door when Dr. Reilly called to us. I turned to see Larry Westphal with him and swore under my breath.

Bernie's eyes flicked to Reilly and Larry.

In a sugary voice, Larry said, "Fancy meeting you here, Callie."

I glared at the man, who appeared thinner than at our last encounter in Cleveland.

Dr. Reilly introduced him to Bernie and suggested she give him a tour of the vet compound. He announced, "Callie, since the new Level 3 will be opening imminently, we're moving our friend Larry directly into the IRF."

Goddamn Reilly! What was he doing putting Westphal in a new lab ahead of me after I'd been waiting for months? "Congratulations, Larry. Your buddy gave you the first Level 3 lab. We'll be in adjacent offices. I hope this time you can behave yourself."

I backed away and asked Bernie to call me when she was free.

Westphal's eyes undressed me before he followed Bernie out the back door.

Reilly snarled, "Callie, I expect you to treat him with civility. Larry has been through a lot."

"I expect the same from him, and I expected fair treatment from you."

Reilly asked what I was working on, and I told him I'd begun reviewing Dad's computer data. After the pathology director had told me Reilly had been snooping into Dad's specimens, I wanted him to know I was working with the data.

"Don't get too engrossed in Nolan's work. Other researchers may be interested in using his data, especially Larry."

Reilly's comment sent ice through my arteries. I tossed my cup in the trash and walked out, trying to cool my anger. I'd wait and see how it played out but decided to get advice from Paul Wilder when I called him about the U.K. question.

I rechecked all the specimens I'd retrieved from the pathology department. I had to be sure Dad's frozen spinal fluid and animal specimens were totally out of sight on the bottom shelf of a bookcase blocked by heavy medical texts. Westphal would not usurp any of my father's research materials. For good measure, I labeled them with bogus names before returning them to their hiding places.

The few items I had left in the pathology department were unimportant, likely treatment preparations Dad had tried in past Chronic Wasting Disease studies. If Westphal took those, it might confuse the thief.

I settled into studying Dad's final documents with Brie on my shoulder. His journals clearly stated he expected me to have exclusive access to his data. Wilder would know the legalities of whether Reilly could take Dad's project information and give it to another researcher.

I dialed Cleveland later in the morning and told Paul of my encounter. "Are there NIH research protocols regarding a deceased researcher's project materials?"

"You were collaborating even before your arrival at the Ridge Lab and have his verbal instructions just before he died. He can't give them to Westphal. If Reilly tries it, you can bring him before the professional ethics board. For God's sake, don't let anyone get their hands on your dad's journals or videos."

"I won't. Then they'd know he was infected."

"So, have you had any interactions with Westphal?"

"Just seeing him was too much and it pisses me off that Reilly is moving him into the IRF today."

"That bastard is moving Westphal in when you and the others have been waiting for weeks?"

"I'm not surprised, but I am furious, but I called to discuss something else. I'm going to contact the Prion Unit at West Midlands University in the U.K."

"What are they up to?"

I explained the crystallography of the prion binding surface. "Monoclonals developed in their transgenic bovine prion mouse study may be able to reverse the abnormal prion structure. It's perfect for use on my baby monkey. What do you think?"

"They'll be proprietary. Help from the top never hurts. How about if I have Greg Andover at Headquarters call the U.K. program chairman?"

"If the monkey doesn't abort, we have about two months before the due date in early November. I need the treatment ready as soon as possible."

"That gives them a little time. It's an opportunity to go from mice to primates immediately. I'll call you back as soon as I can."

Bernie called before noon and asked if I'd meet her for lunch before we checked my monkeys.

"Lunch now sounds good. I'm anxious to hear what you think of Westphal."

She met me in the lunch line. "I found Dr. Westphal charming."

I grabbed a large salad and slammed it on my tray. "All psychopaths are."

Bernie looked around as if concerned someone might hear our conversation. She whispered, "How can you be so negative?"

"It'll take hours to tell you about the trouble he caused me, which ended in a physical attack." I walked to a table near the wall.

Bernie followed. "My God, I'd never expect anything but professional behavior from what I saw."

"Beware. You'll see his true colors. Besides, he and Reilly are old buddies. Now we have two of them to deal with."

"After what you've said, I can see why you wanted to talk. I'm surprised you have any appetite after having to face him again."

"I think Reilly blocked my transfer so he could give Westphal the first available lab just to irk me." I told her what he'd said about sharing Dad's research with Larry.

Bernie looked over her dark-rimmed glasses as she did when she made fun of me. "Did you take an extra blood pressure pill after that?"

"I was so mad I made sure I had most of Dad's specimens locked in my lab. Off-limits to everyone."

Bernie frowned. "Off-limits to everyone except Director Reilly. Don't leave your Dad's journals or logs where he could read or copy them. He has access to all the labs."

I told her what Paul Wilder had said.

"You have ready ammunition if Reilly tries to disperse Nolan's data."

"Let's check my monkeys. I'd like to do another drug injection tomorrow and each week on Tuesdays, if that works for you."

"I'll put it on the schedule."

By the time I left work, Paul had not called back with word on what the U.K. had to say. Time zone differences may be a factor.

I found a message on my cell from Mack saying he'd be in town and would like to buy me dinner. I really enjoyed his company, but he'd destroy my focus. What I really wanted was a glass of wine, a journal to read and my dog beside me. Seeing Westphal spiked anxiety I'd suppressed after years of his harassment. I'd thought I was rid of him. Reilly infuriated me, too, but most of my angst was related to seeing Westphal again. I was in no mood to be with anyone, including Mack, but thought he might distract me from my simmering anger.

I called Sal to tell her I'd be late getting back to pick up Blaze.

"Blaze and I are doing great. Go ahead and join Mack, just remember what I said about him." I thought about her warnings as I drove to the restaurant.

Mack sat at a corner table at the back of the Wildlife Reserve. He had just returned from Missoula after making a late delivery of frozen embryos to UPS, headed for Brazil.

I averted my gaze from blood pooling on the plate around his seared steak. From the look on his face, my salad heaped with tomatoes and sprouts, with a side of steamed broccoli, turned his stomach. "Would you like to try a bite of my broccoli?" I teased. "It's delicious."

Mack shook his head. "No. thanks. How about a taste of steak?"

I declined.

"Before I forget, Callie, I want to invite you to join me at the Beast Feast."

I looked at his disgusting plate and wondered if he was kidding. "That sounds like my kind of party."

"I'm serious. Men do the cooking."

My silence stimulated another encouraging comment.

"It would be an opportunity for you to meet a few people. We serve corn on the cob for vegetarians who dare come to the event."

This made me smile. "I love corn. If I don't have to eat meat, count me in."

"I'll be cooking part of the time, but on breaks I'll walk around and visit vendor booths with you."

We finished eating and talked more about the feast. I was distracted and fidgety but didn't realize my desire to pick up Blaze and go home was so obvious.

"Am I keeping you from something?"

"I'm just wound up after an unsettling day of lab politics and dealing with a new researcher."

"A new researcher?"

"Not really new. My nemesis from Cleveland was transferred here. He arrived today." I told him about Westphal and my disgust after the assault. "I guess I'm afraid of him, even though I believed I was over all that."

Mack clenched his fists. "I'll kill him if he touches you."

I glanced around the restaurant. "Don't say things like that. Someone might hear you."

He glared. "I meant it."

The tension in Mack's voice and angry mannerisms persisted. He gripped my elbow too tightly as we walked out. After opening the car door, he blocked my entrance to the driver seat. "Promise you'll call me if he causes you trouble."

"I'll be fine." I tried to push past him.

He bent forward to my eye level. "Did you hear me? Promise me, Callie, or I won't let you leave."

His intimidation angered me. I wanted him to get the hell out of my way. I hated his controlling me, but I agreed so I could just go home.

Mack stepped aside.

I drove away. His pickup rolled out of the parking lot right behind me. He followed me to the motel and then drove on.

I told Sal about Mack's anger and controlling behavior before heading to the apartment with Blaze. Her eyes opened wide. She took a deep breath.

"What's wrong, Sal? You look scared."

"That's the way he acted with his wife. Milly was a beautiful blonde woman from out East. A rich gal who never fit in because he would never let her out of his sight." She gestured down the street. "I used to go to that little bar on Main for a beer and burger with a girlfriend now and then. One night Milly and Mack were sitting at the bar. He nearly came to blows with some cowboys who were eyeing her. He dragged her out like it was her fault."

I frowned. "He hardly knows me, and I saw that kind of control tonight. I hated it."

"That's part of what I wanted to warn you about."

I sat down. "Is there more?"

"About three years ago, I said hello to Milly one day at the Mercantile. She turned away without speaking, but not before I saw bruises on her arm and face." Sal stared off. "She disappeared soon after that. I think he had beaten her. She had no friends. I should have done something to help her."

"I really enjoyed his company. He's charming. Good-looking. Bright. Talented. But now he worries me."

"Mack told everyone she ran off with a guy working at the ranch. I've never forgiven myself for not helping her." Sal hugged me. "His behavior tonight is a good example of control disguised as caring. It could be the beginning. Psychopaths are charming."

I felt a heavy weight on my shoulders as I said good-bye and walked slowly to my car. Blaze sensed my mood. She pressed her body to my leg and watched my face.

Sal was serious. Dead serious.

I was torn between running away from Mack and wanting to know him better. I admired his intelligence and handsome Indian features. He'd drawn me in. My dad had liked him. Maybe his protective behavior was his way of showing that he cared.

Blaze bounded into our apartment and wagged her tail by the pantry that hid her dog treats. She munched on a bone as I closed the drapes.

A white pickup inched past.

Damn him. Was Mack checking to see if I had gotten home safely, or was he a stalker?

Now what?

Chapter 13 - Prion News

Acute drug reactions such as shortness of breath could have ended the study. Fortunately, the monkeys showed no allergic responses to foreign protein injections, instead, the rat treatment appeared to be working on them. Would it really be the cure we'd all searched for?

After the second week, my hopes sank when both monkeys showed progression. The confused, drooling male fell repeatedly and was unable to ingest enough calories to maintain his weight. The female seemed stronger than the male, but by the following week disease progression in both resulted in myoclonic leg spasms just like Dad's.

I crossed the compound to the vet building dreading our next injection. Bernie greeted me with concern. "They've lost more weight. Let's repeat the ultrasound and see if the fetus is growing."

We watched blurry images of the tiny fetus. Her heart beat rapidly. Her limbs moved. Based on Bernie's assessment, the underweight fetus showed normal development. She assigned two techs to focus on improving the calorie intake on both infected monkeys.

Each day, I walked to the lab to check the prion infected test monkeys. Each day, they looked worse. I asked Bernie if she could perform a CT scan. "I'm wondering if we'd be able to determine if the fetus has brain changes in the thalamus that we see in human prion disease or if she is just small. It would help to know what we can expect to see at the time of delivery."

"We can do a scan, but it may give us little useful information."

I pleaded, "If we see the pulvinar sign in the thalamus, it would correlate with advanced disease. Knowing that would help."

Bernie listened. "I'll ask the radiologist who reads our scans. If he says the fetal brain would be visible enough for the determination, we can do the scan during the sedation for our injection next week."

"Perfect. Paul called to tell me he spoke with the U.K. group. We'll have the antibody in a few days. I hope she doesn't deliver before the package arrives."

My father's computer documentation showed the genomic team at the Ridge Lab provided DNA sequencing in one of his studies on chromosomal codon variations making some humans more susceptible to prion infection than others. He was examining susceptibility of transmission of the wasting disease variant in wild game to humans who consumed infected meat.

Hugh Dalen's call interrupted my reading. "Callie, I am so glad you were in. I have news."

"I hope it's good because things here are not looking great right now."

"What's happening?"

"My monkeys looked better for a while, but now they are worse. They're dying."

"Oh, no."

"The pregnant female isn't due till mid-November. I hope she survives long enough to deliver a viable baby."

"Good luck on that. I'm not sure which piece of news to tell you first."

"The good news."

"Okay. Preliminary studies on your father's spinal fluid showed fewer prions than the original sample."

I gasped. "That is horrible news! It means his treatment was working. If I'd known that when he was still alive, I could have given him the antibody and tried to save him."

"Callie, his disease was so advanced, I doubt if even you could have saved him. But, it means what he was doing had some effect, so that's good news for your study."

"It makes me want to hurry up and try monoclonals. I hope the monkey doesn't abort or have a stillbirth. We need this baby to survive."

"The fact your dad's antibody treatment appeared to be working is hopeful."

"What's the bad news?"

"The latest human death in Wapiti County tested positive for prions, but the CDC has identified an unusual variation and needs more time."

"There'll be hysteria among the hunters if it turns out to be Chronic Wasting Disease, but another mad cow case in cattle country would be just as bad."

"The CDC is blocking the release of any information until they complete their investigation on the source of the infected beef. Maybe after their meeting with the Beef Growers' Association, local ranchers, and slaughterhouses we'll know more."

"I wish them luck. Beef growers have a financial incentive to cover up evidence of contaminated cattle."

Silence.

Hugh finally spoke. "Like you, Callie, I quit eating meat. I'll call you when I hear something."

Chapter 14 – Failure

The female monkey's CT scan showed subtle brain changes in the pulvinar region deep in the thalamus. Similar brain abnormalities were discernible in the tiny fetal brain confirming intrauterine prion transfer, the same findings in variant Creutzfeldt-Jakob disease infecting humans who had eaten beef from infected animals.

The ailing male monkey lapsed into a coma and died within hours of his fourth treatment.

After what had initially appeared to be a rally, the disease in the monkeys followed my father's symptom progression to the end. The monkey's death left me sad but also brought relief that he would no longer suffer. I wondered why the monkeys had shown improvement but then took an abrupt change and worsened. Prion blood levels during the improvement period revealed a reduction in circulating prions. What happened? What did I miss?

I needed to dissect the infected corpse, but looking down at the small body, I thought of my dad and other researchers I'd known who had died the horrible death. All it took was one small slip of a scalpel.

I held out my hands.

Steady. No tremors.

My vision? Colors, vivid. Linear structures, straight. I showed no early symptoms of distorted vision.

Paranoia is another early sign. I certainly had that, but it seemed justified with Reilly and Westphal too close for comfort.

My necropsy took little time. Staff from the pathology department came to the vet facility to collect the monkey tissue for microscopic slide preparation. I asked the techs to perform special stains and prepare slides for electron microscope evaluation. In my justified paranoia, I placed some tissue specimens in liquid nitrogen canisters to stash in my office as a backup, out of view of Reilly's snooping eyes.

More antibody crystallography information from the U.K. study appeared online. Their images of the bovine prion structure appeared identical to the highly aggressive trans-species images from my study. Maybe the U.K. university lab had the cure. If they'd allow me to use it on the primate baby, it could give them another data point in their research. I'd have to call Paul Wilder for his input.

A ring from my cell startled me. I made it a habit to shut off the phone during work hours, but I answered without thinking.

Mack.

After his protective behavior and Sal's admonitions, I had avoided talking to him even though he'd called and left messages. I relented and agreed to go to dinner with him that evening.

Casual conversation at the restaurant drifted to an invitation to my apartment. I made coffee, and he accepted my offer of an Oreo for dessert. He drank coffee while I sipped a glass of wine. I tried to explain that I appreciated his friendship, but that work remained my focus. "I'm sitting on a time bomb. I have to find a cure before more people die. Plus, I love what I'm doing."

Mack's beautiful dark eyes and tone turned angry. Loud words stiffened Blaze. She pressed against me. "Don't waste your life, Callie." Mack gripped my arm causing pain. "Live a little. People have been looking for a prion cure for decades."

I pulled away. "Stop it. You're hurting me."

He let go. "Give it up, rat lady. It's a lost cause, just another one of those incurable diseases you'll never conquer." He smiled. His eyes softened. "Your rats won't miss you, but I do when you stay away so long."

Once again, his charm drew me in. I enjoyed his companionship and interesting life, but on what terms? Mack voiced no understanding of my drive to stem prion disease and no concern when I told him pods of infection were surfacing around the world. He pressed me to work less, but shared he, too, loved his work and talked about Dad coming out to the ranch. "He wanted to learn about the AI and embryo business. Needed reassurance there was hope for the world with proper ranching."

"Did you convince him?"

Mack laughed. "I made headway, but he wasn't ready to eat beef."

"I can relate to that. I'd like to hear more about your conversations with him, but I have to get some sleep. Tomorrow will be a busy day."

Mack stood abruptly. "I can tell when I'm not wanted. Call me if you ever take another break from prions." He slammed the door.

I'm not sure what he'd expected. In one evening he changed from demanding and controlling to acting as if he could care less if he saw me again.

As soon as I locked the door, Blaze's wagging tail beat on my leg. She looked up at me happily, as if very glad he'd left, but I wasn't so sure what I wanted. I felt torn between not calling and getting to know him better.

Maybe he was playing me for the naive person I was.

At work the next few days, my thoughts drifted to Mack. I thought it would be interesting to learn more about insemination and embryo sorting. He'd mentioned that he'd like to show me the process and even get my help. I looked up some sites online to learn a little about the processes to be better informed.

Medical school, internal medicine residency, infectious disease training, and taking the boards had all come easy for me. Relationships with men were another thing altogether. Until now, I'd found research and talking with cohorts more compelling than going out for a drink, movie, or even the opera. Now, at the peak of my career, my thoughts were veering off to a sexy Native American cowboy. I loved his long hair, Western dress, and swagger. Yet something felt wrong about him. Ominous with his history.

An urgent call from Bernie interrupted my thoughts about Mack. "A vet tech just told me of an encounter she had with your old buddy Westphal early this morning. He was charming as usual and said he'd come to the vet facility to check on his rat study, but she found him snooping through files belonging to other researchers, including yours."

"That worries me. I'd never look at someone else's data."

Bernie said, "I wanted to let you know this happened. I told her and others on the prion team to keep an eye on Westphal. They said he's easy to work with but his snooping set them on edge."

I hung up feeling vulnerable. I had to protect the details of my work.

Chapter 15 - Emotional Whiplash

B efore I left work the following Thursday, I relented and called Mack. He didn't answer, so I left a message asking him to meet me at the Outpost the next time he was in town, then headed down the mountain to home. When I entered cell phone range, my phone alerted me to a message. I pulled over to check and see if it was Mack.

Hugh Dalen's cheery voice greeted me. "Callie, sorry I missed you. I have some news from the CDC and am hoping I can entice you to join me here for breakfast, lunch, or dinner in the near future. I would love to hear how things are going with your research."

After hearing his voice and invitation, I was sorry I'd called Mack. They were so different. Both were sexy and charming, but one hated my work and the other took a great interest in it. The choice between the two of them should have been easy. I definitely liked Hugh but found the unusual Native American and his dark side intriguing, drawing me in. I faced the fact that I was willing to take some risk to learn more about Mack.

Before I could call Hugh back, the phone rang. It was Mack. So there I sat at the side of the road, talking on my cell phone as other lab workers drove past and waved on their way home.

I wasn't sure how to orchestrate an evening rendezvous with Mack. Did I want to relive our first meeting at the Outpost and revive the warm feelings we both seemed to have that night? I knew my thoughts were mixed and I wondered what I should do. My mother always told me, "Honey, don't look back. Always look ahead. Learn from the good and the bad." This old memory comforted me. Then, the scientist mind kicked in. With more data I could make better decisions.

Mother's words came back to me at this odd time. Neither she nor Dad had been happy that I had followed Dad's path to the narrow field of prion research. To make that decision, I did look back. I looked back at the joy I had found helping my father in deer pens when visiting the lab when I was growing up, years after he returned from Great Britain. These memories weren't related to my profession. Instead, my personal experiences carried me to the Ridge Lab to do exactly what I wanted to do—and to sitting at the side of the road, confused by men because I hadn't taken the time to date.

Maybe now was the time to forget about having coffee and learn to play.

I was surprised by Mack's first words. "What's up with the rat lady?"

Damn him. I hated the derogatory tone and moniker. It was an immediate put-down and slam to my work that made me want to cut him off. For the moment I said nothing.

"You still there, girl, or did I lose you?" He waited.

"I was calling to see if the invitation to come out to the ranch was still open. If you have the time, I could come out this weekend and learn about AI and embryo sorting."

He sounded pleased. "I'm just driving into town from a Missoula trip. How about meeting me for coffee at the Outpost so we can talk more about it?"

I agreed, thinking about the ironic coincidence that we'd be back at the Outpost in the evening like our first night together. Maybe being there again would ignite a better relationship. There was no time to call Hugh, and I didn't want to break the spell with Mack.

When I walked into the Outpost and saw him, my heart stumbled. I couldn't deny my attraction to him.

He was just sitting down and saw me enter. He smiled and waved his black hat.

Mack greeted me with a hug that was a little harder than I would have liked. "What a great surprise. Thanks for the call."

The overhead music wasn't jazz, but classical guitar provided a soft background to our conversation. While I sipped coffee and ate a veggie sandwich with a salad, Mack drank coffee and talked about his late lunch in Missoula with friends before driving back to Medicine Falls. "I met with a few friends who help me with AI when I need them. We are getting geared up for another insemination. My friend Tim Baird is driving up from Colorado to help after the Beast Feast."

My tension and mixed thoughts about spending more time with Mack subsided as he talked. His enthusiasm was similar to mine when I thought about my research. "I guess my timing is right to come out and watch or help. I wish I could drag you up to the lab to see what I am doing."

His eyes widened. He leaned forward in apparent interest.

"Of course, I can't do that because of all the restrictions at the high-risk lab."

He leaned back. "Dang. You had me going for a minute. Maybe I'd understand why you can't let go if I knew more about what you actually do."

"Things aren't going well right now. I have a pregnant monkey near death, and I am hoping she survives long enough to carry the baby to a viable age." I watched his expression. "I'm planning to use an amazing new antibody treatment developed in Great Britain if the baby survives and they get it to me soon enough."

He didn't acknowledge my concern, just focused on his plans. "The AI process is straightforward, a recipe of sorts. Just the right hormones to stimulate ovulation, extracting eggs, collecting sperm, mix and stir, incubate and sort." He smiled. "It's easy with the help of your friends."

"It sounds impossible. I work with small rodents and monkeys. They can be wiggly and difficult, but cattle?"

"I got Garrett Adcock the elk rancher next door, into elk AI. That is a bit more difficult to accomplish than with cattle."

"AI in elk sounds crazy."

"There are elk ranchers around the country and Canada who need to broaden their genetic base. After the ban on confined hunting, he had to figure out a way to make money. He's been a guide for years, but that's hard work.

Although my father had been at the Ridge Lab for decades, I'd spent little time in Montana in recent years and had no knowledge of domestic elk or hunting. Besides, I hated the killing. "Dad told me about people shooting fenced-in game animals. That's what Garrett did?"

"Other than guiding, he had no real way to make a living. And, it was big money. Guiding in the wilderness is difficult. If those high-paying clients don't kill a trophy animal, they don't come back or send their friends." Mack threw up his arms. "I told Garrett it was a no-brainer. Forget guiding and get easy money from elk AI. There are hundreds of domestic elk ranches around the United States and about a hundred farms just in Montana willing to pay good money for new blood in their stock."

"I'm okay with AI, but don't you hate having an elk ranch next door? If his elk got out, they could infect your cattle with prions and destroy your semen business." The proximity made me worry. "It would be catastrophic."

He snarled, "I don't worry about disease transmission. Health certification on domestic elk ranches is stricter than it is with cattle."

Mack's slashing words struck a blow. Why was he so harsh?

"What about the elk farm in Phillipsburg? When I was at the lab in Cleveland, Dad told me some elk contracted wasting disease and got loose in the wild."

"That was years ago."

I decided to push him. "It's hard to believe Montana Fish, Wildlife and Parks found no Chronic Wasting Disease in the state until the last hunting season. Isn't it true after a break in the fence at the elk ranch, FWP had a big job trying to kill off all the possibly infected free-roaming elk and deer in that area?"

"They killed all of them in an orchestrated hunt. The hard part was convincing the authorities to incinerate the carcasses." He watched me. "Incinerating a carcass that size to ash is difficult. They were just going to push the dead animals into a landfill."

I gasped. "Not incinerating those prion-diseased carcasses would contaminate groundwater and the soil for decades!"

"I know. In the end, they dug a pit and burned them." Mack smiled. "Smoky air carried the delicious smell of grilled elk for miles around."

"None of this is funny. I have nightmares thinking about what would happen if my research animals were released or specimens were stolen by uneducated activists. The transspecies prion would spread rapidly."

Damn. What was I thinking? I shouldn't have divulged that information after the caution I'd received from Headquarters.

Mack didn't seem to comprehend the significance of what I'd said and stared off into the distance. "From what I've heard, no one could penetrate that lab compound with the security you have."

I recalled the comfort I felt driving through the gates to work. "It would be extremely difficult with guards patrolling perimeter fences, one electrified. I feel safe inside, safer than I did in Cleveland."

"Do you like your new lab?"

I wanted to veer off into another topic to avoid the evening ending in another fight. "I love it, but my current study isn't going well." I thought he'd enjoy hearing things were not rosy. "My treatment worked in rats, but instead of curing monkeys, their disease is progressing."

I worried. What I'd said was very close to disclosing classified information. I wanted to change the subject, but Mack leaned in, and his tone flipped as if my earlier statement had just registered. "So, it jumps the species barrier and is rapidly lethal in primates? That's a helluva thought."

Catching myself, I said nothing in response to his question. I had hoped he'd missed what I'd said earlier. No such luck.

"Why are you involved in such a project? Stop before it kills you!"

Damn him. I wished I'd just gone home.

Mack reached across the table and took my hands. "Is that why they moved you, because it's so virulent?" He squeezed, hurting my fingers. "Answer me."

I pulled back. At the moment, Mack's demands threatened me more than prions. "Animal activists bent on destroying research using animals entered the Level 3 laboratory in a high-rise Cleveland facility. NIH and the CDC wanted assurance that no unauthorized person could enter my lab so their decision was to place me in a new lab with state-of-the-art equipment and security. That's why I'm here."

Mack let go. "Prions are prions. They're all lethal."

I talked faster, feeling defensive. "There's no cure, but I'm getting closer."

His dark eyes darted then locked on mine. That look again. My stomach knotted. His long, calloused fingers gripped my arm. "I hate your commitment to research. I thought you liked me. You really won't let go of your work. A cure would be a great achievement, but I don't see why you bother."

Mack raised his voice enough that I looked around the restaurant to see if people were staring at us. Maybe the music and conversational din were loud enough to blunt his voice, but he made me uncomfortable once again. "You may not care, but prion disease is spreading throughout the world and in the U.S. It must be stopped."

He sat up straight and gripped the edge of the table. "We Indians have a different view. My grandmother believed in the land. It lives and breathes life to those who care for it. She taught me the land should be returned to the Natives so nature can rule." His eyes intense. "Our buffalo are gone. Our teepees are gone. Our culture has been destroyed. I told her as a little boy that I wanted to make her happy. Grandmother said, 'Mack, give your people back their land. That will make me happy.'"

Mack sat still, faraway in thought. He spoke so softly I had to lean forward to hear him.

"I've never forgotten what she said. In the military, I fought the enemy to defend the United States, to keep our land. I killed to save this land. I'd kill again." He stroked the back of my hand gently, as if suddenly gaining control. "Callie, you're a star in a starry sky filled with other researchers, but in my sky, you're the only one. I want more of your attention. I want to get to know you better. Can you come out to the ranch Saturday morning?"

His abrupt change away from war to serenity flipped my stomach and softened my reserve to get away from him. I held my abdomen and took a deep breath, trying not to throw up from the stress and to understand this man who had sent my heart racing, leaving me roiling once again.

Why did he flood me with uncertainty?

My life was troubled due to Dad being ill and dying, moving to a new lab, and my monkey trial failing, but none of that set me on a razor's edge like Mack could with a few words.

I had to stop him from whiplashing my emotions.

Before we separated at the door of the Outpost, I agreed to go out to the ranch for breakfast and spend some time with him in the AI barn. Like Dad, my drive for knowledge related to prions and a desire to know him better because my father liked him pushed me toward Mack.

Chapter 16 - The Dating Game

When I stopped to pick up Blaze after meeting with Mack, Sal took one look at me. "You look like you are about to explode. Did something happen at work?" She sat me in Dad's chair at the oak table, where I put my head down.

Blaze pushed her head into my lap and whined. I hugged her. "Sal, I don't know what to think about Mack."

"What brought this on?" She placed a little glass of Dad's favorite brandy in front of me and poured one for herself before sitting down across from me.

The warming liquid trickled down my throat, calming my stomach spasms.

"Callie, you're scaring me. Did Mack do something to you?"

"Yes and no. I stopped to have coffee with him on my way home. At times, he acts as though he genuinely cares. Kind, funny, then suddenly it's as if a pressure cooker blows up. He raises his voice, even in public, not necessarily at me, just in conversation. He has a side that frightens me."

Sal watched me take another sip, waiting.

A warm feeling of relaxation calmed my tense neck muscles. "I just left the Outpost where we've been for the past hour."

"Hmmm. Has he been violent toward you?"

"No. Just demanding. Railing at me about my dangerous work and telling me I should quit."

"Are you kidding? Doesn't he know you're an Archer? He should know you'd carry on your dad's work and yours, pushing forward for a cure."

"I've dated very little, mostly gentleman nerds. Pretty damn boring. Mack sits on the opposite end of the spectrum. Volatile. A live wire. With him, it's like picking up a beautiful snake and suddenly finding it's venomous. I don't know what to do with him."

"You are sounding a little crazy. Callie you're going down the wrong trail. Stay away from this guy. He is nothing but trouble and always has been. Stay away." Sal drank the rest of her brandy and poured more.

"Sometimes I think I should. He invited me to the ranch to learn about the AI process. I'm interested, so I accepted. Maybe I can help him next month when another insemination is planned."

"I'll take care of Blaze, but I'm worried. Leave the ranch immediately if he gets weird."

"Thanks. I have to figure out what to do about him. He could do great things, in spite of his history."

"From the looks of you when you got here tonight, I'm thinking this is a toxic relationship and it's barely begun."

Blaze charged into the back seat and stood behind me, nuzzling my neck all the way home. She obviously sensed my distress. When I crawled into bed beneath my down comforter after a hot shower, Blaze jumped up on the bed and curled beside me.

The doors were locked, the shades, down, and I felt at peace. I was about to turn out the lights when I remembered Hugh Dalen had called much earlier. Eight-thirty, early enough to call. I dialed.

Hugh answered on the first ring. "Callie, I'm so glad you called."

I lay back on my pillow, listening to his calming voice. "I wanted to tell you about the CDC team that's interviewing people in Idaho about those prion deaths. One of them called and gave me a heads up. They are coming here after finishing in Idaho."

I sat bolt upright. "I'd love to talk with them. They might share things verbally they can't write or are waiting to confirm."

"That's why I called. I was hoping you'd come and join me."

"When do you think they'll be here?"

"In about a week. I also wondered about your monkeys. How are things going?"

I gave him an update and told him of my sadness at the prospect of their further deterioration.

Hugh voiced concern and an understanding of my disappointment in the anticipated outcome of the primate project. He suggested I consider staying overnight in Missoula after the CDC meeting, so we could share a nice dinner and I wouldn't have to drive home. "Bring Blaze along. I'd love to spend more time with her, and you."

I breathed a sigh of relief and lay back on my pillow. "I'd love to, and thanks for inviting my dog."

"Blaze is always welcome."

She looked at the phone and wagged.

"I think she heard your invitation. She is wagging her tail."

"Sweet."

I wanted to say, "So are you." God it was great to hear a sane voice. I thanked him and asked him to let me know when we'd be meeting with the CDC.

On Friday morning, Sal was already up before six when I dropped Blaze off for the day. She'd cut a couple inches off her hair, curled it a bit, and looked adorable in jeans and a red turtleneck.

Blaze woofed hello and got a hug.

I looked Sal up and down. "My, don't you look good! Where are you going? Do you have a date?"

She flushed. "Actually, Blaze and I are meeting an old friend in Missoula for an early lunch."

"Who's the guy?"

"A high school flame that burned out decades ago contacted me on Facebook. He's going to be in Missoula for a few days."

"I love it! An old flame." I turned to go. "I want a full report when I get back from work."

I drove happily up the mountain after wishing Sal an enjoyable time.

As I keyed in the entrance code to my office, I could hear the phone ringing. I hurried to answer before the caller gave up. It was Hugh calling to say the CDC investigators would be arriving Monday. He hoped I could drive up Monday morning.

We agreed on the time. "I'm excited they'll be here so soon."

My day sped by with thoughts of going out to the ranch Saturday and then meeting with Hugh on Monday. I felt anxious about the date at the ranch but excited about seeing Hugh. The contrast between Hugh and Mack was striking.

When I opened the motel office door, the bell greeted me. I heard Sal's classical music coming from her apartment. She parted the beads. "I thought it might be you."

Her bright smile told me she'd had a good time.

"He's a lot better-looking now and more interesting than he was in high school. Heck, he had pimples then. Boy, has he changed."

"Nice. Is he going to be in Montana for a while?"

"A few days. I plan to see him again before he leaves."

Chapter 17 - A Big Sky Encounter

Garrett Adcock sat at the breakfast bar drinking coffee with Mack when I arrived at the ranch. Mack pulled me through the door and directed me to a seat next to Garret, who handed me a Beast Feast flyer. "Take a look at this. I stopped by with a stack of these to be distributed around the valley. Mack and I are coordinating the feast again this year."

I read the flier: *Barbecued Beast with baked beans, coleslaw, and fresh corn on the cob. Served by local cowboys and hunters at the Ravalli County Fairgrounds.*

"My freezer is filled with game meat, beef, and a few other options like chicken, lamb, and rabbit, all donated by hunters and local ranchers." Garrett pointed at the menu. "I heard you're not a meat eater, but you'll have fresh corn on the cob to eat. We usually go through a couple of truckloads of corn, picked that morning and delivered to the fairgrounds."

The men talked about the red bib aprons they'd ordered for all the men to wear while grilling. Western shirts, blue jeans, and cowboy hats would be their uniform for the event. "It's a men's affair." Mack explained, "We keep women out of it except for selling the five-dollar tickets at the gate. They like to handle money and watch men do women's work."

"Don't take him wrong. We like women."

"Yeah," Mack agreed. "Montana has sharp-shooting women, so we have to behave."

I listened, saying little while trying not to think about a crowd of people gathered at the fairgrounds to eat meat. "What do you do with the money you make?"

Garrett stacked his flyers on the breakfast bar, getting ready to leave. "Donate it to charities, wildlife and hunting organizations."

"Why not stay for another cup?" Mack refilled Garrett's mug and poured one for me. "It's a popular event, Callie, with good food, a little rodeo, and country-western music. We make more money from the vendors than we do from the food."

Garrett explained, "He's talking about the fees from organizations like the Rocky Mountain Elk Foundation, Ducks Unlimited, Pheasants Forever, and Beef Growers of Montana. They're sponsors, plus they pay a user fee for a promotion booth at our event."

Mack laughed. "We even let the animal rights activists set up booths. They pay good money for the exposure, but around here interest in their causes is lukewarm." He put his arm around my waist, acting loving, showing me a sketch of the booth layout.

He seemed to be playacting in front of his friend. I stiffened, not liking being a prop.

The three of us looked at a sketch of the booth locations. Mack said, "This year, we put PETA between the Elk Foundation and the Beef Growers. Have you ever heard of Natural Order?"

I shook my head.

Garrett pointed out a location. "It's some crazy vegan group. Oops, sorry about the name-calling. I put them between Domestic Elk Ranchers and Feedlots of the West. A perfect location, don't you think?"

Mack laughed out loud. "Vegans surrounded by meat eaters. They won't be thrilled and the guys manning the Feedlots booth won't be interested in hearing about mistreatment of animals or healthy aspects of eating plants."

I grimaced.

Mack frowned. "They're here to make trouble."

I took in their bantering and internalized the derogatory conversation. Their idea of vegetarians was different from mine. I was glad when Garrett finally left because I wouldn't have to endure more of their prejudicial statements.

We followed him outside, then walked across the driveway toward a corral and the big barns. "I wanted you to meet Igor the last time you were out, but we didn't have time. Let's go visit him before we head to the AI barn."

Mack leaned over the corral railing and looked around. He gave a loud whistle. "Igor, Igor, come."

A huge black bull got to his feet and ambled up to the fence. Mack gave him a stem of alfalfa growing along the fence line.

I reached in and patted the bull a couple of times before he wandered off. "Igor has social skills like a lot of people I know."

Mack remained straight-faced and silent at my attempted joke. I had carried the conversation into a quagmire without even trying. "He's very social for a bull." Mack stepped away from the railing and headed off. "Let's go to the AI lab."

After being so friendly in the house, he said nothing as I walked at his side. Did I deserve the silent treatment? I'd seen his off-on emotional switch flip back and forth on Thursday night at the Outback. He turned sullen over issues I didn't comprehend. Something inside told me to be careful.

Mack opened a large double door on the south side of the biggest barn on the property. On the east exterior, the black AI lettering on the white barn was at least my height and could be seen from the road. Inside, glistening white floors reflected fluorescent ceiling lights. An L-shaped desk with computer terminals sat against the wall to the right. We walked into an adjacent, smaller room with black granite countertops, the room I had been in on my previous visit to the ranch. This time, three Native American women perched on stools at microscopes. Each also had a computer terminal. When we entered, their heads turned in unison like robots.

The women varied in age from about twenty to forty, and all three truly beautiful.

We walked into their lab, and Mack spoke. "Mornin' ladies." He introduced each one. "I invited Dr. Callie Archer from the Ridge Lab to come out again and see what we're doing."

They smiled, definitely more friendly than they'd been the last time I was here.

"Her dad, Nolan Archer, used to hang out with us on occasion. After I give her a little tour, I'd like you to show her what you are working on today. She may be able to help us in a couple weeks when we get busy with the next AI." Mack took my arm in a friendly gesture. "She'd like to learn embryo sorting, too."

We walked through a door into an expansive area as big as the gymnasium at the school where we'd met. "Let's look at the chute where we move the cows for hormone injections, egg collection, and uterine flushes for embryos. We also bring one bull at a time in here for semen collection."

The cement floors were clean. In a corner stall, an agitated cow snorted and swayed from side to side, banging against the metal gate. I walked closer. "She looks very unhappy. What's wrong with her?"

Mack reached inside the pen. She shied away.

"The ranch hands brought her in for me to check. She was out in the pasture looking like she might be in pain. They wondered about a twisted gut." Mack climbed up on a railing to look at her more closely. "She's settled down some, but to get her in here and quieted a few minutes for me to do an ultrasound on her belly, we had to hit her with a couple jolts from a Hot-Shot." He pointed at a three-foot rod with metal prongs on one end leaning against the wall near the pen. "Then, I sedated her, but I couldn't see any problem on the ultrasound. I'm waiting for blood tests."

I walked over to the cattle prod. "This looks wicked."

"It gets their attention but doesn't really hurt them." He thumbed a switch on the handle. "The jolt will knock down a human and is very painful, so I'm careful with it."

I followed him from the stockade and the sick cow into the office. He showed me a storage area with tall metal shelves, all lined with the familiar liquid nitrogen bottles I had used in my labs for years. "This is where I keep a large inventory of semen from my four prize bulls, ready for shipment. Igor has the best blood line, so his semen sells for the most money."

I read a number of labels. "You have his semen stockpiled."

Mack counted rows of bottles. "I do, in various quantities so they're ready for a shipment within seconds. With UPS tracking, I know where the product is and when it arrives at its destination."

"Efficient process. I'm impressed." I walked into the lab and sat on a tall stool by one of the techs. "I might as well get started."

Mack disappeared. The techs were efficient and friendly. They talked about processing the semen and labeling the straws and bottles. Their tracking methods used barcodes, and computerized labeling made the process easy to follow. Since they were not sorting embryos at the time, they explained the process using three-ring binders with magnified photos of perfect embryos and images of others that were unacceptable.

One of them said, "It's easy. Once you've done a few, we'll get you set up at your own microscope. If you have any questions, just ask."

After an hour, Mack returned. "If you've had enough of this, could I drag you back to the house for some lunch?"

I thanked the techs. "Sure. I've really enjoyed the time here. Fascinating."

On the way to the house, Mack asked if I'd like to go riding.

I stuck out my foot to show off my cowboy boots. "I'm ready to go. I'd love to."

I sat at the counter sipping coffee while he made sandwiches. Midway through the sandwich making, he disappeared and returned with a large photo album. "I thought you might like looking through some old photos from the reservation, see what I looked like when I was young and good-looking." He smiled and opened to a page with him riding bareback on a spotted pony.

"You're handsome now, but you could have been in movies even as a child." He went back to lunch preparation, and I paged through, asking him who various people were in the photos. I got to see his mother and grandmother. I wondered about his father but found no photo. After a few hunting shots with dead deer, and later photos of his home under construction, portions of three pages were torn out. I found that strange.

Mack put placemats on the table in the alcove and plates with sandwiches and fruit. He beckoned me. "Bring the album if you like."

I left it open to the torn pages and picked up a sandwich with peanut butter, bananas, and sprouts. "Delicious. I should stay here and take cooking lessons, too."

"Fine by me." He sat down. His eyes went to the album opened to the torn pages. In a flash, he flipped it shut and placed it on the counter behind me, out of reach.

Mack sat back down, silent.

The way he had snatched the album made me think he was hiding something, but I dared not ask.

After a few bites, he said, "Sorry about my anger. I try to forget about the day I destroyed a bunch of photos." His face contorted in pain.

He took a deep breath. "You can see I'm not over it. That's why I'm not very pleasant to be around sometimes. I work hard, stay busy, and try to forget." He was silent for a few seconds. "Those were pictures of Milly. She ran off with one of my new ranch hands two years ago. We'd been married about a year. I couldn't bring myself to tell you about her. More baggage I'm trying to get rid of." He pushed his plate away, the sandwich half-eaten.

His words left me weak. I wondered how many more secrets Mack hid, a handsome, successful man, crippled by his past.

Sal's dark words moved through my thoughts. I felt sad for him. I swallowed my last bite and picked up our dishes. "Let's go for that ride you promised."

Mack pulled out his cell phone. "I'll call and see if Andy has time to saddle up the horses for us." After a short conversation, he said, "He's on it. Let's walk out there."

He talked about cutting horses and driving his nonorganic herd along the country road to a feedlot about a mile away. "I wouldn't expect you to drive cattle, but you could be a lookout at road crossings. If you have time to help next month, you could stop traffic while we're moving them along. Sometimes a few cars line up to watch. I just hope we don't have activists causing trouble."

"Could we ride the route today?"

"Sure. I'll tell Andy what we're up to."

I thought about what I'd suggested. "I'm not sure I really want to see a feedlot up close."

Mack stopped. "There is another issue I forgot. We'd pass by the rendering plant, and you wouldn't like that. It stinks."

That made it a quick decision for me. "Let's ride on the ranch today. I'd enjoy seeing more of it."

Mack turned his horse and mine followed. "I'll give you some riding pointers. I'd also like to check a section of fence line on the back quarter where a hand did a recent repair."

We crossed rolling grassland scattered with black cattle framed by the Bitterroot Mountains to the west. Mack dismounted near a stream, letting his horse loose. He helped me to the ground.

I walked up a little rise and sat, looking back on our route to watching the horses graze and drink from the stream. I motioned Mack to join me.

He sat down. "Your dad and I rode out to this spot. He loved Montana and sat just where you are sitting. I hope you'll learn to like it here."

As I thought about sitting exactly where my father had, a feeling of peace blanketed me. I lay back against prickly grass to absorb more of the comfort, watching puffy white clouds track across the expansive sky.

Mack stretched out on his side, leaning on one elbow. He brushed a curl from my forehead, kissed a fingertip and touched my lips. His scent, gentleness, and the peaceful surroundings suppressed my concerns about his past. Acceptance in times of uncertainty could break the barriers of distrust.

I turned toward him. His gentle kiss evolved to a sensual clench of breathlessness. His rough hands loosened my bra, fondling as he rolled to his back, bringing me with him, feeling his bulging interest press against my belly. I unbuttoned his shirt, sliding my hands over hairless skin. My fingers stroked low on his belly reaching for more.

He slid down his jeans.

I reached for him. "I should have worn a skirt."

Mack smiled. "Need help?"

He sat up. We pulled off my boots and jeans exposing lacy black underwear. His dark eyes scanned, stopping on the lace. "Beautiful lady." He removed his boots and jeans, then lay beside me. Stroking, kissing.

I had never intended nor expected this. I was drawn to him, but Sal's admonitions again flitted through my distracted thoughts. A ride in the country turning to a tryst. I was not prepared. No contraception.

Mack removed his shirt and smoothed it on the ground, pulling me from the prickly grass to the soft fabric. His exquisite body exposed to me in Montana wilds blanketed only by blue sky raised overwhelming desire. Lying on his side, he pulled me against his muscular body.

I pulled him closer, wanting him.

Instead, he slowly removed my blouse and bra, lingering kisses held me back, as he eased from his shorts and pulled my underwear aside, teasing me with sweeping light touches stoking the fire of desire. I removed the lace separating us and mounted, gasping with the first touch.

He held back. "Go slow, Callie. Kiss me."

Instead of gentleness, his lips crushed mine, accelerating desire, uncontrolled, he plunged deep, pulsing, carrying me with him. Melted together, hearts pounding. We lay, letting the ecstasy pass. His breathing slowed, hands on my buttocks held us enmeshed. He whispered, "I've waited for this moment from the first night we met."

A breeze rustled the grass around us. Birds sang. I couldn't move, didn't want to. "You lit my fire." I laughed. "I want it to keep burning, but shouldn't we get dressed before some of your employees ride up to see if we need an ambulance?"

Mack laughed. "No worry. They're involved in a project on the other side of the property."

as I pulled on my underwear, I watched him dress, his braid spilling loose strands as he pulled on his shorts. I knelt behind him, unbraiding the black locks before moving to straddle him, combing his long hair with my fingers. His hair fell across my face with a kiss. His hands swept my breasts, and he moved the lace aside easing his penis inside, deeper and deeper, moving and kissing until I fell weak against him. Clinging, hyperventilating, feeling satisfied but wanting more.

We rested till a chilly breeze swept over us and we separated to dress.

Mack whistled for the horses and helped me get my foot in the stirrup. The horses ambled toward the ranch. I reminded him we hadn't checked the fence line.

He reached out to touch me, but we were too far apart. "I'll check it another day. I don't want to break this spell." He blew a kiss and then used a black stretchy band to secure his hair at the nape of his neck.

Before we reached the ranch, I pulled back on the reins, stopping Candy to talk. "I'm worried about what just happened."

He stopped, frowning. "What's the matter?"

"Without protection, I could get pregnant."

Mack raised his arms to the sky. "I'd be delighted." He seemed too eager.

Maybe he thought I'd quit work if I was pregnant. Not a chance. "I'm not ready. I hope luck is on my side."

He shrugged. "No worries. I had a vasectomy after deciding I never wanted kids."

His statement sent a stab to my heart. I'd had a few lovers and we'd always used protection, but I wanted to keep the option for children at the right time open. "Why no kids?"

"It's a long story. I'll tell you another time."

Back at the corral, Andy met us and took the horses from Mack. "We just got a phone call. The Texas semen shipment arrived thawed. They're pissed. We need to get another shipment off to them right away."

Mack snapped, "Damn. Can't the girls do it?"

Andy checked his watch. "They left half an hour ago."

I looked to Mack. "It's okay. I have to get back to town, so go ahead and take care of it."

He wrapped strong arms around me. "Hate to have you leave on this note. Don't forget the Beast Feast next weekend. I'll call you."

The seven miles to town seemed like one. When I arrived back at the motel to pick up Blaze, Sal was busy checking in a guest. I told her I'd had a great time with Mack and would call her, then headed south of town to a river access for boaters. Blaze ran around sniffing and took a quick swim, shaking sprinkles of cold water on me. We walked about a mile to let her dry off some before getting back in the car.

I enjoyed a cheery evening at home with Blaze. She lay on her bed with her eyes closed while I washed clothes and chopped vegetables for soup. I decided to take better care of myself. During the last few weeks before Dad died, I'd lost about five pounds that I couldn't afford to lose.

Mack called to say hello, and I dropped into my recliner to talk. He related details about the Beast Feast. My thoughts distracted me from his words. I tried to listen as I pictured the clear blue afternoon sky, the two of us lying naked in the grass with me enveloped in his arms and charm. A warm stir made me wish he was with me, naked.

On his horse, he was the image of a gentleman cowboy, a Native American movie star.

Mack talked comfortably without a hint of the anger flashes that had left me wary.

I told him I planned to work on Sunday and drive to Missoula on Monday for a meeting. I didn't tell him anything about the meeting for fear I'd disclose something I shouldn't. He didn't seem interested and talked on about other topics.

"Garrett's busy promoting guided elk hunts in the Bitterroots along the Idaho border south of here. He's excited about some outside interests with money who are willing to support hunting in this area."

Dark thoughts of the recent prion deaths in Wapiti County, Idaho, crossed my mind when he mentioned the hunt area. But the confusing part was that the deaths were from bovine spongiform encephalopathy, mad cow disease. I couldn't tell Mack about them until the CDC made the information public. "What do the investors want in return?"

"They're talking about building a private hunting lodge. Garrett would work for them as a guide, and they'd benefit from getting a cut for sending rich friends here to hunt."

"I don't like any hunting and hate the confined hunts Dad talked about. The animals were slaughtered with no chance of escape. The thought of it makes me ill."

"Don't let my buddies hear you say things like that. I didn't like those hunts either, but around here you'd better keep that opinion to yourself."

His words and tone irked me. "That wasn't hunting. I can't stand the thought of those gorgeous beasts inside fences being shot down for their antlers."

"Garrett used to make twenty thousand dollars per trophy elk taken on his property. He had a lot to lose when the law banned his major source of income. That's why he started doing elk AI. He was already in the antler and antler-velvet aphrodisiac business."

"That is gross. I can't believe people would consume those products if they knew about prions."

"Sex is big business. There's a huge Asian market that believes in aphrodisiacs."

"Sick. I'd like to outlaw U.S. shipments."

"Don't say that to Garrett. I believe people deserve what they get. Let stupid people ingest prions and die. It would reduce the population and return the earth to a better place."

"That's harsh, but I guess I don't have to worry about you being infected with prions from taking aphrodisiac supplements."

Mack laughed. "I don't seem to need them."

"No, you don't."

Chapter 18 – Deterioration

I took Blaze to the lab with me on Sunday. Since I was taking Monday off, I planned to make it a quick trip to check on the animals. The halls were silent and the coffee room empty when I walked through and made my way out to the animal compound.

At the isolation monkey pod, I watched the pathetic pregnant monkey crawl on all fours, no longer able to swing or climb. Her wobbly legs carried her along the perimeter as she clung to the cage like a baby learning to walk.

With drool stringing from her mouth, she rose to her feet and inched along the cage over to where I stood.

The female vet tech in protective gear with me said, "This is the worst part of my job, watching these little creatures die. Sure am sorry your special sauce didn't cure them."

I adjusted my gloves and protective glasses and then squatted down to look through the cage at the little female. "It'll soon be over for them. The female looks stronger than the lethargic male. I hope she carries the baby close to term. A couple more weeks would help its survivability." I peered in at her.

She moved closer to me and rested her head against the cage as if so tired she couldn't hold her head up without support. Her eyes looked straight into mine, tired and curious.

I wondered what she saw with her prion-distorted vision. She didn't seem frightened. Maybe she'd become accustomed to the creatures taking care of her.

A little hand reached out between the bars toward me.

I touched her finger.

She reached further, curling her fingers, grabbing.

I took her little hand in mine. "You are a good girl. I'm sorry you're sick. I'm so sorry. I thought you would be a star and save the world." Tears rolled from my eyes. I took a ragged breath and held her trembling hand.

The monkey let go and lay down on her side with her eyes closed, breathing slow, and belly protruding.

The tech held out her hand to help me up.

We hugged each other, crying.

I escaped the lab without having to talk to anyone and found Blaze sitting behind the steering wheel, waiting for my return. Her woofs welcomed me as soon as she saw me exit the exterior gate. Her joyful greeting raised my spirits after the emotional visit with the monkeys. While I was still in cell range, I sat in the parking lot and called Bernie at home to tell her about the monkeys and my plans. "They both look near death. Do you think we should do a C-section and take the baby rather than wait?"

"She's carried it this far. A few more days would be best. I would say let nature take its course. We are giving them daily IV nutritional infusions. If she lapses into a coma, I will wait to do a C-section and only do it if her vital signs deteriorate. Then, our decision would be made for us. You'll get an urgent call from me if that happens."

"I won't be here tomorrow. Hugh Dalen invited me to attend a meeting at the state lab with him and some CDC investigators. I was so glad he called, but after seeing the monkeys I'm torn between going to Missoula and staying here."

"Go." Bernie was emphatic. "That sounds important, and I've done a few C-sections by myself. I have skilled surgical techs. If something happens, I'll call you. In the meantime, don't worry about me and the monkeys."

I felt better after talking to Bernie and decided to go home. I confirmed the trip to Missoula and told Sal my plans. Blaze followed me around the apartment, curious. Her eyes turned sad when I packed an overnight bag. She lay near the bag watching me add a sweater, underwear, and essentials. Her tail wagged when I packed dog treats, a bag of her food, and two bowls. "You get to go. We're going in the car."

She ran to the door.

"It's bedtime now, sweetie. We'll go in the morning." I hugged her.

Blaze curled up on her bed while I laid out a bright green turtleneck sweater, black jeans, and cowboy boots for the next day.

In the morning, I tied a green bandana around Blaze's neck to match my outfit, fed her, and put her outside while I dressed. We were on the road before seven-thirty for a relaxing drive.

Prior to the amazing sex with Mack, I had looked forward to meeting with Hugh and spending the night with him but not now. Mack had gotten my attention and complicated my plans.

Chapter 19 - Missoula Rendezvous

I arrived at the state lab thinking about the time I'd driven away with Dad's body parts in liquid nitrogen in the back of my car. This was a happier day. I lowered the windows, locked Blaze in the car, and walked into Hugh's office with a smile on my face.

Two men and a dark-haired young woman sat with him. Hugh introduced them and took us down the hall to a conference room. Carafes of coffee and water sat in the center of a large oval table. I reached for the coffee. "I didn't stop for my usual morning dose before the drive up here." I poured for everyone before Hugh opened the meeting.

He first noted Paul Wilder had discussed my father's prion death from Chronic Wasting Disease with them. I wasn't sure if the CDC had been informed but was comfortable with them knowing as long as they didn't divulge the information to the Ridge Lab.

Hugh said Paul believed it essential that they understood how the human transmission of CWD had occurred. He gave them an overview of the progression in Dad, faster but otherwise identical to the progression of symptoms seen in the mad cow variant in humans. Dad's Chronic Wasting Dis-

ease was the first on record. I added details about the neurological deterioration I had witnessed from reading his journals and my observations before his death.

The infectious disease officers each spoke in turn about
their completed Idaho investigations of the human cases of
variant CJD found there, all from beef, not the CWD form.
They detailed discussions with family members of the deceased, extensive health and travel histories, physician interviews, and the Idaho state medical examiner input.

The lead investigator said, "We also met with Idaho Fish
and Game representatives and members of hunting and
ranching groups."

The woman reported, "Ranchers were poorly informed
or not interested in hearing about the threat to their industry. The Fish and Game people, on the other hand, were riv-
eted and showed us their excellent website with up-to-date
CWD information. They do limited testing on big game
during hunts, but with the problem on their northern border
along our state and some positives in Montana, they're expanding the testing."

The third investigator quickly added, "I'm worried these
three deaths are the tip of an iceberg. My background as a
veterinarian is in bovine infectious disease monitoring. Callie, I met with your father at the Ridge Lab a few years ago.
I am very sorry about his death. On this trip, we struck out
when looking for a common contamination thread such as a
meat cutter or sausage maker."

The team leader summarized their findings. "We found
no source to tie the deaths together. That makes it more ominous. We need to know the source. We're here to ask Hugh

to be alert to any unusual cases that come into the state lab, same with the Idaho examiner. Given the fact that six mule deer in eastern Montana came up positive for CWD last hunting season we are bound to see more. With Nolan's death from blood contamination, we know CWD crosses the human species barrier. We asked the game departments of both states to increase hunter education and game testing."

The investigators headed to the airport to catch their flight for home right after our meeting. By eleven-thirty, Hugh and I were sitting in a cozy booth ordering lunch at the Mountain Grill. We drove there together in my car with Blaze. The log structure was located conveniently near the state lab, just past the Elk Foundation offices. My eyes stopped on the Rocky Mountain oysters on the menu and then scanned on. There were few vegetarian choices. Seeing all the meat options reminded me of Mack and the Beast Feast scheduled in a few days.

I blocked both from my thoughts and focused on the morning with Hugh. We discussed contingency plans with the CDC should more cases turn up. He had assured the visiting investigators that the state's outbreak action plan had been updated since the discovery of deer infected with CWD in eastern Montana. He'd sent a state employee to the area to help Fish, Wildlife and Parks agents educate locals and hunters about the handling of diseased carcasses.

I ordered salad and vegetable soup, then helped myself to hot bread the moment it was served. "Hugh, before the meeting ended, I was so hungry I considered eating a couple packets of sugar."

He laughed. "I'm glad the meeting didn't go on any longer than it did. They didn't have much information about the Idaho cases to share. I was hoping they'd identified the source so we could take some action."

Our waiter passed by with a sizzling tray for three men drinking beer in an adjacent booth. They cheered when their hors d'oeuvres arrived. Hugh watched them from his position. "Callie, would you like to change places with me so you can watch those guys eating beef testicles?"

I swallowed hard to suppress a gag. "A specialty here, I assume. No. I'll keep my head down and enjoy my bread and vegetarian meal while worrying about the prion deaths that occurred in such close proximity to us. I think it's strange the investigators didn't find some connection?"

"Surveillance is key at this point, but I don't like not knowing. I'll stay in touch with the pathologist at the Idaho state lab. She's astute and called me on the others."

I told Hugh about the pregnant monkey. "Working closely with Bernie Goff over the primate study I've grown to like and trust her. I might get a call if she has to do an emergency C-section."

Hugh looked hopeful; his eyebrows raised. "I hope the baby will wait. I told my secretary I would take the afternoon off unless something urgent came up. How urgent can an autopsy be?"

"Bernie doesn't need me. We did a CT of the mother's belly in hopes we could see the fetal brain. It was a poor-quality scan, but I think the fetus has classic prion brain changes."

"Both of us tend to be focused on our work. Let's see how long we can go without talking about medicine." He smiled and waited a few seconds, watching my expression. "Do you already feel anxious?"

I actually tensed at the thought. "Hmm, what else is there to talk about? I think I'll need counseling."

"I have some ideas. My condo is down along the river. There's a river walk we could try. Blaze would love it. Then, we could do an early dinner at Red Bird on Higgins. They have great food and wine. Then, if there is time, maybe a movie."

"I'm overwhelmed at the prospect of just relaxing. I don't know if I'm capable." I smiled, but inside I knew it was the truth. I hadn't seen a movie in many years.

"You're finished eating. Should we go?"

I looked at his plate. "I am, but you didn't eat much."

"Ordering beef was automatic for me in this restaurant, but the first bite didn't pass my lips. Dark thoughts of prion disease and the unknowns related to the Idaho deaths stopped me."

"I'm glad you didn't eat the beef. Are you still hungry after just a salad?"

"Red Bird opens at five. I can wait a few hours."

Blaze was happy to see us and chomped the piece of bread I'd saved for a treat. Hugh drove my car since he knew the city. Our first stop was at a park near Riverfront Trail. "This is just a couple blocks from my condo. I love the paved trail but don't walk it as often as I should."

We walked about a mile above a river wider and flowing faster than the Bitterroot before turning back. Blaze peered cautiously down the steep embankment not interested in testing the water.

When I had dressed for the day, walking so far in cowboy boots hadn't been on my radar, but I found them comfortable. After a tour of downtown, we parked at his condo and took the elevator to the eighth-floor condo overlooking the city to the southwest, with a view of the river. He pointed out a few landmarks from our perch on a small deck surrounded by a wrought-iron decorative railing.

I followed him back inside and sat at a curved granite counter that arced around his modern, stainless-steel kitchen. He poured red wine into two crystal glasses and handed me one. "This is your first lesson. Sip a little wine on a beautiful fall day under clear Montana skies." He draped a blanket over his arm and took my hand. We went back outside to a love seat. He pulled off my boots and sat close, both warmed by the soft wool. I curled my feet up to the side. Blaze lay by Hugh's feet.

Hugh raised his glass. "Here's to finally having some fun."

"Cheers." We touched glasses. "I wish Dad could join us."

"Yes. A great man, and a good friend. I miss him too."

I thought about my last toast with Dad and looked down at Blaze, asleep, dreaming. legs twitching. "Blaze is relaxed. I'm jealous. She is lying closer to you than to me."

Hugh laughed. "I'm glad she likes me. I grew up with dogs but living here and working long hours makes it impossible to adopt one right now."

I told him of my perfect arrangement with Sal. We talked comfortably about his parents and one sister, all living in the Seattle area where he grew up. His descriptions of the Missoula area, hikes, skiing, and university events enticed me to accept his invitation to join him whenever possible. About four-thirty, we took Blaze for a short walk, gave her dinner, and left her in the condo when we set out for the restaurant.

After amazing food and a little too much wine, we decided to forego a movie and strolled among happy people along brightly lighted streets, arm in arm, taking a roundabout way back home.

Hugh was thoughtful, holding doors for me, and asking my views on political issues. At the condo, I wandered around the living room, reading book titles in his bookcase and looking at paintings on the walls. "Hugh, you're an artist. These paintings are amazing."

"I studied art for a while, but biology drew me in. Maybe like you, my mother is a doctor."

I gasped. "Oh, dear. Does that information count as talking about medicine?"

"No. I think it's been," he checked the time on his cell phone, "five hours. That's pretty good." He looked closer at the phone. "I've had the ringer shut off all afternoon and evening. Looks like I have two messages."

He checked a text message and then put a phone message on speaker: "Hugh. Baxter here with Fish, Wildlife and Parks in Yellowstone County. We've got a problem. Call me when you get this, no matter what the time."

Hugh sat down beside me. "Guess we can't get away. Look at the text message." He handed me his phone. Coroner in Billings: *Think we got a prion case earlier today. I shipped the body to you. Missoula ETA 8 p.m.*

I listened to his side of a conversation with someone at the lab. "Dang. Callie and I just finished dinner. We were having a good time. Please get things set up. We'll be there in about half an hour."

Hugh turned to me. "I'm sorry. We tried to get away. Do you want to come with me?" He raised his eyebrows. His green eyes looked sad. "It's important that I do the autopsy tonight."

"You couldn't keep me away." I sighed. We left Blaze, telling her we'd be back soon. She wagged her tail and rested her head on her paws.

We entered the morgue through the back door at the corpse entrance. Hugh's helper, Dave, a bald, jovial, fortyish muscleman stretched the seams of his scrub suit to the screaming point. I hoped he wouldn't sneeze. I'd met him on a previous visit and really liked him. He'd seen a lot, having helped with autopsies for decades.

Hugh and I split, entered locker rooms and jumped into scrub suits. The horrible smell of death slammed my nostrils when I entered the morgue just behind him. Dave handed us gowns, shoe covers, and masks smeared with Vicks to cover the smell. "Hi, Docs. Sorry you have to spend your evening with me. This is a bad one."

I gagged and put the mask on before donning in the long-sleeved gown.

Dave peeled back the shroud. "This is Fred. The old guy lived alone in a remote cabin in the Pryor Mountains. He usually went to town once a month. His son in Bozeman hadn't heard from him for months, so he went out to check on him. This is what he found."

I stepped back, shocked by the appearance and smell of a partially decayed cachectic body with limbs and other parts chewed or pecked by scavengers. One hand and a foot were missing.

Hugh's eyes passed slowly over the corpse. "This is the type of nightmare case pathologists hate. Callie, why don't you wait in the office? It won't take me long."

I took in a deep breath of the Vicks and ignored his suggestion. "Maybe he just quit eating." I moved closer, wondering how we could identify the cause of death in such decomposed tissue.

Dave handed Hugh a report from the coroner. "Said he'd talked to the owner of a country store where Fred bought supplies. Last time he came in was about three months ago.

Fred was skinny and using a walking stick because he could hardly walk due to jerky legs and poor balance. He thought people were after him."

Hugh scanned the report and handed it to me. "Looks like Fred's milk cow has advanced mad cow disease, stumbling, thin, head swinging. Strange behavior. They want to know what to do with it."

After hearing about the cow, I felt some relief thinking this might be a single case. "Based on circumstances, it looks like Fred might be an isolated case of bovine variant CJD. If his body is too deteriorated to find intact prions for diagnosis, we can euthanize the cow and test it."

Hugh looked closely at the corpse. "I agree, but we may be able to identify prions in the thin dried tissue over his head, neck, and left deltoid. His brain and spinal cord will be mush." He held out a hand. "Dave, could you get me a scalpel and jar of formalin?'

Hugh sliced off pieces of tissue from three different locations.

I held jars for him to drop in the specimens. "So, the proteins may be discernible? My experience is mostly with tissue from the recently dead, not those in advanced states of putrefaction." I labeled the source sites.

With Dave's help, we turned the body, looked at the back side, then took X-rays of his head, chest, and abdomen, looking for boney injuries.

Dave showed us the digital X-ray images. "There's metal lodged in the occipital region behind and below his left ear."

Hugh pointed. "A gunshot wound to the head likely killed him. Entry, right temple with no exit. Probably a low powered 22." He scanned the death scene report. "I don't see any note about a recovered weapon."

"The autopsy details can wait. Dave, I'll help you move him back inside the cooler. We can finish this tomorrow."

Dave agreed.

Hugh covered the body. "I'll call the people in Billings when we get back to the condo to discuss what we need to do with the cow and the death scene. I ask his son if he was right- or left-handed."

"Callie, I usually take a shower after these cases. The smell permeates your hair and skin. If you want to do the same, I'll help move the body, then take my shower and wait for you out in the office area."

It was midnight by the time he finished talking to the investigator in Yellowstone County. Sitting on a comfortable couch, looking out at the lights of Missoula, we talked for an hour about the big picture of this prion case and what to do next. we agreed that this death was likely unrelated to the recent Idaho cases.

Hugh spread out a Montana map and pointed to the location of Fred's cabin. "It's an isolated hunting area where six mule deer were identified with CWD. That means there are many more, but now we have varmints, scavenger birds, and coyotes likely infected from feeding on the guy's body. There may be species barriers, but your prion crosses species lines. What if this is a case of CWD that actually spread to Fred's cow in the wild?"

I looked over his shoulder. "It's ranching country. We need to identify the prion type in the cow. If it's the Chronic Wasting Disease variant spread from deer and not mad cow, we have bigger problems. They'll need to start surveillance testing the cattle in eastern Montana before more people become infected."

Hugh poured us each small glasses of Grand Marnier and went to his computer. "I'm going to alert FWP to orchestrate a massive hunt to kill off as many deer as possible in the area if the cow tests positive for CWD. Many of them could be infected but not yet showing symptoms."

We sat at the breakfast bar looking out over the sleepy city, few vehicles, traffic lights flashing yellow. I took a sip, wondering if I'd be able to finish the drink before falling asleep at the counter. "I think it's past my bedtime."

"You've had a long day."

"Thanks for the invitation and for involving me with the CDC people. It is certainly a memorable date."

Hugh laughed. "I hope you don't write me off after a day like this. Can't say I've ever invited another woman to an autopsy, let alone, one like we had this evening." He put his arm around me. "Please come back so we can get to know each other better. I have the guest room ready for you and Blaze."

I fell asleep with a smile on my face, beneath a white cloud down comforter with Blaze on the floor beside me.

Chapter 20 - Beast Feast

Attending the Beast Feast didn't appeal to a vegetarian, but with the personal turmoil I'd experienced after moving to Montana, I'd taken little time to absorb the local color and events. I decided a country fair would be a new experience and might be fun. Dad's awful death and my intense focus on work had numbed my desire to play. Sal had to work, so I decided to go alone and connect with Mack when he wasn't busy grilling.

The day dawned clear after a cold night. The sun beat down on cars streaming into a grassy expanse where a young man flagged vehicles into parking spots. I walked toward the smell of grilling meat with a throng of hungry people ready to eat steak for breakfast. Cowboys of all ages and shapes, wearing red aprons, joked, and grilled for people waiting in the serving line holding empty plates.

Mack waved the moment he saw me approach.

I had no interest in eating corn for breakfast, so I just waved. He was busy, so I turned away from the food line to wander through a flea market area, reading pamphlets at various booths and admiring the crafts. I bought a beautiful pair of bright blue beaded earrings.

Invigorating sun warmed my pale skin as I moved past the Beef Council booth offering propaganda on the joys of eating steak and burgers. I spent time talking with animal rights activists, listening to their views. I had just left the Natural Order booth when I felt a heavy hand on my shoulder and turned to find Mack.

He pulled me aside. "A friend told me you were hanging around that PETA display. Bad move on your part, Callie." He got into my face. "You can't trust those damn activists. They'll target you because of your research."

I made my retort light because we were in a crowded area, but his harsh touch and reprimand infuriated me. "I consider my conversations with them research. It helps me understand their views."

"And another thing. I don't want you to be seen with them because of my AI business and an elk farm next door. Garrett would blame you if there's trouble at his farm."

I shook free of Mack's hand, feeling like a child in front of an angry father. Six-foot-three and wearing cowboy boots, he towered over me. "Don't tell me what to do, what to eat, or who to talk to. Get the hell out of my way." My anger and sharp response brought a shocked look to his face.

Mack said nothing, an Indian trait I'd already experienced and recognized once again, his cold silence with fire in his beautiful dark eyes. His glare sent a jolt of adrenaline into my core, racing my heart and silencing my voice. Any meaningful interaction with him under these circumstances was hopeless.

I walked away.

He said to my back, "Have it your way, Rat Lady, but in this small town, who you talk to becomes public knowledge overnight."

I turned around. "You're right, Mack. You probably shouldn't associate with someone like me who is open-minded. And don't you ever call me Rat Lady again." I stomped away.

The interaction was devastating after our time together at the ranch three days earlier. It fractured what I had perceived as closeness and a deepening of our relationship.

I had no real interest in PETA or any other animal rights organization, but after Mack's orders, my feeling of outrage sent me back to their booths.

Natural Order turned out to be a strange off-shoot organization with a spiritual base espousing ethical treatment of animals. I talked with a young woman to learn more about their group. I'd used animal specimens in research for years. I'd had run-ins with various activist factions but had never heard of them. Their fundamentalist stance worried me, but I thought getting to know some of them might give me insight into their worldview.

The group presented an ultra-conservative theme of intolerance and ignorance. My words about scientific research brought blank stares.

I recognized a young woman sitting in a corner of the booth breastfeeding her infant. She was the pregnant girl I'd seen checking into Sal's motel. The earthy men and women manning the booth dressed in drab clothing. Thin women wearing long peasant skirts and no makeup, tied back their waist-length hair with triangular bandanas. Bearded shirtless males in dreadlocks sported elaborate body art.

The Natural Order booth smelled of the same pungent perfume exuded by the young couple who had passed me in the Wagon Wheel office. The odd, earthy odor wafted a sweetness, of maybe ginger and orange combined with freshly plowed soil.

I felt faint from the smell and walked away.

I hadn't experienced this weak feeling in a couple of months, since I'd been eating better, but I'd skipped breakfast and had no intention of facing Mack again for a cob of corn.

The sun and the smell of organic perfume blending with smoky meat drippings swept over me in a wave of nausea. I thought of the new mother and hoped she hadn't felt as bad from months of morning sickness.

I frequently skipped menstrual periods when I was underweight, like now. It had been months since my last period, but I'd had no sex since leaving an unsatisfying relationship behind in Cleveland until Mack. The thought of being pregnant made me feel worse; it would be a terrible situation under my current circumstances.

I was sure the feeling would pass, but I felt weaker and headed to a grassy area near a fence to sit down. I barely made it to the fence and lowered myself to the ground.

Sitting in the relentless sun with my head resting on my knees didn't help much. Sweat moistened my scalp and temples. My white sleeveless blouse clung to my skin. After resting a few minutes, I headed toward my car.

The din of the crowd faded.

My vision dimmed, and muscle tone melted.

The blurry face of a young man squatting beside me came into view. A voice emanated as if from a tunnel. "Dr. Archer, you passed out. Can I help you?" He offered his hand.

I smelled the odd perfume again and nearly threw up.

Muscular arms covered with strange tattoos, slick with an oily sheen, pulled me to a sitting position. The man sat beside me.

I rested my head on my knees again.

He left for a moment and returned with a bottle of water.

Acid surged into my throat. I feared I'd vomit but sipped a little cold water.

The nausea improved. "Thank you. I appreciate your kindness. What's your name?"

"Irv Quinn."

"Nice to meet you, Irv."

He looked around. "Do you need a ride home? I could borrow my friend's van."

I shook my head. "I think I can drive after I rest."

"*Think* isn't good enough. One of my friends died trying to drive himself home after he drank too much alcohol." Irv scanned the passing people. "Do you have a friend I could find for you?"

"I'll be okay." I drank another swallow and held the cold bottle to my face. "I already feel better after the water. Thanks. It's too hot for me."

Irv took my arm and walked me to my stifling car. I leaned against the hot metal and handed him the keys.

He started the motor and turned the air conditioner on high. "Please sit for a while until you're sure you can drive."

I convinced Irv I'd be fine. He walked away, but his oily essence glistened on my arm where our skin had touched.

In my rearview mirror, I saw Mack talking to Irv.

Chapter 21 - Birth and Death

D
r. Reilly finally approved my move to the new ground-floor Level 3 biologics lab in the IRF. I moved my important liquid nitrogen specimen bottles myself and hid them behind an array of large textbooks on a bottom shelf in the back corner of a cabinet in my office where no one would find them.

Bernie reluctantly agreed to allow my recovery-phase rats to be moved from the vet compound to the biocontainment portion of my new lab. After I explained I didn't trust Larry Westphal to stop nosing into my records, she acquiesced. I promised her that veterinary personnel wouldn't have to be involved in their day-to-day care.

My treated rats appeared functionally normal, but I continued their weekly drug treatment. They'd be safe in the new lab and closer for me to monitor. I wouldn't have to walk out to the vet building during the coming winter months to examine and treat them.

The move to my new lab brightened my day. Sun streaming in through a wall of windows facing south reflected off the dark green granite countertop. My microscope sat ready to review the recently prepared male monkey slides. A breeze rocked evergreen trees clustered just beyond the fence. The gold of the tamaracks mixed with the dark green pines, imitating the golden mineral flecks in the granite.

White arms of leafless aspens reached through the dense pines toward the compound.

I propped my office door open and found Wagner's "Flight of the Valkyries" on an internet radio station on my computer. The music and thoughts of being with my father in the lab surrounded me as I sat down on the high stool and adjusted the microscope focus on the first slide.

The slide showed advanced disease correlating with the monkey's late-stage behavior. Prions clustered in his brain and body fluids, jumbling his brain into a spongy mass.

In mid-November, Bernie called me one afternoon. "Hurry! She's in labor."

I ran to the vet building and arrived out of breath. Bernie was already dressed in protective garb. I pulled on a long-sleeved gown, full head cover with mask, eye protection, double gloves, and shoe covers. We looked like spacewalkers when we entered the isolation area where the laboring rhesus lay on the floor of her cage lashing out at things we didn't see. She screeched and rolled intermittently during the labor pains.

Not knowing what to expect from the laboring monkey with advanced disease, we stood watching, ready to prevent injury to her baby.

Sedating the mother would sedate the critical twenty-week-gestation newborn, so we waited.

After about fifteen minutes, the limp baby slid out.

Bernie immediately injected the mother with ketamine to sedate her and allow us to clamp and clip the cord. Then, Bernie swept the limp infant from the cage into a warmed, oxygenated incubator.

Our bulky protective garb made working with the tiny creature difficult. We extended gloved hands through apertures on each side of the plexiglass box and began resuscitation. Widely spaced, labored breaths escaped from her small gaping mouth, her fuzzy head lolled to one side. Lax facial muscles revealed little evidence of life. Lids, partly open. Eyes, unseeing.

Death appeared imminent.

Bernie suctioned the baby's mouth and used a miniature oxygen mask to give a few assisted breaths. I listened to the heart and lungs, applied heart monitor leads, placed an intravenous in the cord stump, drew blood for lab analysis, and started an IV dripping.

A tech quickly checked the blood glucose and found it low, contributing to the reduced level of consciousness. The fifteen-ounce baby clung to life on high-flow oxygen and glucose-containing intravenous fluids. She showed only respiratory movements for about five minutes. Then became more alert and opened her little brown eyes. She improved with tube feedings of milk from another lactating healthy rhesus monkey.

A vet tech rushed in to tell us the mother had died. Bernie looked up. "Thanks for letting us know. Get things ready, Dr. Archer will do a necropsy as soon as she can leave me and the baby."

I trusted Bernie's skills and relinquished the newborn monkey's care after the oxygen saturation reached 100%.

The adult female monkey was finally at peace after suffering from the cruel disease. Her tissues had to be processed before post-mortem deterioration from body enzyme activity began. Techs placed the body and placenta on a necropsy table. "Thanks. I'll need specimen containers and instruments but won't need help for the rest."

A HEPA filter mask clamped over my nose and mouth felt like a hand blocking my breath. My thoughts flashed to Westphal's attack back in Cleveland.

Suffocating.

I ripped the mask away from my face and sat down, taking deep, slow breaths.

The impervious gowns usually kept me warm, but I felt sweaty and flushed.

At twenty-eight, I knew the hot flash wasn't menopause. Sometimes I wished I were older, much older. My age and youthful appearance made competition within the research establishment difficult. If the baby died, my progress toward a primate cure would terminate. I'd have to start over. I wished I could talk to Dad. His calm thoughtfulness and support had always been there for me. I had to go on without him. I promised.

After sitting for a few minutes waiting for the flush to resolve, I put on the mask and positioned the dead monkey. Feeling sad for many reasons, I wanted to hurry and complete the dissection so I could get back to the newborn, but my father's horrible mistake doing the same procedure curbed my desire for speed. I paid attention to safety and thought about the hope for effective treatment of the infected baby.

The panic passed, allowing me to focus on preparing labels for tissue samples and cord blood instead of on death.

Gather the data.

Freeze the specimens.

Protect everyone from the rogue prion that jumped species barriers.

A tiny amount of infected fluid or tissue could infect any animal, as it had in the Wisconsin zoo. Meat from an infected "downer cow" killed all species, even birds. That was the same prion I had used in my study that had killed the monkeys.

Dairy farmers and ranchers occasionally had animals that develop undiagnosed health problems requiring they be euthanized. In the disastrous case in Wisconsin, after a cow began stumbling and falling down, the farmer had euthanized the animal and donated meat from the four-year-old milk cow to the zoo for animal food. In hindsight, she'd had classic symptoms of bovine spongiform encephalopathy, mad cow disease.

I often wondered how many downer cows with prion disease unknowingly or knowingly entered human food supplies every day. Meat from abattoirs where mass slaughtering occurs is removed by mechanical strippers, mixing meat and spinal cord material from many animals into hamburger.

The disinfectant smell made its way through the HEPA filter mask. The odors contributed to my queasy stomach. Bernie popped open the door to give me an update on the baby just as I was removing the skull cap to expose the brain. After she left, I removed the brain, with the eyes and optic nerves intact.

I placed the eyes, most of the cord, and a section of the brain in formalin to stabilize and preserve the tissue for slicing, staining, and special studies. The fluid would solidify the gray jelly-like brain tissue and make it easier to cut. I placed a portion of the spinal cord and brain in liquid nitrogen for additional studies.

The optic nerve is a direct extension of the brain, a window into the brain. With this female monkey carrying advanced disease, I expected her eyes to show characteristic cellular changes. Eye abnormalities helped track disease progression, or improvement I could use to monitor the infant's eyes before and during treatment.

My T-incision across the monkey's upper chest and down the midline to the pubis filleted open the chest and abdomen. There was a loud knock at the door just as I reached inside the body cavity to remove organs.

Odd. Why would Bernie knock? I hoped the baby hadn't died.

My heart rate surged.

I wanted to continue the delicate necropsy but decided there must be an emergency.

Would Bernie have sent a tech? A security guard?

Something must have happened.

I tossed my bloody gloves in an incinerator container and shrugged off the gown before removing the tight-fitting mask. I washed my hands. With my hair in tangles and deep mask imprints on my face, I peered through the small window in the door.

Larry Westphal looked in at me.

Damn.

I hesitated, but believing I was safe with Bernie close by, I cracked open the door.

He cocked his head to get a glimpse inside, maybe to see what I'd been doing. "Hi, Callie. I saw you run across the compound a couple hours ago. I wondered if you might need some help. I couldn't get away until now."

How in hell could he think I'd ask him for help?

"Thanks, but Bernie and I have it in hand now. How are things going for you?"

"Not too bad. Montana's a big adjustment from city life."

"That's true for me, too. I hope you're feeling good and back to your research."

"Still plugging away." He stepped back. "Congratulations on getting into your new lab. I'm heading back down the hill for the day. Take care."

I would have considered his offer a nice gesture if we didn't have the Cleveland history. My distrust and profound dislike of the man precluded any acceptance of an offer of help from him, ever.

Larry shuffled down the long hall toward the exit, head down, appearing depressed despite his pleasant words.

Since I had removed my protective gear, I went down the hall to check on the baby and tell Bernie about Westphal's strange visit. His behavior would seem normal, but my suspicion remained high after his sabotage and aggression at the Cleveland lab.

Bernie assured me the spidery creature had improved. There was hope for the frail newborn despite the ominous CT findings.

I returned to the necropsy lab, gowned up, and continued the tedious procedures of removing lungs, heart, intestines, kidneys, and liver. The process reminded me of my first experience dissecting fetal pigs eons earlier in a high school anatomy class. Little did I realize I'd be placing sections from various monkey muscles and organs in specimen containers years later.

I divided specimens between red plastic bags imprinted with "Biological Hazard" and liquid nitrogen containers. The pathology lab secured all the specimens along with cord blood for potential fetal stem cell studies. The bagged specimens would nestle next to the placenta and umbilical cord inside a temperature-controlled freezer in the pathology lab. With that part completed, I turned back to the dissection table to finish.

A small laboratory incinerator in the necropsy lab sat ready for the immediate cremation of infected tissue. I placed the furry remains inside and locked the heavy, windowed metal door. I pressed the incineration button and, through a small, scorched window, watched the inferno vaporize the fur before turning the corpse with its cross-species prions to ash.

Using lye solution and bleach, I washed the table and instruments and then flooded them with water. Burnable items, including my protective coverings, went into the large bin bound for the facility's main incinerator.

I walked back to the nursery, where I found Bernie hovered over the critical newborn with a tech assisting her. They were performing a spinal tap on a baby who had no suck reflex and minimal motor function. We needed a baseline spinal fluid sample before starting treatment. The baseline would tell us if our treatment was effective in lowering prion levels.

Within three hours of birth, we gave the infant monkey the first intravenous dose of rat drugs plus the British antibody. If the prion levels in the blood and spinal fluid fell, we'd know the combination treatment was working.

During the first twenty-four hours, Bernie and I took turns sleeping in her office, not far from the baby monkey. Within twelve hours, the infant began to look around. Bernie held the little head steady while I looked inside the eyes at her optic nerve head and retinal blood vessels.

The literature on bovine prion and Chronic Wasting Disease described unique optic nerve changes. A brain CT of the newborn confirmed changes typical of the bovine variant in humans.

Three weeks later, the infant was still alive. One day, as Bernie and I were working on her, Drs. Westphal and Reilly loomed in the doorway of the treatment room. "What are you ladies working on?" Reilly asked with anger in his voice.

The duo's unusual appearance concerned me. I wondered what the hell they were doing together in the vet building bugging us. I didn't want to divulge information to either of them for fear of sabotage.

Bernie answered. "A premature birth occurred in Callie's study. The infant is improving and gaining weight."

In a forced, happy voice, I exclaimed, "In a monkey this size, even an ounce is a lot." I smiled sweetly, hiding my anger at their intrusion.

Westphal stepped closer to look at the baby. "I suppose that's true, but then what would I know? I'm still working on sheep like I did in Cleveland. You must be onto something big with this primate study." Westphal turned to Reilly. "Callie's made progress since I left the Cleveland lab for rehab."

I answered before Reilly had a chance to ask anything. "I have no news to share."

Dr. Reilly aimed his anger at me. "You do have news. I'm furious you excluded me from this important study. I stumbled around on the phone like an idiot this morning when Headquarters called asking how the baby was doing with the British treatment."

"I've continued working with Paul Wilder. This baby is part of my prion trial in primates that began before my transfer. It's a last-ditch effort for the baby or she'll die like her parents."

Westphal's voice rose. "What's the British treatment?"

"Since Dr. Reilly already knows, I can tell you a U.K. university lab produced an amazing monoclonal antibody targeted to bovine prions. It appears to functionally block and possibly reverse abnormal prions."

"My God! That's what we have been waiting for," Westphal exclaimed.

Since Headquarters had called Director Reilly, I had no choice but to explain. "At first, my rodent study drugs were effective in the monkeys. They seemed to rally, then abruptly deteriorated. I hope the pathology slides will give me some clues to explain what happened."

Reilly's face flushed an ugly red in his anger. "Dr. Archer, was that pregnant rhesus part of the initial study?"

"It was a veterinarian glitch that occurred in Cleveland." Bernie explained, "The vets didn't realize the monkey was pregnant when they placed her in Dr. Archer's study. We've made the best of it. In the end, it may be fortuitous."

Dr. Reilly performed one of his pirouettes. "Thank you, ladies."

Westphal walked out behind him.

When they were out of earshot, Bernie said, "I wondered why I'd seen Westphal around here more often."

"Snooping for Dr. Reilly would be my guess."

A few days later, Bernie and I were having a relaxing lunch together when Larry Westphal walked in with another prion researcher. They ignored us and sat at another table.

I whispered to Bernie, "Larry's limping. I wonder what happened. I hope he didn't injure himself by getting falling-down-drunk again."

Sgt. Collucci joined us.

I apologized for not stopping by to talk with him recently.

"I've seen you run past the control room a few times. Rudy told me you were sleeping here half the time." Sarge frowned. "Don't make yourself sick by working too hard."

Bernie agreed. "Callie's back to her bad habits. The baby monkey is four weeks old and doing well. Now we can go home at night, but Callie needs remedial education on how to play."

Sarge raised his eyebrows. "You're going to develop a bad back sleeping on that couch in the coffee room, Doc. Would you like us to move a comfortable futon couch into your office?"

Bernie said, "She needs to cut back. Instead, she's had me here 24/7. Is prion work contagious?" She laughed. "It is a good thing we both have dog sitters, or it would be hard to keep these hours."

Frosty mornings, crisp fall days, and falling leaves heralded the opening of deer and elk season. Hunters walked around town wearing orange camo clothing. Rifles hung across pickup back windows. On my way home from work, a pickup passed by with an elk carcass in the back with blood dripping out from beneath the tailgate.

In late November, the world turned white with a vengeance. Dr. Reilly went out of his way to tell me the road to the lab never closed due to bad weather. I don't think his prime concern was my safety; instead, he abhorred anyone using weather as an excuse for missing work.

I told him not to worry—even with all the switchbacks, my Subaru would get me to work and back just fine.

Snow accumulation and a few drifts on the road were not problematic. Even on the nights when I left late, I blasted through the snow on my way to pick up my beautiful dog. I'd gained experience driving in Montana winters during my college breaks from Dad's alma mater, UCSF.

One afternoon, Sarge joined Bernie and me for coffee. "I hope you ladies will take a break and attend the Christmas party. Rudy and I will be there. It's the first one I recall in two decades."

Bernie sneered. "It's probably Joy's influence, but it's like him to have it the last day before a holiday, making us stay late to attend his damn party."

I drank the last of my coffee. "Do you think they're in a relationship?"

Bernie peered over her glasses. "I'd say yes, but Joy is effective in her job. Sarge, you can count on me to party with you, but I don't know about Callie. She doesn't cut herself any slack."

I shrugged. "I'd love to spend time with you guys. I'll be working, so I might stop by."

Sarge refilled his cup and waved on his way out. "Don't forget to wear your holiday best."

I turned to Bernie. "Mack has left many phone messages begging me to see him. I feel guilty for avoiding him, but his moods are unpredictable, and he raises my blood pressure by trying to get me to quit work."

"He doesn't sound like a good fit for a top-notch researcher."

"He's not. I like him in some ways. He's good looking, often funny, and I love learning about his ranch, but he's got a dark side."

Bernie rolled her eyes. "There are better men out there."

Later, I telephoned Mack and accepted his dinner invitation and asked Sal to keep Blaze for the evening.

Chapter 22 – Complications

Mack met me at the Wildlife Refuge restaurant. He reached across the table for my hand. "All this time away from you taught me I don't want to live without you. I'm sorry for being so rough. I just lost my head. I love you so much. I want you with me all the time."

I leaned back, disturbed by his statement. This was not my plan for the evening; it was to be a good-bye. "You don't know me. We have so many differences, I doubt our relationship can be more than just friends."

Mack left his food untouched, struggling with words. "Callie, you mean everything to me. You're smart and beautiful. I love you. Please give me another chance."

The busy restaurant provided no privacy. I whispered, "It's too public to talk here."

He suggested, "Let's go out to the ranch. We could relax in the hot tub. You could have a glass of wine."

I looked at him in disbelief. "How can you expect me to go out there after your behavior at the fairgrounds?" I got up to leave. "I don't want you following me around. You don't own me."

I waited outside, wondering what to do while he paid the bill. I'd feel more comfortable inviting him to talk at my apartment if I had Blaze there, but she was with Sal. "Let's go to my place. We can talk for a while."

Mack followed and parked behind me. He barely let me get inside before sweeping me into a passionate kiss. I pushed him away and led him to the couch. He sat on one end, his elbows on his knees and his head in his hands.

I flipped on a small lamp and lit a jar candle on the coffee table, then sat cross-legged on the other end of the couch. I tried to put distance between us for our talk.

Mack moved closer and tried to pull me to him.

I resisted and took both of his strong, calloused hands in mine. "Look, you're the most interesting man I've ever met, but I will not tolerate controlling behavior or violence. Besides, you don't seem to understand, my work is my life."

The flickering candlelight exaggerated his handsome features and smooth skin. Mack clenched his teeth, holding his breath, suppressing his emotion. His eyes betrayed his feeling. He quickly wiped a tear.

I was touched by his caring but was not convinced he could care that much about me when he barely knew me. "Mack, you have to understand. I've never had a serious relationship. I've never loved anyone. My work has always come first. It still does."

"Quit the damn lab. Callie, I love you." He implored, "Move to the ranch. I'll protect you. We don't need your money."

Emotions pulled me in opposite directions. His tears made me sad. "See, you don't understand. I love my work, and until I find an answer, a cure, an immunization, some way to stop prions, I won't be free." I leaned away from him. "I'll never quit. If you want to be with me, you have to accept that fact."

"I'll wait, Callie, I'll wait. I'll be patient. I can't stand it when you don't call me." His hand gripped mine. "Please don't desert me. I couldn't stand it when my first wife left."

"Things are busy and troublesome at the lab. I'm distracted by the project and the politics."

Mack tightened his grip. "Is it that damn Larry Westphal? Has he been bothering you?"

I pulled my hand free. "Stop it! No. Two of my monkeys died, and we are trying to save a sick newborn."

"I'm sorry. I know it means so much to you, but Callie, I'll take care of you." His face, sad, Gaze, intense. "I'd marry you tonight if you said yes."

"Let's talk about something else." I pulled up my knees, creating a blockade against him. I hunched deep into my corner of the couch.

Mack pulled me into an awkward clench, burying his face in my hair. "Please, marry me."

"Marriage? After your behavior? I'm not ready for marriage with anyone. Let's talk."

"Thank you for giving me a chance. I love you. Whenever I see you, I'll think of you like you were out in the grass on the ranch."

"Damn you. I will not be controlled. Until you realize that, and accept my dedication to finding a prion cure, there is no point in talking."

Mack walked to the door. "I have some thinking to do."

I watched him walk out, unwilling to trust him, but torn by his looks and our intoxicating sex.

The next day when driving up the winding road, my thoughts spun from Mack to my failing primate project. His demands and the intensity of feelings he was capable of generating in me were new. I'd never met anyone like Mack, only nerds a lot like me, filled with scientific ideas and emotionally bound to electronic umbilical cords on their belts. Always on call for something more important than me.

Chapter 23 - The Night before Christmas

The snow got deeper as the holidays drew closer. By mid-December, the snowplow berms along the road to the lab had grown higher than my car. The mountain road formed a luge course. The berms made me feel safe. There was no way I could skid off the road and down a steep embankment.

Short winter days gave way to long dark nights. When I looked out the windows, at times I wasn't sure if it was dusk or dawn. Holidays had never mattered to me. In my work, one day was like the next.

Sometimes, I yearned for the college days and medical school in California. Learning came easy for me. I finished college at age twenty. Six years later, I'd finished medical school. During my final MD-PhD studies, I landed a research position with the NIH at the CDC in Atlanta.

Dad's veterinary degree and interest in prion studies evolved to his getting a doctorate in neurobiology. He passed his interests on to me through excitement in his work and by having me visit his university lab. His association with the premier prion investigator had led to his invitation to become a guest researcher with the Ministry of Health during the British mad cow crisis in the 1990s.

His experience with government politics—first hiding the disease from the public and then the collapse of the cattle, feed, and related industries in Britain—gave him a broad perspective for his studies. From all our discussions, I knew what would happen in Montana and in the United States if a prion outbreak occurred.

At work, I dug deeper into Dad's journals and watched the baby monkey thrive. I had to leave Blaze with Sal more than I liked because of commitments at the lab, but I spent nights spoiling the dog and playing ball with her. Having her snuggled up against me at night made me happy.

Blaze was a perfect companion—much less demanding than Mack.

I sought out Rudy, the night security officer, when he worked his twelve-hour night shifts. I'd liked him from the first, and I loved his wife and little son. Plus, Leah sent delicious lunches that Rudy shared with me. On my breaks, we sat in the electronic surveillance room where he told me of his military experiences. I began to understand why Rudy was still jumpy.

One night I told him Mack had been a sniper in the military.

He thought for a while. "Those guys have nerves of steel but don't usually come out normal. I know a couple guys with worse PTSD than mine. One fourth of July, we were having a few beers and a kid lit a firecracker outside. Jimmy McHugh, an old sniper, dived under the table shaking like a leaf when he heard it. He went nuts. I had to take him home. Luckily, his wife got him calmed down."

"Mack is on edge sometimes and quick to anger, but I don't see behavior like your sniper friend. Mack has a bunch of guns, though. That worries me."

"Sudden anger and paranoid thoughts get some of them. Having a bunch of guns in Montana is common but get out quick if Mack acts crazy."

I listened to Rudy, analyzed Mack's behavior, and ruminated on Sal's stories about him. I decided I'd rather spend the holiday working than be with Mack.

Director Reilly insisted on having the Christmas party in the face of a winter storm watch. Because of the storm, many of the scientists said they'd skip the party and take the next week off.

Mack left several phone messages every day. Sometimes I'd call back, but the lab provided a welcome wall between us.

I changed my daily work outfit of jeans and a turtleneck to a festive emerald-green satin blouse with black wool slacks for the holiday event. Sal was already up when I dropped Blaze off on Friday, the morning of December twenty-fourth. I saw her lights on and dashed in to say hello and merry Christmas.

"You look way too classy to be going to work. Hope you have a peaceful, happy day."

"I plan to work tonight and part of tomorrow. I'll call in the afternoon. Hope you and Blaze have a great time."

"I have a new scarf for her and some bones all wrapped up under the tree. She's been sniffing them. I'm afraid she already knows what her present is." From the door, Sal called after me, "Be careful. The storm sounds bad. The wind is already picking up."

The blasting heater and my down jacket kept me warm on my way to work. I navigated a road cleared by a hardy snowplow driver who'd probably worked all night.

I hung my jacket on a hook near the coffee room and dashed out the back door to my wonderful new lab. Wind whipped around the building and blasted my satin blouse, wrapping me in ice. A few steps in the cold air brought me to the airlock door, where I pressed my thumb against the print scanner.

Thankfully, the door opened with a whoosh of warm air.

Brie rushed to her cage door and waited for me to reach inside to pick her up. She climbed onto my cupped hand and looked at me with black beady eyes. I loved her twitchy little nose and whiskers that tickled my face.

"Good morning, little girl. Merry Christmas." I placed the sleek rat on my shoulder. Her paws clung to the slippery blouse like human hands, as she climbed to a warm spot along my neck.

I hated to admit it, but I'd grown to love the little monkey just as much as I loved my rat and dog. I'd named her Amo, *I love* in Latin. When I changed her inventory number to a name, Bernie cautioned me, "She might break your heart."

Both of Amo's surrogate doctor-mothers had become far too attached to her, and the monkey was bonded with her caregivers. I observed Bernie playing with Amo and a tiny plush monkey.

I hadn't talked to Hugh Dalen at the state lab in a week. I wondered if more suspicious prion cases had popped up. I took a break from reading research articles to call and wish him a happy holiday.

Our lunch just before Amo's birth had turned romantic at midday. I felt comfortable with the gentle scientist without anticipation of outbursts like I worried about with Mack who had the ability to rile me every time we were together.

Hugh answered the call. "Great to hear from you, Callie. I've been swamped today. The forensics have proven interesting, but we are, unfortunately, busier with more suspicious deaths, murders, and suicides, than usual. I guess that's better than an onslaught of prion cases."

We caught up on a few issues. I filled him in on the primate study. "We'll be doing another spinal tap to check the prion levels on Monday."

He sounded as excited as I was over the clinical progress with Amo. "Please call when you receive the report. It would be awesome if you saw a reduction like we did in your father's."

Hugh said CDC onsite investigators had not identified any relationship between the three Idaho prion deaths since our meeting. "I found it surprising they all died from mad cow prions. I thought it might be Chronic Wasting Disease since they were hunters from Wapiti County. It must be from eating local beef."

His next comment stopped me cold. "I think they're missing a local source."

"I worried about you ordering that steak at the Mountain Grill.

Hugh laughed. "I saw your face. That was the day I quit."

"It's a relief to know that. I ran across an article this morning I wanted to tell you about, new information from a human study. Researchers found prion overlap with the scrapie form in human cases previously considered sporadic."

Hugh was silent for a moment. "You're telling me sporadic CJD, the one-in-a-million cases, are actually *scrapie*?"

"On crystallography, the structures are indistinguishable from the prion form causing sheep disease."

"That changes everything."

I added, "I don't like it, either, and now, humans in this area are infected from eating beef. We have to find the local source before more people die."

"Please call me with any news. Happy holiday."

"Wait, wait, don't hang up. I forgot to tell you a researcher from the Ridge Lab came here for a visit a couple weeks ago. I had trouble treating him with civility after he introduced himself."

"Who? Reilly?" I wondered what he'd be doing at the state lab.

"No, Larry Westphal."

My heart lurched at the sound of his name. "Bastard. What did he want?"

"Said he was new to Montana, interested in the lab and the forensics we do. Westphal charmed the staff. If I hadn't known his history with you, I would have considered him a gentleman researcher."

I sat motionless after ending the call, still hating Larry Westphal but I realized his scrapie research would be even more important now that sporadic Creutzfeldt-Jakob disease was actually caused by scrapie. I'd like to talk to Larry about it if I didn't hate him so much.

The cause of these cases was no longer unknown. It was not a rare mutation but instead a transmissible prion form. This was different from the bovine in my study that can easily jump species. But scrapie? From sheep? There is so much we don't know.

Now, the mad cow variant of bovine spongiform encephalopathy that had killed the Brits, was slowly spreading around the world. It used to be rare, but the death toll was rising. Every person diagnosed increased the risk of spread from that individual. But our problem was how to identify the local source.

Later that afternoon, I called a guy I had trained with at the CDC. He said their concern was that the beef ranchers around the world were suppressing information on cases of diseased cattle for political and financial reasons. The same response had occurred earlier in Great Britain.

Once mad cow disease was exposed to the public, the economic collapse of beef and related industries had rocked that country and ricocheted where ever their beef had been shipped. Thousands of cows were slaughtered and incinerated to stop the disease. It was too little, too late. Hundreds of people had died. I knew that could happen in the United States, too. The financial costs to the beef industry would literally kill the industry. Even with a cure, spread of the disease would be catastrophic as the disease evolved in already infected man and beast.

The Christmas eve storm struck early with heavy snow and howling winds that carried icy powder into drifts along buildings in the large Ridge Lab compound. Dr. Reilly announced at lunchtime that the party would begin at 3 p.m. so people could head down the mountain before dark.

I changed into scrubs and put on my hooded jacket to walk out to the vet compound along the snow-drifted pathway.

The two deer corrals fenced in chain-link mesh were barely visible in the blowing snow. One herd was infected with Chronic Wasting Disease and the other, normal controls, were located a few yards away. The animals huddled together, partially protected in shelters.

This day, as every day, I checked on Amo with trepidation because of the horrible fate of her parents. Her coordination and activity appeared normal as I took a short video of her playing with a toy monkey. Happy thoughts soared as I made my way back to my new lab, where I slipped into a gown. Shoe covers muffled my footsteps as I walked around checking on prion-infected rats that appeared clinically normal.

I had allowed one of the treated female rats to become pregnant. She carried low levels of prions in her spinal fluid that no longer affected her coordination. Her fat belly looked ready to burst. At twenty-two days of gestation, the delivery could be any time.

Today was her due date, a present from Santa.

The first litter from a treated rat would tell me whether her offspring were normal, which would mean that the blood had carried the treatment through the placenta to the fetal rats. Rat pups would also add interesting data, including fetal growth and neonatal health information.

Planning to just make an appearance at the party, I changed back to my street clothes and called Bernie before walking to the Admin Building to meet up with Rudy and Sarge. I found Rudy in the control room. He said, "Sarge just left for the party. As soon as my relief returns, I'll join you."

"Great! We'll be spending Christmas together. I'm working tonight, waiting for a mama rat to have her babies."

"So, now you're a rat midwife in addition to all your other duties? Be sure to come and have coffee with me later. If she has them, I want to hear about the babies."

During my early dark days in Montana, Rudy and his beautiful wife had made me feel welcome. She had fixed an occasional vegetarian meal for me to take to Dad and had invited me to join them for dinner. They began teaching their son sign language at nine months for fun, and to supplement early communication. Now, nearly one year old, Cole communicated well with his hands and said many words. Rudy shared new photos of his little family with me during our long nights together.

In the lunch area, Sarge and about thirty staff and researchers, including Bernie, had gathered to socialize and partake of holiday food. I sipped punch and talked with Bernie. We joined a couple of likeable researchers who seldom ventured from their labs.

From across the room, Larry Westphal's loud laughs and swagger caught my attention. His behavior made me wonder if he was drunk. He gripped the edge of the serving table for stability and ignored me as he slopped more punch into a cup. Instead, he turned his back. He must have begun celebrating early, a bad sign for someone just out of rehab. I had thought he might be friendly after our last encounter when he'd offered to help me.

I joined Rudy and Sarge, who were standing against one wall. Rudy said, "Dr. Callie, you look beautiful. You should be out dancing or meeting up with Santa somewhere."

Sarge held up his punch in a salute. "Here's to a sharp-lookin' doctor. I agree. You should be out riding in Santa's sleigh."

"I'd rather be here with you guys. I'm happiest behind bars." I meant what I said, but it brought a reaction.

"Do you have a fever? You must be sick." Sarge rubbed his belly. "Actually, I'm not feeling great. I think I ate too many spicy shrimp. I have to get home. Ann has a ham dinner planned for tonight, but right now, I don't feel like eating." He waved and called, "Merry Christmas, everybody."

Moments later, Sarge returned and made an announcement. "The storm is howling. Wind and heavy snow are threatening to close the road. If you want to get home tonight, you'd better head out."

His announcement triggered a mass exodus. By 4:30 p.m., Rudy and I stood at the Admin entrance watching a parade of vehicles moving slowly out the gate and heading down the mountain road in drifting snow. "You better go home while you can, Doc. The road may be impassable by morning."

"I want to be here when my rat delivers her litter. The offspring are important to my study." I didn't tell him the other reasons: one, I wanted to be sure the mother didn't eat her young, and two, I didn't want to deal with Mack.

After going to my lab to check the rat and review more pathology slides, I returned to Admin and found Rudy in his cushy swivel chair inside the warm control room. One handheld his coffee, and the other flipped a switch on his silent board. Security points dotted the wall diagram with little green lights. "Hi, Callie. It should be quiet tonight. You and I are the only ones inside the compound other than the Vet Building interior guards and a skeleton crew taking care of the animals."

I understood why some nights, just thinking about what could go wrong, made him sweat. Security in such a large complex harboring fatal diseases was potentially dangerous work.

Rudy appeared on edge, scanning the board and testing alarms and lights. "Equipment failure or a problem in the IRF Level 4 high-risk contamination area would set off a piercing alarm and flashing red lights." He tested a strobe alarm for Level 4 that nearly blinded me. "The place is deserted. I don't expect anyone to roam the halls tonight. I'll keep a watch on you. Don't stay up too late."

"I always feel better knowing you're keeping an eye on me. Most of the weekend, I'll be in my lab catching up on work." I sat with Rudy for a few minutes as he answered a call from a guard outside the double fence and then headed to the lunchroom.

Ventilation ducts chattered along the route. Heating pipes drummed an erratic beat, like Rudy's description of his heartbeat whenever he startled from the "twinge" of PTSD he had from the war.

It was more than a twinge, but it was certainly not as bad as his friend Jimmy's.

I went out the back door between the IRF and the Admin Building. It was just a few feet from Admin, beneath a canopy, to the IRF entrance. My rat hadn't yet delivered, so at midnight I walked back to the control room to say good night to Rudy. "I'm going to take a nap and check on the rat in a couple hours. The storm is frightful. I feel sorry for the deer."

Rudy and I walked to a window at the entrance near the control room. He said, "The deer have some protection in the stockade, but in the forest, they'd be able to find a better windbreak and bed down." Snow swirling in the bright lights obscured parts of the razor-wire fences and drifted into the Admin door alcove.

We stood in silence for a few seconds listening to the howling wind. "At least we're warm in here. My perimeter guards will have a tough night in this weather." Windows rattled. "Usually this old building is silent but listen to it tonight. She's talking to us. The wind is making her moan. It's giving me the creeps." Rudy shuddered.

I sensed what he meant. "It's like a caged tiger. Pacing, uneasy."

"When I arrived about three this afternoon, powdery snow dimmed the perimeter lights like a dense fog. Wind off the mountains had already blown up a blinding ground blizzard." Rudy tripped his radio, testing its function.

I left him in the control room and walked back to the couch in the coffee room, happy to be isolated and safely asleep inside the high-risk lab compound.

Chapter 24 - Merry Christmas

Just after 2 a.m., radiators clanged as Rudy strolled down the hall a short distance from the control room. The troublesome amber warning light indicated a problem in the coffee room. The light had flashed so many times, he had once told the electronics crew, he was afraid the stupid thing would burn out.

He recalled earlier that the IRF door had opened and closed, showing him Dr. Callie had probably returned to her lab after their conversation. Later, the board showed the same doors open and close. He thought he might find Callie in the coffee room.

Researchers brought no food or drink to their labs because of health risks. Instead, they gathered around tables in the coffee room and sometimes left coffee pots scorching on the burners. Distracted scientists forgot bread in the toaster and burned that, too. Both situations had triggered board alarms in the past.

Rudy doubted Callie had done anything to set off the alarm. Her vegetarian menu usually didn't require heating food. She ate salads. Occasionally, when they sat together at night, he'd seen her eat a boiled egg. The skinny young doctor wasn't much of a cook, and she'd convinced him of that when she placed a boiled egg in the microwave to warm it. The egg blew up, leaving behind a mess of sticky shrapnel.

He knew Callie worked in a Level 3 biologics lab located on the ground floor. Level 4, one floor up, secured the worst biologics, but Level 3 worried him, too. Many labs contained common microbes like deadly viruses, and those causing tick-borne diseases. Sgt. Collucci had told him some Level 3 projects were dangerous, although not as lethal as prions. No one entered the IRF without special clearance.

An airlock and oxygenated isolation suits protected researchers in Level 4 from rapidly lethal airborne diseases. There was rumor of a Level 5 being planned. Rudy didn't understand what could be more dangerous than Level 4 containment organisms, and he didn't want to know.

Before Rudy reached the coffee room, he startled at the sound of a distinctive building alarm pulsing from his control room—an IRF breach!

His heart pounded as he ran back down the hall. Sweat drenched his armpits. The jogging left him winded.

Before he reached the control room, a white strobe pierced the dim hallway, joining the alarm. The blinding strobe only came on when there was an IRF door breach.

The deafening wail continued. Rudy could not override this signal with a flip of a switch. He covered his ears and scanned the board, looking for a malfunction.

Then, a different alarm sounded. The perimeter siren!

Red lights flashed all over the board.

No malfunction. A real crisis!

The radio on his belt sounded. He keyed the mic. "What the hell is going on out there?"

Rudy could hardly understand the frantic voice. "Hang on. I have to get this damn alarm shut down in here before I can hear you." Rudy flipped open a control panel on the wall and silenced the brain-piercing noise. "Okay, Gary, go ahead."

The guard spoke a bit slower. "I ran back from my rounds when the alarm sounded. Ted's lying by the open gate. Blood all over. Somebody slit his throat."

"Activate code red lockdown and call for backup! Shoot to kill. If you see any deer on the loose, kill them."

"Perimeter lights just went out. It's dark out here. I don't see nothin' movin'."

Rudy keyed his radio. "Lyle, report now! Check in! Where are you?"

No response.

Rudy autodialed Sgt. Collucci.

No breach had ever occurred in the history of the Rocky Mountain Ridge Lab. Compared to this, practice drills were like kindergarten children crawling under desks for earth-quakes.

The phone seemed to ring a hundred times before his boss answered.

"Sarge, Rudy. We have a major breach and a fatality. The IRF was penetrated. I need you up here, fast."

"What the hell happened?"

"A guard is dead. Lights are flashing all over the damn board." Rudy scanned the wall as he spoke. "Shit! Level 3 animal cages in IRF just alarmed."

Rudy clicked his buzzing radio.

"Lyle hasn't shown up out here from his rounds. Maybe they got him, too. From what I saw before the lights went out, I think the fence is intact. They came in through the gate!"

Sarge snapped orders in Rudy's ear. "No one in or out. Shoot intruders. I'll be right there. I'll call the FBI." The call ended.

Gary keyed the radio and cut in again. "I'm in the shack calling everyone on our code red list."

Rudy's hand shook as he punched in 9-1-1. Gary had called them already, but Rudy wanted to be sure help was on the way. Could this be an inside job? Was Gary involved? Lyle?

A harsh voice answered, "This is 9-1-1. What is your emergency?"

For an instant Rudy wondered if his call on such a stormy night had angered the dispatcher.

"NIH Security, Jonsrude at the Ridge Lab. The lab's been breached. A guard is dead. We need help now, right now! Send officers."

The same nasty voice, "Another guy just called from up there. This is a helluva night! Roads out your way are closed. Drunks are in the ditch everywhere." He took a raspy breath. "Plows are busy just trying to keep the main roads open. I'll see what I can do."

"Divert a plow. We need help. Hurry." Rudy hung up and radioed Gary. "We're gonna have to handle this ourselves for a while. The road is impassable. They have to divert a plow to get to us. We'll get help, but not soon."

Gary reported, "I got ahold of my boss in Medicine Falls. He has a powerful snow cat he thinks will get him here ahead of the others."

Rudy called the guards at the vet compound and put them on alert before he ran down the hall, gun in hand, to check doors and see what had triggered the first alarm. As he neared the coffee room, he smelled the familiar odor of scorched coffee and worried about Callie being in there. The back door from the coffee room led directly outside to the short walkway connecting the compound's buildings. That was the route Callie always took.

Rudy rounded the doorway and stopped short.

Callie sprawled motionless on the floor.

Blood streaked her white face and pooled beneath her head.

Rudy's eyes darted around the room looking for perpetrators. Clear. He knelt beside her.

Red clots in her dark curls spread into maroon splotches down her neck onto her shiny green blouse—the red and green of Christmas gone terribly wrong. Her beautiful face was a death mask.

Rudy had seen death in Afghanistan.

He lifted her limp arm.

Blood spurted from the stump of her missing left thumb.

Chapter 25 - Prion Chaos

Emergency vehicles caravanned up the mountain to the high-risk laboratory behind a slow-moving plow. Blue strobes from responding county sheriff cars stabbed the darkness, sparkling off snow swirling around the line of vehicles.

An all-wheel-drive ambulance with medics fueled by Red Bull and Mountain Dew arrived on scene, frustrated by the slow progress up the access road. The only report they'd received was one body.

Laboratory perimeter lights were out. The driver parked, leaving the ambulance running and headlights on. He aimed a spotlight on a uniformed man waving to them. "I wonder if there are others with injuries. They'd freeze to death if they were outside for long in this weather." He jumped out, grabbed the door to steady himself, and fell to his knees. "God, I'm dizzy." He sat on the snowy ground.

His partner rounded the vehicle and helped the man get back in the rig. "Sit for a while. I felt it, too. Vertigo. Lack of visibility and swirling snow will do it to you. I've had vertigo a few times skiing in fog. Join me when you feel better." He dragged a medical bag out of the back and headed toward the guard.

Gary directed the medic to Ted's body, where snowmelt from the gush of blood from a large neck wound had crusted the snow to red ice. Snow frosted Ted's face. His frozen eyes stared at them. Under the glare of ambulance lights, it took the medic one second for his assessment. *DRT—dead right there.* "Let's call the coroner."

The second medic walked over to the body and pulled up on the sleeve of Ted's jacket.

The arm didn't budge.

The medic scanned the body. "Looks like the slash cut through his jugulars. Based on the blood pattern, they got a carotid artery, too." The three men backed away. "Sorry about your buddy. Don't move him. Investigators will want everything left as is."

Two sheriff's deputies approached. "What'd you find?"

"The guard's dead. Bled out from a neck wound."

A deputy radioed dispatch. "We've got one confirmed dead. Send the coroner and detectives up here to the Ridge Lab."

Following the initial shock of seeing Callie, Rudy's automated military discipline took over. He located her rapid pulse and grabbed clean towels from the kitchen to press on the spurting stump of her thumb and her bleeding scalp, then radioed Gary. "Send medics to the Admin coffee room right away. Dr. Archer's bleeding and unconscious. Looks like someone tried to kill her."

Soon he heard rapid footsteps thudding down the hall. He called, "She's in here."

Rudy held pressure on her wounds while the medics knelt to assess her. "This is Dr. Archer. You can see she's lost a lot of blood from her scalp. Hasn't moved since I found her."

Callie took shallow breaths.

Rudy hoped to God she'd survive. He felt responsible. She'd counted on him to protect her, and he'd failed. He reluctantly relinquished her care to the medics.

A siren in the control room blared, sending Rudy on the run. He froze in the flashing doorway.

Chaotic lights and alarms shocked his senses.

Panic surged.

Rudy was back in combat. Blood everywhere—choppers—loud noises—a deafening blur of sound—jets screaming overhead—bombs and artillery all around.

His anger exploded when he realized he was in the Ridge Lab, not in combat. With clenched fists, he seethed at the unknown perpetrators, "You'll pay. I'll see that you pay for this."

Sarge burst into the control room. "On my way in, Gary looked stunned, just standing there outside the booth. What's he been doing?"

"Everything's gone to hell!" Rudy focused on the board signals. "I called a code red, and Gary called his team for help."

"Where the hell are they? The perimeter isn't secured."

"I'm surprised you made it this fast."

"My new Jeep got me up here right behind the county cops."

"What about the FBI?"

Sarge scanned the flashing board. "It'll be awhile. Roads from Missoula aren't passable. There's a DEA chopper at their disposal, but it's grounded in this storm."

Rudy picked up the phone. "I called in the bio emergency team and Reilly. He's on the way. I was just going to call in more of our security officers."

"It's an all-out alert!" Sarge spoke rapidly. "I'll send them home once we have things under control."

Running footsteps got Sarge's attention. He stuck his head into the hall and saw a medic. "Hey, man, what do you need?"

"A stretcher." The medic ran out the exit.

Sarge felt a gush of icy air and turned back to Rudy. "What's going on?"

"Somebody tried to kill Dr. Archer. She's unconscious."

Sarge's face contorted in sadness. "No." His anger flashed. "What'd they do to her?"

Rudy explained her injuries and what had happened. "I saw lights about an hour before the alarms. Looked like she'd left the IRF and was back in the coffee room where she'd napped earlier. Maybe they followed her when she left the IRF."

Sarge tried to understand exactly what had happened. "Did anything else on the board flash?"

"Nothing until alarms sounded. After they killed Ted, I think they got to Callie and entered the IRF. They were fast."

"How could they get in there?"

"Hell, grocery stores have surveillance cameras but not us!"

"No shit. And they knocked out the perimeter lights." Sarge raged, "It's as dark as the inside of a dead cow out there. We can't see a damn thing on the compound."

Rudy opened a metal control panel on one wall and flipped a switch.

Nothing happened.

He said, "The emergency backup should have lit everything up. I think they disabled a main circuit."

"Damn them to hell! So much for high-tech security!" Sarge's eyes scanned the control board. "All of Level 3 is flashing. Keep everyone away from the IRF until Reilly gives us biosafety instructions." Sarge left Rudy and rushed to the coffee room to check on Callie.

The stench of burned coffee met him at the door. Inside, a medic kneeled by Dr. Archer's motionless form, securing an airway tube protruding from her mouth. "Hey, Sarge, I need a little help. Could you squeeze this oxygen bag while I start an IV?"

Sarge had to get back and take charge, and Callie needed better care than a security chief who couldn't even keep a high-risk lab locked up. This breach could cost him his job. He squatted on the floor beside Callie's head, pumping oxygen into her lungs. Before the medic could hang a bag of saline, Sarge's arthritic knee gave out, forcing him to sit on the floor. He looked down at his young doctor friend, alarmed at her appearance.

The back door stood ajar, sending an icy gust along the floor to Sarge. Was he delivering enough oxygen to her? He prayed the medic would hurry and take over her care.

Sarge's hand cramped from squeezing the oxygen bag by the time the second medic arrived with the wheeled gurney and backboard. The two medics secured Callie's limp body to the board and lifted her onto the gurney. Sarge watched Callie's white face, hoping to see some movement, some sign of life. There was none.

They rushed her down the hall past the control room, with Sarge squeezing in the oxygen and helping guide the gurney.

Rudy stuck his head out of the control room. "How bad is she, guys?" He frowned.

A medic said, "Unconscious, in shock, and head injured. Like you said, she's lost a lot of blood."

Rudy called out. "Take good care of her."

On a portable monitor, a medic watched Callie's rapid heart rate. "We will. Doc Maxwell is working in ER tonight. He's the best."

The other medic asked Sarge," Is she contagious? We've heard she works on bad stuff."

"I don't know. Around here, they tell us to wear gloves. Wear a mask. Wash our hands. That's what they say to do for everything."

Rudy followed them and held the door. "Dr. Reilly's on his way."

Sarge said, "After we talk to Reilly, we'll radio you or call the hospital if you need to do anything else to protect yourselves."

The three men struggled to move the gurney through drifted snow to the back of the rig, where they loaded Callie inside. On his way back in to join Rudy, Sarge stopped to talk with Gary, who walked him over to Ted's body. Gary said, "It's a damn shame. He has a wife and two kids."

The white sheet the medics had placed over the dead man had tumbled in the wind and gotten stuck against a perimeter fence like a flapping Halloween ghost. Sarge shook his head at the ugly scene and hurried back to the control room, wondering what to do next.

All the practice drills in the world couldn't have prepared him for this breach. He knew police procedure and should have cordoned off the coffee room to preserve trace evidence, but Callie's injuries had destroyed his focus. Saving her life outweighed any investigative protocol.

Another NIH security officer arrived. Rudy turned the control room over to the new man and joined Sarge to survey the IRF. They walked through the coffee room, taking the same route Callie had taken. The wind blasted Sarge the second he opened the door. He wondered exactly what had happened to Callie and how much she had suffered.

A bright emergency light blinded him. "They didn't cut these lights. They are so damn bright, I feel like I just stepped out of a bar at high noon back in my drinking days." Dizziness swept over Sarge again as it did when he had walked into the Admin Building from the ambulance. "Rudy, I don't even remember driving home. I think somebody spiked my punch last night."

Rudy tromped through a snowdrift ahead of Sarge before rounding the side of the IRF out of the wind. "All I drank was my coffee from home. Joy said there was no alcohol in the punch." He touched his weapon out of habit. "We're sitting ducks out here, Sarge. Anybody with good aim could take us both out."

Sarge peered into the darkness beyond the floodlight. "They're probably gone by now and based on the method they used to kill Ted, they were silent—in and out before we knew what happened."

The men walked to the main entrance and found it locked. Blood stained the print scanner. Sarge signaled Rudy to follow him out of the wind, where Sarge cupped his hands against a window.

Rudy shined a bright beam into the window and peered in. "This is Callie's lab. Shit! Animal cages are scattered on the floor. Refrigerators and freezers are wide open." Rudy cut his light. "I'm getting the creeps." Sweat beaded on his forehead despite the biting wind. "Let's get out of here."

Sarge recalled the emergency lighting circuitry. "My guess is they got access to the primary emergency Knox Box on Level 3 and flipped the right circuit breakers to cut the emergency lighting and the perimeter electric fence." Sarge scowled. "All our fail-safes failed." He tried to think on his feet and dredge up basic rules to handle the crisis. Usually, the job was boring as hell. It had been a long time since he'd handled a true emergency.

The two men were walking around the corner of the building onto the lighted walkway to the coffee room when the sharp crack of a rifle flattened both men to the ground.

A bullet struck the building above the door.

They scrambled back into the shadows with guns drawn.

Another shot rang out, striking the Admin Building.

"Damn it. They must still be on the grounds. We have to get back inside." Sarge shot out the floodlight. "Okay, run. You, first."

Inside, Sarge radioed Gary about the shots. "Tell everyone we're okay. We're going to douse all the lights in Admin."

Rudy went directly to the electrical panel in the control room and began flipping circuit breakers. Soon, the Admin Building was dark except for a few hallways and a couple of windowless rooms, including the conference and control rooms.

Sarge heard voices and walked to the conference room, where he found a few more officers had arrived. "At this time, we have to stay put." He pointed at two men. "I want you to take flashlights and search the Admin halls and unlocked rooms for intruders. You probably heard the rifle shots. Stay away from windows. The rest of you, sit tight." He checked his watch. "We have about three hours before daylight."

More men gathered in the hallway outside the control room, all talking at once. Sarge brought them in to join the others. "Thanks to all of you for getting here so fast. I'll bring you up to date. Of the three perimeter guards on duty, unfortunately, one was murdered, another is missing."

They talked all at once, wanting more information. He had to quiet the men before continuing. "Intruders vandalized the IRF. Harmful biologics and animals with fatal diseases are missing."

Sarge headed back to the control room. As he approached, Reilly strode into the building. Through the open door, a wind gust caught his stiff comb-over, raising the dome flap up like a sail in the wind. He smoothed his hair and pulled off his red parka. "Collucci! What the hell happened?" Dark, spidery veins across Reilly's cheeks matched his maroon sweater.

Sarge snapped, "We've had an IRF Level 3 breach, and they killed a perimeter guard."

Reilly's expression changed from anger to panic. His wide eyes fixed on Sarge. "The animals? Frozen specimens?"

"Gone. Looks like they're all gone from Dr. Archer's lab."

"Those specimens can kill! The IRF is off-limits." He spun around "Where is everybody? Did you call the Level 3 researchers?"

Sarge headed to the conference room. "Come with me. After shots were fired, I put everyone in the conference room, where it's safer with no windows."

They entered the crowded room.

A tall man wearing a parka with FBI insignia entered the conference room and stood behind them. He waited in the doorway listening to Sarge and Reilly.

Reilly raised his voice. "Where's Dr. Archer? She should be here. It's probably her fault this happened."

Sarge snarled, "She stayed here last night to work after the rest of you left. She might die because of it."

Reilly turned toward Sarge. "What do you mean?"

"The bastards tried to kill her. She's in an ambulance heading down the mountain to the ER."

"Did she say what happened?"

Sarge clenched his fists at Reilly's words. "It's difficult to talk when you're unconscious with an oxygen tube sticking out of your mouth,"

Reilly made no comment about Callie's condition. "So, how'd they get through our security?"

"By killing a guard and disabling electronics."

Reilly scanned the crowd of officers. "I thought we had safeguards on everything."

Sarge fought to stay calm. "We do, but once they got access to the main IRF control panel, they shut down everything on the lower floors and our perimeter electricity."

Reilly glared at him. "This is Archer's fault."

Sarge shook his head. "No way. Somebody knew how to navigate within the compound without tripping alarms. This is an inside job, and it wasn't her."

"You're a fuck-up, Collucci. This never could have happened if you'd trained your men!" Reilly swept a hand toward the room full of officers. "We're all doomed if they got inside the IRF."

The officers watched the angry exchange and moved aside to let Special Agent Hal Vater come forward. His six-foot-six height was imposing next to the five-foot-five Reilly. "Dr. Reilly, you're out of line. We don't need anybody punching up the anxiety in this chaotic mess. Your job is to remain calm, secure the biologics, and leave the rest to us."

Dr. Reilly walked out.

Special Agent Vater called to him. "I suggest you ask your researchers to come in and check their labs under our supervision."

The sound of Reilly's slamming office door reverberated down the hall and pulsed Sarge's anger. "Good to see you, Hal. This is the kind of catastrophe I thought we were ready for."

Vater addressed the men. "We're professionals and don't need finger-pointing. A man is dead. We're on high alert and in damage-control mode."

Sarge's confidence returned with Hal at his side. Over the years, they had worked together on many issues. He told the men Special Agent Vater would be in charge. "As soon as there is enough daylight, we will be working in pairs. Hal will give you specific orders at that time."

Sarge's radio sounded. "Gary here. We just heard snow-mobile engines. Are you expecting anyone?"

"No. Maybe that's how the perpetrators got here."

Seconds later, Gary keyed his mic. "The sound is fading. I think they're leaving.

In the hours before dawn, four men, including two sheriff's deputies with two perimeter guards, took turns manning the gate. Without lights and in the bitter cold, they used a portable light to illuminate part of the area, and every half hour they rotated inside to warm themselves, drink coffee, and join the discussions with other law enforcement personnel.

Vater, Sarge, and Rudy sat together in the control room reviewing the break-in timeline, security protocols, and safety plans.

Reilly gathered the bio-emergency team and researchers in his office to discuss damage control.

At sunup, the entire group of law enforcement personnel, except the four gate guards, gathered in the board room for instructions. Hal Vater took control, directing NIH guards to survey the grounds and coordinate with the county sheriff's deputies. "You have thirty minutes to do a sweep of your assigned areas, then meet back here. Stay together. We don't know what we are dealing with. Shoot to kill."

Reilly, Sarge, and Vater dressed in impervious jumpsuits and gloves to go into the IRF. Reilly removed a glove and reached out to touch the print pad. When he saw blood on the controls, he jerked his bare hand back. He steadied himself with one hand on the door, looking back at Sarge. Color drained from his ruddy face.

Sarge saw Reilly's reaction, and after the accusations the director had leveled at Callie, he decided to needle the man. "Don't worry about a little blood. It's Dr. Archer's. They chopped off her thumb."

Reilly sat down, head in his hands, as if he might faint. He mumbled, "I don't like blood."

Sarge cringed, thinking about Callie's torture, but winked at Vater. "They used her amputated thumb to trigger the print lock. That's her blood frozen on the sidewalk beside you."

Reilly moved away from the red splash and retched.

After a few minutes, Reilly slowly got to his feet and touched the pad, releasing the lock. Then he put his protective glove back on and held the heavy door open, allowing the others to pass.

Inside the entry alcove, the door of a complex electrical panel stood open. Sarge examined the array of labeled controls. "Looks like they flipped switches to disable IRF Level 3 but not Level 4. Some of our board alarms are also unarmed."

Reilly led the men down the hall to Callie's lab and pushed the damaged door open wide enough to allow entry. Files and books scattered the floor. "Her computer is missing."

A look in the interior lab area revealed empty animal cages strewn on the floor. Reilly looked inside a freezer, standing with the door open. "Devastating. This will be a terrible setback for her research, but they didn't take everything. A few specimens are left." He closed the freezer door.

Reilly checked other doors along the hall and returned. "I hope they were smart enough not to breach Level 4. It appears they only targeted Dr. Archer's research and knew right where to find it."

They returned to the exit and removed the protective gear. Reilly tossed his gown into an incineration barrel. "Archer's given me trouble right from the start. This is her fault. Whoever it was, they targeted her lab and she's paying the price."

"None of this is her doing and you know it." Sarge fisted his hands, wanting to slam the words back down Reilly's throat. "She was the only one working. Everyone else went home to celebrate Christmas."

Reilly stood tall, facing Sarge. "Exactly. Very suspicious. She probably let them in."

Vater snapped, "So, let me get this straight, Dr. Reilly. You think she cut off her own thumb and handed it to them?"

Sarge stormed outside mumbling obscenities and left Vater to walk back to Admin with Reilly.

From Reilly's office, Vater and Reilly called NIH Headquarters to report the breach. Within minutes, a CDC representative and the director of the Department of Homeland Security telephoned back on a conference call. Sarge joined them and listened.

On speaker phone, Reilly explained the known extent of facility damage to Eric Dryer, the head of Homeland Security, who said, "This is exactly what we tried to avoid, Clint. How the hell could you let this happen at the most secure biologics facility in the U.S.?"

Reilly looked at Sarge. "You should be asking my head of security that question. What do you have to say, Sgt. Collucci?"

"The system didn't fail. Based on our initial analysis, they had insider help. After killing a guard and nearly killing Dr. Archer, they entered the IRF Level 3 biocontainment area and gained access by disabling the electrical circuits."

Reilly clenched his teeth and violently shook his head.

Dr. Dryer's words were crisp and curt. "We'll get a team from the CDC and DHS on a flight as soon as we can assemble them. Clint, call me when you've determined the specifics of the biologics breach."

Vater said, "The FBI has taken control. Our forensics team is en route."

The call ended and the three men made their way to the conference room, where they found Reilly's secretary setting up snacks.

Dr. Reilly rushed over to her. "I'm so glad you could make it."

Joy's blonde tendrils straggled from a twisted knot atop her head. She smiled at her boss and arranged boxes of gooey sweet rolls on a table next to a gurgling coffee urn.

Reilly's eyes followed her movements. "How did you find treats like these on Christmas morning?"

Joy smiled slyly. "If I told you my secrets, I might lose my job." She adjusted the snug top of her red jogging outfit over her unfettered breasts.

A pleased look from Reilly assured her that she was very unlikely to lose her job.

Men returning after their survey of the lab acreage hung their heavy jackets on the backs of chairs and headed to the coffee and rolls. No one asked where Joy had found the goodies. No one cared. The cold officers circled around the coffee and the sweets, which from their expressions included Joy.

Vater asked Sarge to begin with his facility report after talking to some of his men. Sarge reported that they'd found sled tracks starting behind the IRF that led to a hole in the perimeter fence and continued outside the grounds. The grooves tracked down a steep slope to a creek bed, where three sets of snowmobile tracks disappeared downstream. Sarge stressed that the deer corral was empty; large, adjacent holes had been cut through corrals and through the two perimeter fences. Although the wind and the snow made it difficult to see, it was obvious deer tracks led out of the compound.

"It would have been tough going in the deep snow, both for the snow machines and the deer. Now we have our answer as to how they accomplished their feat. In my opinion, it took a small group of people a lot of preplanning and only minutes inside the compound to accomplish their goal."

Sarge called on Rudy to review the timeline from the first alarm. "I put the vet guards on alert as soon as the perimeter alarm went off. They had no problems in the animal complex."

Dr. Reilly accepted a cup of coffee from Joy and expounded, "I personally checked the labs in this building. They looked fine. Then, I notified Chief Veterinarian Bernie Goff of the breach and checked with the night guards in the vet compound. They heard the alarms but had no building breach."

Sarge noticed it was as if Dr. Reilly hadn't listened to Rudy's report because he was too busy paying attention to Joy.

Reilly paced, lecturing the group. "The fools went for prions. They weren't interested in anthrax or other killers. They went for the goddamned cross-species prions! They have no idea what kind of danger they're in."

Sarge countered Reilly. "I think they do, otherwise why would they just target Dr. Archer's lab?"

Vater inquired, "What exactly was she working on?"

"Prions. Monkey research." He addressed the roomful of men. "We'll return in a few minutes after I speak to them privately." Reilly motioned Vater and Sarge to follow him to his office, where he closed the door. "This information cannot be leaked to the media. We don't want panic." Reilly's voice shook. "She was working on an especially virulent form of mad cow disease, highly contagious and universally fatal. I hope it doesn't spread to the cattle ranches around here."

Vater took a notebook from his pocket. "So, fill us in."

"Dr. Archer and three other scientists here are working on prions, an unusual class of infectious proteins that cause various forms of neurological disease similar to mad cow disease in humans. They are all fatal, but her prion shows interspecies transmissibility. In other words, it's capable of crossing species lines, infecting humans, cattle, wildlife, birds, cats, dogs—you name it. If an eagle feeds on a carcass, the eagle dies."

Vater squinted. "Are you saying Dr. Archer's prion can kill everything?"

"Not fish, but yes, probably everything else. It came from a dairy cow in Wisconsin that was euthanized after falling ill. The meat was donated to the zoo, where it infected and killed most of the zoo animals." Reilly had their attention. "Then, when the zookeeper became confused and stumbled like his sick animals, the doctor thought the forty-year-old had Pick's disease, a type of Alzheimer's that affects younger people. After the man died, his brain was sent to Dr. Archer at the Human Prion Disease Center. His brain samples clearly showed prion damage."

Sarge looked more concerned. "That's what's in her monkey study?"

Reilly nodded. "She thought if she targeted that virulent cross-species bovine prion, it could be the pathway to developing a broad immunization for man and beast.

"Before the zoo incident, we all thought there was a species barrier. Mink disease spread to mink. Cow disease spread to other cows—that is, until it spread to humans in Great Britain."

Sarge asked, "So, did the zookeeper eat the donated meat or get the disease by just handling it?"

"He didn't eat it. It was only a few months from the time he handled the bad meat to when his brain was riddled with holes from prion infection."

Vater clarified. "So this is similar but more aggressive than the one in the U.K. years ago."

"This one jump species and kills rapidly. It could cause extinction without containment. There is no cure." Reilly explained, "Under my guidance at the Ridge Lab, Dr. Archer had great results treating infected mice and rats, and then she became involved in a monkey study. Because of my strong support, I think she's close to a cure." Dr. Reilly looked at the men to be sure they were listening. "No matter what animal gets it, humans, too, they become aggressive, psychotic, then stumble around for a few months and die. There's no hope."

Vater asked, "How fast would it spread?"

"We aren't sure. That's why the feds moved her here." Reilly paced. "Dr. Archer talked the zoo administrators into letting her examine diseased brain tissue from all the animals, right down to ostriches, a jungle cat, bears, lions, and wolves. They all had cow prions in their brains. The animals that ate the meat all died, so this looks like a form that could spread through animal and human populations and kill within weeks instead of years."

Vater said, "So, last night they took animals from her lab that carried the aggressive prion?"

"Yes."

The men remained silent, waiting for Reilly to continue.

"The typical disease in cattle follows a three-year course ending in stumbling, drooling, and inability to eat. In deer, the disease takes about half that time to show symptoms." Reilly paged through a file and handed them a photograph of a dying whitetail deer. "As Sarge knows, before retirement, Dr. Archer's father researched prion diseases in cattle and big game. He was our local expert after years of working with the Brits and NIH."

Reilly stopped to take a deep breath. He exhaled and stared at the two men. "You could be eating an infected venison or beef and not know it was infected because there are no physical signs for years with the common varieties. All bets are off with Dr. Archer's strain. We just know it kills more species and faster."

Special Agent Vater made notes. "This is critical. We need her help."

Reilly sat at his desk, studying his buffed nails. "Can't say that I like her much, but in the field of prion research, she's top-notch. If the disease escapes control, it could cause a prion pandemic, infecting people, animals, even carrion-eating birds. They may not all develop the disease but could carry and spread it. We know from one study that crows don't get sick from mad cow but do spread prions. We think fish are spared."

Sarge asked, "Why don't more people know about this disease? Are the feds covering it up like the Brits did?"

Reilly explained, "Only one person per million in the world would die each year of a sporadic form. Authorities don't get too concerned at that rate."

Vater commented, "I think it's possible the information has been suppressed by the beef industry."

Sarge said, "Around here, I believe it's been suppressed because of ranching, hunting, and all the related businesses like sporting goods stores and gun dealers."

Reilly's heels clicked on the old tile floor as he paced. "We've had no mad cow disease and only a few cases of Chronic Wasting Disease identified in eastern Montana. We also know CWD has been slowly spreading in wildlife for decades along a Wyoming-Colorado corridor. If a rapid prion form spread in our wildlife, it would destroy the hunting economy in the Bitterroots and the Rockies."

"It's not *if*," Sarge corrected him. "I guess you didn't hear me. The men said our deer corral is empty. They released the whole herd."

"God, no! Are you sure?" Reilly's face paled. "They were in a secure double corral inside the electric fence!"

"*Were* is the operative word." Sarge emphasized, "The deer are gone. Unless they starve and die in winter storms, they'll be spreading the disease. Even then, whatever eats the carcasses will be infected."

Vater looked more worried, his brows furrowed. "I'm convinced this group knew what they were doing. If the infected deer contaminate our local wild elk and deer populations, we'll have to shut down hunting for good. And, I assume if they mix with cattle, prion disease will spread and collapse the beef industry."

Sarge said, "Any idea who would want to do something like that, destroy the world around us?"

Saliva gathered at the corners of Reilly's mouth. Droplets of spittle spewed with his angry words. "That would suit the vegetarian just fine. Archer hated hunting and killing animals but used them in her studies. A goddamned wing-nut with double standards." He stopped pacing. "She helps her beef rancher boyfriend with his Angus artificial insemination and embryo business but never eats meat. Go figure." Reilly sat down, exasperated. "Archer's brilliant, yes, but she's crazy like her dad. They never stop working. We're all in big trouble without her. Nolan's dead and now Callie's incapacitated."

Sarge looked sad, his words soft. "The woman is brilliant and loved. I sure hope she does well and gets back to work soon." He frowned. "We can't even eat chicken if it spreads to birds. We'll all be eating lettuce and fish."

Vater asked Reilly, "Can't we just make sure the meat is well done before we eat it?"

"Cooking doesn't kill prions. Surgical sterilization procedures don't work either. Hospitals learned the hard way by spreading the disease from patient to patient after usual instrument sterilization methods failed. Everything prions touch has to be treated with lye solution, concentrated bleach or incinerated."

Vater looked askance. "Incinerated?"

Reilly repeated, "The only absolute way to kill prions is to burn them to ash."

Silence.

Reilly ranted, "No one else is as advanced as Dr. Archer. She'll be in line for a Nobel Prize in Medicine if her treatment works."

"I still don't get it," Vater stated calmly. "You said prions are proteins. How can they be infectious?"

"They're strange, contagious proteins that, on contact, snap normal proteins into an abnormal shape that causes neurological disease. Simple as that."

"Sounds crazy." Sarge said to Vater, "I like to read science fiction. When I asked Dr. Callie about prions one day, she compared them to Ice-Nine in Vonnegut's *Cat's Cradle*. Prions have a domino effect on normal body proteins, just like Ice-Nine had on water molecules. Instead of freezing everything they touch, prions snap normal proteins into disease forms."

"Why do Colorado and Wyoming have so much Chronic Wasting Disease and we don't?" Vater asked Reilly.

"Colorado's been tracking and trying to control the disease since 1968, when Mary Williams discovered it had spread from sheep diseased with scrapie to deer. Scrapie is also a prion disease that crosses species, but it's not as aggressive as Dr. Archer's."

Sarge asked, "So, what do we tell the public?"

Reilly glared at him. "Nothing. You don't scream fire, Ebola, or prions in a crowd."

Vater stood. He looked out a frosty window, staring into the fenced compound. "One serious breach with this cross-species type of disease could infect every food source. If carrion-eating birds are a vector, it would be impossible to contain."

Reilly said, "That's why I brought you in here. We can't let the public know how serious this is. With Archer's rodent success, there's hope."

Sarge said, "I trust her. I'd take her rat drugs any day."

Reilly gave Sarge a condescending look. "Drugs have to go through a proper test phase to qualify for human use. She'd be in deep kimchi if she used rat drugs on people."

"Dr. Reilly, we have to tell the public." Vater's tone was firm. "We have no choice."

"We can't. Lives are at risk, but the international beef and poultry industries depend on how we handle this. No one would buy our beef if cattle started falling down with mad cow disease. There would be a U.S. economic collapse."

Sarge and Vater watched the agitated lab director.

When he saw their reactions, Reilly stood erect, his chin in the air. In a soothing voice meant to encourage them, he said, "I just meant we need to avoid bad publicity. Maybe we'll get the animals back."

Sarge muttered, "Yeah, and maybe we won't."

Chapter 26 - A Dire Holiday

Rudy felt terrible. Dr. Archer had counted on him, and he'd let her down. He couldn't believe what had happened on his shift at the most secure high-risk facility in the United States. He might lose his job. Dr. Archer might die. A buddy of his in the war had looked like she did when he found her.

His buddy didn't make it.

The rotor wash from the medical helicopter lifting off struck Rudy as he trudged to the front door of the Medicine Falls hospital. He had a good idea of the hospital layout after his son's birth at the facility. Popsicle-orange frizzed hair framed the wrinkled face of the same woman who had been on duty at the front desk obstructing the way to all who entered the afternoon he had rushed Leah in.

Rudy walked up to her and pushed back his hood. She didn't even look up from filing a talon that matched her hair. He cleared his throat to get her attention. "Ma'am, could you tell me what room Dr. Callie Archer is in? She was just brought in this morning." He unzipped his jacket and wiped sweat from his neck. His stiff posture and NIH guard uniform gave him the appearance of a tense military officer.

Popsicle Hair looked up. Her voice snapped at him like a drill sergeant. "Sir, there's no one by that name registered here."

Rudy exploded. "Bullshit! I know she's here. They brought her by ambulance from the Ridge Lab." He stormed down the hall toward the intensive care unit.

With each step, his anxiety increased.

Maybe she had died.

The receptionist stood, her eyes following Rudy. She sat down and jammed buttons with a pencil eraser. Her head bobbled as she spoke into a boom mic. "An unauthorized person is heading toward intensive care. Stop him."

Two FBI agents strode toward Rudy.

He recognized them. "How's Dr. Archer? Is she gonna make it?"

One agent shook his head. "Alive but not good. That was Dr. Archer headed to St. Pat's. We just help get her into the chopper."

Rudy froze.

"The blood clot expanding on her brain got worse. She needs emergency surgery."

The second agent cautioned, "We aren't supposed to release any information, so keep it quiet. She'll be on 24-hour protective guard. We have men waiting on the roof helipad at St. Pat's."

A hospital security guard, a friend of Rudy's, joined the three men. "Rudy, you look pretty hot, man. Don't make trouble for yourself."

"Sorry guys. I won't. I was there during the night when all hell broke loose." Rudy tried to slow his breathing as he'd learned to do when stress had twisted through his body in combat. "I couldn't believe it when I found her on the floor almost dead."

The agents looked at each other, acknowledging Rudy's pain. The first guy said, "You know how it is, Rudy. Everybody's a suspect until we get more information, so keep your cool."

Rudy motioned to the admissions clerk. "Is there a no information order on her?"

"Yes. We don't want the perps trying to off her so she can't ID them."

"Okay." Rudy zipped his jacket to leave. "Thanks."

One guard said, "Special Agent Vater will give us periodic medical reports on her."

"Everybody's a suspect," the other guard warned. "Don't try to go and see her, Rudy. They have orders not to let anyone in the room. If anyone pushes to see her, the men have orders to arrest them."

Rudy left, exhausted and deflated. Now he wasn't just worried about Dr. Callie, he was worried about his job. Were they insinuating he had something to do with the break-in?

He didn't trust that damn Reilly, who would send his own mother to prison rather than take responsibility for anything himself. Dr. Reilly would say one thing and do another. How could someone with his lack of principles have ever been placed in charge of anything as important as an NIH lab?

Rudy calmed down once he had talked things over with his level-headed, optimistic wife. She and the baby snuggled up against him in bed until he fell asleep. Once Rudy was snoring, Leah and baby Cole sneaked out of the bedroom.

His wake-up alarm sounded seven hours later, but Rudy had already awakened to the smell of baking bread. Leah had homemade chicken barley soup and rolls for dinner. His lunch sat near the door with a thermos of strong coffee.

Rudy ate dinner, kissed Leah, hugged Cole, and walked out the door. The December daylight faded early, but the clear skies had improved visibility. Recently plowed roads made the trip to the lab less treacherous than his trip home had been.

A cold front had moved in with subzero temperatures. Snow crunched and squeaked underfoot as Rudy walked to the gate. Instead of one guard at the entrance, three armed men with FBI insignia were standing at the gate, ready for trouble. Sarge was with them. Yellow crime scene tape cordoned off an area of red-splashed snow.

Sarge looked at Rudy through red-rimmed eyes. "Rudy, I'm counting on you, man. I'm too tired to talk." His voice hoarse, "I left a stack of stuff on the control room desk for you to fill out. I started, but I'm too tired to finish. I have to go home and sleep."

"I'll get at it. Any special instructions?"

"Stay close to the control room. Tonight, we have six guards walking the perimeter, three FBI at the gate. Our NIH officers are assigned to each major building inside the compound, and an extra one is in this building with you. Two in the vet compound as usual. The IRF is secured."

"Did you get the fence fixed?"

"It's patched, but on Christmas we couldn't find anyone to repair circuitry damage. IRF Level 3 is lights out and off grid. Locked up tight. No one is allowed in the building."

Rudy confirmed the plan. "So, everyone on the premises has a radio with instructions to check in with me hourly?"

"Yes. A grid sheet with their names and locations is on your desk. Check them off when they call in."

"I'll get started on the paperwork."

"Write your report down the way it happened. Don't leave out anything." Sarge walked with Rudy. "More feds will be here at 0700. I want you to stay for the meeting. I'll be back at six."

Rudy asked a question but dreaded the answer. "Any word on Dr. Archer?"

"A neurosurgeon removed a blood clot on her brain. She's lucky to be alive."

Rudy sighed. "I'm really upset over her, Sarge."

"Me, too. Doc Maxwell told Hal Vater the sample of her blood he sent to the lab for analysis measured a high level of the date-rape drug Rohypnol. She won't remember anything."

"Damn. So, they drugged her? God, Sarge, I feel like shit. She was counting on me."

"It's not your fault. Things would be worse if you'd been drugged, too. You saved the day, Rudy. Remember that."

"I saw the IRF door open and close when she'd left that building and returned to the coffee room to nap on the couch. Right after the board lit up, I found her on the floor bleeding. The sirens started screaming at 2 a.m."

Sarge took a small notebook from his pocket and made a notation. "None of this should have happened, but we won't know how bad it really is until she's able to tell us what's missing." Sarge zipped his parka, flipped up the hood, and left.

Hourly check-ins from the many guards and writing his report in the comfort of his electronic cockpit made the time pass quickly. Rudy couldn't believe it was morning when Sarge walked in at 6 a.m. His stress ebbed, standing with Sarge when everyone gathered in the board room for the meeting with arriving dignitaries.

Special Agent Vater, Sgt. Collucci, NIH Officer Jonsrude, and Dr. Reilly talked privately before the others arrived. Vater announced, "Dr. Archer is stable. She's still on a breathing machine. If all goes well, her doctor says she may come off it this morning."

Sarge asked, "When can we talk to her?"

"The neurosurgeon told me he expects a full recovery. She'll be in ICU for a few days. If he can remove the airway tube, she may be able to talk to us tomorrow."

Purplish veins etched Dr. Reilly's nose. "Don't turn her statements into a media circus."

Vater remained calm. "Dr. Reilly, this is an investigation. The press is banned. Dr. Archer's life is at risk because of what she might have seen."

Dr. Reilly faced Vater. "After this fiasco, I don't want the Ridge Lab getting a worse image than it already has. I've tried hard to keep things here low key and out of public scrutiny."

Vater said, "I understand, Dr. Reilly, however authorities far higher than me or you will make the legal and political decisions on this disaster."

Sarge's angry voice cut in. "We're all here to solve a crime, but we're also here to protect the public, and we're not doing it unless we alert them to the dangers of the prion breach."

Reilly struggled to control his rage, resenting his subordinate position.

Two additional FBI special agents arrived from Helena. Sarge had also called Cy Cass, an NIH officer, back from vacation. They discussed aspects of their investigation with Dr. Reilly until the dignitaries entered just before 8 a.m.

On this cold day, the radiators were turned on full, and their clanging added to the conversation when Governor Evan Howard and Mason Boyd, a director from NIH, entered the room. The dignitaries dragged their metal chairs away from the table to sit. The legs screeched on the floor and echoed off the stark walls. Wearing new puffed-up down jackets and carrying briefcases, the men slid into their chairs on either side of Director Reilly at one end of the scarred wooden table.

Special Agent Vater sat at the far end. He spoke first and introduced himself as the investigator in charge. His calm demeanor set the tone for the meeting. He asked Dr. Reilly to introduce the Ridge Lab personnel and the new arrivals.

Reilly smoothed his unruly hair. "It is my honor to introduce Governor Evan Howard and NIH Biologics Director Mason Boyd. The CDC representative remained at the Montana State Crime Laboratory in Missoula with Dr. Hugh Dalen to discuss public health issues related to the Ridge Lab breach. You'll meet him later."

Vater began, "Thank you for your help in this grave matter. The surrounding area is crawling with FBI and county investigators searching escape routes the perpetrators may have used, but at this time we have few facts. This is what we know. Notable prion researcher Dr. Archer's laboratory seems to be the primary target. Sedated and bludgeoned, she's hospitalized with a head injury but is expected to survive. The unknown perpetrators took biological specimens that carry a lethal risk to the community and possible risk to the world. We don't know their intentions. No one has claimed responsibility."

The men sat in silence.

"We need expert assistance for damage control and FBI forensics to carry out the internal investigation. Dr. Reilly insists that Dr. Archer was responsible for the break-in, but in my opinion, based on our current findings, it is unlikely that she was involved. It appears to be an inside job with hallmarks of a professional team."

Reilly glared at Vater and gripped his pen like an ice pick.

Vater said, "We need federal and state involvement related to public health and welfare. I'm pleased the CDC is speaking with Dr. Dalen at the state lab."

Governor Howard asked, "Any leads?"

"Nothing solid. We have a lot of ideas. We believe someone in the group knew the new IRF building and its electronics setup. It points to a participant from within the lab. Their actions were stealthy and lethal. We are poring over the records of all employees, researchers, on-site workers, contractors, and lab staff to see if anything was missed."

Reilly jumped to his feet. His chair overturned, and the crash emphasized his rage. "I will not have Special Agent Vater blaming my staff for this!"

"Dr. Reilly, please sit down. You have no authority to run this case. In fact, you are a suspect until we say otherwise. I'll call it the way I see it."

NIH Director Mason Boyd pushed back from the table and stared at Reilly.

The director righted his chair and sat. His eyes stabbed Vater.

Director Boyd said, "We never want to believe anyone we vetted could turn on us, but it happens. NIH is determined to limit public harm and damage to our programs. One of the reasons we forced Dr. Archer to move her project here was because of the safety and isolated location of this lab." Boyd directed his comments at Dr. Reilly. "We thought it would be safer and easier to defend her from nut cases and terrorists, especially with a primate study. Obviously, we were wrong."

Boyd scanned the men at the table. "There were also some personnel issues at the Human Prion Disease Division in Cleveland that concerned her safety that prompted our decision to move her. I also understand her life was threatened a few months ago by activists here who knew of her studies in Cleveland." He looked at Vater. "That needs further investigation. What's her condition this morning?"

Vater brought them up to date on the information he'd relayed earlier to the other team members.

In spite of the cool room, sweat beaded on the brow of NIH Director Boyd. "I know Dr. Archer personally. We need her brilliance and drive in this field. Dr. Reilly, what is the extent of the damage to her laboratory and work?"

"Trashed. The animals and most frozen specimens, gone. Computer, gone. A refrigerator, presumably containing test drugs, empty." Reilly toned down his response. "We need her to check things over when she is able. She may have lost everything unless she had data saved off-site. I don't know if she'll be physically or mentally able to continue her work."

The NIH Director stressed, "The Prion Project here is high priority. She's our top NIH researcher. Nevertheless, Dr. Archer is also a suspect at this time so we will be watching her carefully."

Vater glanced at Sarge after watching Reilly in action. In a private conversation, they'd discussed Reilly's disdain of Dr. Archer and his blaming her for the breach. Vater tried to keep the interactions on track so he could get back to work. "Our team of experts from Quantico is due in this afternoon. Under Dr. Reilly's supervision, the FBI forensics team will begin work inside the breached IRF.

Governor Evans's brow furrowed. "What are we looking at regarding other damage and state issues? On the ride up here, I learned they released infected deer."

"Our small herd of twenty is gone. Many of the diseased ones were quite ill and wouldn't make it very far." Reilly explained, "Others are infected but look healthy. In deer, it takes about a year and a half for them to show signs of prion disease."

"If you're saying we have infected deer roaming the Bitterroots, we have to kill all of them immediately." Governor Evans stood. "This is a disaster in every sense."

Sarge spoke up. "I used to be a hunter. There is no hope of tracking them in this weather. The few tracks near the fence were covered by blowing snow long before sunup." He directed his next comment to Dr. Reilly. "I put a rush on completion of the video surveillance project. If the camera installation had been completed on schedule, we'd know what happened last night. We might have stopped them."

Rudy reported, "Disabled connections to our control board will be repaired this morning, so electronic surveillance will be back online by noon."

Special Agent Vater responded. "Great, Rudy. I ... "

Dr. Reilly interrupted him, "Agent Vater, my researchers are upset about being locked out of their labs by the FBI. Some have time-sensitive projects. You have to allow them entry."

"I already said we'd escort them with your supervision. I thought most of them were taking the week off between Christmas and the New Year."

"Some are, but here we are on Saturday, Christmas Day. Some of them will want to be back on Monday to at least check their work after the break-in."

"My team will talk to each of them and escort them to their labs on an individual basis. But, Dr. Archer's lab and the IRF are part of a crime scene and closed to everyone. If possible, have researchers on that level stay away until after the New Year. That would give us time to process the facility without people contaminating the investigation any more than they already have."

NIH director Boyd supported Special Agent Vater. "I'm in full agreement. Dr. Reilly, find out from your Level 3 researchers if they must enter that wing."

Director Reilly addressed the whole group. "I'll be available to escort the FBI investigators anywhere they need to go in the IRF. Governor Howard, regarding risk of spread, worse-case scenario is the spread of disease from Dr. Archer's lab will start a pandemic because of the ability to spread across species. But the freed deer were not part of her study. They are infected with a different prion, that always kills but not as fast. Terrorists could systematically infect animals and contaminate our food supply with animals and specimens taken from Dr. Archer's lab. Carrion eaters could spread the infection, too."

Vater said. "If the perpetrators don't have a clue what they've done, they may save us a lot of work by contracting the disease and dying off with all the infected animals."

Boyd stared at Special Agent Vater. "Don't make jokes. This is more serious than we realize at this point. My staff, along with the FBI and Dr. Hugh Dalen at the state lab, will analyze what we know about the spread and develop public health recommendations. In the meantime, on my authority, secrecy about this breach and the potential health impact is mandated."

Sarge made his views known again. "I don't see why we can't just tell people. Make an announcement that until it's all sorted out, don't eat meat. Period."

The governor said, "We can't do that, Sgt. Collucci. Our economy in Montana is driven by beef and hunting. The other part is tourism. They'd all be destroyed."

Reilly raised his voice. "I've told you before, Collucci, people would panic. Montana would be in financial ruin if ranching and hunting collapsed."

"He's right, but it's not just the local economy. Most of the world relies on U.S. meat exports. After the mad cow crisis in Britain, we saw everything from the beef to the animal feed industries fail. Protein slurry from all the rendering plants went to animal food. They had to recall everything and burn the food for farm animals, fowl and pets." He raised his brows. "Can you imagine what would happen if the world thought our food was contaminated? The U.S. would be in economic free-fall. The stock market would collapse. Until we've determined the impact, tell no one."

Vater asked, "By whose mandate?"

"The president of the United States. She's in agreement and has given us 24-hours to give her an update. It's critical to our national economic security."

Chapter 27 - Mack's Shock

On Monday morning, December twenty-seventh, a Ridge Lab security guard knocked at the ranch house door. Mack answered with a cell phone to his ear. "God damn it, Sal. What's happened? What have they done to her? ... A helicopter? ... I wanted her to quit that damn job. Someone's at the door. I'll call you back."

"I'm Cy Cass, Security from the lab. If you're asking about Dr. Archer, that's why I'm here

Mack gripped the door. "Is she dead?"

"No. She was airlifted to St. Patrick's Hospital after she was injured in a laboratory break-in. I'm here to escort you to the hospital if you'd like to see her."

"I'll drive myself, thanks." Mack grabbed his jacket from a hook near the door and pushed past the agent.

"Mack, we're not allowing unaccompanied visitors. If you want to see her, I have to escort you."

"What happened to her?"

"She suffered a serious head injury."

Mack stopped. "A head injury? Oh, no!" He raised his voice. "Why didn't someone notify me?" Mack jerked the car door open. "I have to see her. Let's go."

Officer Cass gave Mack minimal information as he pulled out onto the country road and headed north. "Dr. Archer is more stable. She is off the breathing machine and able to talk. Special Agent Vater got word you had called the laboratory asking for her many times. She authorized your visit."

"Damn her! I didn't want her working at that lab." Mack pounded a fist on his knee. "I've been trying to get her to quit."

"You may be shocked at her appearance."

Mack glared at him. "Why?"

"They shaved off half of her hair for the surgery."

Mack's face twisted from anguish to anger. He could usually control his emotions, but after his combat experiences, sometimes when anxiety took over he exploded in anger. He knew that if he could block his accelerating hyperventilation, the feeling would pass. Mack held his breath and looked out the side window, hiding his face from the driver. He hated having things out of his control.

His panic subsided, but the thought of going inside the hospital knotted his gut and fired misdirected anger at Callie. "I never wanted to set foot in the damn hospital again. They killed my mother. They let her die of alcoholic liver disease. The doctor said there was nothing they could do." Mack lay his head against the headrest. "He lied."

Cy slowed, allowing another car to pass on the icy roads. "Sorry about your mom, Mack. I hate hospitals, too. I hope Callie will be off the breathing machine when we get there."

Mack's thoughts remained dark. "After watching my mother die, I vowed never to drink. I think they let her die because she was just an Indian. They didn't care. I hope they treat Callie right. I don't want her to die."

The officer glanced at Mack, whose face was contorted in anger. "Why the hell didn't they tell me before now? I would have gone to see her sooner. Some ass told me she wasn't working when I called the lab Christmas Day."

Mack had left many messages on Callie's cell begging her to come to the ranch for Christmas dinner and stay the weekend. Sal had called Mack for information after hearing a rumor about Callie from a hospital worker. She told him her assault had occurred on Christmas Eve. Christmas Day had passed with no word. Now, a day later, they'd finally gotten their act together to inform him.

Instead of being with her on Christmas as he wanted, she lay in a hospital bed where he couldn't just go and visit her. She wasn't avoiding him and she wasn't with that damn pathologist at the state lab. He didn't have to worry as much about losing her.

His thoughts drifted to the exquisite two-carat Yogo sapphire ring he'd bought for her, planning to formally propose. The timing hadn't been right.

Cy slowed as they approached Highway 93. "It's hectic at the lab. You need to understand, for her safety she's on 24/7 guard because someone tried to kill her."

After questions the officer couldn't answer, Mack turned silent. As a child, he'd hidden from his abusive father, in a closet, in the woods, under a step, in his own world where it was safe. His grandmother demanded silence and spiritual thoughts. Silence had always been his means of escape.

Mack looked at the guard, resenting the man's control over him. Did they think he was a threat to Callie? A suspect? Is that why they hadn't called him? As a juvenile in detention, he had made it a practice to never offer information to law enforcement. He wanted to remain low profile, but after half an hour on the road, the unknowns plagued him, firing up his nerves. If he'd been alone, he would have parked and walked off his emotions.

To keep the thoughts of Callie possibly dying out of his mind, Mack decided to pump Cy for information. His request for details about what happened at the lab went unanswered.

"The break-in is under investigation, so I can't tell you anything, Mack. Sorry. I'm not saying you're a suspect, but we aren't allowed to talk about cases like this. I saw you once last year at the lab meeting in the Medicine Falls school when you escorted the researchers out."

"I met Callie that night. I love that woman, but she's married to her work. Maybe now she'll quit and move to the ranch with me." Mack sized up the officer and tried to relax. "Callie has never told me exactly what her research entailed, but, like everyone else around here, I knew it was about prions and finding a cure. With my beef business, I know a little about prions."

Cy said, "All I know is that it causes cows to go crazy."

The comment made Mack smile. "I hadn't thought about it in quite those terms, but yes, mad cow disease. Before her dad died, he worked at the lab studying a form called wasting disease spreading in wildlife."

"Are you concerned about prions infecting your cattle?"

"Scares the hell out of me, being an Angus rancher with an embryo and insemination business. Anything related to mad cow disease is bad."

Mack told Cy about Garrett Adcock, his neighbor who owned a domestic elk herd. "The wasting disease has been found in domestic elk on a few farms in Montana, North Dakota, and Saskatchewan. But Garrett thinks elk ranchers are being unfairly targeted by authorities."

"Aren't environmental groups opposed to elk farming?"

Mack agreed.

"Could your neighbor be involved in the lab break-in?"

"Garrett hates the government, including Fish, Wildlife and Parks, anyone in authority—a lotta people in Montana do. He carries grudges and can be violent."

"He was a bit out of control at that community meeting. I believe the FBI wants to talk to him."

"Good luck getting him to talk. He's an angry man. His family lost a lot of money when the timber mill in Darby closed down. He also nearly lost the elk ranch when the state outlawed confined kills"

"We have to look at every possible angle."

You might want to check out that damn lab director. He invested in the Adcock elk herd to keep Garrett afloat. Neither of them is stupid, but maybe Reilly wanted to steal her data."

"How about activists?"

"Animal rights activists are always hanging around my ranch because of my insemination business. I treat my animals humanely, like the Ridge Lab does, but activists don't like either one of us. Harassment from them goes with the territory."

"Have you talked to your neighbor in the past week?"

"We're not what you'd call friends. We work together on a charity project each year, and I taught him how to do the elk AI business."

"AI? I saw that on your barn."

"Yeah. Artificial insemination. I use semen from chosen Angus bulls to impregnate a whole herd of purebred Angus cows, or I freeze the semen and sell it." Mack felt a little more relaxed and distracted. "The process caught on in the domestic elk ranching arena, too. Garrett's making quite a bit of money selling sperm to elk ranchers around the U.S. with limited breeding stock."

The officer remained silent for a moment. Then asked, "How in hell can anyone get a bull elk or an Angus bull to cooperate in the procedures?"

"I'll tell you some other time. Right now, I'm worried about Callie." Mack fell silent.

As they entered Missoula, Mack thought more about Callie and feared what they'd find. He had enjoyed the fact that he and Callie had been an odd couple for the past few months, a tall Indian rancher with a petite scientist city girl. As far as he knew, neither of them dated anyone else, but recently she'd been less available, and he worried about her relationship with the guy at the lab in Missoula.

Mack recalled the night they'd met and how he'd immediately thought the attractive researcher was an amazing bundle of brains, energy, and beauty. He found Callie's fascination with his high-tech cattle business a plus, but they were both so involved in their professions, they didn't see much of each other.

Losing his wife had taken a toll on him. Meeting Callie had turned his head and fired his soul. He wanted to control her and keep her to himself, but her stubborn streak made that impossible. He hadn't forgotten her anger when he called her rat lady. That had not done his cause much good, but he thought she'd come around to his way someday, especially if he helped her through this crisis.

Mack was dressed all in black except for a red beaded hatband and a twist of red in his braid. The gentleman rancher looked like a dapper bad guy from a Western movie. Sweat slicked his forehead and palms as he followed the officer into St. Patrick's Hospital, up the elevator, and down the hall to her ICU room. A guard with a weapon on his belt sat outside her room.

After Mack was cleared to enter, his hand trembled when he opened the door.

Chapter 28 - Callie Fights Back

Dr. Braden rewrapped the gauze bandage covering my craniotomy scar while talking to me about my surgery and expected recovery. When he bent forward to listen to my heart and lungs, my blurry vision focused on Mack's approaching image. Tall, handsome, and dressed in black. I hadn't heard the door open. After Vater asked me if I wanted to see him, I was unsure. After hearing he'd called many times, I agreed but seeing him jarred my senses with mixed emotions.

Mack took my bandaged hand gently in his. "You had me worried."

A fleeting kiss on my cheek brought tears. "I'm okay now."

"I don't think so. You're as white as that gauze turban. But beautiful, like you just stepped out of a shower and wrapped your dark curls in a towel."

My voice came out raspy after having an endotracheal tube. "Dr. Braden, this is my friend, Mack Janns."

"Pleased to meet you, Mack." The doctor shook his hand. "Drew Braden, neurosurgeon. Callie's stable but has a way to go." He finished checking my pupil reactions. "From a blow to the head, she developed a subdural hematoma, a collection of blood beneath the skull that pressed on her brain."

Mack turned pale.

"I stopped the bleeding, but to adequately expose the area, the surgery left quite a scar. She lost nearly half her blood volume, but it wasn't from her brain bleed. She lost the baby."

Mack dropped into the nearest chair and covered his face.

I gasped. "How could that be true?"

I recalled not eating much and *losing* weight. I often missed menstrual periods because my baseline weight remained so low. I'd had that pattern for years.

Pregnant?

No way. I tried to sit up, but pain zinged to my forehead. My head felt like a lead weight.

Mack had said he'd had a vasectomy. A *vasectomy*. I couldn't be pregnant.

Dr. Braden stared at Mack, and the two guards who had heard his statement stared at me.

What were they thinking?

Dr. Braden's voice interrupted the silence. "Callie, because of your injuries and medications, you may not remember everything I tell you. If you have questions, you can call me."

Mack stared off into space.

"Basically, you were about ten weeks along and had an abruption. The placenta detached from the uterus. By the time you reached the Medicine Falls hospital, profuse vaginal bleeding had dropped your blood pressure and placed you at risk of dying from the hemorrhage. Between the head injury and the vaginal bleeding, Dr. Maxwell had a challenge keeping you alive."

The information blurred through my troubled brain, making little sense.

Dr. Braden explained that Dr. Maxwell had delivered the dead fetus and the placenta and stopped the bleeding.

Mack's voice was barely audible, "They nearly killed you and they killed our baby. A baby I was unaware of." His eyes bored into mine.

"Dr. Braden, I didn't know I was pregnant. Missing menstrual periods is not unusual for me. You'd think a doctor would know if she's pregnant, but I work long hours, never eat regular meals, and have been underweight most of my life."

Mack clenched his fists.

Maybe I made a mistake to let him visit me. I'd experienced his violent outbursts and hoped he'd control himself. I wanted to scream at him "You lied!" but held my tongue, confused, not sure what to think.

"The second CT scan of your brain showed enlargement of the bleed. You were airlifted here. I was able to open your skull and stop the bleeding."

Brain fog from my injuries, the drugs, and a truly splitting headache jumbled my thoughts. I'd already decided not to marry Mack, no matter what. Seeing him again made and hearing about the pregnancy, his lies. I never wanted to see him again. I hadn't told him my decision because I feared his reaction. A pregnancy would have made no difference in my decision.

Marrying him would have meant going from prion prison to literal prison on the ranch. He would have made me give up work, my research. That wouldn't happen.

He had lied. What else didn't I know about him?

Why did he lie?

Because he wanted to control me.

He didn't want me to work and would have demanded I stay home and have more kids.

I'd be willing to become a mother, something I'd treasure at the right time and under my terms. I would have stayed in my own home and hired a nanny. Sal would have helped me.

Dr. Braden talked to Mack. "Before you walked in, I had just told Callie she has blood typed and cross-matched in the lab, ready to hang, but she refused the transfusion. She's still groggy. Maybe she isn't thinking straight. Can you talk some sense into her?"

I was angry at Braden for trying to get Mack to override my decision.

What would Mack say? I waited.

"She's a bullheaded doctor and will do what she damn well pleases. I wouldn't argue with her if I were you. You'll lose."

Mack looked through me. His expression angry.

Dr. Braden's attractive face and unruly blond hair gave him the appearance of a teenage skateboarder in surgical scrubs, way too young to be a neurosurgeon. "Callie, you'll need to be here a few days. If everything goes as expected, I'll discharge you, but only if someone can stay with you, make you take iron pills, vitamins, and eat right." He handed me a lab report. "Your blood work suggests malnutrition. You were probably anemic before you bled. On discharge in a few days, you'll need antibiotics, pain pills, and an orthopedic follow-up for the hand."

Mack said, "What's wrong with her hand? I hope it isn't her trigger finger." He flashed me a fake smile.

"Her left thumb is gone. The attacker hacked it off."

Mack sat back down, pale. He looked at Dr. Braden. "I could easily kill a man with a sniper rifle at five hundred yards, maybe a thousand, and do anything to cattle, but the thought of Callie being hurt makes me sick. Why would anybody do that?"

I answered. "That's easy. My thumbprint gave them entry to my lab."

"God damn them."

"I have a bad headache and feel weak, but I have to get back to work. I'll eat better and be stronger in a few weeks. I'm sure Sal will give me a hand at my apartment, and Blaze will protect me."

Mack stood over me. "That is totally insane. You have to come home with me to the ranch."

I doubted I could take care of myself from the way I felt but knew damn well that I didn't want to be under his suffocating control. Sal would help me.

"I wouldn't have it any other way. You'll be comfortable and eat right. I'll see to that."

I shook my head. Each movement hurt. "I need to rest." I closed my eyes and turned away, wondering why the son of a bitch had lied.

Mack leaned over and hugged me too tightly. "Have it your way. I'll be back so we can talk."

Dr. Braden left, saying he'd be back later in the day to check on me.

Mack didn't leave.

I closed my eyes and listened to agents informing him that I was in protective custody and would have a twenty-four-hour guard, even after discharge because they feared for my safety.

I heard more voices outside the door and opened my eyes to see two men entering. They spoke to the guard stationed inside by the door who said, "Let me ask her. Wait a minute." The guard asked if I'd see them.

I agreed.

Hugh Dalen and a CDC investigator I recognized from our recent meeting walked over to the bed. "Hi, Hugh. Thanks for coming."

"Callie, I'm so sorry this happened to you. Your injuries and the break-in are horrible."

Hugh touched my shoulder and turned to the other man. "I brought Bill Hatcher from the CDC with me."

"Hi, Bill. I didn't think I'd see you again so soon."

"Sure sorry about everything, Callie."

Mack stood back, frowning.

"I probably won't make much sense. I'd like to talk to you when I'm stronger." I motioned to Mack. "This is my friend Mack Janns. Mack, this is Hugh Dalen, the state medical examiner, and Bill Hatcher from the CDC."

They greeted Mack, who was solemn.

Before they left, Bill handed me a business card and Hugh wished me well

Mack said little and left with Cy Cass a few minutes later.

My heart pounded, partially from blood loss, but surged at the thought of Mack's lies and my being trapped at the ranch.

I had to call Sal.

Chapter 29 - On Guard

Five days after my surgery, Sal and Ann Collucci showed up with two FBI agents to drive me home. The women wheeled me out of St. Patrick's with a guard on each side. When the automatic doors whooshed open, a blast of arctic air swept in sending a chill beneath my down jacket.

I took a deep breath. The cold air made me feel alive.

Two black SUVs with darkened windows waited near the door with motors running. I sat in the middle of the back seat of the first vehicle with a friend on each side. The twin SUV followed us to Medicine Falls while the girls filled me in on events.

What had happened to me at the lab was a blank. I had no memory of either the helicopter or the ambulance ride. "I have no recollection of going to either hospital."

Sal patted my hand. "It's probably best you don't recall any of it. They took good care of you. That's what matters."

I closed my eyes and rested my head back as we headed south. My mind traveled into dead-end tunnels. Wispy figures without faces threatened me from shadows. Sleep stopped my aberrant thoughts.

I awakened when we slowed and turned off Highway 93 into Medicine Falls. Ann said, "Good morning. You had a nice snooze."

I appreciated having good friends to help. "Thanks for coming to get me. Mack was intent on taking me to the ranch, but I want to be home. I'll do fine."

The SUVs parked side by side at the Wagon Wheel Motel office. "Why are we stopping here?"

The guard turned around. "Dr. Archer, you won't like this. Someone trashed your apartment."

I choked. "What did you say?"

"Your apartment is a crime scene. Our forensic team is still dusting for prints and collecting trace evidence."

I sat up too fast and felt woozy.

Sal put her arm around my shoulders. "I found it a mess after they flew you to Missoula. I went over to pick up some clothes for you and found the door standing open with keys dangling in the lock. I backed out and called the police."

The guard said, "Maybe we should have told you sooner, but nobody wanted to stress you out with more bad news. Files were strewn around, and if you had a computer, it's gone."

I gripped Sal's arm. "I had important research data on my laptop."

She opened her car door and got out. "I'm sorry. Come on in Callie. Blaze will be excited to see you. I'll feel better having you and Blaze with me. I'll take good care of you." She held out her hand to steady me.

Ann slid out carrying a plastic bag. "The guards stopped on our way to the hospital so we could buy you a couple comfortable jogging outfits, undies, socks, and slippers. Until the FBI releases the apartment, you can't even go inside to get clothes."

Sal opened the office door. Blaze met us woofing and wagging.

I patted her, afraid to lean forward for a hug because of my throbbing head. "Hi, sweetie. I missed you."

Ann walked me inside. I removed my jacket and sat in Sal's recliner. Ann adjusted the back position and put a lap robe over me.

Blaze sat close enough for me to reach her. "It feels great being with friends and out of the hospital."

The guards followed us inside and looked around, examining the windows, doors, and locks. I introduced them to Blaze.

Sal took two keys from their hooks and handed one to each guard. "I reserved the room next to the office for you. It's a kitchenette with two queens. I thought you'd want a microwave and refrigerator since you may be here awhile."

One of them left to check out their new residence. He returned a few minutes later. "Thanks Sal, that will work out fine. Comfortable, and a second door leading into your apartment makes it safer."

We looked at each other in awkward silence while Sal made coffee. One guard sat near me on the couch, Ann and the other guard, at the table. Sal filled my cup first and handed it to me. "It's time for a party." She filled the other cups and then sliced banana bread. "Ann made this and brought it over for us."

Silence.

Why weren't they talking? Did my appearance scare them? "You guys don't look like you are having much fun at my party." I took a bite. "Delicious. Thanks." I pushed back the gauze turban that had slipped down over my ears. "Dr. Braden said I could take this off tomorrow, but based on his description of the horseshoe scar, it might be frightening."

Ann smiled, "You won't scare us."

The guards, Nick and Rex, had been with me for days at the hospital. They were friendly but professional, always scanning and ready for trouble.

Nick, a husky dude with bulging muscles a little more talkative than Rex helped himself to a second slice of bread. "We have no good leads on who broke into the lab and nearly killed you. Investigators want to talk to you as soon as you're strong enough."

Rex added, "Any recollection you have of events that night might help."

"I have hazy memories. I'm not sure if they are real or dreams, but about a week before the break-in someone had moved a data file in my lab. I took the file home for safekeeping."

"Who had keys to your house?"

"Mack and Sal."

Sal jingled hers after removing them from a hook on the wall. "I have mine. The one still hanging in the lock on your door had an electronic car key on it which looked like yours."

Rex confirmed, "We verified the Subaru key on the ring matches your car."

"Mine were in my jacket at the lab. I used it to cover myself when I returned from checking on the newborn rats. I remember lying on the couch in the coffee room with it over me." I smiled thinking of the babies. "I hope Bernie's techs are taking good care of the little rat pups."

Silence.

Nick, a tall athletic man who had stood looking out the window, turned with a frown. "I guess I'm the one to bring you all the bad news. Reilly says your lab computer is missing and all the animals are gone."

I gasped. "Oh, no."

Sal put her arm around my shoulders. "We're all horrified, but there is nothing you can do right now. You have to rest and get stronger. I have wild rice vegetable soup simmering. We can all eat and then let you nap."

Data from years of work, stolen.

Animals, gone.

Years of research destroyed.

How could I recover the data? I sat in stunned silence wondering how anyone could have penetrated the high security lab.

I had to fight.

Chapter 30 – Recovering

The bell on the motel office door jangled. Sal started toward the front desk, but heavy footsteps followed by the bead curtain striking the wall stopped her. Blaze barked a sharp warning when Mack walked in.

Sal stepped back as he entered. "Hi, Mack. We just got Callie settled. I'll get you a cup of coffee."

She had just let a traitor into her home. Sal had no clue about the pregnancy, Mack's lies, or the fact that blood loss from the abortion had contributed to my near-fatal injuries.

I'd had no time to tell anyone about what transpired between me and Mack at the hospital.

Seeing him enter flipped my fuzzy brain into alarm mode. Mack's lie about something as important as a vasectomy was unforgivable. I would have taken an emergency contraceptive to prevent pregnancy after our unplanned intercourse had I not believed him.

I glared. "What the hell are you doing here?"

Sal's shock at my reaction to his presence made her slop hot coffee on her hand. The guards came to full alert, both on their feet.

I sure as hell didn't want to talk about personal matters in front of them but had no choice under the circumstances. I'd been too groggy and sick to focus on the lost pregnancy while in the hospital. He'd returned to visit each day, maybe thinking I'd forgotten because of the head injury and drugs, still believing I'd go home with him.

Pregnancy. Hearing that one word from Dr. Braden's lips had snapped my liking, maybe even once loving, Mack to hate.

He took the steaming cup from Sal, pulled a kitchen chair close to the recliner and sat facing me.

"Callie." His voice soft and apologetic, "I've come to beg your forgiveness for lying."

I shook my head.

I spoke as if we were alone instead of in a room full of people. "Please give me a chance. I lied because I love you so much."

I sat up straight. "You expect me to believe that? A good relationship is based on truth and respect. You've shown me neither. You're a liar. Get out!"

He didn't move. "My home is yours. I had everything ready for you. I thought you'd relent and let me take care of you. I spent time with the dietician to make sure I fixed you the right food to build back your blood and strength. I'm so sorry. Forgive me."

The guards positioned themselves a few feet from me.

If Mack didn't leave voluntarily, I doubted the two of them were strong enough to throw him out without breaking up Sal's nice home.

I had to get him to leave. "You can never own me. I'm not for sale and will not be herded around like a favorite cow. You can't control me. Leave."

Sad dark eyes locked on mine. "I've never loved anyone so much. Could we at least be friends?"

I said nothing.

"We have so much in common. My techs loved working with you and send their best wishes. They're hoping you'll come and spend time with them again when you're feeling better." He pleaded. "You could bring Blaze. She could run through the grasslands while you ride Candy."

I shook my head, zinging pain across my surgical scar. "I'm wounded physically and emotionally. You are part of my pain. I have no strength to fight with you or talk. Maybe, after I've had time to rest and recover, I'd be willing to talk, but at this point, I want you out of my sight."

He walked out.

Chapter 31 - The Investigation

Two days after my hospital discharge, Sal helped me dress in a pale blue jogging suit. I fell asleep in the recliner waiting for the investigators to arrive. She awakened me about noon when the team parked near the office door. "They're here. I hope you don't scare those guys with your surgical scar." Sal fluffed a soft pillow behind my shaved head.

Sarge and FBI Special Agents Hal Vater and Rod Page walked in. Sarge took a close look at my face. "You look puny, Doc. Maybe we should wait a few days."

"I'm okay. Sorry if I'm scaring you. I looked in the mirror this morning and scared myself." I smiled at their shocked faces. "I look worse than I feel. I couldn't stand seeing half my hair gone, so I had Sal shave off the rest." I showed them and then sat back. "I'm fine.

Hal examined the staples. "Dr. Archer, you look beautiful bald and sound great after all you've been through."

Sal smiled at Hal's compliment.

"I'd look more presentable with my head covered, but I'd have to go to my apartment to get a hat."

Sarge leaned forward protectively. "Don't worry. You look fine."

He made me feel more comfortable and directed my thoughts to the lab. "Did they hurt Rudy?"

Sarge shook his head. "He's concerned about you."

"Please tell him I'll be okay."

Hal introduced Rod Page to me and Sal. "If you're ready, I'll start firing questions so we can get out of here and let you rest."

"I'm ready, feeling better each day with Sal's good cooking. She threatened to feed me raw liver to build back my blood if I didn't eat a lot of spinach. I'm eating the spinach."

Sarge laughed. "Being a vegetarian, I'd guess liver isn't on your basic food list." He readied his pen and notebook. "Hal's in charge of the investigation, so he'll ask most of the questions."

Vater started a recorder. He began by stating the date, location, those in attendance, and the purpose of the interview. "Dr. Archer, the night you were injured, they killed two guards. Dr. Reilly tells us your lab was the only one targeted. He thinks you're responsible for the break in."

"Bastard. He'd sell his own mother into slavery to save face."

"Perpetrators knew a lot about the lab's security measures. Has anyone shown a special interest in your work?"

"A lot of people are interested in mad cow disease. In Cleveland, our labs were less secure, and I feared sabotage. A couple weeks ago, I think someone was snooping in my lab. Reilly is the only one that could have entered. As director, he has access to all the labs."

"Let's go to the afternoon of the Christmas party."

"I'm not much of a party girl, but I was working on a special project. On a break, I joined the party and talked to a few people at the gathering."

"How many were there?"

"About thirty out of about a hundred researchers and staff. A lot of researchers are reclusive and only attend mandatory meetings. Many left early because of the storm."

"What about the food?"

"Great hors d'oeuvres, even for a vegetarian. I liked the punch. Joy said it was mango and tangerine juice mixed with ginger ale, no alcohol."

"Who did you talk to?"

"I wandered around for about fifteen minutes talking to Sarge and Rudy, a couple researchers, and the chief vet, Bernie Goff. I didn't stay long."

"Anyone look suspicious?"

"I knew all of them and in their odd ways, they seemed normal."

"Did anyone hang around you close enough to spike your drink?"

"I left a cup of punch in the coffee room refrigerator before I headed out to the lab. I suppose someone could have spiked it there."

"Why didn't you just go home?"

"I had a pregnant rat about to give birth, and I wanted to be there when she delivered to be sure she didn't eat any of her offspring. I know that's gross, but sometimes it happens, and these babies were very important."

Vater made a face. "Yuck."

"I was anxious to see if the babies were born with any evidence of disease. She delivered while I was at the party, and they were doing fine when I checked on them. After I set up a file to do genetic mapping, I took a logbook of data to review in the coffee room before sleeping."

"What else?"

"My stomach was upset from the shrimp. I think I talked to Rudy, then drank the punch before falling asleep reading."

"Anything else?"

"Waking up with a tube in my throat."

"You don't remember the thumb?"

"Only that it hurt when I was still drugged in the hospital. It felt like someone was crushing the tip, phantom pain because that part is gone." I looked at my bandaged left hand.

Vater continued, "Look at your arms. They're still bruised, and it's been a week. What happened?"

Bruises encircled my wrists, extending to both forearms. "Maybe I fell down. It could be from IVs."

Rod Page commented, "Doc Maxwell in the Medicine Falls ER said those are defensive injuries from a struggle, trying to fend off someone. He didn't think you'd fallen. Your legs aren't injured."

"I don't remember."

Sal put her hand on my shoulder to comfort me, looking at my bruises.

Vater went on. "Dr. Braden said you were struck from behind, almost on the top of your head. That injury isn't from a fall."

"Someone made sure you were out cold and didn't care if you survived." Vater emphasized, "They left you for dead, Callie."

Sarge suggested, "Maybe not for dead, Hal. If they'd wanted her dead, they would have left her outside to freeze to death."

"I think you're right, Sarge. If they didn't care or wanted you dead, they could have dragged you outside in the freezing weather to finish you off. Maybe they were interrupted."

"I've tried to remember, but it's like trying to recall a dream."

"A drug screen ER docs always do on unconscious patients includes sedatives. They specifically checked for Rohypnol. It was positive."

"The date-rape drug? Really? If I survived, they didn't want me to remember anything."

Page said, "You're still at risk, so don't try to ditch your guard."

Rex looked up from a magazine. "We're keeping her covered. She's slow right now so we can keep up with her. But we've heard it may be a challenge when she's feeling better."

I smiled. "Watch out, I'm feeling stronger."

Vater asked, "Can you think of anything else about that night?"

"What about my lab? They never should have been able to get inside."

"Your animals and most of the specimens are gone."

"I heard. My project is highly damaged. I tried to prepare for every contingency, but since my apartment was burgled, too, I may have lost more data."

Sarge explained there was no logbook in the coffee room.

"No one else is supposed to enter my lab, so when I noticed a file I'd left on a corner of my desk had been moved and the papers inside jumbled, I brought the file home."

Vater asked, "Was anything missing when you found it?"

"I don't think so, but it made me wonder why Reilly was nosing around."

Sarge leaned forward. "Did you say anything to Reilly about him being in your lab?"

"I don't talk to him unless I have to. If any of the surveillance cameras were working, maybe we could see who went in."

Sarge made a note. "I'll check for a video, but I doubt there's anything to be seen because that section wasn't fully functional at the time."

"What about your file in the lab that someone messed with?" Vater asked. "How important was it?"

"Very. I was analyzing my final data on the rodent study with plans to publish it. I had the drug combination and dosages of the only successful treatment known."

Vater looked down at his notes. "Tell me about a researcher named Westphal."

"I reported him for assault in Cleveland and they sent him off to detox, then later transferred him to Ridge lab. I doubt if he had anything to do with this."

"What's his full name? We need more info on him." Vater checked the recorder to be sure he'd get the details.

"Lawrence R. Westphal III, PhD. He'd been doing scrapie research, prion disease in sheep. Since his transfer here, I rarely saw him. He wasn't a problem."

My thoughts sorted through shadowy images from Christmas Eve. "Larry's an alcoholic just out of rehab and was boisterous at the party. Maybe he's drinking again."

Sarge said, "I agree. He was inappropriate at the party. I think he left before I did."

I struggled to get up. "When we're finished, will somebody take me to my apartment? I want to see if they took all the data I had hidden. It's catastrophic if they did."

Page pulled out his cell phone. "I'll see if the evidence team is finished." Following a short conversation, he affirmed, "They're done. We're cleared to enter."

I added, "Something I didn't tell you is that Dr. Reilly and Larry Westphal are old friends, classmates, buddies."

Vater asked about activists. I described the scene with Hannah and the threats.

"I didn't hear about that. Did you, Sarge?" Vater sounded surprised.

"The group harassed Callie outside the lab gates the morning after the town meeting. I found out about it and called the car license into the sheriff's department."

Hal asked a few more questions then said, "Okay, last question. Who do you think is responsible for the lab break-in?"

"I don't know. Doubt it's locals. They seem afraid to venture near the lab."

I talked them to into taking me to my apartment. I walked in with trepidation and stood at the entry, stunned by strewn books and files. Desk and file drawers, open. Black fingerprint dust powdered surfaces. Fortunately, my traumatized brain blunted any emotion. I left the men standing in the kitchen, headed to the bathroom, closed the door and closed the toilet seat.

Dizzy from the walk to the house from the car, I sat and rested a moment, then balanced one knee on the toilet and lifted the tank lid. A loud clunk occurred when it slipped.

Sarge knocked on the door. "You okay?"

"Fine. I'll be out in a minute." Moments later, I walked out waving a key chain in my injured hand. "The killers didn't find this!"

Vater came forward. "What is it?"

"Paranoia to keep computer files safe paid off. Most are in my dad's gun safe in the garage, but I stored this thumb drive with my latest laptop data above the water in the toilet tank."

Special Agent Page grinned. "It's an old trick but you outsmarted them."

Later that afternoon, Rex drove Blaze and me back to the apartment to watch Sal, and a friend clean up all signs of the invasion. The joyful dog bounded around the snowy back yard a few times then curled up at my feet. After coffee, I talked Rex into going for a walk with me. A red hooded parka and matching knit hat covered my bald head and kept me warm.

We circled through town on shoveled sidewalks. Rex slowed when he realized I was breathing fast and having trouble keeping up. I accepted his arm for the last block. "I guess I need more time to build back my red cell count before much exercise."

Sal opened the door. "I heard you tromping up the steps. Here's some hot chocolate to warm you up."

"Thanks. I had to hang onto Rex but being in the fresh air gave me hope for better days." I told Sal that Rex was driving me up to the lab to say hello.

Sal offered to take care of Blaze, but Rex said, "It's okay by me if we bring her along." Rex patted her head. "She's a special dog."

I sat in the back seat with her head on my lap as we drove up the winding road. When we parked, Blaze curled up to wait when we got out and headed for the entrance. Rex and I paused at the perimeter gate guard to explain our intentions. After a call to security, they let him through the metal detector with his weapon. Our first stop was to thank the duty guard in the control room for not harassing Rex over the gun.

Rudy met us. "Dr. Callie, you look great in that hat. Are you reporting for duty already?"

"Just here for a visit. I look like Frankenstein underneath the hat and didn't want to scare anyone. Sure glad you're okay. Is Dr. Reilly around?"

"He's here." Rudy scanned the hall and in a low voice said "Yesterday, he told me to turn off alarms because they'd be going in and out of your lab. Said he was cleaning it with someone."

I stared at Rudy. "Who was with him?" I was thinking, if it was Westphal I'd file a complaint.

"Not sure, but you can't get in until I reprogram the scanner to your other thumb."

"When can you do that? I want to come back as soon as I get the okay from my doctor."

He pointed to the corner of his office. "The new digital fingerprinting machine is set up, but I'm in the middle of something right now. I could do yours after you talk to Reilly." Rudy removed the cover to show us his new equipment. "This is the best. The FBI wants us to redo the entire staff and send all the prints to AFIS, the Automated Fingerprint Identification System."

"Dr. Dalen told me about AFIS when I toured the state lab. Do you think you'll find any surprises?"

"That's one of the reasons we got it, to turn up possible information related to the break-in."

"You aren't coming back to work already, are you?"

"I want to, but it may be another week or longer. What are you doing here in the daytime?"

Rudy grinned. "Got promoted. The Feds decided I'm a good guy and not the one who wacked off your thumb."

"Congratulations. I'll miss your company and won't feel safe without you here at night."

"Lotta good I did you Christmas eve. I'm sooo sorry. Glad you have a guard."

Rex shook his head. "Not your fault, man. They knew all the angles."

Rudy smiled. "It's great to see you both."

I walked down the hall to Reilly's office with Rex at my side. We walked right in through the wide-open door to find Reilly was pressing Joy against one of his perfectly arranged bookcases.

Joy snickered when she saw us. "Oops, Dr. Reilly and I were just reviewing some interesting data."

Reilly's flush exaggerated the nests of capillaries tangled across his cheeks.

"Looks like something pretty personal. I'm here to see what happened to my lab."

Reilly regained his composure. "I think you'll be pleased. We cleaned it up and I ordered a new computer for you."

Joy exclaimed, "It was a mess."

Shocked he would bring his secretary into a biosafety area, I stared at him. "Is Joy bio-trained?"

"I cleared her myself." He snarled. "We wore hazmat suits and wiped everything down."

"Unless you used concentrated sodium hypochlorite it won't change prion concentration."

Reilly shook his finger in my face. "You ungrateful bitch!"

Rex stepped in front of Reilly. "Cool it, man. That's no way to treat her. Remember, she nearly died here."

Reilly sidestepped Rex. "You shouldn't be here. How can I trust someone who's just had brain surgery?"

"It wasn't brain surgery. My brain had pressure on it from a blood clot on the surface. It was recognized early on CT scan and treated." I removed my hat. "My brain is fine. It's my scalp that looks bad."

Joy's eyes popped wide, staring at the ugly scar closed with a row of staples.

Reilly turned pale and sat down. "You look like a brain-damaged freak. I don't want you scaring people. You are banned from all biosafety areas until the staples are out and can prove I can trust your judgment."

Wrath-fueled comments came close to spewing from my mouth, but I remained silent with fire in my eyes. My clenched fists sent a shooting pain like a shock to my injured thumb. "Dr. Reilly, you've broken NIH regulations by bringing Joy into my IRF lab. You know how to protect yourself, but she's at great risk for contracting a fatal disease without thorough training."

Joy stepped away from him. "Clint, you didn't tell me that!"

"Don't' worry, I'd never let anything or anyone, hurt you." He pulled her close to him.

I took a deep breath and addressed Joy. "Exactly what did you do?"

Joy tensed, eyes frightened. "Clint showed me how to wipe surfaces with bleach solution while he mopped the floor. We closed the empty cages and put them back on the corner cabinet instead of scattered on the floor."

Reilly added. "On that first morning, I closed the refrigerators and freezers so residual contents would be preserved."

I turned to go. "Thanks for trying and for the new computer."

Reilly followed. "Believe me, it wasn't for you. It's my responsibility as lab director to oversee every detail." Joy watched our interaction. "I tried to get you transferred again, but DHS vetoed my request. I'm stuck with you."

I resented his attitude. The cutting words convinced me his time in my lab was a coverup for prying.

"I need Bernie to order more hooded rats for me." Rex and I headed for the door. "I'll have my staples out tomorrow and will be back to work part-time a few days later."

"How can you possibly continue if you lost your source specimens?"

"As soon as I survey the lab, I'll know how to start. I was very careful to hide specimens." I backed away from him. "In this work, I've learned the hard way. I expect sabotage."

Reilly snapped. "You weren't cautious enough. You got your head bashed in." He followed us into the hall, talking as we walked away. "You're a liability, Archer. I'm making a report that will be placed in your permanent record. You're still on guard and jeopardizing lab operations by parading around here looking like a sideshow."

"I look like this and nearly lost my life because you didn't do your job to keep us all safe. I have a bodyguard because someone tried to kill me as I worked in your secure facility. Aren't you pleased I care enough about my work to come back so soon?"

He stood in the middle of the hall as we walked back to the control room.

Rex glanced back to be sure he was out of earshot. "I wanted to punch him out."

"He's been like that since day-one." We walked into the control room office where I placed my hat and coat on a chair. "Rudy, I haven't talked to Bernie, and I need to do that before I go home. Could I use your phone to see if she can come over here? I think I'm too weak to walk out to the animal compound."

Rudy called. "She'll be right over." He handed us each a cup of his strong coffee.

Rex took a sip. "This is what I call coffee."

When Rudy finished my prints, the guard and I took our drinks to the coffee room to meet with Bernie. The back door burst open a few minutes later, she shed her parka and gave me a gentle hug. Bernie peered over her frames. "Girl, what *are* you doing here? Don't get me wrong, I'm happy to see you and your friend here." She said hello to Rex. "I tried to visit you at St. Pat's, but his buddies wouldn't let me in."

Bernie went to the coffee warmer and poured herself a cup. Rex pulled out a chair for her. "We're still worried about Callie being a target. The perps may believe she recognized some of them. We have to keep her safe."

"Callie," Bernie gripped my arm. "I'm so excited. Amo is thriving! I can't believe our little monkey has gained more weight. I did a second spinal tap and gave her another dose of your drugs. She hasn't missed any treatments."

"Thank you. Amo's been on my mind. Even in the hospital, my foggy thoughts circled back to her. If I had the energy, I'd be jumping up and down with the good news about her improvement."

"It's a breakthrough!" She spoke a little too loudly, looking around to see if anyone else had heard.

"I still have grant money. Could you order two more monkeys? We can use our healthy ones from the last study as controls. I want to get projects started on both rats and monkeys."

"It won't take long to get them here." She rolled her eyes. "Should I order a pregnant one?"

"I guess that's a joke but let me think about it."

Rex mentioned the interaction with Reilly.

"He can't keep you away from here! What does he think he's doing?"

"I was too weak to fight today, but no matter what he says, I'm coming back. I'll be here part-time a few days from now when the neurosurgeon releases me."

"Call if I can help."

"I don't think I'm ready for another baby monkey. Just order two adults. Let me know when they'll arrive. I'll call Paul Wilder to tell him the great news about Amo."

Blaze curled up beside me on the way back to Medicine Falls, and I was sound asleep when Rex parked at the Wagon Wheel. He helped me out of the car. "You better get stronger before returning to work."

I didn't like being a weakling, so I walked into the office with quick steps that made me short of breath, something I hoped he didn't notice.

We told Sal about Reilly.

"He's trying to make you look bad and push you out of the lab. Your dad never trusted him." Sal sat me down at the table. "How long will it take for your blood count to rise? It's been less than two weeks."

"I think it takes about six weeks, but I want to move home and be working full-time long before that."

Rex reminded me, "Before you move to the apartment we should wait until the investigation proceeds, until it looks safe. It's easier to guard you here at Sal's."

"Mack stopped by while you were gone. He wants you to meet his partner from Colorado."

The thought of having to talk to him sent a chill through me. "He's a manipulative liar. After what I learned in the hospital, I can hardly speak his name."

Rex and Sal remained silent, not sure what I might say.

"His partner Tim Baird is a large animal vet who helps him with semen and embryo collections. I've never met the man but feel like I know him because Mack talked about him a lot."

Sal held up a bottle of Merlot. "Mack brought you a gift. Said it would be good for your anemia. They're starting an insemination process soon and he thought you might like to watch."

Rex looked at me as if worried I might want to go to the ranch.

I shook my head. "I'm not going out there. I don't even want to talk to him."

Sal placed a glass of brown liquid in front of me.

"What, pray tell, is this? It looks more like motor oil than wine."

"It's prune juice. I called a dietician at the hospital here. She gave me a list of things to feed you to build back your blood. I bought some iron pills, raisins, and spinach. You don't have to eat them all at one meal."

"The juice looks nasty." I took a sip. "It's not too bad."

Sal laughed. "You'll probably like the spinach better."

Rex said, "Why would Mack want you out at the ranch?"

I downed the rest of the juice to get rid of it, hoping Sal wouldn't refill the glass. "Before the break-in, a couple of beautiful Native women who work for him taught me how they freeze the semen and sort embryos under a microscope to choose perfect ones to freeze in liquid nitrogen for shipment or use at the ranch."

Sal took the glass and replaced it with a bowl of raisins. "Sounds like quite the process."

I absentmindedly ate a few raisins. "Mack and Tim inject hormones in cows, then aspirate eggs at just the right time. Technicians mix sperm with eggs in little dishes, letting them grow some before sorting perfect embryos from imperfect. I found it fascinating."

Sal sat down beside me. "Are you in any condition to go out to the ranch? You look like you need a nap, not a job in an insemination laboratory."

"I'd like to watch if I didn't have to see Mack. The people at the ranch seem talented and nice. He says he employs four Native American ranch hands who live in the bunkhouse. They're ex-military like he is and needed jobs."

Rex sat at the table with me. "We have to look at everyone who could be related to the break-in. Tell me more about Mack and Tim. Mack is already on our list to interrogate."

"I don't trust Mack for personal reasons but can't imagine him being involved with the lab crime. Tim lives near Denver and helps ranchers with AI in Colorado and Montana. He's thinking about moving here."

"Are you suspicious of Tim?"

"I don't know him, but Mack would trust him with his life, just like the ranch hands. I've met a few of the Indian guys. I got the feeling they were spiritually bonded through bloodlines and the military. Mack says they're not all from the Pekisko nation like he is. Some are from Southwest tribes."

A boom shook the ground, rattling windows and sending Rex through the beaded curtain, gun in hand. "Sounds like an explosion. Get in the bedroom and lock the door."

Blaze barked wildly.

Sal grabbed her and pulled me inside, locking the door. We sat on the floor, listening to approaching sirens. "I'm glad Rex is here."

Blaze pawed frantically at the door, panting, trying to get out.

I held her close, calming her. "I've never seen her act like this. Have you?"

"Once. Just before your dad retired, he left Blaze with me one day. When a guy came to the desk to get a room, the fur stood up on her back and she went nuts barking and growling. He ran out, jumped in his car, and drove off."

"Weird. I've never seen her that upset before, only wary when Mack was in my apartment one evening."

The bell on the door jangled fifteen minutes later. Rex called, "It's me. I'm back. Come on out."

Blaze greeted him with her tail wagging but positioned herself on guard between us and the door.

"A meth lab caught fire and blew part of a wall out of a small house down the street. A deputy sheriff just arrived to back up local police. They sent the ambulance away." Rex pulled out his cell phone. "I'm calling Nick to give him a heads up. He'll be relieving me tonight and will be here the next few days."

I watched Blaze sniffing Rex's legs and shoes. "Interesting. Blaze was distraught and sure is interested in where you've been."

"Which house is it?" Sal looked out the window. "There's a lot of activity around that old duplex."

"You can't see it from here, but part of the south wall is gone."

Sal closed the curtain. "I wonder if the guy who wanted to rent a room here smelled of meth when Blaze went berserk. We don't know her history before Nolan adopted her. Maybe it was meth users that left her for dead."

I hugged Blaze, recalling her condition when Dad had found her. "A meth lab explosion in Medicine Falls not far from the meth recovery house is going to send locals into a tizzy."

Rex spoke softly. "It's hard to screen people checking into a motel, Sal. Be sure to alert me or Nick if you sense anything suspicious. Doubt if they are involved with the lab break-in, but meth-heads are dangerous when they're high or scrambling for drug money."

Chapter 32 - Artificial Insemination

Nick arrived in time to drive me to Missoula for my appointment with Dr. Braden. He and Rex exuded the same professional confidence. Rex, a fair-haired bulky guy, gray in the temples, flashed a smile that was quick like everything he did. He moved fast, and his blue eyes flicked back and forth, constantly scanning. Nick was thinner, with dark curly hair, younger, and about six inches taller; he looked like a college professor I'd once loved. I didn't feel frightened and hated to have the officers babysitting me when they could be doing something important.

I invited Nick into the room for my exam. I told Dr. Braden I felt strong and ready to return to work. He cocked his head. "You're still pale." After some discussion about what I'd like to do he said, "I'll agree with your plan if you're on track. Let's run you through a few clinical tests for balance and strength. How's your memory?"

"Memory is fine except for that night."

He had me stand on one foot, then the other, close my eyes, and hold my hands out, touch my nose with my eyes shut, and do a few other standard neuro checks. "I wouldn't expect you to recall much of the night of the break-in due to the head injury and the fact that you were drugged." Dr.

Braden examined my surgical scar. "I'll remove the staples but want to see you again later this week to be sure the wound is healed before you set foot in the lab.

Braden asked a few more questions before sending me to the hospital laboratory for a blood draw to check my hematocrit. "Come back Friday. If the scalp looks healed, you can work half-time beginning Monday. By half-days, I mean four hours."

He called me on our way home with the favorable result on a rising hematocrit.

Sal and Blaze greeted us with exuberance. "How'd things go?"

"Super. My blood count is on the rise. I need to see him one more time, but it looks like I can work on Monday."

Nick sat on the couch, frowning. "She's going to have to protect me from bad bugs, and I have to protect her from the bad guys. I'd rather stay here with you, Sal."

I removed my hat. "It's only four hours a day at first. You can just sit and watch me, like you do here."

Sal handed me a glass of prune juice. "You left here without breakfast. You'd better eat something. Are you sure it isn't too soon to work?"

"I don't think we can slow her down. I'll be keeping an eye on her." Nick sat at the table with Sal and me for our lunch of vegetarian sandwiches stacked high with sprouts, avocado, and tomatoes. "I'll miss this good food when they cut out the guard duty."

"Maybe you'll be free from taking care of me by Monday."

"No. There are still some suspects on our interview list. Mack and Reilly, to name two."

I sucked in a breath. "Mack? I don't think he'd harm me or steal stuff that would destroy his business. No way. Reilly, yes. He's weird, mean, hates me, and is buddies with Westphal."

"Westphal is a prime suspect, but we can't find him. Hasn't shown up for work."

Sal appeared thoughtful. "Did you tell them about Mack's past? I forgot to tell you he called today and wants you to come out to the ranch tomorrow for dinner."

Nick put his sandwich down. "We haven't found much on Mack but are compiling a profile and list of questions. I'd like you to take him up on the ranch visit so I can look around."

I felt suddenly weak at the thought of seeing him.

Nick looked at me. "Did you see a ghost?"

"Sort of. It felt like one just passed over me. I don't know quite how to say this because it makes me look stupid and naive. I thought I loved Mack before this happened." I sat back, my hands folded on the table. "Neither of you were with me at the hospital the day they took me off the vent. Mack stood by the bed all lovey-dovey and sweet, holding my injured hand, while Dr. Braden informed me of my injuries. My thoughts were muddled from the injury, surgery, and drugs. When he said, 'She lost nearly half her blood volume, but it wasn't from her brain bleed. She lost the baby.' I just about had a stroke."

Sal choked, eyes wide. Nick grimaced.

I felt tears welling, tears of humility for being so dumb. "I didn't know I was pregnant. I often miss periods because I'm so underweight. Mack told me he'd had a vasectomy, so I couldn't get pregnant. I think he wanted me pregnant, not working, and under his control."

Nick stared at me. "I saw Mack's reaction when Dr. Braden talked to you, but I didn't hear what the doctor said. What a shock."

Sal stood up. "That son of a bitch. His past has always troubled me. I know you wanted to take care of him. You're soft-hearted and trusting. He used you."

"I believed in him. His behavior is unforgiveable, but I don't think he'd ever hurt me." I thought for a moment. "I'll help, Nick. You'll be with me and it will give you time to talk to him before he knows he's a suspect."

I took a nap and then called Mack to set up a time to visit and have dinner.

We drove beneath the log entrance with AAI inscribed on the arch. "Angus Artificial Insemination is the name he uses for his primary business, but he also sells organic Angus and ships embryos everywhere." I gave Nick an overview of the buildings, the workers, and their living quarters.

Nick parked near the ranch house. Mack met us at the car and held out a hand to help me up the three plank steps to the expansive porch where the chair swing rocked after a wintry gust.

I looked around. "There's a lot of activity around the embryo barn."

"We're rounding up a hundred cows over two days. Tim is next door helping Garrett with the elk. Since he was in town and the timing is okay, I decided to have him help get my herd ready for insemination, too."

Mack placed three cups and a pot of coffee on the breakfast bar. "I had helpers all lined up, but a guy just left for Wyoming on a family emergency. That leaves me critically short."

I poured the coffee. "Is there something I could do to help?"

Nick looked at me as though I'd lost my mind.

Mack thought for a moment. "If you feel strong enough, you could be a recordkeeper for a couple of days. It's a clean job. I assigned that guy to another job and we'd have enough help."

The guard looked skeptical. "Where would she be?"

"In a clean area of the barn. It's where we run cows into confinement stalls, give them hormone shots to stimulate ovulation and use a vaginal insert to get the uterus ready for insemination. Callie could scan their ear tags to track the process on registered animals."

"Amazing. You can do that to a hundred cows in two days?" Nick's eyes wandered around the kitchen. He spun on the bar stool, peering into the great room.

Mack shrugged. "We've done as many as thirty per hour when skilled wranglers keep the cows organized and moving. With Tim and me doing the technical work, it goes fast."

"For a city guy like me, watching the process will be something to write home about." Nick motioned to the fireplace. "Beautiful rock work. You sure have a nice place out here."

"Thanks. I'll show you around later. A beef roast has been in the oven most of the day while I've been rounding up cattle." Mack pulled out a chair and held it for me to sit. "I fixed spinach lasagna for you."

Mack placed the roast and a pan of bubbling lasagna in the center of the checkered cloth draped over the oak pedestal table. Nick sat across from me. From the dining area, we looked out at the huge white embryo barn with black lettering nearly the height of the building. More pickups drove in.

I served myself two pieces. "I'm glad you made lasagna. I'm really hungry."

Nick helped himself. "I had no idea you had such a high-tech operation. You do that and cook, too. About all I can do is boil wieners."

"Hope you like it. Callie doesn't eat meat, so I've taken to eating vegetarian with a meat side dish. Pretty soon, I'll be a quiche eater."

"Not likely." I laughed and passed the lasagna to Nick.

I wondered about the procedures. "So, you want me out here in the morning?"

"Before eight, if you can make it that early. It's messy and smelly, but you won't get dirty in your job. In a week, we have to run the cows through again to remove the insert and do another injection."

Nick took another serving of beef. "What then? What's the second injection for?"

"The first one is a gonadotropin. The second one is prostaglandin to stimulate estrus. We shoot injectables into the neck muscle with a power injector. It goes fast."

"Then, you turn them loose with the bulls?"

"No. The next step is time critical. In about two days, fifty-six hours to be exact, they're ready for artificial insemination with the specific semen. That's the third step where timing is critical."

Mack got up from the table, went in his bedroom, and returned with a computer spreadsheet. "This document shows each calf we produced. They wear a tattoo and an ear tag with the birth date, registration number, and parentage." Mack scanned the list. "These are purebreds registered with the state Department of Agriculture in Helena."

He gave us an overview of the insemination process. "We try to do AI at fifty-six hours after the second injection. If it's done later, even twelve hours after standing heat, the conception rate goes way down."

I said, "I know a lot about human reproduction, at least I did right after medical school." Mack glared. We hadn't spoken further about my pregnancy.

The guard said, "You lost me. Standing heat sounds like a hot flash."

Mack said, "It is irritable, aggressive behavior in cows."

"Kind of bovine PMS?" I asked to lighten Mack's frown.

The men laughed. Mack said, "If you're interested, tomorrow I can answer a few questions and tell you more about the embryo part of the process."

Nick drove back to town. I looked over at his smile. "So, what do you think?"

"I'm still laughing about cow PMS. And I totally see your point about him being charming. It would be very easy to be taken in by him. Don't blame yourself."

"Thank you. I'm feeling bad about a lot of things. I was duped by a man I loved. Seeing him in action pulled at my heart, but I actually hate him." I sat silent till we turn on to Highway 93.

Nick looked at me. "You okay?"

"I feel like I should be talking to a shrink. My dad is dead. My rodent research stretching over years has been destroyed. My monkeys died in November after they appeared to improve with the rat treatment. I almost died. A baby I didn't know I was carrying died. Death is stalking me."

"Look at it this way. Your baby monkey is doing well, and your dog needs you. The world needs you. With your saved specimens, soon you'll be back on track."

"I know. I don't feel suicidal, but with all the pain, I wonder why I don't."

"Because you have hope and you give us all hope for the future. I understand why you want to get back to the lab. I called Sarge while you were napping and told him about us going out to Mack Janns' ranch tomorrow. He is enthused about the prospect and will pass the information on to Special Agent Hal Vater, who is in charge of the lab investigation. Vater and another guy who just arrived are going to interview Reilly tomorrow."

"I would love to see his face when they walk in. Reilly is excitable. Being under investigation will turn him into a Ferris wheel."

Chapter 33 – Harassment

Sal sent us off before seven after mushroom-spinach omelets, toast, and prune juice. Needless to say, Nick skipped the juice. He drove the seven miles south and beneath the AI International arch to the barn. Dressed in coveralls and gloves I stood along the animal chute with a scanner. From the lower rung of the fencing, I had a clear view to scan ear tags of black cows being rushed forward past Mack and Tim who injected and inserted suppositories into the frightened animals.

While I scanned, Nick wandered around the building looking at photos, and surveyed the semen storage room. Three hours of intense focus not to miss an animal left me exhausted. By the time someone took over for me, I felt shaky and needed a rest.

Nick and I walked to the ranch house for a break and sat at the table drinking coffee. A few minutes later, Mack strolled in without a word and went to the refrigerator. He pulled out a tray stacked with sandwiches. He had always been jealous. I wondered if he was simmering, and we'd have to deal with one of his outbursts. He surprised me by placing the sandwiches in front of us. "I knew we'd be hungry and busy, so I had the bunkhouse cook make these last night. He's serving all the hands during this process. Thanks for coming out to help."

I rested my feet on a chair listening to Mack's conversation with Nick as we devoured the sandwiches. "The ear tag scans Callie is doing are fed into our computer where we keep records of everything. After the insemination, we will ultrasound the uterus to see if the AI took, to see if we have evidence of embryo development."

Nick poured more coffee for all of us. "How do you get a cow to stand still for any of this?" We waited.

Mack smiled. "It's easy. We lead them into a darkened stall."

I sat back anticipating a joke. "Do you tune in a jazz station to add to the atmosphere?"

"No fancy music. The window right in front of them sort of serves as a TV for distraction." He explained the next step, a rerun of directing all the cows through the chute again at the exact time they were hormonally ready for insemination. "We remove the semen straw from the liquid nitrogen and, once thawed, insert it using shoulder-length gloves."

Nick rolled his eyes as Mack continued. "We do ultrasounds later to see if the cows are pregnant. If there are no embryos, the cow is turned out to pasture with a bull for natural insemination." He hesitated. "Are you sure you want me to be talking about this stuff after you just ate?"

"Heck, yes, if it doesn't bother Callie. My wife's an ER nurse, so I'm used to listening to some crazy stories."

I agreed. "I haven't heard all of this, so I'm interested."

Mack talked about procedural details, how they timed and collected the embryos, flushing them from each cow in about a week. "We usually get seven or eight embryos from each. Those are sorted. We freeze the perfect ones in liquid nitrogen, ready for shipping."

I told Nick a little about the embryo sorting I'd done but had never asked about calf development. "So, Mack, when will the cows deliver?"

"Angus gestation is two hundred and sixty-three days. We time them to deliver in early spring, so they'll fatten up for the fall auction."

We headed back out to the cows and worked nonstop till 6 p.m. When they'd finished, Mack brought his vet buddy Tim Baird over for a quick introduction. The sweet-talking blond cowboy about Mack's age didn't stay long enough for me to get a feeling for him. He was congenial but in an un-explained hurry.

Mack invited me and Nick to stay for dinner, but we opt-ed out and headed home since we'd be returning the follow-ing day. On the way home, Nick frowned. "Callie, how does he sell all that semen he has in the storeroom?"

"AI International has an online catalog for insemination products, embryos, organic beef, Angus cows and stud bulls. Most purchases are made that way, then UPS drives out to the ranch and picks up the shippable orders. Frozen semen is sold for ten to fifteen dollars per straw."

We rounded a sharp corner shortly before reaching Highway 93 and heading north.

"I was surprised at how much more he charges for semen from a prize bull like his favorite one named Igor. Mack gets fifty dollars or more per straw. He paid nearly a hundred thousand for Igor when he was a yearling."

"No wonder the price of hamburger has gone up."

Three days of scanning ear tags and watching AI procedures was too much physical and emotional stress. It gave Nick time to wander around both in the house and the barns while Mack was distracted, and I was busy. I wondered why in hell I agreed to help Mack after what he'd done to me. I hated being in the same room with him. It set me on edge. Nick and I both came away knowing more about the process than we cared to, but he reminded me the time spent on the ranch was valuable for the FBI investigation.

On our drive to Medicine Falls about noon on Friday, my energy surged at the thought of getting back to work. "Every minute away is time lost. Lately, I've awakened in the middle of the night wanting to be at work with my microscope, rats, and baby monkey."

"That's a little scary. Some people would call it a nightmare, but it's great Doc Braden thinks you're doing well enough to get back to what you love."

"I also want to move back to my apartment. Maybe my injuries were accidental, like I just got in the way."

"No. Think about it as attempted murder." He sounded serious. "They knew exactly what they were doing. They drugged you, fractured your skull and cut off your thumb for the print to get into the IRF. That's why you have to put up with me, remember?"

"You're right. I actually like being with you and Rex. I've spent more time with you guys than any other man." I watched for a reaction. "I'm always working, so guys never stay around me very long. I rather like being with a good-looking man carrying a weapon."

Nick flushed. "I want you safe and healthy so you can get back to those rats and save us from prions." Then he cautioned, "Maybe you should give yourself a little more time. Let's wait for the FBI's report. Look at the bright side, you'll be getting back to work soon. The bastards just slowed you down."

"My treated rats are gone. Since the break-in, I've felt so sad for them and furious at the perpetrators."

"You do sound like you could use a shrink, but remember, you didn't lose everything and you're alive."

"I know, but someone has stolen data I didn't want to share. And prions live for decades. They released deer infected with a different prion, but my animals and the tissue specimens are the cross-species form that could kill everything rapidly, including the thieves."

"Wouldn't it serve them right?"

"Maybe, but who will they take down with them? It could be the town, the region, the country ... the world." I closed my eyes and rested my head against the seat back. I sat up when we turned into town. "I'd like to stop at my apartment for some more clothes before we go to the motel."

At the Wagon Wheel a boisterous greeting from Blaze made me happy. The dog didn't seem to notice my funny appearance. When I sat on the floor in the motel office to pet her, she lay beside me and snuggled close.

The guard reached down and petted her head. "From the look in her eyes, Callie, that dog loves you."

"The feeling is mutual." I hugged her furry body. "Sal, I want to move back to my apartment as soon as I can, maybe in a week."

Sal arched her dark brows.

"Dr. Braden released me to return to the lab on Monday."

Nick turned to Sal. "Today I learned how to do AI in cattle. What do you think she'll teach me at the lab?"

Sal threw up her arms. "Hard to tell. It depends on how much you like rats."

He stepped back. "I don't do rats or mice. Snakes are okay."

I smiled at the strong gun-toting man. "I won't make you hold any rats. They're harmless, unless infected with prions."

Nick grimaced. "I'm not a happy man. I think I'll demand hazardous duty pay."

I told Sal we were heading up to the lab to give Reilly my work release.

She offered food.

I quickly answered no because I wanted to get to the lab. "We won't be gone long. Tonight, we'll go to the Wildlife Refuge for dinner."

Sal walked with us to the registration area. "So, how did Mack treat you? I've been worried."

"Okay." I looked at Nick.

"Mack seemed fine. Too busy and distracted to harass Callie."

Sal examined my knit hat. "You look cute. In a month, your hair will be about an inch long. Soon, back to your usual length." With what appeared to be an afterthought, she said, "Did you tell Nick about Mack's wife?"

Nick's eyes bored into mine as he opened the jangling office door.

Blaze and Sal followed us out to the unmarked FBI car.

I closed my car door and buckled up for the ten-mile drive up the mountain. Sal waved as Nick backed up, then drove out of town. Before we reached the highway, he jerked the wheel when he looked at me. "So, what about Mack's wife?"

I was feeling great after getting my work release, getting hugs from Sal and Blaze, and a stop at the apartment. I hated breaking the spell. "Sal thinks he killed her."

Nick pulled over and stopped. "Shit, Callie. How could you not tell us that?"

"I keep thinking it couldn't possibly be true. He cried when he told me about her leaving him and running off with one of his ranch hands. He was very sad even after a couple years. I thought that was why he wanted me with him all the time. Insecurity."

Nick shook his head and pulled back on the road. "He killed his father when he was fourteen. We verified that story. It sounded like self-defense. You said he was a sniper in the military. We're still working on that. Anything else?"

"I guess you should know he has a lot of guns, including an Uzi. I've seen them in his gun safe in his bedroom. Said he's a collector and used to hunt."

Nick drove in silence at first, then said, "In Montana, that could be normal, but they're red flags."

I fell asleep trying to recall anything aberrant in Mack's recent behavior.

At the lab, we headed directly to Dr. Reilly's office. Just to irk him, I walked in hat in hand with my shaved head bare and surgical wound exposed.

Reilly sat pawing through an array of papers strewn across his desk, some on FBI letterhead. When he saw us, he stood up, shoving his chair unceremoniously against the bookcase behind his desk.

"What are you doing here, Archer? You look frightening. I told you before, I can't have you disrupting the staff by reminding them of the devastation you've brought on us." He snapped, "What the hell do you want?"

"I'm here with wonderful news. My neurosurgeon released me to return to work on Monday." I placed the work release in front of him on top of the papers. "I thought you'd be delighted."

"Archer, you're brain-damaged and can't be trusted. You're a liability."

Nick stepped forward as if to protect me from the verbal assault.

Reilly didn't move toward me, but his barbed words continued. "I was just reading the FBI overview of their investigation of the laboratory breach. Their conclusion is: *Insider knowledge led to the success of this penetration.* Until proven otherwise, you're my prime suspect. I don't trust you."

"Thank you for your kind words of support. I have a witness to your accusations. From here, I am going directly to Human Resources to report your verbal abuse and unprofessional behavior. I'll also report the accusations directly to Headquarters."

Seeing I was on the attack, Nick stepped back.

I asked, "Where's your friend Larry Westphal? He should be on your short list of suspects."

Reilly's jaw clenched.

I threw another barb. "I told the FBI about your relationship with him and about your elk ranch investment with Garrett Adcock. Don't worry. They're already investigating you. It does make one wonder why you as a scientist would invest in an unstable local business. Take your time, I'm sure you'll come up with an interesting answer."

Reilly's eyes squinted in anger. "God damn you. That's why they showed up unannounced. I thought they were here about the break-in with news about who did it. Instead, they made me feel like a criminal in the laboratory I direct."

"I hope you were truthful. So, where is Larry? He was drunk at the Christmas party. Did he fall off the wagon again?" I put my hands on my hips, waiting for an answer that never materialized.

Nick and I walked out, leaving the flustered man gripping his desk. Nick whispered in my ear, "Good job, Doc." We walked down the hall to HR, where I filed a complaint stating details of the harassment and accusations, along with a request that copies be sent to Paul Wilder and Headquarters.

The HR director took my written complaint. She appeared hesitant. "Are you sure you want to do this, Dr. Archer? Director Reilly can be vindictive."

"I've already found that out. This is not the first time he's threatened me. He has also publicly defamed me to staff members. This time I'll press charges if I need to. I have witnesses."

Nick signed my report as a witness. I emphasized to HR, "I'm calling Paul Wilder tonight. He'll expect a scanned copy by email tomorrow."

We walked down the hall to the coffee room. My cohorts cheered when we walked in. Some of them kidded me about my dark stubble not yet being long enough to cover the scar.

I made an announcement to their table. "I just left Reilly's office. He told me I'd scare you and didn't want me back." Their voices melded into protests and head shaking. One of the men stood and put his arm around my shoulders. "You have our support. You come to work whenever you're strong enough."

One of the guys stormed out. "I'm going to tell him he is out of line. We want you back."

After a cup of coffee, I dragged Nick into the IRF dressed in a protective jumpsuit, booties, and gloves. He had full approval through Security but would have to wait for me in my office outside the lab area because of bio restrictions.

Chapter 34 - Déjà Vu

Nick and I entered the high-risk integrated building where research on the most infectious dangerous agents was confined. He remained hesitant even after I explained the precautions for entry. I was his charge and he had to keep me safe even in the off-limits research area. I told him the Level 3 biocontainment office area on the ground floor was safe due to the strict rules. But even with all the precautions, he wouldn't be allowed in the higher, Level 4, area that allowed no one but the highest trained staff. I assured him he wouldn't be going upstairs where they performed work wearing environmentally controlled space suits with individual oxygen supplies.

"Well, that's a relief. I've always thought being an astronaut would be amazing, but claustrophobia would get to me if I had to be in a bubble suit."

Nick sat at my desk in the office located just off the hall while I surveyed the devastation. He explained, "I don't even like being in this jumpsuit because I can't get at my gun." He pulled open the front and folded back the fabric so he could reach his underarm holster. "This place gives me the creeps. Get me out of here as soon as you can."

"I will." I looked around. "The office wasn't a prime target except for my computer. I'll start here. This will be your spot while I clean the lab. I don't trust Reilly to have cleaned it adequately. Since my life depends on avoiding unseen contamination, I want to do it myself."

I checked the office. "This shows what a great job Reilly and Joy did cleaning. There's print dust everywhere from the forensics team."

Nick checked to be sure the door into the hallway had locked behind us. "The dust isn't the problem. It's the prions I'm worried about." He settled back into the chair with his hands folded in his lap.

I talked to him as I worked. "Here we are in the most secure high-risk NIH compound in the U.S., yet my project and research animals were destroyed. At least the baby monkey remained safe in the veterinary compound."

The likelihood of contamination in the office, away from the lab animals and specimens, was low, but I usually wore scrubs. Prion specimens never left the lab except inside liquid nitrogen bottles or special pathology containers. After purifying my desktop, other surfaces and the bathroom with the lye solution, I wiped everything again with Clorox.

I'd purchased a piece of Plexiglas before the break-in to protect the desk surface from my pet rat's cage. I removed its adherent plastic wrap and covered the desk with it. Behind books on the lowest shelf of a corner cabinet, I found my father's untouched biopsies in liquid nitrogen canisters. Reilly didn't find them.

Feeling more positive, I added a mask, gloves, and shoe coverings before entering the laboratory. Nick removed his arms from the gown sleeves and relaxed while I set to work thoroughly cleaning the lab.

After defrosting the freezers and cleaning the insides of the refrigerators, I placed anything submersible, including animal cages, one at a time into the largest sink filled with lye solution and hot water. In the end, after scrubbing granite countertops, cabinets, microscope and my stool with lye and Clorox, my eyes burned.

The granite countertops sparkled, and the floor looked clean. I stacked the clean animal cages in a corner. The refrigerators and freezers were nearly empty, but I'd found a small plastic package on the bottom freezer shelf and scraped off the ice. The label said it contained a portion of prion-infected tissue from the original source, a rat specimen I'd infected from the zookeeper's brain.

Prions survived all but physical destruction by lye or fire. These prions would still be infectious and could be used to continue my work on the cross-species prion. The infected tissue stored in my refrigerator-freezer at the apartment was safe, too. I wasn't crazy. It was inside double vacuum-sealed bags to avoid contaminating anything and to avoid freezer burn.

I ask you, would anyone touch a package labeled *lutefisk?*

I'd planned for the worst after my paranoia had spiked a few months before the break-in.

I didn't trust Larry Westphal. His behavior had seemed suspicious to the vet techs and Bernie, too.

With Larry and Clint Reilly being old buddies, I feared their camaraderie could be at the heart of the lab break-in. But, why would they orchestrate such a thing and kill people?

It made no sense.

The blood loss anemia made me weak. I rested on my high microscope stool whenever I felt short of breath. Pacing myself was something I'd never had to do. The cleaning took almost three hours, something I could have done in half the time before the assault.

Invisible prions could be anywhere. Like bacteria or viruses on hands and surfaces, minute quantities of protein could spread to large areas. I didn't know what the intruders might have touched. Live rats housed in my lab, including the treated mother with newborn pups, were all potentially infectious. Reilly, in his wisdom, had come in and *cleaned*. If there was contamination, he had likely smeared it around instead cleaning it up.

I filled the autoclave with instruments and glassware for sterilization at high heat with steam after the lye treatment. While waiting for the autoclave to finish and exhaust, I sat down at my microscope. The light on the scope had burned out. A scorched, cracked slide sat beneath the lens. I must have left it on the night of the break-in.

Foggy bits and pieces of that night drifted in and out of my memory bank.

I finished the cleaning and returned to the office area.

Nick appeared relieved to see me.

"The lab may have been perfectly clean before I started. Maybe the intruders were knowledgeable enough to avoid contaminating themselves. I couldn't take that chance."

Brie's cage sat empty. "I wonder what happened to my pet rat and the mom with a new litter."

"You had a rat in this office?"

"A pet. They're intelligent and cuddly, just like a little kitty. I am so sad she is gone."

"Oh, Callie, I think you spend way too much time locked in here."

As I straightened the books hiding the nitrogen bottles, a yelp startled me.

Nick jumped to his feet. "A goddamned rat just ran over my foot! I hate rats."

I heard a noise from my desk where he'd been sitting and opened a lower drawer. There sat Brie. She cowered in a corner amid a mess of crackers and wrappers from trail mix bars. After being frightened by Nick, she'd crawled back inside her food haven from beneath the desk

"Brie, baby, you're alive! You found my stash!" I picked up the rat. "You're okay. They didn't get you." I showed her to the guard. "Isn't she adorable? Don't worry. She won't hurt you. I kept her isolated in my office and she sat on my shoulder as I worked."

Nick backed away, obviously worried about being close to a rat.

I put Brie in her cage. "I'm ready to leave. From your pale face, you're ready, too."

I left fresh water and rat food. "She probably got to water in the bathroom, or she'd be dead."

Nick removed his gown and went to the door. "Your rat gives me the creeps."

I discarded our gowns in bags located in the garbage vestibule where they were collected and burned daily. I'd be happier when my cleaning towels and the gowns were nothing but ash.

We left the IRF and entered the Admin Building via the coffee room like I always did. "How about some coffee before we drive to town?"

The guard held out a hand for the cup I offered him. "I haven't had my quota."

"Are you hungry?"

"Starving. Coffee will help."

"I'll see if Bernie can join us for a minute. And I'll make a fresh pot."

Nick sat at a table.

Bernie arrived a few minutes later. "Don't you look cute? Not many people look that good without hair. At least it won't blow in your eyes in the wind." The cheerful woman greeted Nick. "It's been quiet around here since the break-in. I haven't seen Larry Westphal in the vet compound recently."

One smelly pot had concentrated coffee tar scorched on the bottom. I placed it in the sink and filled it with water to soak. I found a clean pot and started the coffee brewing while we chatted.

Nick said, "You know, Callie, this is where they found you on the floor that night. Do you have any recollection of being here?"

I pondered his question and went to see if the coffee was ready. As I reached for the fresh pot, I felt movement behind me.

My heart pounded.

A ghost image, a strange smell, a struggle. My head hurt, and my vision and hearing dimmed. I felt a piercing pain in my left hand.

Falling. Arms around me. I fought.

Sensing the cold tile floor stimulated my brain. I opened my eyes to blurred images of Bernie and Nick looking down on me. Bernie placed a cold, wet towel on my forehead.

My vision improved. My hearing returned. They helped me to a chair.

Bernie asked, "What happened? Are you all right?"

Nick looked worried. "Maybe I should take you to the town doctor."

"You're white as a ghost." Bernie looked closely at my eyes. 'You look like you saw one."

My hands trembled. My eyes focused on the healing stump of my left thumb. "I think I'm all right. I came close to fainting. Thanks for catching me."

"You weren't *close,* Callie, you fainted dead away, and you don't look so good right now. I'm glad you didn't bump your head." The guard stared at me. "I really think you should see a doctor."

I looked around the room, stopping on the coffee pot.

My brain searched dim images floating in the periphery, not clear enough to recognize. I shivered.

Nick and Bernie looked at each other and back at me, waiting for me to speak.

"I think that scorched coffee smell triggered my memory of head pain and searing thumb pain, a déjà vu moment. Nick, did you come up behind me? My brain sensed danger. Very weird. I felt the attack again, but I couldn't make out who it was."

Chapter 35 – Fear

A panic deep in my core surged to the surface whenever I thought of the break-in. I tried to block the break-in from my mind for fear I'd faint again. I wondered if, like Rudy, I was developing PTSD or, like Mack, some strange residual emotional element, which in his case came from abuse or his sniper activities.

Nick's eyes focused on my clenched fists. "Let's get out of here. I think Reilly set you off. You don't need this stress."

"I've never been prone to fainting, but I'm ready to leave." By the time we got back to town, I felt good. Seeing Sal and Blaze lowered my anxiety. I called Dr. Braden to discuss the fainting and make sure it wasn't a complication from the head injury. He asked me to meet him in the clinic early Monday morning or to go to the ER if I developed a headache or fainted again.

We took Sal out to dinner. Blaze and I rode in back. Just her presence distracted me from my fears. I wanted to be well and get back to work, not worry about my health, so ate a double order of creamed spinach for good measure. Sleep came easy, probably due to exhaustion and knowing a guard was close by. I was spending so much time with the guards, I knew I'd miss them.

Rex took over Monday morning and drove me to Missoula. We talked all the way. He filled me in on some of the interview with Dr. Reilly. The investigation had turned cold.

Dr. Braden allayed my concerns, agreeing it was probably a strange combination of events that brought on the fainting episode. On our drive to the lab, I mulled over all the things I had to do. I made a checklist that included calling Hugh Dalen and Paul Wilder.

Having to face Reilly again dragged my thoughts back to the negative environment he'd created at the lab.

Rex and I stopped in to talk with Rudy, and I told him about the fainting episode. "I think it was where you found me after I was attacked. I'm beginning to remember who did this to me."

Rudy got up and closed the door. "With Rohypnol in your blood, is that possible?"

"I suppose it depends how high the level was at a particular time. Maybe Hugh Dalen would know or someone in his lab could tell me my level and correlate the timing. I need to talk to him anyway."

"I think you're frowning for good reason." Rudy studied my face. "Bernie told me Reilly has been harassing you. Remember when I told you he cleaned your lab? I was surprised he wouldn't order someone else to do it."

"Me, too. And, that he took his untrained secretary with him instead of following strict bio-protocols. What was he trying to hide?" I got up to go. "I don't know what he was thinking! Most of the time Joy acts like a ditsy blonde, but I'm getting suspicious about her, too."

Rex laughed. "Joy's a looker. Reilly wasn't thinking about typing skills when he hired her."

From my office, I called Paul Wilder to see if he'd received my HR report against Reilly. He had read it and was furious. He'd called Headquarters about it. He had no information on Larry Westphal but had heard the FBI investigation was at a standstill.

On an early February evening Hal Vater called to report the FBI had terminated my bodyguard protection because of no identified ongoing risk. "I thought it was time to set you free and not have guards with you everywhere you go."

Rex and Sal listened to my side of the conversation.

"I have mixed feelings about not having guards but understand your reasoning. I was waiting for the okay to move back to my apartment, but now that I can do it, I'm scared."

Hal gave me his personal cell number with instructions to call at any time.

I didn't want Rex and Nick to leave. The safety of having one of them close during the weeks when I'd felt frail had been reassuring. The thought of losing them produced a stab of sadness and insecurity.

"You're not happy?"

I shook my head. "I'll miss you and the comfort of knowing you're with me."

Rex frowned. "Hal called me and Nick this afternoon. It makes me uneasy because we still don't know who the enemy is. I don't want to leave, but the least I can do is help you and Sal move your things to the apartment."

Sal put an arm around me. "You'll just be down the street and will see me every day when you drop Blaze off. Look at it as graduation. You are stronger and meaner every day, but, know what? I'm still worried."

Her hug and words infused strength into my resolve to get back to normal. But then, for me, what was normal? After all the instability and uncertainty I'd seen recently, I wasn't sure.

"I won't be far away and will take good care of Blaze when you are working. Just let me know anytime you need anything. You are ready for this. Be strong."

After we moved everything inside the apartment, Sal and I followed Rex out to his car. Nick drove up and got out. "I couldn't go on to a new assignment without saying goodbye."

Blaze walked around the men, wagging and getting a few pets. Nick squatted down to hug her. "Take good care of Callie."

These were the same words Dad said in the video; they stabbed my heart.

The two guards were deserting me like Dad had. Tears welled. I felt small and alone.

Rex said, "The FBI has strict orders of discipline about not fraternizing with the people we guard. Don't tell our boss, Dr. Archer, but we want you to know Nick and I have special feelings for you. We'll miss you."

Nick wiped a tear from my cheek. "Carry bear spray. Keep Blaze with you. Lock your doors."

I smiled through tears while being crushed in a hug from two men wearing stiff Kevlar vests and weapons. "I love you guys. Thank you."

Sal and I waved at two disappearing black SUVs.

Chapter 36 – Reflections

As February faded into March, brilliant white snow gave way to icy ridges along roadways. I worked hard, designing a new rat study and arranging to get enough guaranteed monoclonal antibodies for another small primate study. Amo thrived, evidence of the disease in her decreased. I took most weekends off and drove to Missoula a few times to meet up with Hugh Dalen. One lazy Saturday, Blaze and I drove north out of town, heading to the Bitterroot River boat landing.

Along the way, winter wheat rose green in expansive fields beneath a morning sun. I welcomed warm weather that would bring wildflowers and vees of geese flying north.

So much had changed since my arrival in Montana in late fall. Less than a year earlier, life in Cleveland had been routine. Dad and I consulted with each other, often talking daily. At the end of a humid Midwest summer, activists hit my lab and changed everything, sending me to the Montana Ridge Lab. Dad's untimely death in late fall left me in grief. My monkeys died. The break-in left death and chaos at the Ridge Lab, destroying my research and nearly killing me. I ran fingers across my constant reminders, the numb scar on my scalp now hidden from view by inch-long curls and the ugly base of my missing thumb.

Thoughts transported me back before my injuries to a safe city high-rise, then to a ranch in Montana with an unpredictable man who had enticed me with his good looks and charm, then crushed me with his lies.

I drove down to the river and parked, letting Blaze explore while I sat on a boulder listening to water rushing over stones near the shore, taking in earthy fresh smells of the country around me. Above, turkey vultures wheeled in lofty winds over fields to the south toward Mack's ranch. They circled down over something on the ground. I wondered what the scavengers had found for breakfast. My thoughts segued to one of my visits to the ranch after the community meeting, when Mack was teaching me how to ride. I'd sat on the porch swing waiting for him after he'd received a call from his men to go out to the barn.

Three angry male voices, one of them Mack's, their words indistinct, had carried across the driveway. I was curious about what was going on, so I walked out to the barn and around the end of the building out of sight and out of the wind where it abutted the corral. Curious black cows moved closer to stare at me.

The door opened. "If we can't trust our own people, who can we trust?" Mack's voice increased. "Tim's not Indian, but he's one of us. Indians, first. Marines forever."

What were they talking about? I pressed myself against the building, listening.

The men got into Mack's pickup and sped south. He'd left me alone without a word, so I drove back to town.

Mack had called me later the same day. "Could you please come back out to the ranch right away? I need help with sorting in the embryo barn. We're behind, and I have to get some big shipments out."

I didn't feel like leaning over a microscope, but he sounded anxious. I agreed to come after eating. I changed into jeans and a long-sleeved shirt, armed with a stomach full of yogurt and fruit, I had driven back out to the ranch. I asked a beautiful Native woman for a quick refresher. She tested my skills before releasing me to proceed on my own.

I felt like an outsider. None of the three techs talked to me, but then they seldom spoke to each other. Sorting was interesting, but I felt an uncomfortable silence. No happy chatter or camaraderie existed among the four of us sitting side-by-side at microscopes for hours.

Mack walked in. "Ladies, three more embryo orders just came in. Thanks to all of you for pushing ahead and increasing our stores." He walked to a counter where dozens of liquid nitrogen containers sat near me and scanned a logbook. "Based on this, we have more than enough to meet the new orders, but we still need to build our supply and finish what we have started. They embryos don't wait."

A man snatched open the side door and signaled to Mack. He went outside and closed the door. In the hum of their voices, I made out only one word, "elk."

I stood at the door and watched Mack's double-cab pickup speed out to the road and turn south. He hadn't returned by quitting time when the sun dipped behind the Bitterroots, sending a golden shimmer across the yard as I walked to the house. I turned up the thermostat, flipped on some lights, and put a pot of water on a burner for tea. While the water heated, I stood on the porch scanning his property, wondering where he'd gone.

I went back inside to make a peanut butter sandwich, and then donned a jacket and dragged a lap robe out to the swing. I rocked in the waning light, sipping steaming tea and enjoying the fresh air, when I heard a vehicle approach and then speed on past. A white pickup headed north carrying an elk carcass with its stiff legs jutting skyward.

When Mack returned, I was snuggled in his recliner with more tea, a blanket, and a medical journal on emerging infectious diseases. I found it interesting to see what other researchers around the world were doing. He opened the door with such force it struck the wall and startled me.

"Hi. What's up? Was that you driving past with a dead elk?"

"Garrett found one of his prize bulls down at the back of his property. We couldn't tell what happened to it. The guys winched it into my truck and we took it to the rendering plant."

"You weren't gone long. The plant must be real close."

"On a side road about two miles from here. It always stinks out there. I'm glad the wind usually blows out of the west and carries the smell away from us." He disappeared into the bedroom. After making a couple of phone calls out of my hearing, he emerged in clean clothes. "I'm taking a delivery to Missoula. UPS can't make it in time to get the order on the next flight. I'm sorry I have to leave again."

Before I left that day, I had walked along the AI corral and into the huge barn with numerous empty stalls where they performed the inseminations. The office and sorting area sat empty. The door to the large semen storeroom stood ajar as if someone had left in a hurry, failing to secure it. Shelves of liquid nitrogen canisters with hundreds of valuable semen products made me wonder why he didn't keep the place under lock and key.

Anyone could have walked in and left with an armful of canisters.

A couple of pickups were parked near the bunkhouse. No human activity, just cattle sounds, the occasional chirp of birds and the yips of far-off coyotes.

It all seemed strange, eerie, after the bustling activity over the previous weeks when work had continued into the evenings. Then silence.

One busy evening when Mack had invited me out for dinner, he had barely stopped to eat. He introduced two Native American men about his age who had come to the house upset over something. The three spoke in whispers. Mack pulled them out on the porch to talk and then bounded down the steps behind them without an explanation, returning short of breath about half an hour later. "We had a problem with a ranch hand. They needed my help."

"Are those men Pekisko?"

"No," he'd said, "they're from other tribes. We got back together after the military."

A week later, Mack showed me his collection of weapons. I wondered why he had so many guns, especially the Uzi I'd seen when we first met. I'd never been around weapons except to do some target practicing on the ranch with him. It made me uncomfortable knowing there were so many weapons in the house. I'd asked him, "Why do you and your ranch hands walk around with pistols strapped to your belts? It's safe around here. Guns make me nervous."

The conversation that followed didn't ease my anxiety. He'd said, "Get used to it. We never know when we'll run across a varmint or a rattlesnake."

I'd felt better after he taught me to shoot, but I needed more education to feel comfortable with guns. I admired Mack's accuracy. His shots were dead center in the chest or head on our human silhouette target. I asked him if I'd ever get to be as good.

"Sure. It's easy. Just takes a steady hand and practice. Growing up on the reservation with a small hunting rifle in my hand, I killed deer for food my grandmother fixed for us. I was a good shot." Mack had given me a wicked laugh. "After killing the man attacking my mother, I realized the power I had in these hands and joined the Marines. I spent a couple years working my way up to sergeant in charge of a sniper platoon. I'm really a nice guy, but I learned how to be a cold-blooded killer."

"You scare me."

It was as if he was trying to reassure me. "That's all behind me now, but for some, after their experiences in the military they never adjust and are left with demons. The guys that work here were aimless, sleeping on the streets, ducking unseen bullets. I gave them a new life on the ranch, lives with purpose."

He said his grandmother had hated him joining the military but accepted his decision. She feared he'd be killed, and he assured her all the teaching she had drilled into his young mind wouldn't be lost. He would carry on Native traditions.

Blaze shook icy water on me after her swim in the river and brought me back to the present. I drove to see Sal. We talked about my freedom and being back in my apartment. She suggested a walk. I had trouble keeping up with her. My dad had died at sixty-nine. I figured Sal was about ten years younger than Dad, but she was in terrific physical shape. She talked as fast as she walked. "We should take more walks. It will build up your endurance."

Back at the apartment, I played ball with Blaze and then roamed around straightening things. I opened the gun safe to be sure Dad's journals were secure and placed the all-important thumb drive I'd saved from the burglar inside for safekeeping.

Living in Dad's home required some adjustment. I felt uneasy. Seeing his journals in the safe made me lonesome. It had been months since his death in September and more than two months since the lab breach. If only I'd had developed the treatment working on Amo sooner and used it for him. I awakened in a nightmare of trying to save a dying baby monkey that morphed into a dream state of saving my own baby's life, a little girl with dark curls. I awakened in a cold sweat and reached over to the other side of the bed. My hand found Blaze's fur.

Reassured by her presence, before returning to sleep my mind tracked back through recent months. I'd been underweight, grieving the loss of my father, exhausted, and so intent on a prion cure that before the lab break-in, I often forgot to eat. My menses stopped, but that had happened before. I knew, now, that my periods stopped because I was pregnant, not from secondary amenorrhea like I'd experienced previously, similar to anorexics or runners who stop menstruating because of excessive exercise and poor nutrition.

Food had never been a priority for me, but how could a physician be so dumb as to be pregnant and not realize it? I guess I had too much on my mind to worry about myself.

Mother had harped on me to eat right. She never bought chips or salty or fattening food. There was always fruit, yogurt, and healthy bread for snacks. We ate meat when I was young, but when Dad's prion research brought him to the United Kingdom, they gave up meat. The risks were too high to tempt fate. Mom was creative with vegetarian meals, but her art interests and photography filled the long hours she spent alone while Dad worked.

My years of schooling kept us apart, but our family was close. Newsy emails were electronic hugs. When I came home from college for a visit, Mom railed at me about needing to eat more. I smiled, "Hey, Mom. Look at you. Maybe you should follow your own advice." We wore the same clothes and same shoe size, and in baby photos, we looked identical.

I'd never paid much attention to personal needs. Never had a manicure or a massage. Sometimes I cut my own hair, not wanting to take time away from work to go to a beauty salon. I'd pushed on with a nerdy focus on science and disease. Now, with both parents gone and alone, I found solace with Sal and Blaze, my companions, my new family.

I decided to go out to the ranch on Sunday and talk with Mack about the pregnancy and his lying about the vasectomy. I wanted my mind clear of distracting thoughts. Spending time in his presence with Rex at my side calmed my fear but left me wary because of Mack's charisma. His size and control issues weighed heavy, but I didn't think he'd hurt me. I had to confront him about his lies, alone.

I hoped that Rex's visits to the ranch had given the investigative team some additional information. I thought I'd hear about it from Mack if they had showed up at the ranch to question him. I pictured him blowing up and blaming me for involving him.

I brought Blaze over to Sal's before heading to the ranch. She didn't want me to go and offered to go with me. I assured her I'd be back soon with the difficult discussion behind me. I called Mack to see if he was up for a visit. He sounded positive.

The drive was peaceful enough but seeing the AI arch entrance increased my heartrate. As I drove toward the house, Mack ran out the door and jumped in my car. "We have to get over to Garrett's."

I drove back out and turned south. "What's wrong?"

"He just called for help with a guy stomped by a bull elk. Two of his hands were starting early to round up some of the cows for AI so Tim could start the process this morning."

I said, "I hope he called 9-1-1 for help. There isn't much we can do if the man is seriously injured."

Mack directed me to the turnoff about a mile south. We found Garrett in a corral kneeling by a motionless cowboy lying on the ground. We ran inside the stockade through a tall metal gate. A horseman herded elk away from us.

I tried to recall ER training. I never did like trauma. That's why I went into internal medicine and infectious disease study where I had time to ponder and consider differential diagnoses, not just jump into action, thinking on the run. But anyone could see the cowboy was dead. His neck was bent at an awkward angle. Wide-open dead eyes.

I pulled up his bloody yellow T- shirt revealing a caved in chest and swollen belly. I checked a carotid pulse. None.

"He's dead, Garrett. How long ago did this happen?"

"Ten minutes at the most. He'd dismounted to tighten a stirrup when the elk charged and stepped on him. He didn't have a chance." He looked for the other rider. "I'm glad his partner could drive it away, but it was too late."

Mack scowled. "This will be bad for your business. It'll be all over the news."

"It's clearly an accident, not foul play. Could've happened anywhere. I know the sheriff. He'll cover for me. I'll go call him." Garrett turned away. "Thanks for coming over."

We expressed our condolences and left him and the man's partner to handle the problem.

I started the Subaru. "For an accidental death like that, they'll have to call a coroner to pronounce him. His body will go to the state lab."

Mack slammed a fist on his thigh. "Damn state agents will be all over Garrett's place trying to close him down."

His agitation and anger worried me. We walked into the ranch house. Mack grabbed a chair at the table. "Here, have a chair. Let's sit down and talk to get it over with."

This was the moment I had wanted yet dreaded.

Mack appeared grimy and mean. Based on the look of his clothing and dirty skin, I wondered if he'd been wrestling steers. Would this be an adult conversation or a blow-out?

"What do you have to say for yourself? You're released to return to work, and your sweetie-pie guard is gone. He's not here to protect you from the big bad Indian." He studied my face, as if anticipating an outburst. "Remember, I love you and you killed our baby. That's the starting point. We have a long way to go to make amends."

I had difficulty finding words after the threatening beginning and proceeded with caution. "First of all, I trusted you. How could you lie to me about a vasectomy?"

He glared and pounded on the table.

"Stop it. You lied and impregnated me on purpose to control me."

Mack's knuckles blanched across his closed fists.

I felt threatened and pushed my chair back thinking of Sal's stories about Mack's wife. "I wouldn't have terminated the pregnancy, but before the lab break-in I'd decided to end our relationship because of your violence and controlling behavior. Wanting me to quit my life's work." I pushed further back.

Mack jumped up. His chair screeched on the floor. "Rat Lady has it her way. Get out, bitch." He walked outside, letting the screen door slam. His boots reverberated on the porch steps. I stood on the porch watching him stomp toward the corral.

I sighed in relief inside my car with the doors locked, driving to Medicine Falls on my journey to a new life in Montana. My breathing slowed as I put more distance between me and Mack.

Sal poured two glasses of the wine Mack had left me as a gift. We celebrated my successful end to any further contact with him. I left with Blaze, ready to sleep and return to work.

Chapter 37 - Good and Bad

I unlocked my apartment door, turned on a dim light, then locked us inside. The dead bold I installed after the break-in brought comfort. Following a hot shower, I crawled beneath the down comforter, pushing Blaze over to make room for me.

The next morning, I awakened refreshed and ready for my first half-day back at work. When I dropped Blaze off, Sal invited me to come for dinner that night. With a scone from the Coffee Outpost and an Americano, I started my drive up to the Ridge Lab at about ten-thirty, recalling the exhilaration of my first day at work in Montana. Now, I faced a new beginning.

New NIH security officers guarding the compound went out of their way to be friendly after I showed my ID.

Rudy stood in the doorway. "Welcome back! Video surveillance is up and running." He explained that security had improved, with more guards and motion sensors. "Don't be picking your nose or doing other unladylike things, Doc. We'll have it all on camera. Big Brother really is watching you."

"Actually, I like the idea. You'll be able to see what I do with my time and not just stalk my travels electronically."

"You're always busier than the others Dr. Callie. I'm worried you'll return to your normal work schedule."

"Back to normal? I'll have to figure out what the new normal is going to be."

Sarge walked up to us. He looked around to be sure no one could hear him. "Any cure for prion disease in the near future? I'm starving for a good steak."

I laughed and suggested we go have lunch. I wasn't hungry after eating the scone on the way up the hill, but I wanted to spend time with them before starting work.

I looked at Sarge's waistline as we walked down the hall. "You've lost weight." His shirt hung so loose I could barely make out the lines of his Kevlar vest.

"Fifteen pounds." He rubbed his flat belly. "Now that the heat is off, with no arrest prospects in sight and nobody dropping over dead from prion disease, I'm thinking it's okay to go back to eating rare steak. What do you think, Doc?"

"You look good with that weight off, Sarge. There is no evidence local meat is contaminated, but it's like Russian roulette. You might get the bullet, and then again, you might not. If I were you, I'd eat fish."

"Maybe the people who broke in were an inept violent group without prion knowledge." Rudy looked at Sarge and me for our reactions. "But I think they knew what they wanted and had a plan. We just don't know what it is yet." He ordered a salad and bread. "Leah and Cole and I are still working on the venison I took last fall, but I'm not hunting anymore. We're switching to chicken and fish."

After I ordered lentil soup and bread, Sarge hung his head. "I'll have the same. This could put a real crimp in the Testicle Festival and eating cowboy caviar down the road at Rock Creek." We all sat down, and he continued, "The Beast Feast in the fall might end up serving tofu."

We all laughed and were still laughing when Reilly's appearance flipped our laughter switch to off. Uninvited, he sat down at our table. "You were certainly having a good time. I thought I'd better come and see what was so funny."

Sarge chuckled. "Serving tofu at the Beast Feast."

"You are sick. That kind of talk will provoke total panic. Anyone who doesn't eat meat is crazy." Reilly took a bite of his burger.

I looked straight at him. "What is Stan Heath as regional director of Fish Wildlife and Parks doing about the deer that were released in December? Have the FBI and Homeland Security clued him in on the high risk of spreading Chronic Wasting Disease in this area directly from the Ridge Lab? Have you demanded an organized hunt to kill all the deer in this area to stop potential spread? You wanted to hide all the information. If people die, it's your fault."

I got up to leave the table. Sarge spouted, "I read recently vegetarians live longer than meat eaters. My grandmother was a Seventh Day Adventist and lived to be a hundred."

I addressed Sarge, "I hate to tell you this, but a recent study showed prions are taken up from the soil into vegetables, including spinach and tomatoes."

My comment put terror in his eyes. "That's horrible. Soon we won't have anything safe to eat."

Rudy sipped coffee from his thermal cup. "Dr. Callie sets a good example for all of us. You cut out red meat and lost weight in the process."

Sarge pretended to savor a bite of spinach and directed a comment to Reilly. "I was telling them I'm about to fall off the wagon and start eating raw steak."

Reilly added ketchup to his burger. "None of this is funny, Callie. You shouldn't even be here after your brain injury and talking about this topic is inappropriate. No wonder I don't trust your judgment."

I couldn't let his comment stand. "Dr. Reilly, we were discussing public information about mad cow and Chronic Wasting Disease. I wish we had an easy way to test live animals to make our food supply safer."

"Yeah, it would be nice if somebody came up with a urine test like they had for Leah's pregnancy. Then we could easily tell if an animal was infected." Rudy sipped his coffee. "But it would be difficult to get a deer or a steer to piss in a cup, don't you think?"

I turned to Rudy. "It would, but researchers are working on that exact test. We need a quick, easy test to diagnose early. Diseased cows that appear healthy probably enter our food chain every day at the big slaughterhouses."

Sarge stared at me. "I'm eatin' fish."

"That's ridiculous!" Reilly supported his statement. "Our food supply couldn't be safer, and even the wildlife is fine. I just read the statistics put out by the Department of Agriculture and the Beef Growers' Association."

I chided him. "Consider the source. It takes about three years for cattle and more than a year for deer to show symptoms." I watched for his reaction. "The diseased ones without symptoms can mix in with all the others. Infected meat is diluted and hard to trace. It's as simple as that."

Reilly choked and spit a bite of burger into a napkin.

I said to Reilly, "You're a high-risk lab director. What the hell have you been doing to keep people safe? You need to hear this. I called Hugh Dalen at the state lab over the weekend. The CDC just released the information. They identified another human prion death in Wapiti County, Idaho, just a few miles away. That makes three in two years—two in the past few months."

Dr. Reilly's expression changed to shock.

I added, "I'm wondering about Larry Westphal. Have you heard from him?"

"Larry hasn't been here for three months. I guess the holiday temptations were too great. When he missed a meeting after the New Year's break, I called and found him in rehab. I've called him since, but his phone's been disconnected."

I suggested, "Maybe he's in a long-term facility now because he failed the first spin-dry. Some rehab programs block all outside contact."

"We shouldn't be discussing Larry, but I am worried. If you hear from him, please call me." Reilly started toward the door. "I'll get ahold of Stan Heath and the Governor."

"I will. But I'd be the last person Larry would ever call."

Paul Wilder at the Human Prion Center in Cleveland telephoned. "Hi, Callie. I figured I'd find you back at work. I can't believe the FBI stopped providing you a bodyguard."

"I'm back at work part-time. This is my first day."

"The details that you were critically injured, and two guards were killed didn't make it to our departmental memo. Your mandated move to the most secure facility known to man nearly got you killed, and they're keeping it quiet here."

"We now have full video surveillance and more security."

"Has Reilly given you any more trouble?"

"He stopped by the cafeteria a few minutes ago, and in the presence of NIH security he told me I shouldn't be working after a brain injury because he said he doesn't trust my judgment."

"I'd call that harassment. I'm furious he was so incompetent he didn't have the Ridge Lab surveillance system finalized. You'd been there for months."

"I try to avoid him."

"How are things otherwise?"

"My research is going great guns. Note the Montana slang I'm picking up."

Paul laughed.

"The baby monkey is thriving, and I'm ecstatic."

"That's the best news I've heard in years."

"Have you heard anything about Larry Westphal?"

"After you left Cleveland, Larry Westphal III, the jerk, convinced someone in rehab he was doing well and got out ahead of schedule. That's when they sent him to Montana. I haven't heard anything lately. So, are both Reilly and Westphal harassing you now?"

"No. Westphal has gone missing. I think that is suspicious, but being paranoid about them probably saved my research. I'd hidden a pure PrF sample from the infected zookeeper's brain and saved electronic copies of all my data."

"Thank God you didn't lose your work! What does the F stand for?"

"I made it up ... the F is for firestorm."

"I like the name. It's apropos. I was hoping it wasn't the other F-word."

I laughed. "No, I wouldn't do that. I just received another supply of antibodies from the U.K. and am continuing baby Amo's treatment. I had to name her, Paul, she's so adorable. Her spinal fluid shows fewer prions, so the treatment is really working!"

"Have you told anyone?"

"I hadn't planned to. Only the chief vet who helps me with the injections, Hugh Dalen, and the supplier knew. Then Reilly showed up in the Vet Building with Westphal and walked in on Bernie and me treating the baby monkey." I told Paul about Reilly's anger about being excluded from the U.K. cooperation. "I think he brought Westphal along as a witness."

"I don't know what to make of that."

"I could come up with a few scenarios."

Paul said, "Me, too. Orchestrate the break-in, get you out of the picture, steal your work, make it look like animal activists, call you incompetent, and transfer your project to Westphal. They could share in your great achievement, a cure that would change the world. I wouldn't trust either of them."

"Same here, but Westphal hasn't come back since the break-in."

"They'd both end up in prison if they stole your information, of course, but there are the two dead guards and murder charges, too. You better ask the researchers in the U.K. to let you know if anyone else from the U.S. tries to get their monoclonals."

"I told them my suspicions and updated them on the success of the baby monkey. They are pushing forward with a small human study. News of a cure is bound to leak. I hope I can publish my findings first. Of course, I'll give them credit."

Paul continued, "I'll tell Andover your great news since he got them to send you the antibody. He'll keep it quiet. How are you doing physically?"

"Good. I don't scare people anymore. It's been about three months. My hair is about two inches long, so it covers the craniotomy scar. At half an inch a month, I had to be patient. At first, Reilly unmercifully badgered me about scaring people."

"Why is he doing this?"

"He wants me gone because I'm ruining the lab's image."

"That's bullshit. File another formal complaint. Don't let him intimidate you."

"I'm keeping notes. Headquarters will think I'm a wimpy troublemaker if I file another charge."

"Do what you think is right. Are any activists bothering you?"

"I feel safe. NIH security is high, and we have more perimeter guards. Cameras are online. I haven't seen any activists hanging around. Maybe they go south in the winter months like the birds."

"It's reassuring to talk to you. Please let me know if you need my help."

After discussing potential approaches with Bernie, I asked her to get a total of four dozen hooded rats and four whitetail deer yearlings, two does and two bucks.

During the time I wasn't working, I had run across a Wisconsin study on the transfer of abnormal prions through soil contamination into plants. My planned deer project was a trial of infecting one of each sex with the wasting disease prion through eating infected plants.

I had a location for the test: the prion-infected empty corral left behind after the release of the Chronic Wasting Disease-infected deer. It was the perfect use for the contaminated area. I had discussed plans with the lab to test the soil and plants before releasing the deer to the area. By the end of the summer, I could begin monitoring the deer for signs of infection.

Reilly couldn't refuse my plan for that study. A few packets of vegetable and grass seeds wouldn't cost much, and I had residual monies in my prion grant to purchase research animals.

The second pair of whitetails would be housed in the clean deer stockade to use as controls. I could compare their normal growth and development with that of the infected deer.

I decided I'd infect the cadre of rats by inoculation to generate rapid disease progression. Then, treat them with the antibody intravenous in conjunction with a compound that disrupts the blood-brain barrier. This would allow the antibody to reach the brain and then add P-glycoprotein to remove the abnormal proteins. I hoped this combination would provide transmission of the reversing antibody to the brain and nervous system, followed by rapid prion clearance.

Life in Ohio had been simple. Moving to Montana was like moving to the shores of an alien planet. I hoped the summer sun would bring warmth and happiness after a tough winter.

Rat injections kept me late one night, so I called Sal to keep Blaze overnight. On my way home, I stopped at a gas station with a small grocery store, where I filled my tank and purchased yogurt, fruit, and bread. For some reason, I had an uneasy feeling, like someone was watching me.

I scanned the area around my car when I left the store and walked with my finger on the pepper spray trigger inside my pocket. On my other arm, I carried my bag of food and the car key remote. I clicked the door opener, got in, and locked the doors. Driving after midnight along empty streets was creepy.

I let myself in to my apartment and secured the dead bolt. A night light provided enough visibility to drop the groceries on the kitchen counter. I felt safer with the outside world blocked out after closing the drapes, but I still felt uneasy, wishing I'd picked up Blaze.

I tossed my jacket on the bed.

Before the jacket landed, a figure stretched out on the bed sat up.

I screamed.

"Why are you so late? I've been waiting for hours." Mack sat on the edge of my bed.

I flipped on a glaring ceiling light.

He stared at me with burning eyes, making my heart stumble.

"You scared me. How in the hell did you get in?"

"I still have the key you gave me. But I have more important things, Igor is dead."

"Oh, I'm so sorry. What happened to him?"

"I don't know. Did you do it with your damn prions?"

"Don't be crazy. Was he sick?"

Mack snarled. "He was fine. We did semen collections last week, and there were no problems. He looked perfect." Mack's tone changed. "Today, I was out riding the fence line and found him dead, belly-up in a gulley. It looked like he slipped, rolled over on his back and couldn't get up. He was kind of wedged in a depression."

"Couldn't it just be a fluke?"

"With a young healthy bull like him? Four years old? No way."

"Are you doing a necropsy on him?"

"Hell, no. If it got out that he was prion-infected, I'd have no business. His lucrative semen product would be worthless. It would be your fault."

"You aren't making sense. If he was infected, there is no way I could have done it. Maybe Adcock's friends, or an elk. Did you test that elk that died?"

"Hell, no!"

"You took it to the rendering plant without testing it? That's criminal. It would contaminate all the protein slurry they put in animal feed just like it did in Great Britain."

Mack was silent.

"You have to stop all semen shipments. All of them."

He bowed his head. "I'm too upset to think straight." He pleaded. "Could you please come out to the ranch with me and take a look at a couple of my other bulls? I want you to see if you think they are showing any early signs of disease."

"You're the vet. I'm working at the lab tomorrow morning until eleven doing injections. Then I'm going to Missoula for a noon meeting with Dr. Dalen at the state lab. He wants me to consult on a case he just got in. It could be a prion death."

"First Igor dies, and then you'd rather meet with some other guy than help me. Dalen, isn't he the one I met in ICU? He came to visit you. Do you two have something going?"

"Stop it. I can be at your ranch by 3 p.m."

Mack jumped to his feet. "You didn't say no to my last question. Fine! Work and meeting another man are more important than doing this for me. I can see I'm at the bottom of your priority list." He stormed out, slamming the door and knocking a picture of me riding his beautiful quarter horse off the wall. The glass shattered.

I wished I had remembered to ask him for my key. Having him in my house was frightening and even with the dead bolt, it took hours to get to sleep.

Chapter 38 - The Beginning

I walked into Hugh Dalen's office at the state crime lab, excited to see him again. He sat in a soft, dark leather chair at a desk with neat piles of files on one corner, busily typing on a keyboard. When he saw me, he jumped up and walked around his desk with open arms. "Callie, you look wonderful. Your curly hair is back." He held me at arm's length and then hugged me. "You look a lot healthier than the last time I saw you."

Our cheeks touched. A hint of his aftershave clung to my skin. "It's great to see you."

Less than a year ago, we were talking about my father's death. Last September seemed like forever. Now the snow is gone, the birds are singing and spring is just around the corner.

Hugh held the door for me. "I'm so glad you could come. I have two worrisome cases. The second one came in last night."

I followed him down long halls, where he introduced me to some of his skilled staff. We stopped at the fingerprint lab, where a tech lifted prints from a plastic cup. In the ballistics lab down the hall, a crime scene investigator talked with a technician, comparing tire-track impressions from a hit-and-run homicide.

"The print lab really interests me after cleaning up dust in my lab and apartment and with the new Ridge Lab security upgrade to digital fingerprinting. They're redoing the entire staff and sending them to AFIS."

"Fingerprinting is much better than it used to be, but DNA has become more important than prints in many cases." He pointed, "We do DNA sequencing here in some situations, but send most of it to regional labs."

"Thanks for calling me. I'm so isolated at the Ridge lab compound, it's a treat to see what you're doing."

On the way to the morgue, we walked past a classroom filled with men and women, many of them in uniform. "These officers from around the state are attending our Montana Law Enforcement Academy crime scene course. Part of our job is to train law officers so they provide us with the best possible forensic material from their crime scenes."

Hugh punched in a door code at the end of a long hall. We entered a large, cool room with a line of stainless-steel tables where we'd done the autopsy on the decomposed body months earlier. Refrigerated body drawers lined one wall. The smell of death mixed with an array of medicinal odors.

He led me to a side room designated Biologic Hazard. Before entering, we donned full protective gear, including masks. An empty steel table reflected the overhead lights. Another held a shrouded body. Hugh opened a labeled drawer and pulled out a metal slab, peeling back a sheet to expose the dead man's head. "This is the one I called you about."

I moved to his side. Instead of the odor of death, a strange, earthy smell wafted out. The unusual smell raised goose bumps on my forearms. I stopped short.

"Sorry, I should remember you work with animals." Hugh looked at me. "Are you al right?"

"It isn't that. I've seen many bodies." I walked closer to stand by the dead man's side for a better look at his white curled fingers with dirty, broken nails. Long hair circled the waxy, bearded young face that had a lax expression fixed in time. An oily film coated the thin body decorated with tattoos. A familiar smell washed through my body, making me weak.

"We don't know which of the two IDs they located is valid. They found his body in a camper near Lost Trail Pass, south of Medicine Falls."

I looked closer at his face. "It's Irv, a guy I met last October who was with a group of activists at the Beast Feast."

Hugh checked the toe tag. "One of the IDs we have is for Irvin Quinn."

"That's the name he gave me when he came to my rescue after I fainted."

"His brain is riddled with holes, Callie. A classic prion death."

"I liked him. He was kind and seemed normal except for his crazy idealistic Natural Order beliefs." Hugh pulled up the sheet and I walked closer. "They believe the earth should be returned to a natural place of beauty and serenity, with few people, no modern transportation, and no government. That day, he had the same god-awful stinking oil on his skin."

"It's patchouli, an essential oil that is supposed to treat depression, reduce inflammation, stop infection, and is an aphrodisiac." Hugh smiled. "Maybe we should all wear it."

"I don't think it helped him. From October till now, six months, he went from normal to dead."

Hugh looked aghast. "Fast deterioration. This is a very aggressive prion."

"How soon can we get a tissue sample to the Human Prion Center in Cleveland for identification?"

"It went out yesterday morning. We could get a preliminary report late today." Hugh closed the drawer and removed his gloves. "What do you know about him?"

"Not much. Natural Order is a concept, a system functioning in line with the natural laws of the physical universe. Not human or supernatural laws. I'm not sure I understood their theme entirely, but they believe there's no place for government."

"I've never heard of them."

"They're vegans, so Irv didn't get this eating meat. We need to know the prion subtype."

Hugh's eyes lit up. "If it's your subtype, he's the first clue to who orchestrated the lab break-in."

The smell of patchouli made me feel dizzy. I sat down on a stool. "The break-in was December 24th. That would mean this prion kills humans in less than five months. I'm liking this less and less."

"After I called you yesterday, I got this one." He pointed to the shrouded figure on the other steel table. "This one's an older guy. I just opened his skull and removed his brain this morning so we could look at it together. Let's do it before we call Paul Wilder. I sent the specimen directly to him."

"Who is this?"

"No ID. He died in a motel in Frenchtown, north of Missoula. The transporters brought a load of empty medication bottles and syringes in with the body. I haven't had time to go through them."

Hugh put on new gloves and walked to the autopsy table. "At first glance, I thought he was a cancer victim who killed himself. His brain tells another story."

Still thinking about the first man, I followed Hugh, talking. "Irv offered to drive me home the day I fainted—an animal activist offering to help an animal killer."

"So, he was a likeable sort."

"I thought so at the time. That day, I felt nauseated and the smelly oil on his body made it worse. I'll never forget that smell." My hands went cold.

Hugh saw my pale face. He removed his gloves and helped me to a stool. "Put your head down. You look like you're about to faint."

A cold sweat drenched my upper lip and forehead. "I think the oil smell triggered my memory."

Hugh held me close. His warm hand on my neck eased my symptoms.

"I think he's the one, the one who nearly killed me and cut off my thumb." I leaned my head against Hugh. "I don't remember much from that night, but I remember the smell."

Hugh dragged an armed chair closer and helped me move from the small metal stool to the chair. "Sit here until you feel better. I don't want you falling off that stool."

I leaned back. "Forgive me for being weak. It makes me furious that I'd feel this way."

"Don't feel sorry. You've been through a lot."

"Something similar happened last week at the Ridge Lab in the room where they found me on the floor after I was attacked. I experienced a weird sensory wash and fainted."

"The brain is strange. That smell triggered your memory in spite of your being drugged with Rohypnol." Hugh looked in a file. "If Irv is the same man, his address is Colorado. Law enforcement shows a long rap sheet for assault, breaking and entering, and a weapons charge."

"From what I found with a little research after meeting Irv, Natural Order is a violent anarchist subculture. There are small, organized pods of true believers around the world that hate all forms of government."

"I haven't met any of them and hope I don't." He handed me gloves. "When you feel okay, let's take a look at the second body before we examine the brain slides I set up on alias Irv Quinn and the guy on the table."

Hugh turned back the cover exposing the whole body. I walked around the table to get a better look from the foot.

Prominent ribs. Eyes sunken, similar to Dad at the time of his death. Dark hair sprinkled with white, untrimmed gray beard. My eyes stopped on the man's face.

Hugh frowned. "You don't know him too, do you?"

"It's Larry Westphal, the prion researcher from Cleveland, the surly alcoholic. He is the one that attacked me and was transferred here last fall. You said he came to visit you. You liked him."

"Right, but I didn't recognize him. He was working with you?"

"Not recently. He disappeared in December after the Christmas Eve party, the night of the break-in. Dr. Reilly said he'd talked to him in rehab."

"Maybe he used alcohol in an attempt to disguise his disease symptoms. Pitiful. He did a good job. None of his cohorts diagnosed him."

My anger surged. "It's pathetic. I didn't even diagnose my own father."

"Nolan did a good job of hiding it from everyone, too."

Hugh went to the microscope. "Let's look at Westphal's brain first."

"Could I see the drugs and syringes you found with him?"

Hugh pointed at the array of medication bottles on another autopsy table. Wearing gloves, I held a zip-locked bag up to the light and read labels through the plastic. "Oh, my God, Hugh, my handwriting is on some of the labels." I pointed. "This one is an old trial drug from Cleveland that didn't work on the rats. I didn't bring it to Montana, so he must have." I looked at other labels. "The others are drugs I used to treat my monkeys that died here last fall."

"He stole your monkey drugs to treat himself." Hugh looked over my shoulder at the drugs. "We have some answers, Callie. But this may be the beginning of the crisis we feared."

"You're right. I'm sad for Westphal and my monkeys."

"The meds probably helped him survive as long as he did."

"He killed the monkeys and couldn't save himself. I bet I was giving the monkeys saline."

Hugh snarled, "Shit. No wonder they died."

"Larry was desperate. Contracting prion disease for Westphal and Dad was a terrible blow. Like some with HIV, they wanted no one to know. Unlike HIV now, for prion disease there were no treatment options available."

"Except yours." Hugh pulled my thoughts back to the present. "Are you ready to look at these?"

I followed Hugh to the microscope, feeling weak and empty. We looked at magnified brain tissue from both victims. I removed my gloves and gown. "Two doesn't make an outbreak, but this is a rare disease."

"With three confirmed in Idaho's Wapiti County. Irv's body was found near the Idaho border and if related would make four in that area. Westphal would make five."

"I think we'll find Larry's subtype is scrapie from the sheep study he was doing in Cleveland." I thought for a moment. "Scrapie may be a slower prion in humans until it gets to a critical stage. Maybe that's why Larry was able to hide the disease and live longer."

"That makes sense. I'm not familiar with the scrapie prion in human infection."

"No one was until a recent study showed the scrapie prion to be indistinguishable from the sporadic human form that kills in about six months once symptoms occur."

"He stole your monkey drugs. They probably slowed his disease, but he ran out."

"Right. If Irv Quinn's prion turns out to be the aggressive form stolen from Ridge Lab, we'll begin seeing more disease. How many of his friends are out there right now, dying?"

The oily patchouli essence clung to my nose and distracted my thoughts.

Chapter 39 - It's Spreading

Hugh and I sat in his office behind the closed door. He placed the phone on speaker and stabbed in Paul Wilder's phone number. "Paul, Hugh Dalen here. Callie Archer is with me. We have bad news. It's started."

Paul raised his voice. "What do you mean?"

"I have two prion bodies in the morgue here at the state lab. Do you have a preliminary on the brain specimen I sent to you yesterday?"

"They were working on it. Hold on."

He came back on the line. "Bad news. Bovine origin with your PrF prion Callie. I'll inform the CDC. They'll probably be on the next flight to Montana."

My anxiety shot up. "I'll call the FBI here. This is a big break in the lab investigation and horrible news."

Hugh said, "Paul, another case I got in last night is also a prion death."

I blurted out, "It's Larry Westphal."

"Shit. Are you sure?"

"I didn't recognize him at first because he's bearded and so skinny. The Ridge Lab has his fingerprints, so we can confirm his identification, but I'm sure it's him."

Hugh said, "We printed the body because he came in with no ID. The prints may be online already. I'll let Callie tell you the next part."

I told Paul about the stolen drugs from my lab in Cleveland and the Ridge Lab.

"Shit. He wasn't drunk. He was stumbling around two prion centers infected with prion disease and no one recognized it. Even his crazy behavior correlates. My God, we're morons."

"I can't believe we missed it. But then, I missed it in my father."

"This is awful." Paul's voice carried sadness and anger. "He took your drugs from our Cleveland lab and your Ridge Lab to treat himself."

I said, "Some of the medication bottles were left in a refrigerator after the break-in. We can have them analyzed. I bet he replaced my drugs with saline. That explained why the adult monkeys died and Amo survived. She actually got the drugs because Westphal was gone."

Paul sounded sad. "Larry was desperate."

"Paul, Callie is a bit shaken by what she's seen here."

"I recognized the other dead man, too. I think he was the one who tried to kill me."

Hugh described my sudden reaction to Irv's stinky oil. "The smell triggered fear. She's still shaking."

"Amazing. At least now the CDC and FBI will have more details to track to a source and find the perpetrators responsible for the lab breach.

Hugh said, "I appreciate your help with the CDC reporting. I'll wait for your call regarding the print ID on Westphal and his prion subtype."

"I'm feeling better, now. I think Westphal's prion is most likely scrapie because of his work. Do you want both bodies shipped to you?"

"Yes. Ship them, Hugh. I'll take care of reporting Quinn's death to the CDC, Westphal's too. They need to start the investigation immediately. The FBI will retrace Quinn's trail."

Hugh walked me out to my car. I forfeited his invitation to lunch. I'd lost my appetite and wanted to get back to Medicine Falls to go to the ranch. I asked Hugh if the medication bottles could be fingerprinted and matched to Dr. Reilly's prints. "I wonder if he helped Larry Westphal get my monkey drugs."

"That would crack open the case. I'll probably have to get the FBI to access the NIH print file on Reilly. Since you're calling them, ask them to get his prints released to the crime lab to speed up the investigation. I'll try AFIS in the meantime."

I called Hal Vater in the Missoula FBI office on my way back to Medicine Falls and told him about Natural Order and Irv Quinn, or whoever he was, and Westphal. I asked him about getting Reilly's prints for comparison.

"I'm on it, Callie. Don't tell anyone about the deaths until we have more information." He thanked me for the call. "This is the break we'd been looking for. I'm glad you've recovered and are back in the thick of things."

We hadn't talked since the interview when my head was shaved. "At least, I have hair again and won't have to make a living doing hair-loss commercials."

"I thought you looked great without hair."

"You're kind."

He chuckled.

Before the end of the call, I asked him about progress killing off deer in the area around Medicine Falls that might be infected. He said, FWP had a task force working on it, with accelerated carcass testing, setting up a cremation pit for large game and had just announced an orchestrated kill by volunteer hunters. That report made me feel better about containment.

I replayed interactions I'd had with Larry Westphal in Cleveland in my mind. Now, I understood why I had seen so little of him at the Ridge Lab. He had done his best to hide the disease. That's why he tried to get information on the drugs I was using. Just like Dad, he searched for anything that might work. Oh, my God, I could have helped him. Maybe I could have helped both of them, but they were too proud to reveal their errors and the prions had muddled their brains.

Driving to Medicine Falls, I worried about the human prion deaths and my own safety, but not from risk of prions. If the break-in perpetrators learned of Irv's death from my lab prion, what would they do next? I also had concerns being isolated at the ranch but had to see for myself if Igor or the other bulls might be infected.

I arrived at the ranch earlier than estimated. Mack wasn't in the house. My concern about his behavior the night before and Igor's death made me wish Rex and Nick were both with me. Maybe the FBI terminated the guards too soon.

Wearing black slacks and polished boots, I wasn't dressed for a barnyard. I got back in my car and drove out to the AI barn. There were no visible vehicles, but Mack had said the ranch hands usually parked in the back. I entered the side door and found him at his desk.

He didn't hear me at first and was startled when he looked up in anger. "Glad to see you finally made it." He held up a computer spreadsheet. "I'm tallying up our sales for the past month. It was great." He flashed a satisfying smile. "I've shipped more embryos and semen to more locations than ever. UPS will be picking up another shipment today." He turned back to his keyboard. "I'll take you out to look at the bulls as soon as I'm done here. Sorry about last night. I was out of line."

He was way out of line too often. I sat down to wait.

His cell rang. "Adcock, what the hell are you talking about? A bull is down? Others are sick? Callie and I will come over and have a look."

He got up and headed toward the back door. "Come with me. My truck is parked on this side. We need to drive over to Adcock's."

As we sped down the road to the adjacent ranch, Mack told me one of Garrett's prize elk had collapsed. We found him standing outside a tall wire-fenced corral staring at a gorgeous bull elk lying on the ground unable to get up. The elk's beautiful brown eyes filled with fear as he struggled, then fell back.

Garrett paced. "That's thousands of dollars down a rat hole if he dies."

I squatted near the large animal. "When did this bull get sick? He looks starved." Six elk huddled along the fence. One lay on the ground.

Mack scanned the corral. "What the hell is wrong with you Garrett? Haven't you been feeding these animals? Are you drunk?"

"Haven't had a drink since last night. Call Tim. Get your vet meds over here." Garrett spun around as if he were taking a swing at Mack. He looked at me with unfocused eyes and pitched forward in the dirt. Uncontrollable muscle contractions evolved to a generalized seizure.

I dialed 9-1-1. "It's Dr. Callie Archer. Mack Janns and I are at the Adcock elk ranch about seven miles south of Medicine Falls. We need an ambulance for Garrett. He just had a seizure ... That's right. Just south of Mack's ranch, on the right."

Mack's eyes widened. "Looks bad. They've both got it, don't they?"

I agreed. "Look at his herd. They're all sick."

Garrett regained consciousness but lay on the ground, still confused when the ambulance arrived. I relayed medical and contagion information to the crew. Using proper protection, they loaded him and screamed off toward town, trailing a cloud of dust.

The elk stopped breathing. Unless I could get the monkey serum to him, Adcock would soon die like his elk.

Mack drove back to his ranch without a word and stopped at the AI barn. "I want you to look at the bulls." We walked to a corral enclosing six big black Angus bulls. "These look healthy to me. So, did Igor."

Two shied away as Mack walked to the fence, one stumbled, the other stood, menacing, swinging his head back and forth. Drool stringing from his mouth. "I'm no vet, but they both need to be tested for prion disease."

Instead of being upset at the thought of his friend and elk along his property line dying of prion disease, and now prize bulls appearing infected, Mack sounded exhilarated when he answered his cell. He confirmed with the caller the past month was his most lucrative and that a UPS truck would be arriving in minutes for another pickup. He cut the call, and before he could say anything, I screamed, "Stop shipping your damn products! AI stock may be contaminated. Maybe prions killed Igor."

I headed for the door. "I'm going to the lab. I have to get antibodies into Garrett. It might save his life."

"Forget Garrett. If he was dumb enough to get it, he deserves to die." Mack blocked the door. "If they find you injecting him without human testing, they'll crucify you."

When Garrett had visited Mack before the Beast Feast, I liked the man. His simple approach and love of Montana showed in everything he said. He even loved wolves. That tipped my liking for him. "I hate his hunting and what he did to elk, but he deserves a chance. Get someone out here to test the bulls."

My trip back to the lab didn't arouse suspicion. I came and went at all hours of the day and night, so this trip wasn't unusual. My new batch of study rats were running around and looking healthy. They needed the prepared drugs, but Garrett needed them more. I made sure all their water bottles were full and that they had enough food.

Then, I verified the intruders had missed some of the monkey drugs I'd left in a back corner of the refrigerator. Later, Dr. Dalen could analyze them and see if they were diluted or contained only saline. I left carrying a satchel of anti-prion rat medications and the antibody I'd prepared to use on the baby monkey for the next four doses. I ordered more antibodies, so they'd be shipped immediately. My supply was inadequate for Garrett's size, but I decided to give him all I had on hand. Combined with the rat meds, I hoped it would buy him some time until the shipment arrived.

I went home to shower and change before going to the hospital. Dr. Reilly wasn't in when I called to tell him about Larry Westphal's death. I left a voice message with the information and suggested he contact Paul Wilder in Ohio in two to three days giving them time to identify the prion that killed Larry. I said the FBI and CDC would likely be contacting him related to their investigation. Before preparing the injection, I called Hal Vater at the Helena FBI and Hugh Dalen to tell them about Garrett's prion disease, the infected elk herd and my concerns about Mack's bulls.

My decision to secretly inject Garrett with potentially life-saving animal drugs was foolhardy and could jeopardize my professional standing and medical license. Injecting untested animal drugs into a human was outlawed by the

FDA but Garrett's death was imminent. He would likely be long-dead by the time the often-lengthy approval process to use a research drug on a human facing certain death occurred.

Paul Wilder was minimally reassuring after I told him what I was doing. He said he'd file an emergency compassionate request for approval through an NIH study, but it could take days.

My parting words were, "I can't wait. He's already unresponsive and on a ventilator."

I entered the hospital through the ER late that evening after visiting hours and found my way to Garrett's isolation room. From an empty waiting room in view of his room, I watched for an opportunity for me to enter, inject and leave without being seen. It would take seconds to inject the contents of a single syringe containing monoclonal antibodies combined with rat meds and steroids. His nurse rushed in and out, sometimes gone for ten minutes, more than enough time

When the nurse left his room again, I donned a gown and gloves from a supply stacked outside his room and entered. He lay comatose. The ventilator cycled in and out like end-stage adults I'd treated unsuccessfully at the human prion center in Cleveland. I quickly found an injection port in his IV line and injected the fluid. I carefully replaced the needle cover and backed away from the bed. As I turned to leave, bedside monitors alarmed.

Shit. I'd killed him! An allergic reaction from the foreign protein was my first thought. I'd added a whopping steroid dose to reduce the risk, but like a bee sting, anaphylaxis could result in death.

I realized he would have died anyway, but I was horrified and expected the nurse to burst into the room. I watched the heart monitor tracing track across the screen over his bed.... Normal. A dangerously low oxygen saturation triggered the alarm. I checked his finger clip and found I'd dislodged the oxygen probe, probably when I'd moved the sheet to expose the IV line.

His nurse ran in, eyes wide with surprise at my presence.

I'd palmed the syringe and repositioned the oxygen probe.

Garrett's oxygen saturation rose, silencing the alarm.

Behind my mask, I faked a smile and bright voice, "His finger clip came off. How's he doing?"

She elbowed me away from the bed. "He's to have no visitors. Who are you?"

"A friend. I wanted to check on him."

"Only family can visit."

I walked to the door. As I removed my gloves and gown, I dropped the empty syringe.

The nurse stared at it. "What's that? What did you inject into him?"

I grabbed the syringe and opened the door to leave.

She pressed a code blue button on the wall beside Garrett's bed generating a thundering herd of hospital staff running to help with a cardiac arrest. They met me in the hallway. There was no cardiac arrest. Calling the code was the nurse's way of getting immediate help.

With her backup team arriving, the chunky nurse lunged, pinning me against the wall.

The confused team watched as I struggled to free myself. One nurse put on protective gear and checked Garrett. "He's stable. His heart rate's 90 and O2 Sat is 100%. What's going on?"

Her screech hurt my ear. "Get Security! Call the police! She just injected something into my patient."

I quit struggling and slipped the syringe I'd retrieved from the floor into my pocket. I waited for security to explain the situation.

A large male with a respiratory therapist name tag took over, looming over me. "Aren't you the research doc somebody tried to kill?"

Chapter 40 - Cure!

Fingerprinted, mug-shot and jailed, I sat on a cot in a dank cell in the Medicine Falls jail, furious. Not sure what to do without an attorney. I made my one allowed phone call to Mack after midnight and explained what happened. His loud words spiked my anger but before I could respond, he ended the call.

Half an hour later, a surly jailer wearing a tan uniform shirt stretched across his belly reached into my cell to hand me a piece of paper. "This here's the name of a high-powered lawyer Mack Janns asked to defend you."

The next morning, I looked my worst appearing before the judge with Mack's attorney. After a tortuous night of wanting to get out of jail and considering scenarios to obtain more meds for Garrett, I stood next to a tall stranger with graying temples, his black hair drawn back in a sleek braid. Dressed in a dark three-piece suit, white shirt and string tie, his height exaggerated by cowboy boots, I felt like a child with an imposing guardian who held my life in his hands. I wondered if Mack and his lawyer were related.

The gavel silenced a full court room. "Dr. Callie Archer, you are charged with assault and battery for injecting drugs into a comatose patient without his permission. How do you plead?"

The attorney answered. "My client pleads not-guilty to all charges. She is a brilliant scientist at the Ridge lab and has never been in trouble with the law. She is no risk to society. Her intentions were honorable. She was trying to save a man, not harm him."

The judge addressed us. "Lab director Dr. Clint Reilly, Dr. Archer's supervisor, informed me she is brain-damaged and cannot be trusted. Further, Dr. Archer, you are barred from returning to the Ridge laboratory. A restraining order will be enforced."

Bastard. I should have expected as much from Reilly.

The judge set bail at $100,000 in spite of my lawyer's arguments. Reilly barring me from the lab meant total obstruction of my urgent plan to save Garrett.

Mack met us in the hall outside the courtroom. He secured a bail bond and with his heavy hand on my shoulder, we left the courthouse. He steered me to his truck. "I need you at the ranch."

"I have to get more drugs for Garrett. It's his only chance for survival."

"Hell, no." Mack opened the truck door. "Get in. Dealing with you and your idiotic behavior put me further behind. I can't keep up with orders that are piling up. You owe me."

I thanked him for getting me out of jail, but I didn't want to deal with him. I just wanted to go home. "I want to get my car from the hospital parking lot."

Mack drove past the hospital. "You can get it later." He turned south.

I'd be better off in jail than trapped at the ranch with a volatile man. We'd been in the house for a few minutes when he received a phone call, barked orders and hung up. He opened the ranch house door. "Come on out to the barn with me. We need to get to work."

His demands pissed me off. I followed, but he walked so fast I could hardly keep up. "I'm not helping with any shipments! You have to assume they're contaminated with prions."

"They're not. My business depends on quality. You know how careful I am." He was convincing, but I refused to help with shipping. Mack kept me busy in the AI barn helping him organize records into three-ring binders and entering data into his computer tracking program. My first stack of invoices tallied in the thousands. Although my left thumb stub still hurt some, it didn't slow my typing speed.

He'd leave for a few minutes and then return to the back office as if to be sure I hadn't sneaked out. I worked diligently wanting to finish his backlog and get the hell out of his control. I schemed to come up with a plan to get my hands on more drugs for Garrett. I had never thought Reilly would actually bar me from the lab. When Mack left again, I called Chris Turner, my cohort whose wife had developed Alzheimer's. He had already left the lab but picked up my message when he reached cellphone range.

I didn't want to reveal my treatment protocol to anyone, but under the circumstances, had to trust someone who had ready access to the Level 3 in the IRF. "One of my regular shipments of antibodies should be in the pharmacy. Could you get those and bring them to me at Mack's ranch?"

"I'll go back up and give it a try but Reilly made an announcement at the meeting this morning. Your arrest sealed his vow to get rid of you. From what he said, he'll have my head if he found out I helped you."

While waiting for Chris to call back, I called Bernie at home to hear more about the lab situation. She said she'd have the techs take care of my rats and would continue with Amo's treatment. I gave her the info to order extra antibodies since I was planning to use the latest supply on Garrett. I told her I was worried about how long it would take to get out of the legal mess and back to work? Her reassurance that she'd defend me to Reilly lowered my anxiety.

Mack still hadn't returned so I called Paul Wilder in Cleveland. "Callie, it's a serious charge to use animal test drugs on a human without proper approval. There is no word on my emergency request for compassionate use of your drugs. I call them in the morning and let you know."

I was crushed by Chris' report. My antibody order hadn't yet arrived so there was nothing he could do. I called Sal to tell her what had happened and heard alarm in her voice. "Now you're in his control. I don't like you out there alone with him. Should I come and get you?"

Mack walked in brusque and irritable, demanding to know who I'd been talking to. I cut my call, but knew Sal heard him.

I backed away. "Look, I'm not a flight risk. You won't lose your damn bail money. I was trying to save your friend and got myself into this mess."

"He's not a friend of mine. Garrett's a dumb-shit slob. If he'd known what he was doing, he wouldn't have infected himself with prions or have his elk falling over dead."

One of Garrett's ranch hands I'd met in the past walked in. Mack spun around. "Sam, what the hell do you want? Are you in trouble again?"

"Hey, man, simmer down. I just came by to thank your little lady, Dr. Callie. I thought she might be here."

"Hi, Sam." I walked closer, glad to have someone interrupt Mack's tirade.

"I just wanted to thank you in person. Garrett's breathing on his own and they are taking him off the breathing machine tomorrow. That's good juice you shot into him. We've got another downer elk. Do you have any stuff we could inject into it?"

"I might in a few days." I doubted I'd get enough quantity to treat an elk, let alone a herd.

"He looks bad. We might not have that long."

Mack sat at his computer and leaned back in the chair. "My men and I used our lift truck to take the elk and Igor's carcass to the rendering plant, a waste of money and meat!"

Sam made a face. "I ain't eatin' meat after what happened to Garrett. Scrambled eggs is about the only thing I've eaten in days."

Before Sam left, I assured him I'd call if I could get a dose of anti-prion serum for the elk.

Mack closed the door. "Don't offer to help anyone. That's his problem."

"What's happened to you, Mack? You're acting crazy."

Mack stomped around the office. "Let's get back to work."

"You took those carcasses to the rendering plant? That was stupid. You know they had to be incinerated to kill prions."

"Don't call me stupid, bitch! You were stupid getting caught. It destroyed your job and reputation." Mack grabbed a newspaper from his desk and thrust it in front of me. "Here. A ranch hand brought it from town. You're front-page news! Clint Reilly says you're a brain-damaged criminal and no longer fit to continue at the lab as a researcher. You may never work again, but that's the way I like it. Maybe now I can get you to marry me. By the way, I called my lawyer to get Reilly charged with libel."

With all the turmoil and distraction my mind stuck on the amazing news from Sam. "Mack, do you realize, Garrett is the first human to ever show recovery from prion disease? I am so excited!"

"Since he's better, maybe my lawyer can get the charges against you dropped. But you're banned from the lab and out of business until your legal situation is solved."

"The rendering plant has to be shut down immediately. The protein slurry has to be burned or prions will enter animal food like it did in the UK during the mad cow outbreak. It has to be stopped or poultry, dogs, cats, all of them will get prion disease."

"Don't tell me what to do!"

I had to get more prion drugs to help Garrett, one dose would buy time and help but I doubted it was enough. "Maybe Hugh Dalen could help me get more drugs."

"So, what is he, your new boyfriend?" Mack's badgering accelerated, and I headed for the door. I didn't have my car but could drive his truck. He always left it unlocked with the electronic key in it. A push of the starter and I'd be gone.

Mack grabbed my arm, pulling me back. The phone rang. He held my arm while he talked.

Mack slammed the receiver down. "That was Tim. Our last shipment to Brazil went bad. Somehow the nitrogen bottle opened, and the contents thawed. They're furious."

He ranted on. "Where the hell did you think you were going? I have to get another shipment to them right away. Help me. I can't wait forever!"

I didn't move.

"What the hell are you waiting for, Rat Lady?" He shoved me toward the storage room. "Get to work!"

Mack blocked the door. "Go get a liquid nitrogen storage bottle with an Igor label and a blank bottle for transport."

I'd be an accomplice to murder by shipping contaminated AI products. "You're taking chances that could kill people."

Mack pinned me against a cabinet. "I've heard your views. Do what I say."

Chapter 41 – Firestorm

Frightened by his violence, I scanned dozens of metal cylinders labeled *Igor* lining shelves in the storage room. I chose one labeled *Igor12.24,* picked up a shipment bottle and brought them to Mack.

He was on the phone again, yelling. "What do you mean, Irv is dead?" Mack covered the receiver. "Hurry, Callie. UPS will be here any minute."

I shook my head. "You could be spreading fatal disease." I slowly unscrewed the cap, trying to delay. Then, with forceps I grasped two strings attached to frozen sperm straws and pulled them out. The strings dangled in an icy fog.

Mack dropped the phone, his eyes wide. He grabbed for the transfer bottles. "Dammit, you got the wrong bottle!"

I looked at the dangling strings. Hanging from one was a semen straw and from the other a frosty chunk of white flesh with an attached fingernail that matched my missing thumb.

In an instant the truth surfaced.

Scenes flashed in my thoughts, the numbers on the bottle were a date, the date of the break-in at the lab.

Irv Quinn lay on the morgue slab, brain riddled with prion holes. Irv attacked me. He had worked for Natural Order. Why did Mack have my severed thumb?

I flung the strings at Mack and rushed for the door.

His foot sent me sprawling. As I went down, he caught a fist of my short hair. My scalp over the scar felt like it ripped.

Mack held my shoulders. Satanic eyes burned with hate as he laughed in my face. "You aren't leaving, Rat Lady."

He'd used me from the day we met, but in my naïveté, I'd believed in him. A psychopath, so smooth. Unknowingly, I'd made love to a madman.

The sniper platoon leader.

Ex-military followers were part of his army.

Mack was the leader of Natural Order.

I had believed the pathological liar who'd orchestrated the lab break-in. He employed the cult on the ranch and sent prion-contaminated AI products around the world. Mack had charmed me to get access to the deadliest prion from the beginning of our relationship.

I jerked to get away, but his strength and anger overwhelmed my attempts. "You nearly killed me. You killed our baby. I loved you. I trusted you. You're a fucking liar!"

"You're a stupid bitch with a one-track mind to save the world. You and I have opposite goals. You lose, and I win. Natural Order wins."

I landed a kicked to his knee sending him off balance and tried to rip free of his grip.

Mack righted himself and tightened his grasp on my arm. "Listen, bitch. Tim and I built this dream after our time in the military. I was always good at getting people to do as I said. They taught me well back in juvenile lockup, but after I killed my dad, I had a head start."

Mack looked around the empty office.

We were alone.

I jerked.

He held tight. "Tim liked my plan. Neither of us is a veterinarian. He faked his vet credentials and mine. He learned about prions growing up on a ranch in Colorado. Tim got us certified in Montana as AI techs. Anyone can do it."

I kicked and jerked.

Mack's breathing calmed, his speech slowed. "We knew our time would come when we could return the earth to its purest form. Clean, simple. Reduce bloodshed, cripple governments, and stop overpopulation."

"That's crazy. Let me go"

"Hell, no. Hear me out. Our goal is equality. Our cause is global. I want to return the land to my people and our brothers of the world."

His hands squeezed my upper arms. "You're hurting me. Stop it."

"Massive AI shipments have supplied Natural Order followers in numerous countries. Our earlier prion was weaker and slower. Since December, all of our frozen shipments have been contaminated with your prion. Our AI products have infected every inseminated cow and calf, in turn the contaminated ground spread it to other domestic and wild animals, butchering plants, homes, and even scavenger birds and animals." Fierce eyes glared. "You should be proud. Look what I've accomplished with your help." He laughed. "You've spread disease to the world, not cured it."

I spun away and dropped my dead weight. His height and long arms made me dance like a marionette. He dragged me into the adjacent barn area and kicked open a stall.

Mack reached for a rope. "I'll wrap this around your pretty little neck and torch your body with the barn. No one will ever know. Fires happen." He laughed. "This is your fault. I didn't expect to fall in love with you. I told you I wanted you to quit, but no, you wouldn't marry me."

"You never loved me. You used me. You're a lying psychopath."

"You shouldn't be calling me names." Another wicked laugh. "Your name will be in the news again, in the obits. You'll be on the front page, famous and dead."

I looked around for an escape.

"No. Maybe instead of torching you, I'll take your body to the rendering plant with the next dead elk. Don't you think it's fitting that a vegetarian becomes animal feed?"

Mack swung the rope, taunting me with it. "I didn't tell you what really happened to my cheating wife. She and her boyfriend disappeared at the rendering plant up the road. No one ever suspected I killed them."

I spun out of his grasp and grabbed a cattle prod leaning against a wall of the stall.

He lunged.

I swung the yellow prod around and jammed it into his midsection. He screamed with the jolt and fell limp like the dying elk. He looked up at me with frightened eyes.

Footsteps and voices neared outside the side door. Mack moved, trying to get up.

I gave him a burst of three shocks.

He stopped moving.

With prod in hand, I ran through the office to his pickup and jumped inside, locking the doors as I pressed the starter. I accelerated on the road to town as soon as I cleared the arch, adjusting the seat and fastening my seatbelt en route. My legs shook so much I had trouble keeping my foot on the gas.

A pickup pulled out from the ranch drive, following me. In the rearview mirror, it loomed closer.

A loud crack shattered the back window.

They were shooting. My life depended on maintaining control. I drove down the center of the dirt road until a UPS truck heading south toward the ranch forced me to slow and move over. As it passed, I hit the shoulder and fishtailed. Hard braking and correction brought the truck into better control. The cloud of dust behind me made visibility poor, hopefully slowing those in pursuit.

I had nowhere to go for help, was out on bail, and the Medicine Falls police believed I was a nut case. I reached Highway 93, turned toward Medicine Falls, and sped up.

My thoughts raced. Where could I go before Mack's people got to me?

I didn't know what to do except speed toward Missoula.

Many phone numbers were programmed into my cell phone, but I didn't dare look at it because of my speed. Taking my eyes off the road for an instant could put me into a ditch and a rollover. I concentrated on driving but dug into my pocket for the phone. I tried a voice command, something I rarely used. "Call Hal Vater."

The phone rang. "FBI, Special Agent Vater here."

"Hal, help me! It's Callie. I'm in real trouble. I'm just south of Medicine Falls on 93 headed north, being chased and shot at by hands from Mack's ranch. He tried to kill me, but I escaped."

"What the hell?"

"His ranch has shipped semen contaminated with prions all over the world. Mack is involved with Natural Order. His men are in a pickup chasing me."

"Slow down so you don't kill yourself."

"I can't. They just shot out a window."

"Hold on, hold on. Let me scramble some help for you. What are you driving? What color?"

"Mack's white double-cab pickup. What should I do?"

"Head to Missoula. State troopers will come from both directions. We have a drug chopper gunship on a training mission on the ground in Missoula. I'll try to have it overhead in minutes." He continued, "Keep talking while I get things going. I hope I don't lose you. I'll call back if I do."

I heard him barking orders.

"Just keep driving, Callie. Shit, girl, you sure know how to find trouble."

"Hal, I hear a siren and see flashing lights. A cop is chasing me."

"Don't stop. We don't know who your enemies are at this point. Keep going. I'll contact Ravalli County dispatch."

"I'm going eighty. I've never driven this fast before."

"Slow it down. There are logging trucks all over and too many curves."

"Where should I go in Missoula?"

"If you make it to Missoula before we rendezvous with you, go to the police compound right next to the crime lab."

In minutes that seemed like hours, the police car backed off and shut down his siren. I slowed to seventy.

I heard a chopper and saw a black helicopter just off my left side providing escort. "This is like the movies, Hal. I can't believe it's for real." My voice cracked. Tears blurred my vision. I wiped them with a trembling hand.

"It's real. Now, slow down. My office is on the phone with FBI Headquarters. They checked with Interpol. International offices have confirmed reports of prion disease spreading throughout the world. Crazy people are filling ERs and jails. Animals are stumbling and dying."

"We have to get more drugs mobilized for worldwide treatment. Garrett Adcock improved, so we know my treatment works."

"We'll talk about treatment when you're safe."

I fell silent, but my brain went into overdrive. "Reilly blocked me from the compound. I have to get some data and drugs from my lab."

"The chopper will take you to the lab so you can get what you want as soon as we can find a place to land. The pilot is telling me to have you pull off at the next wide area. They'll land and get you out of harm's way. Hold on." He came back on and reported a county deputy had shot out the tires of the truck following me. "One man dead, one in custody."

"Thank you." I took my foot off the gas.

"Good luck, Doc. After you get your drugs, I'll meet you at the crime lab with Dr. Dalen. It's a good place for a temporary headquarters. Hugh says for you to be careful."

"I'm banned from the Ridge lab, Hal. They won't let me in."

"You'll be in a gunship, Doc. You can have *anything you want*."

Chapter 42 - And the World Changed

Rotor wash from the helicopter beat down on the evergreens outside the Ridge Lab parking lot when it settled to the ground. Perimeter guards with shocked expressions and guns drawn holstered their weapons and backed away.

The main rotor slowed.

A door popped open, and an agent dressed in black exited with his weapon drawn.

He scanned the area and then held out a hand to steady me as I stepped to the asphalt.

I led the way, a cowgirl, followed by a man in black who walked through a screaming metal detector, protesting his weaponry.

Sarge and Rudy stood at the Admin door, smiling and giving me a thumbs up. I returned the greeting with my stump and pushed past Dr. Reilly, who stood red-faced, babbling and waving his arms. The agent in black waited near the door with the security officers.

I strode down the hall, through the coffee room and outside to the IRF, using my intact right thumb to press the scanner. The air-lock door whooshed open.

Minutes later, I returned carrying two bags filled with medication bottles. My laptop hung from one shoulder, and in front of me I carried my pet rat Brie in a small cage.

Sarge and Rudy said they were proud of me and wished me well.

I climbed back into the helicopter and dropped into a seat with the agent beside me. I snapped restraint straps around me and felt safer than I had in years.

The helicopter lifted straight up, rotated 180 degrees, and headed north, bound for Missoula.

Hugh waved from the police department tarmac as the loud DEA chopper landed. As the blades slowed and the guard opened the door, the smell of jet fumes reminded me this wasn't a dream. It was the beginning of a nightmare of enormous proportions to stop the extinction of man and beast.

THE END

Epilogue

Natural Order ideologues partially accomplished their goal to cause economic collapse and reduce the world population. They didn't foresee the firestorm that would follow.

Prions are resistant to destruction.

To kill them, they must be burned.

Instead of returning the earth to a pristine, less-populated place, the air was filled with smoke and the stench of death.

In the effort to destroy the prions in human remains and animal carcasses large incinerators belched smoke day and night.

Natural Order's plan to infect food sources through contaminated insemination and embryo products proved effective. Their choice of the aggressive prion in Dr. Archer's primate study gave them the perfect vector. Behind a façade of professionalism, the two ex-con vet techs and their anarchist followers first used a less virulent prion form to test their success in spreading the disease. After learning of the PrF "firestorm" cross-species prion in Callie's study, Mack Janns orchestrated the Rocky Mountain Ridge Lab breach with his skilled ex-military cult to obtain the more virulent prion and used it to contaminate shipments in his international business.

Within days of the outbreak announcement, doctors' offices and ERs across Montana and the United States filled with frightened patients. Violent people in various stages of the disease filled jails.

In cooperation with Interpol, the World Health Organization tracked insemination shipments to numerous countries and triggered the destruction of entire herds of diseased cattle.

Centers for Disease Control and Prevention investigators found many cases in the town of Medicine Falls had resulted from eating meats purchased at a local butcher shop. Contaminated equipment spread prions to all meat products. In addition, wild game hunters who processed diseased venison and elk contaminated their homes and infected their families. Reports of prion cases around the United States and Canada mounted, some of them resulting from domestic elk products shipped by Garrett Adcock's business.

Under presidential order, the Department of Homeland Security, the CDC, and the Department of Health and Welfare commandeered large pharmaceutical labs to escalate treatment serum and immunizations for the United States and cooperate with labs around the world.

Medical teams rallied in Missoula to provide support to treat the large disease outbreak in the area. They used Dr. Archer's only known successful treatment combination supported by mass production of the British monoclonal antibody.

Mack had planned to use Callie, not fall in love with her. With their divergent goals and failing relationship, he gave up courting Callie and proceeded with the Natural Order plans. His violence toward Callie were in part his psychopathic behavior accelerated with prion brain involvement. Mack's symptoms worsened in jail. He recognized the disease and begged for help, but like so many innocent people he had infected, Mack died before treatment became available.

FBI investigation of the residual drugs from Dr. Archer's Cleveland lab and the Ridge Lab revealed marked dilution. The findings confirmed Larry Westphal's attempt to save himself by stealing her drugs.

Fingerprints on medication bottles confirmed Dr. Reilly's collusion in obtaining Callie's drugs for his friend. The prion that killed Westphal was the scrapie subtype used in his research. He had met Natural Order operatives in Ohio and assisted them with insider knowledge after requesting his transfer to Montana.

Fingerprints found in Dr. Archer's apartment after the burglary belonged to him.

Dr. Callie Archer received the Nobel Prize in Medicine for her work on prion disease. Her approval for use of the animal treatment as a compassionate drug to save Adcock's life absolved her of wrongdoing and criminal charges were dropped.

Author's Note

F*atal Feast* is fiction, but prions are real and universally
fatal. Prions are abnormally twisted proteins that re-
cruit normal proteins to change conformation and clump,
damaging the body. In the diseased state, the abnormal proteins are found throughout body fluids and in muscle, but
the nervous system and the brain are most affected.

Prion disease is easily transmissible via surfaces contaminated by contact with infected body fluids and tissues. These
deadly, infectious proteins kill people in the United States
today as they did in Great Britain in the 1990s. Patients have
died from blood transfusions, contaminated neurosurgical
instruments, and tissue transplants. Some forms of prion disease are inherited.

The fascinating history of the discovery and conse-
quences of abnormal prions can be found in many sources.
The most recent outbreak occurred in the United Kingdom
killing more than two-hundred people who contracted the
deadly disease by eating beef from infected cattle. Prion disease spread by consuming the bovine source is called variant
Creutzfeldt-Jakob disease or vCJD. Millions of cows were
euthanized and incinerated to stop the spread, but shipments of infected meat products spread the disease to other

countries during the U.K. epidemic. Initially, this outbreak was concealed by authorities until it could no longer be hidden from the public.

Wildlife across the U. S. and in Canada have been found with a prion infection called Chronic Wasting Disease. The infected animals become unable to eat, develop muscle wasting and die. Attempts to stop the epidemic spread are hampered by the stability of prions in soil for years and because it is taken up into plants that may be able to transmit the disease to grazing animals. Studies are ongoing.

Sheep infected by prions develop scrapie, manifested by a rubbing behavior resulting in large patches of missing fur. Mink also contract the disease. Hundreds of house cats died during the UK outbreak. Since then, jungle cats and other zoo animals have died. Recently, infected cows in Scotland were euthanized. Infected elk shipped to South Korea have introduced the disease to that country. Reindeer are also affected. Chronic Wasting Disease recently killed primates who ate infected venison.

Researchers around the world are focused on improving techniques for the early diagnosis, treatment, and prevention of prion disease. Species barriers are incomplete. At this time, no human has been diagnosed with prion disease from eating wild game, but bovine source prions killed hundreds who ate infected beef in Great Britain. At the time of this publication, there is no cure and no effective treatment.

ACKNOWLEDGEMENTS

Writing a prion disease thriller has interested me since the outbreak of mad cow disease three decades ago in Great Britain. My skilled critique partners shepherded the final product through many iterations. I especially thank Debbie Burke who brought me from zero to seven finalized books in the past seven years, and for introducing me to the *Scene & Structure* format in modern fiction writing by Jack M. Bickham. Special thanks to Bev Erickson for the cover designs on all of my books.

My dedicated critique partners include Deborah Epperson, Marie E. Martin, Susan Purvis, Phyllis Quatman, and Rebecca Schuster, writers across genres, some of them bestselling authors. I thank all of them and, in particular, former writing partner Jim Satterfield, retired Regional Director of Fish Wildlife and Parks who provided significant insight into wildlife management and community interface. For all of us, Dennis Foley is a former Hollywood screen and television writer, consultant, author, educator and esteemed guru, who with Deb Burke, launched a dynamic growing group of writers helping writers in Authors of the Flathead.

Jerry Cunningham and I share an intense interest in prion disease. I am greatly appreciative of his input and detailed plot enhancement suggestions. Thanks also to Jim Bruckner, retired coroner, former NIH high-risk laboratory security guard, and my long-time friend. Hours of nocturnal discussions with him over coffee in the ER and attending crime scene courses contributed immensely to writing realistic law enforcement scenes. Thanks also to the cattle insemination experts who clarified their processes for me.

Questions and Topics for Discussion

1. Did you find the premise of *Fatal Feast* believable?

2. How did the mountainous setting contribute to the story's intrigue?

3. How did the death of Callie's father contribute to your understanding of human prion disease? Realistic?

4. How did you feel about Callie's reaction to her father's death? Would you have behaved the same?

5. Have you ever worked in a similar setting? Harassment? Physical isolation? Always looking over your shoulder? Did you relate to Callie's professional problems?

6. Were ranch scenes and insemination processes understandable and clear?

7. What did you think of Mack Janns? Could you relate to her attraction to him?

8. Were the medical aspects and procedures clear?

9. How did you find the pace of the story? Fast enough? Too fast?

10. Was the ending satisfying?

Please consider writing a *Fatal Feast* review at your chosen retailer.

For updates and information on new books, please subscribe at:

https://www.bettykuffel.com

About the Author

Betty Kuffel MD is a pilot and retired ER physician who lives in Montana. Medical and wilderness experiences, flying, dog sled racing in Alaska, and surviving a plane crash in the mountains of Idaho fuel her writing.